I0788446

REFORMING KENT

USA TODAY & WSJ BESTSELLING AUTHOR

SIOBHAN DAVIS

This print edition © July 2024

ISBN-13: 978-1-959285-79-3

Edited by Kelly Hartigan www.editing.xterraweb.com
Cover design and logo by Shannon Passmore
www.shanoffdesigns.com
Cover imagery © depositphotos.com and © elements.envato.com
Interior graphics © Robin Harper www.wickedbydesigncovers.com
Formatted by Ciara Turley using Vellum

BOOK DESCRIPTION

Kent

Rogue. Troublemaker. Bad Boy. Delinquent.

Everyone thinks they know who I am, but they know *nothing*.

And that's how I prefer it.

Keeping my demons under lock and key is my only survival tactic.

Until a gorgeous feisty bartender enters my life, turning it upside down. Presley captivates me in a way no woman ever has, and I can't get her out of my mind.

She's determined to resist me, but I'm equally stubborn and more than up for the challenge.
Winning her trust, and her heart, becomes everything because she shows me a future worth fighting for.

But the consequences of my tortured past are far-reaching, and if I don't let her go, I'll only drag Presley down this dark hole with me.

Presley

Since I aged out of the foster system, I've worked hard for my dream future, and it's so close. Too close to let some arrogant rich playboy distract me.

I've heard all about Kent Kennedy, and with my history of troubled bad boys, I need his attention like a hole in the head.

Except he's nothing I expected and everything I never dared to dream of. As I slowly uncover the truth, I discover a broken man with a big heart who desperately needs someone to see him.

I want to be that person, but his demons loom large, and I don't know if I'm strong enough to do this again.

When the past rears its ugly head, shattering everything, will there be anything left of my heart to protect?

Note From The Author

While you do not need to have read the previous books in this series to enjoy *Reforming Kent*, it is recommended you start at the beginning to have a greater understanding of the *Kennedy Boys* world and to avoid spoilers to the earlier books contained within this book. However, you can read it as a **stand-alone romance** if you prefer as it focuses on a brand-new couple with a HEA. For readers who are following the series, this book picks up directly from the end of *Adoring Keaton*.

This is an angsty, emotional romance with some dark themes that may be triggering for certain readers. I cannot be more descriptive without spoiling the story. For a list of triggers, refer to my website.

For my loyal readers. Thank you for patiently waiting for Kent's story, and I hope I have done him justice. This book would not exist without your love and enthusiasm for all things Kennedy! Thank you for your amazing support.

REFORMING
KENT

Prologue
Kent

"Hey, you!" I barely lift my head, clicking my fingers in the direction of the bartender. I slam my empty glass down on the counter. "Another whiskey."

Footsteps approach, and I raise my head fully, blinking repeatedly in an effort to focus on the blur in front of me.

"I think you've had enough," a sultry, female voice says, sending shivers of awareness cascading down my spine.

"Where's Ford?" I ask, still struggling to see clearly. "He always looks after me."

"Unlucky for you, Ford went home. I'm behind the bar now, and I'm saying you're done."

Fumbling in my pockets, I extract my wallet and slap a hundred-dollar bill down on the counter. I slide it toward her. "I'm saying I'm not. Get me a whiskey, and you can keep the change."

She pushes the money back at me, folding her arms across her chest.

My vision solidifies, and I stare at her awesome rack. She's wearing a plain black T-shirt, but it's tight, highlighting the generous swells of her tits.

"Your money's no good here, Kennedy, and stop staring at my tits."

My lips curl into a seductive smile of their own volition. "Your tits are awesome," I say, examining her gorgeous face for the first time.

She has beautiful big brown eyes, full lips, high cheekbones, and thick, long lashes that are the real deal. None of that fake spidery shit for this girl. My eyes roam appreciatively over the rest of her. Ink adorns the inside of both her lower arms, and there's a hint of a tattoo peeking out from the top of her shirt. Leaning forward, I peruse the rest of her body, really liking what I see. She's wearing a short leather miniskirt with scuffed biker boots, and she's rocking an incredible body, one I want to get acquainted with.

My dick turns to steel behind my jeans, and I lick my lips as I meet her disgusted gaze full-on.

It doesn't deter me.

It only spurs me on.

"You're hot, and I'm horny. A perfect combination." I stand, gripping the edge of the counter when I sway a little. Straightening up, I tower over her, flashing her the grin that makes countless women drop to their knees. "How about you bend over the counter and I rock your world, baby."

She laughs. "Holy shit. Does that crap really work on women?"

"All the fucking time," I truthfully admit.

Her arm darts out, and she grabs a fistful of my shirt, yanking me toward her.

Hell yeah.

That's more like it.

"Word to the wise, Kennedy. That shit won't work on me. *You* won't work on me. Quit while you're ahead." She lets me go, stepping back. "And you're cut off. Go home."

This woman doesn't realize it, but she's just thrown down the gauntlet. I cannot remember the last time a woman rejected me, and my blood is ON. FIRE. "What's your name, beautiful?" I ask, undeterred.

She rolls her eyes. "You're drunk, Kennedy. Go home. Trust me, it's in your best interest. This isn't the type of place you should be hanging around anyway."

"I like it here," I reply. "Even more now that I've met you."

She shakes her head while drying a few glasses. "Not happening, Kennedy. And if you won't go home, I'll have Bugger throw you out."

"Bugger?" I ask, frowning.

She points over my head. "That big motherfucker at the door. One whistle, and he'll haul your ass outside."

"I'll leave," I say, leaning my elbows on the counter. "On one condition."

Her lips twitch as she rolls her eyes again. "It's cute you think you hold any bargaining power here. I'm the bar manager on duty, and what I say goes."

"Your name," I say. "Just tell me your name, and I'll leave with no trouble."

"Why the hell does it matter?" she asks, placing the dry glasses on the shelf behind her head.

"Because I want to know."

She smirks, leaning her elbows on the counter so we're face to face with barely any distance between us. "And I bet you always get what you want. Am I right?"

I shrug, flashing her another one of my trademark smiles.

I get no reaction.

Not even a flinch or a blink of her eye.

"Just tell me your name."

She straightens up. "No." She grabs a cloth, wiping down the counter. "Go home, Kennedy. I won't tell you again."

"Pres, is this guy bothering you?" a gruff voice says from behind me. I glance over my shoulder, and wouldn't you know it, it's Bugger, and he's even bigger in the flesh. But I'm not worried. I've got enough shit flowing through my veins to be completely unconcerned.

I grin, straightening up. "Pres?" I arch a brow at her in question.

"Presley. You need me to kick this asshole out?" Bugger asks, telling me exactly what I want to know.

Presley groans, pursing her lips. "I have it handled. Get back to the door."

He shuffles off, and I stand there grinning like a loon. "Presley. I like it. Were your parents big Elvis fans or something?"

She rolls her eyes again, and if she keeps doing it, she'll give herself eye strain. "Like I haven't heard that a million times." She leans into me again, and I silently fist pump the air when her gaze rakes me from head to toe.

She might feign disinterest, but I know when a broad wants me, and Presley wants every inch of this body. "Liking what you see, babe?"

She snorts. "How original. You got my name. Now, be a man of your word. And *leave.*"

I grab my jacket from the back of the bar stool. "I'll go, but this isn't the last you've seen of me, Presley baby." I blow her a kiss and walk off.

And for the first time in a long time, something, or some*one*, has pulled my head out from under the black hole I've been living in.

Presley thinks she's immune to my charms.

I can't wait to prove her wrong.

Chapter One
Kent

Year 1 of Law School (March)

"I'd rather boil my balls than sit through another one of those lectures," my buddy Lance says as we exit the old-fashioned gray-brick building after our property law class.

"Just do what I do." I shrug, gripping the strap of my book bag as we make our way through campus toward our next class. Most of the nineteen Harvard Law buildings are situated on the northwest corner of Harvard Yard, which means walking time is short.

"Not all of us can get away with sleeping through classes, when we show up that is"—he arches a brow—"and putting in minimal studying time and still graduate in the top ten percent."

I shoulder check him. "Envy is not a good look for you." And I'm the last person he should be envying or emulating. "And that was the old me. I haven't missed any classes since the start of the year." Honestly, it's a miracle I graduated with my business degree at all. I'm lucky I have an uncanny ability to remember stuff and a decent level of intelligence. I generally only have to read something once to understand it and retain the knowledge.

"You sleep through every property law lecture," Lance reminds me, grinning at two girls as we pass by them.

"Only because it bores me to unconsciousness. And I always download the course notes and study them so I don't fall behind." In some ways, it feels like I've sleepwalked through my entire college life so far. A lot of it is a blur. Especially the past couple of years because things got fucked up again after all that shit went down with one of my triplets. Keaton coming out messed me up. Just as I felt I was emerging from the dark haze I'd been living in.

Now he's getting married, and I know I'm going to be forced to confront this head-on. Only it's not cut and dry. And I can't go back there again. The nightmares and flashbacks had been fading, but now they lay siege to me again, almost as bad as it was in the immediate aftermath. It's why I spent all weekend drowning my sorrows.

It's not my brother's fault. It never has been. But I can't help how I feel. Even if how I feel is unfair to Keaton and Austen. I just don't see how I will ever come to terms with it—with *them*. I legit feel ill every time I think of them together like that.

It's driven a huge divide in the family, and apart from my parents along with Eva and Kade and Keanu and Sel, I don't see much of the others anymore. I'm closest with my other triplet, Keanu, and I only see Kade because of my friendship with his wife. If it wasn't for Eva, I wouldn't visit Kade because he hasn't hidden the fact he has disapproved of me for years.

"Dude. We're here." Lance tugs on my elbow, pulling me to a stop outside the entrance to Pound Hall.

I snap out of my head, grinning as we stride toward the door. "My favorite building," I joke, and it's got nothing to do with the stylish glass and gray-brick façade and everything to do with my immature humor.

"You coming to the WCC for lunch?" Lance asks as we pile out of the classroom after our criminal law lecture has ended.

I nod, following my fellow students out the door. "I'll grab a quick bite before the library."

We enter the dining hall a few minutes later, joining the line. A shrill whistle rings out, and I jerk my head to the left, nodding at Topher. He's bagged a table near the window, and he and Mitch are already sitting and chowing down. Lance accepts a heaped plate of creamy pasta from the server, and I stick with two chicken breasts and a generous serving of vegetables.

"Your lunch is almost as boring as property law," Lance says as we make our way through the crowded room toward our friends.

I poke his fleshy abs. "Tell that to your jelly belly."

"You're an asshole."

"You're just figuring that out?" I ask, abruptly holding my tray aloft when I spot the tiny little thing barreling toward me.

She slams into me, but she's so tiny I scarcely feel the impact. "Ohmigawd." The petite blonde blushes, straining her neck as she stares up at me. I'm six foot three, and she's like five feet nothing, so she barely reaches my chest. She looks so young, and if we weren't in a Harvard dining hall, I'd question if she's even legal. Her blush deepens, and she's looking at me with these big googly eyes, being obvious in the extreme. I might be tempted if she didn't look like jailbait and I wasn't irritatingly fixated on a fiery brunette with killer curves and a potty mouth.

"I'm so sorry, Kent," she squeals, placing her hand on my stomach. "I wasn't watching where I was going."

I hate how everyone knows me, but it's par for the course when you're a Kennedy because everyone knows who my family is.

Welcome to my fucked-up world.

"Don't make a habit of it," I grunt, removing her hands from my body.

Her tongue darts out, wetting her lips, and her cheeks are fire-engine red when she speaks. "I have a free hour," she blurts. "And I booked a study room upstairs."

"Good for you, sweetheart." I move to walk away, and she grabs my arm.

"You could join me?"

I should take pity on her, because her face is on fire, but I'm not the good guy in this scenario. Lance is shaking his head at me, but I ignore him, fixing a neutral expression on my face. "To study?"

"No. To...to, you know." Even her ears are red at this point.

I lean down, putting my face all up in hers. "Use your words, baby."

"To fuck," she blurts, cringing when it comes out loud. A few titters ring out around us, and she's so red now I half-expect her to burst into flames.

Unfolding to my full height, I literally look down my nose at her. "I don't fuck kids."

"I'm not a kid," she pouts, placing her hands on her hips, attempting to glare at me. "I'm nineteen."

"I prefer my women like fine wine. Aged and full-bodied. Now run along back to the playground, toots."

Her hands ball into fists, and I almost want her to hit me, but she storms off, taking her red face with her.

"I rest my case," Lance says, rolling his eyes.

"Not my fault she didn't get the memo I'm an asshole," I say as we reach our table. Considering she knows who I am, I'm guessing she got the memo but didn't care. I find most women don't, which is really pathetic.

"You got a fever or something?" Mitch asks, stretching his arm toward me, his hand hovering in front of my forehead.

Dumping my tray on the table, I swat his hand away before dropping into my seat. "She wasn't doing it for me."

"She's female and she's got a pulse," Topher adds, leaning back in his chair, eyeing me curiously. "That's usually all it takes. What gives?"

I can't get the woman from the bar out of my head is what gives. But I don't tell my buddies that because I'm not the sharing-caring type and we're not close. "I'm turning over a new leaf." My friends crack up laughing, and my lips turn up at the corners. I flip them the bird. "Motherfucking assholes."

They drop it, and Mitch starts giving us a blow-by-blow account of the girl he and Toph tag-teamed over the weekend. *Did I mention my friends are assholes too?*

"Why don't I ever meet those kinds of girls?" Lance grumbles, shoving another mouthful of coronary-inducing pasta in his mouth.

I elbow him in the ribs, and he almost chokes. "It's the jelly belly. I'm telling you," I tease. Truth is, the dude is tall and lanky as a bean-pole. I doubt there's an inch of fat anywhere on his body despite his poor choice of diet.

Mitch flexes his biceps. "You need some guns, man. Chicks dig muscles."

I scoff. "The only muscle you're sporting is the one behind your pants, and even that's not impressive."

"Spout that shit at Cindy," Mitch retorts, puffing out his chest. "She loved the muscle in my pants so much she rode it three times."

"It's Sandy," Toph says, emitting a loud burp. "Chick's name was Sandy."

"Who cares?" Mitch says, shrugging. "Bitch fucked like a pro. That's all I give a shit about."

"How did I end up friends with a bunch of dicks?" Lance asks, finishing his pasta. "It's no wonder Emma never wanted to come to Boston on weekends."

"Your ex was too fucking selfish and lazy to make the effort to see you," Toph replies, leaning his elbows on the table. "Good riddance to the bitch, I say."

Lance drops his head to the table, and I caution the guys with a stern look. None of us understand it because we don't do the girl-friend thing. But Lance is a relationship guy, through and through, and he's heartbroken. Emma was his childhood sweetheart from back home, and he was devastated when she broke things off with him last year. Dude still isn't over her, and I don't think he's even gotten someone else underneath him since.

"You need to get laid," Mitch says. "You were too good for that prissy bitch."

I roll my eyes because, honestly, the guy has a brain the size of a pea.

"Look on the bright side; at least your brother didn't fuck her to get back at you," I supply.

Lance looks up at me. His brow is scrunched in confusion. "Why the hell would you say that, man?"

Toph and Mitch lean forward, eyes alight with interest.

Fuck, why the hell did I blurt that? I suck at trying to cheer someone up. Now, I'll have to fess up; otherwise, Lance will bust a ball worrying about his ex hooking up with his brother.

"I fucked my brother's ex to get back at him," I admit, lowering my voice so no one else hears.

Toph laughs, and Mitch leans across the table, punching me in the shoulder. "You're my fucking idol, man. I worship at the altar of Kent Kennedy."

"You seriously had sex with your brother's ex?" Lance asks, failing to hide the disgust from his face or his tone.

I eyeball him. "You know I'm an asshole. Why does this surprise you?"

"Because that's fucking low, even for you," he says. "Which brother?"

"Keats."

"Is that why you and Keaton don't talk anymore?"

"Yes," I lie.

"It's that Melissa chick, right?" Toph says, drumming his fingers on the tabletop. "The one who talked shit about your brother in that interview."

I nod.

"Damn, dude. She's hot. I'd do her," he adds.

My friends have no class and zero standards. A lot like me.

"She was a terrible lay. I'd get more enjoyment out of fucking a corpse."

Toph and Mitch whoop and holler. Lance wears his usual mask of disappointment when he looks at me. "Yet you risked your relationship with your brother for a shitty lay." He shakes his head. "I don't get you sometimes, man."

"I know the feeling, dude," I mutter under my breath.

Chapter Two
Presley

"**Y**ou want to get a drink?" Jimi asks when the class ends, his face holding on to hope where there is none.

"I can't. I've got a shift at the bar." And even if I didn't, I still wouldn't go for a drink with him. I like the guy. He's a decent dude and a fucking kickass artist, but I'm not attracted to him. I won't lead him on because that's not how I roll. He's one of the few people I like in art class, and I don't want to lose his friendship. It's not like I'm drowning in friends, because I have trust issues bigger than Kanye West's ego.

"Maybe next time." His smile is brittle, and I know I need to set him straight. I've been avoiding it because I suspect he's only coming to class for me, and I don't want to hurt his feelings.

Shoving my portfolio under my arm, I turn to face him, deliberately softening my features. "Jimi. If you want to go for a drink as friends, I am happy to do that any night I have no plans. But if you're hoping for something more, it's not going to happen." I don't add a "sorry" because I won't apologize for how I feel or *don't* feel.

His face drops, and his Adam's apple bobs in his throat. "Message received. Loud and clear." He turns to walk away, and I grab his elbow, holding him back.

"I value your friendship so much, and I think you're a really great guy, Jimi. Please don't take this personally."

"Hard not to," he mumbles, jerking his arm out of my reach and shoving his hands in the pockets of his jeans. "Is there someone else? Is that it?"

An image flashes in my mind. Blue eyes as vibrant and deep as the ocean. Messy dark hair I can imagine grabbing hold of. Muscles stretched over muscles. And an ego the size of a planet with plenty of attitude to match. I hate how often my mind has conjured up images of Kent Kennedy since our run-in last Saturday night at the bar.

"There isn't anyone." I don't elaborate because I won't insult the guy by throwing out the usual platitudes, and I can't admit the truth without hurting him. No one wants to hear the person they're crushing on doesn't reciprocate.

He gulps again. "Okay. I appreciate you setting me straight."

"Have a good night." I smile, hoping I see him again, as I head off in the other direction toward Ramshackle, the bar where I work.

I wear my backpack on my back and hug my portfolio to my chest as I walk the streets in this less than desirable part of Boston. Rent is much cheaper in Mattapan thanks to crime rates that are thirty-one percent higher than the national average. It's not the ideal place to live and work, but it's home, and the cheaper rent means I can put money into my savings account each month, bringing me closer to my goal.

It begs the question how the hell does a wealthy, notorious celebrity like Kent Kennedy even stumble across a place like Ramshackle anyway? My brain—just like it has on numerous other occasions—takes a detour to asshole town, and I let my thoughts wander.

Kent Kennedy personifies trouble. No matter how tempting his exterior is, there is no denying Kent is a bad boy who breaks hearts all over the place. I need another broken heart like a hole in the head, so

Reforming Kent

I'm glad I shut him down last weekend. I've zero desire to be another nameless, faceless notch on his considerable belt.

Rumors about the guy have been rampant for years, and I've heard personal tales of his escapades in recent times. Kent has been coming to the bar on weekends for a couple months although Saturday was the first time he was there when I was on shift. Ford—the other bar manager—and I alternate nighttime shifts over the weekends, so we have some semblance of a normal life. One week, I do days, while he handles the nights, and then we swap. During the week, we rotate as necessary, depending on what else we've got going on. It's a system that's worked well since the owner, Rafe, promoted me from waitress to bar manager eighteen months ago.

I might have only just met Kent in the flesh, but Ford has regaled me with tales of him for months. He always arrives alone, proceeds to get trashed, and then he either takes a girl out back or he leaves with her. Always a different girl, according to Ford, and he never even glances at them again.

Until I met him, I wondered how he gets away with treating women so terribly. Now, I understand it better. It's not just because he's fucking gorgeous or that he exudes this masculine sexual confidence that conveys he knows how to show a woman a good time.

It's just *him*.

He has this aura around him. It's like an electrical charge that's out of control. I can visualize him surrounded by it—sparkling and sizzling, prickling and crackling, it's orangey-red light both dark and bright, hypnotic in quality, drawing you toward him like an invisible rope is around your waist and he's slowly pulling you in. You know that even one touch might kill you, but you're powerless to resist the forward trajectory. You don't fight it, because you realize it's worth the risk, *he's* worth the risk, because that one touch will change you forever.

There's no denying how dangerous Kent is. To himself and others. To *me*. Because he radiates this dark, destructive energy that is as alarming as it is appealing. That fact is the single biggest issue I face because I've always been drawn to dark, reckless, broken boys who hide behind a mask. I don't know if I have a hero complex or I'm just too damaged myself, but I gravitate toward these guys like it's a compulsion. Like I've no choice.

It never ends well because you can't fix someone who doesn't want to fix themselves, and you should never try. It only ends in failure and self-loathing on all parts.

My mind instantly recalls my painful history with Chris, reminding me why I must forget about Kent. Pressure sits on my chest as I think about my ex. It's been a couple months since I've seen him, and I'm worried. He usually checks in with me monthly. I've searched the usual places, but it's as if he's disappeared off the face of the earth. Clay could probably locate him for me, but they despise one another these days, and Chris wouldn't thank me for involving Clay in his business, which is why I haven't raised my concerns with the guy who is my de facto big brother.

"Pres." Bugger tips his head at me when I approach the door to Ramshackle. The name is fitting because the place is in a state of disrepair, and it could definitely use a makeover. The structure is sound, but inside, it's like the seventies threw up in there. "You got a visitor," he says.

I arch a brow.

"At the bar," he adds, but his facial expression doesn't change. Bugger has two looks—bored and menacing—and he never mixes it up. Right now, he's bored, and I know that's as much as I'm gonna get.

"Love you too," I quip, knowing it will aggravate him, brushing past him as I enter through the narrow doorway.

Music pulses through the room from the old jukebox, and I skim the place, noticing it's busier than usual for a Thursday night. Half the tables on the floor are full, and all the booths that line the far wall are occupied—with a higher than usual percentage of female customers. That's the only clue I need to guess the identity of my mystery visitor.

I make my way across the scuffed, dark hardwood floors toward the bar, instantly spotting the back of Kent's head. He's sitting on one of the stools at the long bar, his head bent over, books sprawled across the counter, and he's jotting notes on a pad with his right hand.

My interest piques before I swat it away.

Remember he's the enemy, I caution myself because the only way I'll avoid falling into his trap is to remind myself of the threat he represents and to treat him accordingly.

"Hey, Pres." Tommy greets me from his usual perch at the end of the bar, directing his toothless smile in my direction.

"Hey, stud." I kiss his leathery cheek. "You waiting for me?"

"Like always, darlin'." He scrubs a hand across the patchy gray stubble on his chin and cheeks. "Just one look at your face and everything is right with the world."

Out of the corner of my eye, I spot Kent's head lifting, amusement clear in his expression. I pretend I don't see him, focusing all my attention on Tommy. He's been coming to the bar for more than twenty years, and he's as much a part of this place as the worn furniture. "You give me too much credit, Tommy." I give him a quick hug before slipping under the counter.

Ford approaches with a towel draped across one shoulder and a bottle of lager in his hand. "You're early," he says, setting the bottle down in front of Tommy.

"My teacher had to cut class a little short," I explain, grabbing a glass with ice and a bottle of chilled water from the fridge. "Just give me five to get ready."

"Take your time." Ford squeezes my shoulder, leaning his mouth in close to my ear. "I'll continue entertaining your admirer. He's been here for over an hour, and he must've asked for you at least a dozen times."

"You should put him out of his misery," I say in a low voice. "And send him on his way."

Ford grins. "We're already taking bets on you two."

Of course, they are. I inwardly sigh. Ford, Rafe, Bugger, and

Digger—our other bouncer—love making bets, so this isn't a surprise. I shove at his chest. "I hope you bet big. I'll enjoy watching you lose your shirt this time."

He laughs. "My money's on Kennedy."

I flip him the bird.

"He's got all the moves." He waggles his brows. "The guy is legendary."

"You sound like *you* want in his pants." My lips fight a smile. "You have my permission to go for it."

He rolls his eyes, slapping my ass with the towel. "Get your sexy delusional butt in the back and get changed. I want to get out of here. Promised Michelle I'd take her to see that new Theo James movie."

"Awww." I pinch his cheeks. "You're so romantic."

He swats my butt with the towel again. "You're pushing it, little lady. Be gone."

I'm still chuckling to myself when I emerge from the staff room five minutes later, having changed into my tight, black leather pants with an off-the-shoulder ripped short-sleeved top that reveals one of my red bra straps. My hair is pulled into a messy bun on top of my head, because I was too lazy to wash it this morning, and I've left a few strands framing my face.

"It's busier than usual so I called Imogen in. She's just waiting on Kady's babysitter to arrive."

"Cool." Imogen is my best friend, my only female friend, and I don't get to see nearly enough of her. She's a single mom to her daughter Kaydence, so she only works part-time and mainly during the day because she doesn't like leaving Kady at home with a babysitter too often at night. Kady's dad takes her every second weekend, so I have coordinated my nighttime weekend shifts to align with hers.

"I'm out of here," Ford says, raising his fist for a knuckle touch.

"Later, old man."

"Hey." He turns around, frowning. "Quit that old man shit. I'm only five years older than you."

"But thirty is sooo old," I tease, laughing when he flips me the bird. "Shouldn't you be married with a bunch of little rugrats by now?" Ford is a serial dater. In the seven years I've worked here, I've lost count of his girlfriends. Most don't last past the three-month mark, yet he's been with Michelle for five months, so maybe she's the one. Or maybe he's finally growing up.

"Just wait. You'll be thirty before you know it."

A throat clearing claims my attention, and I wave at Ford before turning my attention to Kent. "You again." I purse my lips, purposely keeping my eyes trained on his face so I don't gawk at how freaking hot he looks in that tight black button-up shirt he's wearing. He has the sleeves rolled up to the elbows, and the arm porn is to die for. Let's not even mention how broad his shoulders are, how ripped his chest is, or how bulging his biceps are because that's irrelevant. He's dangerous to my health, and I need to remember that.

"Hey, beautiful."

I roll my eyes.

"I've been waiting for you." He waggles his brows, flashing me a blinding grin. His teeth are perfect. Straight and white, and they fit snugly behind his full lips.

"Why?" I prop my hip against the back of the bar. "Because you're still horny and you think now you're sober you've got a chance?"

His grin expands. "One thing you should know about me, Presley baby, is I'm always horny." His eyes drill into mine, and a girl could get lost in those depths if she's not careful. "And I always get what I want."

"That's two things," I drawl, grabbing the wet cloth and wiping down the counter.

"I *can* count."

"Wow. Shocker." I plant a hand on my chest.

"Go out with me."

"No."

"Why not?"

"Because I don't want to."

"Why?" He leans forward, resting his arms on the counter, looking genuinely curious.

I wonder if girls ever say no to him. "I have my reasons."

"Such as?" He quirks a brow.

I lean my elbows on the counter, propping my chin in my hands. "One, you're a manwhore." I fake-sweet-smile at him. "Two." I pause for dramatic effect. "You're a manwhore. And three—"

"I'm a manwhore," he finishes for me.

"Now he's listening." I straighten up, continuing to wipe down the counter.

"You shouldn't believe everything you read online," he calls out as I move down the other side of the bar.

"Is that young pup bothering you?" Tommy says, pinning narrowed eyes on Kent.

I pat his hand, grinning. This guy is the sweetest. "It's nothing I can't handle."

He sits up straighter. "Just say the word and I'll flatten him." He flexes his shaking hands, balling them into fists. "I had quite the punch in my day."

"Stay out of it, old man," Kent hollers. "You're messing with my game."

"Ignore him," I pretend to whisper, knowing my voice is loud enough to reach Kent's ears. "I intend to."

"Now that's just mean, beautiful," Kent says when I move closer. "Throw a guy a bone here."

"You're not getting in my pants," I say, moving past him to serve the customers who have just approached the bar.

"Famous last words, Presley baby," Kent calls out, looking like he's up for the challenge, and I know it's going to be a long night.

Chapter Three
Kent

"What are you reading?" the annoying blonde asks, smashing her tits into my arm. I'm not looking at her. I'm too busy watching Presley joking and laughing with the blue-haired waitress as she loads her tray with drinks.

"*The Glannon Guide to Criminal Law*," I deadpan, not even glancing at the blonde as I reply.

"Cool." She titters, right in my ear, and I'm about to reach my breaking point. She's the sixth girl to approach me tonight, and they are all getting on my last nerve. Any other night, I'd probably be drunk or high or a combination of both and I'd fuck one of them in the bathroom, but the only woman I'm interested in fucking is the spitfire behind the bar. "You a lawyer or something?" Blondie adds, and I swear I see her gold-digging claws come out. She's seconds away from digging them into my flesh in some form of claiming-slash-branding.

"Law student," I confirm, removing her hand when it lands on my chest. "And I need to study." I gesture at the materials laid out in front of me. "So, fuck off. I'm busy."

"I can be quiet," she says, making no move to leave.

"I'm not interested." I glare at her, but she's not getting the message. "Now or ever. I'm not fucking you, so you're wasting your time. Take a hike." I make a shooing gesture with my hands. "Make sure to tell all your skanky friends I'm not interested in any of them either."

The stool screeches as she pushes it back and stands. "You're an asshole."

"Yeah, yeah. I know." I return to my books, wondering why I thought it was a good idea to come here on a Thursday night. Under my new self-imposed rules, I focus on school Monday through Thursday and cut loose Friday through Sunday. Coming to a bar on a Thursday night is tempting fate, and though I've been nursing sodas all night, my liver is craving alcohol like it's sustenance.

"You could've let her down more gently," Presley says, replacing my soda for a fresh one without me asking. I'll consider that progress because I'm that pathetic now it seems.

"Why would I bother? She's nothing to me," I truthfully admit.

"She's still a person. A human being with feelings," Presley retorts, folding her arms and glaring at me.

"News flash. I'm a person with feelings too. All she wanted from me was my dick. Go lecture her instead."

She leans back against the far counter, examining my face in a way I wish she'd examine my body. With sharp eyes and keen curiosity. I've never met any chick who intrigues me as much as this woman does.

"You can't honestly tell me you expect anything else when it's commonly known that's all you want from women. You fuck girls like they're a dying breed."

"Don't pretend you know me because you don't. No one does."

She straightens up, moving closer. "That's the way you like it though, or am I wrong about that too?"

I shrug because I'm not giving her shit until she tells me something. "What's with the portfolio?" I ask, and her eyes pop wide.

"You saw that?"

I nod. I'm drinking everything in about this girl for reasons unknown to me.

"You're deflecting," she adds, leaning over the counter, and it takes mammoth effort not to ogle her gorgeous tits. She's got an impressive rack and I'm dying to get up close and personal with every part of her rocking body.

"I'm trying to get to know you. Though it'd be easier if you just let me take you out for dinner." I glance over my shoulder, noting the heated stares from several corners of the room. I hate having a fucking audience.

"Why me?" she asks.

"I don't know," I truthfully reply, and she seems to like that.

"You're wasting your time," she says before moving to serve a few other customers.

I go back to my book, but it's futile even pretending I can focus in a noisy bar.

"I'll make a deal with you," she says, popping the top off a bottle of lager.

"Add that to my tab," I say, knowing it's for the old dude at the end of the bar.

She nods, handing it to Tommy. He lifts the bottle in the air in a show of gratitude, and I smile at him. Best buddies now. Perhaps he can help with Presley. She seems fond of him, and he's definitely got a soft spot for her.

"What deal?" I ask when she returns.

"You answer one of my questions, and I'll answer yours." I don't point out that I've already answered several of her questions though I'm tempted, 'cause I like winding her up. She's hot as fuck when she's irritated.

"Shoot." I take a sip of my soda, waiting for her to hit me with it.

"Why law?" Her eyes drop to the books on the counter, and I know she overheard my conversation with Blondie.

I could give her a bullshit answer, but something tells me this girl would see right through it, so I go with part of the truth.

"Because I want to do good in the world. I want to be known for more than my family name. I want to fight for justice. To battle on behalf of people who might otherwise be overlooked." I can't give her more because it's too close to home, even though what I've just said probably sounds like something a thousand other law students would say.

She stares at me, and a frisson of electricity crackles in the space between us. These tiny little gold specks flicker in her warm brown eyes as she looks at me like she can't figure me out.

Join the club, babe.

"It's my art portfolio," she admits after a few heavy beats of silence. "I attend an art class once a week at the local community college."

"Can I see?"

She shakes her head. "You have to earn that right."

"Go out with me," I repeat as I have intermittently all night.

"No." She dumps all over me again, but it only strengthens my resolve. Girls don't reject me, and her attitude excites me. It's not often I'm challenged these days, and I'm getting off on the thrill of the chase. If she genuinely doesn't want to have anything to do with me, she'd be better off agreeing to the dinner date because her stubborn streak means I'm definitely invested in seeing where this could go.

My cell pings with an incoming call, and I break our eye lock to find out who's calling me, groaning when I see Whitney's purple-haired image staring at me from the screen. I hit the ignore button, sighing.

I don't know what to do about Faye's half-sister.

Faye is married to my older brother Kyler. She's also my cousin. It's complicated as shit—even more so because Whitney and I have been fuck buddies, on and off, from the time we met when I was fifteen. If the timing had been different, maybe we never would've hooked up, but we've been trapped in this vicious cycle ever since, and I want out.

I managed to break all ties, and I didn't screw her for over a year, but every time life drops a bomb in my lap, I seem to end up back in her bed.

We're not good for one another.

We're too alike, and we're toxic together.

She knows it. I know it.

And it's not like we've ever been boyfriend-girlfriend or been exclusive.

If I'm a manwhore, Whitney is a slut, but she has feelings for me, feelings I don't share, and it's why I need to cut her loose. For good this time.

If I was going to confide in anyone, it probably would've been Whit. The fact I haven't speaks volumes. While I don't love her, I care about her, and I don't want to hurt her. She's broken, just like me, and all we are doing is enabling one another, excusing the behavior like it's normal when we're intelligent enough to understand it isn't.

She deserves better than me, and I'm trying to do the right thing by her now. I fucked her two weeks ago when I was up in New York, and I told her that was the last time. That we are over for good. We had a massive argument, and she's been blowing up my cell ever since. I'd block her number if I thought it would do any good, but Whit's resourceful. She'd just get a new phone, and it's not like I can avoid her. She's part of my extended family because Adam—her and Faye's dad—is close friends with my parents, and Mom always invites him and his kids to family events. Whether I like it or not, Whitney will always be a part of my family, and I have to find a way of making it work that doesn't involve drilling my cock in her pussy.

"Is everything okay?" Presley asks, bringing me back into the moment.

"Yep." I gather up my things. I want to call Whitney back but without prying ears. Also, it's late, and I have an early morning class. "I've got to go."

"Giving up so soon," she teases, her eyes lighting with mischief, and I'm transfixed. It's like this girl has cast a spell on me.

I pin her with my infamous panty-melting smile. "Not a chance in hell, Presley baby. I'm only getting warmed up," I say, as the blue-haired waitress slides behind the bar, knocking against a crate of bottles on the floor. Glass rattles and screeches, the sound piercing my skull, and I'm transported back in time.

Imaginary pain tears the skin off my left cheek, and I grab the counter, squeezing my eyes shut, as the sound of jangling glass reverberates in my ears. Tightness spreads across my chest, and my breath oozes out in strangled spurts as I struggle to get enough air into my lungs. On some level, I'm aware I'm in public, so I don't totally lose it, keeping my back to the main floor as I silently decompose on the inside.

A hand lands on my lower back, and I jerk to one side, blinking my eyes open. "Don't fucking touch me!" I hiss, straightening up on shaky legs. The environment comes into clear focus as I stare directly into Presley's concerned eyes. She's come around the counter to check on me, and I realize how badly I've fucked up. It's been years since I've had a panic attack in front of anyone.

"Kent. Can I—"

"Drop it," I snap, not waiting around to hear the rest of her sentence. I rush out of the bar, shoving past the bouncer and almost falling onto the sidewalk. My chest heaves, and I caution myself to get a grip before someone notices and starts recording my meltdown. The very last thing I need is something like this going viral.

A familiar guy steps out from under the shadows at the corner of the bar, his eyes asking a question. Fuck it. I've been steering clear of illegal substances during the week, but emergency situations call for emergency measures. I claw my hands through my hair, quickly scanning the area before gesturing for him to fall back under the awning where it's dark and private.

"What you want, man?"

"Just weed."

He arches a brow but says nothing, removing a baggie from his inside jacket pocket. I get it's not my usual weekend order, but I need to show up for class in the morning looking like a human not like a druggie.

Let's just say my less than pristine background and my rep as a womanizing bad boy did me no favors when I applied for Harvard Law. Only letting myself bleed on the pages of my personal statement salvaged it for me. Along with my parent's substantial yearly donation. And glowing recommendations from Dan Evans, our family attorney, and the governor of Massachusetts, who happens to be a personal friend of Evans' and a man who is an alumnus with strong current ties to the college.

I know there is an extra spotlight on my head, and I can't afford to fuck up. It's why I haven't missed any classes, have turned all my assignments in on time, and why I'm focusing on studying during the week so I stay on top of my classes. Getting high during the week is a recipe for disaster, but I can't go home and easily fall asleep after a flashback. I need something to numb my mind and take away the pain.

"Kent." Presley's disapproving tone echoes at my back, and I silently curse as I hand the cash to Jet.

"Later, dude." He gives Presley a quick once-over before walking off. I shove the baggie in the pocket of my jeans and turn around to face the music.

"You forgot your books and your bag," Presley says, handing my black backpack to me. It's zipped up, so I'm assuming she put my stuff away. "They are all there," she adds, as if she's a mind reader. A muscle clenches in her jaw, and I know she saw what went down here. She won't say anything because at least every second customer in the bar is high on the weekends, and it's not like the owner or either of the managers don't know Jet sells his shit on the street corner.

"Thanks."

She spins on her heel, ready to walk off, before halting and turning back around. Her jaw relaxes. "Are you okay? It looked like you had a panic attack inside."

"I'm fine," I snap. "It's none of your business," I add in a clipped tone.

Her eyes flare with instant anger. "Damn right it isn't, and that's the way I intend to keep it. Good night, Mr. Kennedy."

She storms off and all I can do is watch her retreating with the sinking knowledge I have probably fucked up any chance I had with her now.

Chapter Four
Presley

"Night, Bugger." I swoop in, kissing his rough cheek, laughing when he pushes me away with a scowl.

"You love winding him up," Clay says, pushing off the wall, grinning as he walks toward me. He flicks his cigarette to the ground, grinding the butt with the heel of his boot.

"I've got to grab the laughs where I can." I loop my arm through his, sliding my portfolio under my other arm as he grabs my backpack, slinging it over his other shoulder. "I didn't know you were stopping by tonight."

"Was in the area. Thought I'd walk my favorite girl home." That's code for he was up to shady shit that is gonna get him killed one day. I sigh, and he presses a kiss to my temple.

"Uh-huh." I narrow my eyes at him as we walk in the direction of my apartment. "I wish you'd go legit."

"Pres. Quit with that shit. What the fuck else do I know?" His eyes implore me to drop the subject as he drags his free hand through his long dirty-blond hair. Usually, he wears his hair to the nape of his neck, but the strands are brushing his shoulders now, and I can't decide if he looks like a wannabe rocker or a homeless bum.

"I don't want anything to happen to you," I explain. "I can't lose you too. You're my only family."

He slams to a halt, jerking his head at two tall, skinny guys wearing hoodies, lounging on the street corner. Giving him a terse nod, they walk off. "Pres." Clay clasps my face in his hands. "Nothing's gonna happen to me. No motherfucker would be brave enough to take another pop at me."

"Don't bullshit me, Clay." I wrap my fingers around his wrists, staring into his red-rimmed hazel eyes. "Rival gangs aren't the only reason I could lose you."

He places a tender kiss on my cheek, and it's completely at odds with the whole 'don't mess with me' vibe he exudes from his every pore.

Everyone knows to give Clayton Cooper a wide berth around these parts. He's almost as notorious in the underground scene as Kent is within celebrity circles. Although he never tells me shit, and I don't ask because the less I know, the better, I know he's mixed up in all kinds of illegal activities. I've no doubt his face is plastered upon the walls of police stations up and down the state, and he's constantly getting into street fights over control of the drug supply in the area.

"The pigs would've arrested me by now if they had anything on me." He slings his arm around my shoulder, urging me to start walking again. "You need to chill, Pres. All this worrying will give you wrinkles."

I thump him in the arm. "You're my brother." *And a known criminal.* "Of course, I worry."

"And you're my little sister. It's *my* job to worry about *you.* To protect you."

I roll my eyes. *What is it about guys and their constant need to protect?* As if we're not able to protect ourselves. "I've been living by myself since I aged out, and I've held down a full-time job since I graduated high school. I know how to protect myself."

"You still got that gun I gave you?" he asks while I look left and right before we cross the road.

"Nope."

Air expels from his mouth, and a muscle pops in his jaw.

"Don't do that. I'm not keeping an unregistered weapon in my possession. I bought my own handgun. It's legit, and yes, I know how to use it. I haven't forgotten."

After I left the foster system at eighteen, one of the first things Clay did was teach me how to shoot and how to defend myself physically. He'd been living by himself for four years by that time, and he'd already gotten heavily involved with The Vipers, the main gang who controls the streets of Mattapan and other neighboring towns. He'd seen enough shit go down to know I wouldn't survive living around here without the ability to defend myself. I work out a few times a week at a local gym to keep myself fit, and I do refresher self-defense classes every couple years to ensure my skills are sharp. I carry my gun everywhere with me, thankful I've never needed it.

Most people around here know Clay and I grew up in the same foster home. That we're as close as blood siblings, so no one gives me any trouble.

We arrive at the triple-decker I call home, and Clay follows me up the stairs to my second-floor one-bedroom apartment. I open the door, turn off the alarm, switch on the overhead lights, and walk into the open plan kitchen-slash-living room, dropping my bag and my portfolio on the kitchen counter. "You want something to eat or drink?" I ask him, sticking my head in the refrigerator. "I've got beer."

"Gimme a beer." He flops down on my couch, kicking his feet up on the coffee table.

I pop the caps off two beers, toeing off my shoes and padding barefoot into the living area. I hand him a beer before shoving his feet off my table. "Don't be an ass. I eat off that table sometimes."

He chuckles. "This place is a dump." He waves his hands around. "Why do you even care?"

Hurt blossoms in my chest, quickly replaced by anger. "Don't be a fucking jerk." I drop down beside him, pinning him with a glare. "It's not a dump. It's just a little dated, but I've worked hard to make it a home. I take pride in where I live, especially because it's the first place I've called my own since aging out. I don't give a fuck that it's not modern or that I don't have the latest, most expensive furniture."

I scan the homey room with a lump in my throat. "I carefully selected every single thing in this apartment, and it's a representation of who I am to my core." I rub a hand over the ache in my chest. "This place means something to me. You can't disrespect it just 'cause it's not to your liking."

I'll admit it's not the world's biggest apartment, and it definitely needs modernization, but it has character, something a lot of newer places lack. Plus, it's clean and tidy. The muted gray walls are freshly painted, and I sanded and stained the original hardwood floors myself last year. The furniture might not be trendy, but it's in good condition, and I scoured the consignment stores to find hidden treasures that perfectly fit the vision I had for my first proper home since my parents died. Most of the drawings on the walls are my own, and I painted the colorful mural on the back wall in my bedroom. I even sewed cushion covers and made the matching drapes.

"Don't get your panties in a bunch. I didn't mean to offend you," he says, looking mildly sincere. "It just frustrates me you won't take me up on my offer. You could live someplace better. You just have to say the word, and I'll make it happen." He swigs from his bottle, removing a pack of cigarettes from the inside of his worn leather jacket.

"I'm not taking your money, and I'm not arguing over this again."

"Let me pay for a nicer place." He squeezes my knee, and his eyes are pleading. "Come on, li'l heartbreaker. It would make me happy, and I know you want to."

Clay is so pigheaded when it comes to getting his own way, and it pisses me off that he can't see things from my perspective. I don't want his drug money, which is why I refuse all offers of financial help. I'm saving my hard-earned money to pay for art class and my apprenticeship. There have been occasions where I've been sorely tempted to give in to him, but I'm glad I stuck to my guns.

My future plans include setting up my own tattoo shop, and I want everything to be legit. I don't want anything from my past crawling out of the woodwork to ruin my plans. So, I keep on saving, and I reckon within the next year I will have enough to cover my years of apprenticeship and the courses I'll need to attend.

"Wow, you haven't called me that in forever." I'm deliberately deflecting, and he knows it. I've never admitted part of the reason I don't want handouts is the fact it's dirty money because I could never outrightly hurt him like that. Not after everything he has done for me. I owe Clay so much, and he's the only person I can truly count on to always have my back. Thoughts of ever losing him make me break out in a cold sweat. He might not be my blood sibling, but I doubt I could love any brother more.

"Break any hearts lately?" he quips, happy to leave the heavy stuff aside.

"Unfortunately, no."

"You should get back with Lync. He was crazy about you, and I liked him."

"Don't you read the tabloids? He's enjoying fame and all the perks that come with being a rock star. We broke up two years ago, and he's forgotten all about me."

"I wouldn't be so sure."

I shrug, because it makes no difference now. "I haven't regretted ending things when he got his big break. I'm not cut out for a long-distance relationship, and I've heard enough stories of life on tour to know he'd never stay faithful."

"He might have." Clay waggles his brows. "I bumped into him in New York a couple weeks ago, and he asked me if he should call you."

"You were in New York?"

"Just some business." He shrugs, averting his eyes. "You should call him."

"I'll call him when you find a girl to settle down with." Clay has never had a serious relationship, and I'd love for him to meet someone nice.

He finishes his beer, putting the empty bottle down on the table. "Nah." He toys with his nose ring. "Couldn't tie myself to one pussy. Variety is the spice of life."

I swat him with a cushion. "You're a walking STD. I should make you wear a hazmat suit before letting you sit on my couch."

Throwing back his head, he laughs. "Tales of my conquests are vastly exaggerated."

"Uh-huh." I take another sip of my beer. "I work in a bar. I hear things." Clay doesn't hang around Ramshackle much these days, but word travels fast in this neighborhood.

"I always wrap it before I tap it."

I swat him with the cushion again. "I don't need deets, thank you very much. Not unless you want me to reciprocate." I smile sweetly at him, and he gags.

"Hard pass." He stands, stretching his arms up over his head, stifling a yawn.

"You look tired. I can make up the couch for you."

Leaning down, he kisses the top of my head. "Got someplace to be. Maybe next time."

I walk him to the door. "Thanks for walking me home."

"Anything for my fave li'l heartbreaker." He rests his forehead against mine. "You know you mean the world to me, Pres. Right?"

"I know, Clay. You're that person for me too."

"It's you and me against the world," we whisper at the same time, sporting matching smiles when we break apart.

"I might be gone for a while," he adds. "Call me if you need anything, and I'll send someone around."

"Gone where?" Concern bubbles to the surface again.

"Just some business. Nothing for you to worry your pretty little head about."

Like that isn't condescending as hell, but I let it go as it's late and we've already shared heated words tonight.

He opens the door. "I'll call you when I'm back. We can grab dinner at The Pit Stop."

"Sounds good. Be safe."

"Always." He flashes me a devilish smile I know all too well.

"And cut your hair," I call out after him. "You look like a hobo."

His booming laughter follows me back into my apartment, and I'm still smiling as I turn off the lights and head to bed.

Chapter Five
Kent

"Dude, what the fuck is wrong with you?" Mitch stares at me like I've had a brain transplant as Casey and Savannah walk away from us in a huff. He's obviously not happy I instantly declined their foursome proposal.

"Trust me, I did us both a favor. They're bitches." I still remember the nasty things Casey said to my sister-in-law Selena, and that was the last time my dick went anywhere near her pussy. I intend to keep it that way.

Swiping my beer from the floor, I lean back in the couch, spreading my thighs wider as I survey the room with a new set of eyes. Music pings off the walls as an energetic crowd dances in the large living room. Every chair and available surface in the space is occupied with couples making out or fucking. A few guys are snorting lines of coke off the coffee table, and a cluster of girls is popping pills in the corner. Empty red cups litter the floor, and the myriad of booze on the table is in short supply. Mike and Paul's college parties are legendary, and I've had plenty of good times here, but for some reason, I'm not feeling it tonight.

"You're in a pissy mood," Mitch grumbles, draining his beer as he eyes the room with a trained hunter's lens.

He's not wrong. I've been in a pissy mood since I left Ramshackle after discovering Presley wasn't working. It's not like Mattapan is convenient, and I wasted hours of precious party time waiting for a girl who won't give me the time of day. I swallow the rest of my beer, gesturing at Mitch to grab us a couple more before all the bottles disappear.

He flips me the bird, cussing me out under his breath, but he still gets up, like a good little minion. When he returns, I snatch the beer from his hand, swallowing a few greedy mouthfuls as I watch the curvy redhead approaching.

"Hey, baby." She drops onto my lap uninvited, and it annoys the fuck out of me. I shove her away, and she falls to the floor, protesting loudly.

"Did I say you could sit on me?" I glare at her. "Do I look like a fucking chair to you?"

"You had no issue with it last time." She returns my glare, climbing to her feet.

I wrack my brain for any recollection of this chick, but I've got nothing. She stomps her feet and purses her lips, and it might be comical if I wasn't in such a shitty mood. "You don't even remember me, do you?"

"Come here, baby." Mitch pats his thigh. "You can sit on me anytime."

She gives me the evil eye as she plonks down on Mitch's lap. "Well?" She stares at me, waiting for an answer.

"Nope. Did we fuck?"

"You're an asshole."

I roll my eyes, thinking about getting it stamped on my forehead —for the one percent of the population who isn't in the know.

"It mustn't have been very memorable," I add because I'm a complete jerk when I'm pissed and Presley has me tied up in knots.

Tears well in her eyes, and if I had a heart, I might just feel bad about that. Instead, I drain the rest of my beer and stand. "I'm out of here."

Mitch wraps his arms around the redhead, and I'm betting he'll kiss her boo-boos better. I don't bother saying goodbye to Topher or Lance, wherever the fuck they are, calling an Uber and heading outside.

Silence greets me when I return to my apartment, and for once, I don't mind it. I grab a beer from the fridge and settle on the couch in the living room, kicking off my shoes. Lying back, I stare up at the ceiling, restless anxiety pricking at my skin.

I can't remember the last time I was home before midnight on a Friday night, relatively sober with no illegal substances humming in my veins.

I can't decide if I like it or not.

This is all Presley's fault.

Since I met her last weekend, I can't get her out of my head, and I don't do this.

I get drunk, get high, fuck random girls, rinse, and repeat.

That is what I'm good at. Not pining after girls who think I'm a worthless piece of shit. This is all new, and it feels like I'm an imposter in my own skin.

I consider calling Keanu, but I think better of it. If he knows there's *a girl*, he'll jump all over that shit, and he'll be planning double dates before I know what's hit me. An idea comes to me, and I sit up, dialing my brother Keven's number before I talk myself out of it.

"This better be good," he grunts when he eventually picks up.

"Forget it," I snap, my finger hovering over the end button.

"Don't hang up! Just give me a minute," he pleads. I hear the rustling of sheets and a soft feminine voice. Shit. I think I just interrupted him and Cheryl mid-banging.

"Kent. You still there?" Kev asks a few seconds later.

"I'm here."

I hear a door closing.

"Are you okay? Do you need me to come get you?"

"I'm twenty-fucking-three, Kev, and I know how to use a cell phone. There's this thing called Uber, and—"

"Always such a fucking smartass," my brother replies. "Excuse me for being concerned when you call me late at night after not hearing from you in months."

A pang of remorse hits me in the chest. I should probably apologize for that.

But I won't.

"You wanna help me out or not?" I ask.

A heavy sigh filters down the line before he says, "Always, brother. What do you need?"

Emotion clogs my throat at his words, and a part of me wishes I had told Keven. Out of all my brothers, I think he's the one I came closest to confiding in. Then I remember he was at Harvard, and he barely came home because he was pissed at my parents, and he wasn't there for me, just like everyone else. All too wrapped up in their own problems to see I was fucking drowning, right in front of them.

I squeeze my eyes closed, and the same intense pressure sits on my chest, making breathing difficult.

"Kent? What's wrong? You need me to come over?"

"No," I grit out, pulling myself together. "I was wondering if you could check up on someone for me."

"What trouble are you in now?" His voice sounds resigned.

Anger rushes to the surface. "Why the fuck does everyone jump to that conclusion all the time?" I shout, pacing the floor.

"Calm the fuck down, Kent, and just tell me what's going on. I left my wife naked in bed, and I'd really like to get to the point."

I hang up on him, tossing my phone across the room in a fit of rage. Fuck him. Selfish prick.

Turning the sound system on, I raise the volume, blaring heavy metal, not giving a shit if the neighbors call the cops. Our apartment is on the top floor of the building, and while the other residents are professionals, this part of Cambridge is full of students, so parties and loud music aren't exactly uncommon. Still, it's been a couple of years since this place has been party central.

Keanu and I bought it the summer before our sophomore year, and we partied hard for a while. Until Selena came back to my brother. After she moved in, I put a stop to all the partying because she was dealing with a huge amount of serious shit, and being around that scene wasn't helping her heal.

Finding out what happened to Selena had a profound impact on me, and things settled down for a while. Until...

"Fuck." I grab handfuls of my hair, dropping to my knees. I can't think about that now. I drain my beer as if it's water, returning to the fridge to snatch another one. Then I grab a joint from my room, light it up, and lie back on the couch, nodding my head in time to the music, as I let the effects wash over me, numbing me to all painful memories.

Closing my eyes, I picture Presley. That vivid spark in her gorgeous big brown eyes. How tempting her plump lips look when she's mouthing off at me. The determined set to her jaw, as she puts me in my place, that cranks my arousal to new heights. All that thick, long, gorgeous dark hair I imagine fisting in my hand while I—

The music cuts off abruptly, and I bolt upright, startled, my heart racing as adrenaline floods my system.

"Jesus fucking Christ, Kent," Kev says, staring at me like I'm an imbecile. "There are noise ordinance laws in effect from eleven. Your neighbors could lodge a complaint for disturbing the peace."

"Do I look like I give a fuck?" I flop back down, staring at the ceiling like it's the most fascinating thing.

"Do you give a fuck about anything, Kent?" Keven asks, sinking onto the end of the couch.

I give a fuck about a lot of things, but it's telling he doesn't know.

"Why are you here?" I ask, sitting up and swinging my legs to the floor. Swiping my half-empty bottle, I chug a few mouthfuls of warm beer.

"You hung up on me, you little prick." Kev rubs the back of his neck. "And you didn't answer when I called you about a hundred times, so I thought I'd come over and see if you were okay."

"How'd you get in?"

"I still have a key from when I organized the security system. Guess I forgot to return it to Keanu."

"You didn't need to come all the way over here." While traffic is minimal at this hour of night, it must've taken Kev at least thirty-five minutes to drive from Chelsea to Cambridge.

"Well, I'm here now, so you might as well tell me what's up."

"It's nothing," I mumble, embarrassed to say it to his face.

"Bullshit." Air whooshes from his mouth. "Look, I know things are shitty between you and Keats, and I can't pretend to understand why, but—"

"I'm not talking about that," I snap, cutting him off, my bad mood back in full force.

"I'm not asking you to. I'm just saying I can be your brother and Keats' brother even if you two aren't talking. Stop shutting me out. You've barely spoken to me since my wedding, and you acted like you were only there because you were forced to be." Hurt glimmers in his eyes. I'm a selfish prick. Keven is the most selfless of all my brothers, and he's done so much for our family.

"I was happy to be there," I truthfully admit. "I'm happy for you, man. Cheryl's great, and it's nothing personal. It's just..." I look down at my feet. I can't explain to my family without telling them the whole truth, and after all this time, what's the fucking point?

"Just don't be a stranger," Kev says, slapping me on the back. "We miss you. Mom misses you."

"I see Mom," I protest.

"You refuse to come to family dinners. It's hurting her."

I grind my teeth to the molars. "If you only came to lecture me, you can leave. You know where the door is."

Kev rests his head in his hands, and I'm betting he's silently counting to ten. I know I exasperate my entire family. Honestly, you think they'd be happy I'm keeping my distance. I just can't fucking win no matter what I do.

The silence is suffocating, and I wish Kev would leave so I can smoke another joint, drink another ten beers, and hopefully pass out.

Eventually, Keven lifts his head. "I didn't come here to lecture you or argue with you. I came to offer my help. Tell me what you need and it's yours."

"I met a girl," I blurt, like I'm ten.

Kev's lips twitch. "I thought you'd met plenty of girls."

I flip him the bird. "I'm not talking about a random hookup. I haven't even kissed this girl."

"Why the hell not?"

"Because she won't let me. She'll barely even look at me."

"I like her already." He can't contain his amusement anymore, and a massive grin slips across his mouth.

I jump up. "Forget it. I shouldn't have said anything."

"Kent." Keven stands, losing the smile. "I think it's great you've met someone. Tell me about her."

"That's the thing," I say, dropping back down onto the couch. "I don't know much about her because she won't give me the time of day, so I was hoping you'd do a search on her." Kev is a computer genius and an FBI agent, so he has the skills to pull this off.

His eyes pop wide. "You want me to investigate a girl you're interested in? Is there something I should know about her? Is she involved in something illegal or—"

"No." I shake my head. "It's nothing like that. I just want you to find out everything there is to know about her. And get me her address too."

"You want me to help you cheat," he surmises, narrowing his eyes in my direction.

"What the fuck are you talking about?" My brows scrunch up.

"You can't investigate someone you're interested in like she's a research topic. What about her privacy?"

"I just want to get to know her," I sulk.

"So get to know her."

"How?" I throw my hands in the air. "I told you she won't even talk to me. I have asked her out a million times, and she keeps saying no."

"Kent." Kev moves in closer to me, and he's fighting a smile again. "If you're serious about getting to know this girl, then you do the work like the rest of us mere mortals." He rolls his eyes. "Do you think Cheryl made it easy for me after what I did to her in high school? Look at what Selena and Keanu have been through. Faye and Ky. Lana and Kalvin. I could go on. We all had to fight to make things work. If you want to date this girl, then you've got to let her see the real you. Show her why she should say yes."

"How the fuck do I do that?" He's talking in riddles, and it's not like I've got any experience with this stuff.

I know how to get a woman into my bed, period.

Getting a woman to spend time with me outside the bedroom is a foreign concept, and I'm more than a little out of my depth. I've never wanted to get to know a woman until I met Presley, and it terrifies me as much as it enthralls me. I have zero clue what I'm doing. Or even why I'm doing it.

I accepted a long time ago that I wasn't destined to find love. Not like the kind my brothers have with their girls. I doubt there's a single girl on the planet who could put up with my shit. I come with a truck-load of baggage, and it's not attractive.

"You fucking woo her, you dumbass." He thumps me in the upper arm. "Send her flowers or cupcakes, or walk her home from work, or write her a letter, or—"

"I'm not writing her a fucking love letter. That's lame ass."

Kev chuckles, slapping me on the back. "'Much you have to learn, young padawan.'"

I groan. "Not you too." I blame Keaton for the fact all my brothers can quote random movie lines at the drop of a hat. Keats is movie obsessed and a lover of all the big blockbusters. If it's not *Star Wars*, it's *Twilight* or—I stop my train of thought as a tight pain spreads across my chest, like it does anytime I think of my triplet.

"Just be yourself, dude."

"I don't think that'll help. She hates who I am."

Kev shakes his head. "I'm not talking about the perception the public has of you, that face you show the world." He pins me with a serious expression. "Show her who you really are. Let her know the real you, and if she turns you down after that, then she's not worthy of you."

Chapter Six
Presley

I stroll into the bar Monday evening, stopping at the counter to kiss Tommy on the cheek. "Miss me, stud?" I tease, sliding behind the bar.

"For sure, sweetheart. Ford's pretty, but he's not in your league."

I bark out a laugh, waggling my fingers at my coworker, as I push through the door into the staff room. I slam to a halt as a delicate floral scent slaps me in the face. Blinking repeatedly, I stare at the massive bouquet of flowers perched on top of the small counter that runs the length of the back wall.

"They came earlier," Ford says from behind me, and I detect the grin in his tone. "Kennedy is slick. And persistent. I'll give him that."

"They're for *me*?" My voice betrays my disbelief. No one has ever bought me flowers before.

Ford nudges me forward. "That's your name on the card."

I stare in awe at the beautiful flowers, burying my nose in the soft petals. I recognize the roses and lilies, but I don't know what the peach and cerise pink flowers are or what you call the green foliage interwoven between the more colorful blooms. They are tied in a big white bow, and the card does indeed have my name on it.

I open it up, hoping Ford hasn't noticed how my fingers are trembling.

Go out with me? Because I'm "All Shook Up" over you.

I choke out a laugh over the lump wedged in my throat. Throwing the Elvis reference in there is kinda cheesy, but it's oddly sweet too.

"Dude must want in your pants *real bad*," Ford says, leaning over my shoulder, not even pretending he isn't reading the message.

Turning around, I punch him in the upper arm. "Don't rain on my parade. Whatever the reason, it's still a thoughtful gesture." But it'll take a lot more than this to worm his way into my bed.

Kent shows up a couple hours later, sliding onto the stool directly beside Tommy, shooting me with a panty-melting grin that has my ovaries weakening. Wetting my suddenly dry lips, I ignore the strange fluttering in my chest as I walk toward him. "Kent." I plaster a smile on my face. "What can I get you?"

"I'll take a Coke and whatever he's having." He jerks his head sideways at Tommy.

"My usual, sweetheart," Tommy says, never one to turn down free booze.

Tommy is the only guy in this bar that gets a free pass to call me sweetheart. With anyone else, it would be sleazy as fuck, and I'd get Bugger or Digger to throw them out on their ass. But Tommy is a true gent, and in his day, sweetheart was a genuine endearment and not a term used by douchebags to fake charm women into their bed.

I fix their drinks, sliding them in front of both men. "They're on me." I stare into Kent's wide blue eyes. "Thank you for the flowers. They're beautiful."

He cocks his head to the side, his lips curving at the corners. "So, when are we going out?"

I bark out a short laugh, shaking my head. "You think I'd make it that easy on you?"

His grin expands. "Challenge accepted, Presley baby."

"I'm not a challenge or some prize for you to win."

"I know you're not. You're so much more than that." He looks sincere, but I can't tell if it's real or part of the game.

"Don't set the bar too high, Romeo. You'll only be disappointed."

"I can be very determined when I want something." Kent waggles his brows, eyeing me over the rim of his glass with a pointed look that does funny things to my insides. "And I want you."

Tommy chuckles. "I think he's growing on me."

Unfortunately, I'm afraid he's growing on me too.

Footsteps pound across the floor the following morning while I'm doing inventory, and I shout over my shoulder, "We're closed. Come back in an hour."

"I just came to give you this," Kent says, and I spin around, watching him approach the bar.

"How did you get in here?"

"Bugger let me in."

I narrow my eyes because Bugger isn't known for his charitable gestures. I prop my hip against the counter as Kent places a coffee cup and paper bag down on the scratched laminate surface. "How much did you pay him?" I inquire.

Kent smirks. "Who says I paid him? How do you know it wasn't my legendary charm and wit that got me through that door?"

"He doesn't have a vagina, and he's not exactly your biggest fan."

Kent pushes the coffee at me. "I've been known to charm even the grumpiest motherfuckers. Consider it a warning." His blue eyes sparkle with confidence, and it's hella sexy. Almost as sexy as the dark scruff covering his chin and cheeks.

In daylight, Kent is even more hazardous to my health. He's wearing dark jeans that hug his muscular thighs and a tight white T-shirt under a grayish-blue shirt that really makes his eyes pop. Scuffed, unlaced boots adorn his feet, and he's wearing a ball cap backward, showcasing his high cheekbones, strong nose, and chiseled jawline.

He's truly beautiful in a strictly masculine way.

He hands me a tissue, his lips twitching. "For the drool."

I snap out of it, straightening up. "Ugh. Thanks for the reminder."

"I'll bite." He leans forward, bringing his stunning face closer to mine.

"I was almost in danger of falling for the sweet act."

The smile falls off his lips, and he takes a step back. "It's not an act, Presley. I'm interested in getting to know you. Why is that so hard to believe?" He shoves his hands in the back pockets of his jeans as his jaw tenses. "Enjoy your breakfast." His expression is devoid of warmth, and the sparkle has faded from his eyes as he shakes his head before walking off.

My eyes stay glued to the door long after he has exited. He seemed genuinely hurt by my comment, and I wonder if I haven't completely misjudged him. Taking a sip of the coffee, I groan appreciatively as familiar notes of cinnamon and nutmeg coat my tongue and swirl around my mouth. Pumpkin spice latte is one of my favorite drinks, and what are the chances Kent guessed correctly?

Opening the paper bag, I remove the bacon, egg, and cheese sandwich as my tummy rumbles in appreciation. I had to skip breakfast, thanks to waking up late, so this is exactly what the doctor ordered. I devour my food while opening the small envelope inside. It's another note, and I can't stop the cheesy smile creeping across my face.

Go out with me? Because "A Boy Like Me needs A Girl Like You."

"Why are you grinning like you've just won the lottery?" Imogen asks, ducking underneath the counter and coming up alongside me.

I show her the note, quickly explaining what's been going on because I haven't had a chance to fill her in since the first time Kent came into the bar. "So, you *have* won the lottery," she teases, wrapping an apron around her waist. "The boy lottery." She waggles her brows, and I snicker.

"Trust me, there's nothing boyish about Kent Kennedy. He's all man."

"Why are you resisting then?" she asks while she empties the dishwasher.

Tucking the note in the back pocket of my jeans, I finish my coffee and toss the cup and bag in the trash. "I don't want to be another notch on his bedpost."

"Makes sense," she agrees while I finish my inventory. "But you've got to get back out there. It's been two years since Lync left, and I haven't seen you show the slightest interest in any other guy, until now."

"You know my history, Mo. I've got to stop falling for the bad boys. It only ends in disaster."

"You can't tarnish every guy with the same brush, babe."

"Google Kent's name and tell me you wouldn't feel the same way in my shoes." Bending down, I unpack bottles of water, stacking them neatly in one of the fridges.

"You shouldn't believe everything you read online, and you won't know if it's true unless you give him a chance."

A thought occurs to me. "He didn't pay you off too, did he?"

"What?" Her brow puckers. "What are you talking about?"

"I wouldn't put it past him to bribe my friends into convincing me to go out with him."

"I wish he would," Imogen quips. "The extra money would come in handy now Kady's at middle school."

"If you need cash, I can—"

"Nope." She folds her arms across her small frame, giving me one of her fierce looks. "I'm not taking any more cash from you. You have already helped me out so much, and you're close to reaching your goal. I won't get in the way of your dreams." A look of nostalgia washes over her features. "I'm gonna miss you so much when you leave."

I yank her into a quick hug. "I'm not going anywhere for a while, and it's not like I'm moving to Mars. I'll still be in the area. We'll just have to find time to hang out around our busy schedules."

"I'm proud of you, Pres. You have worked so hard for your dream, and it's getting close now."

"I'm proud of you too, Mo."

She slants me with an incredulous look. "What have I done?"

"Only birthed one of my favorite little people in the entire world, and you are a fucking incredible mom. I know Rob helps out, but you're raising Kady alone, and you're doing an awesome job. You're my hero."

"You really think so?"

"I know so." Tears stab the back of my eyes, and I'd give anything to rewrite history.

"Thanks, babe. I couldn't do it without you. I hope you know that, and when it's your turn, I will be right there by your side, every step of the way."

Kent doesn't show up the rest of the day, and I'm oddly disappointed. Then again, it is spring break, and I'm sure he has better things to do with his time.

Wednesday is my day off, and I stay in bed for an extra hour before making my way to the local gym for a workout. I'm walking back to my apartment when my cell pings with a new message.

Ford: You have a delivery. Want me to stop by your place later and drop it off?

Reforming Kent

I shower and spend a couple of hours working on some new sketches before I take off for my afternoon shift at the youth support center. I volunteer once a month to man the helpline, and it's always a reminder of how lucky I am and how far I've come. Some of these kids are in terrible situations, and they have no one to confide in except a stranger at the end of the phone. Some days, I wonder if I should have studied psychology or sociology and gone into that line of work. Except there was no money for college when I left the foster care system, and I'm not sure I have the type of personality that could leave it all at the door after the working day has ended.

Besides, for as long as I can remember, my life has revolved around art and pursuing my dream of working in, and eventually owning, a tattoo shop. That is all I've wanted from the time I was thirteen when I first discovered *Ink Master*. I am freaking addicted to that show, and it's been a big source of inspiration.

When I return to my place, I see Ford has already come and gone. A medium-sized rectangular box is propped against my apartment door, a hastily scribbled note on the front from my friend:

Was in a hurry, couldn't wait. See you tomorrow.

I carry the box into my apartment, depositing it on the kitchen counter as I retrieve a pair of scissors to open it. I remove the contents, and my mouth hangs open in shock.

Two sketch pads rest alongside two Caran d'Ache gift boxes. One contains their graphite line, and the second wooden box has three layers of colored pencils. This stuff is ridiculously expensive, and I cannot believe Kent spent this much money on a girl he barely knows.

It's too much. I can't accept it, even if my fingers are twitching to test them out.

An unfamiliar sensation spreads across my chest as I stare at Kent's latest offering. This is nuts. *Does he think I have a fucking magical pussy? Or does he truly want to know me? Is Mo right? Am I judging him unfairly?* While I could say it's easy for him to whip out his platinum card, it's more than just the money. It's an extremely thoughtful gift, and I'd be lying if I said I wasn't tempted to give in to his request and go on one date with him.

Extracting the note from the small envelope, I read his words with growing concern for my heart.

Go out with me? Because you're my "Mona Lisa."

Is that even an Elvis song? Contrary to popular opinion, I'm not an Elvis fan, but Google is my friend, and Kent is on the ball. I press play on the YouTube video, listening to the legendary crooner, paying attention to the lyrics with an ever-spreading grin on my face. The notes are still corny as shit, but little by little, Romeo is chipping away at the walls around my heart, and I'm not sure how long I can continue resisting his undeniable charm.

Chapter Seven
Kent

Leaning against the wall, with one leg bent at the knee and the box resting at my feet, I watch men and women spill out through the doors of the community college, searching for the feisty brunette who has my balls in the palms of her hands.

I was disappointed Presley wasn't at the bar last night or this morning and more than a little pissed when Ford returned the gift I gave her yesterday. I don't understand why she won't accept it, and it's part of the reason why I'm here now. The other is I simply cannot evict this woman from my head. She has taken up residence there, and she shows no sign of leaving.

Coming up with new ways to "woo" her is giving me a fucking headache, because I don't know enough about her to make the gestures really count, and I'm running out of ideas.

I might possibly go insane before she agrees to date me.

I straighten up as Presley emerges from the building, an immediate scowl appearing on my face when I spot the dude walking by her side.

With his untamed hair, shabby mismatched clothing, lanky frame, and the obvious paint splatters on his wrinkled T-shirt, he looks like the stereotypical starving artist. I instantly hate him, and the second he places his hand on her lower back, I grab the box and storm off in their direction, ready to flatten his scrawny ass to the asphalt.

Presley's eyes widen when she spots me approaching, and the guy frowns, turning slowly to face me.

Landing in front of her, I ignore the nerd. "There you are, baby." I dart in, pressing a kiss to her cheek before she anticipates the move.

She narrows her eyes in suspicion. "What are you doing here, Kent?"

I flash her a cocky smile, pulling her into my side, pleased when the nerd glares at me as his hand falls off her back. "I'm escorting you to Ramshackle."

"I'm perfectly capable of walking by myself," she says, extracting herself from my side.

"I've driven all this way, so you might as well accept the ride." I'm forcing myself to be polite instead of indulging my inner caveman and just throwing her over my shoulder and carrying her to my SUV.

Her eyes lower to the box tucked under my arm, and I don't miss the pang of longing on her face, which spurs me on. "We need to talk about this," I add, patting the box before extending my hand to her. "We can discuss it while we drive."

She stares at my hand for eternity, and I feel like a tool, especially when the asshole smirks, clearly enjoying my discomfort. I'm seconds away from dropping my hand and hightailing it out of there when her fingers wrap around mine, spreading warmth up my arm. A deep sense of contentment washes over me as she laces her fingers in mine, and I know I'm grinning like a goober, but the reaction is automatic.

We're only holding hands, but fuck it, it's everything.

"Let's go." I tug her forward, eager to get her away from the geek.

"You're seriously going with him?" he huffs, folding his arms. "Is *he* the reason you blew me off last week?"

Presley moves to withdraw her hand from mine, and I hold on tight. Nuh-uh. It's the first time I'm holding hands with a woman, and she is *not* ditching me that easy. She flicks her gaze to me briefly before focusing on the nerd. "Kent has nothing to do with it, Jimi. We're just friends."

Kill me now, why don't ya.

At least friends is a step in the right direction, I suppose, so I try to remind myself it's progress. Still, I wouldn't be me if I didn't say what I say next. "For now." I level Jimi with a dark stare. "Presley knows my intentions." I shoot her a cocky grin. "And she won't be able to resist my charms for much longer."

She wrenches her hand from mine, pursing her lips and glaring at me. "You were doing so well until you opened your mouth."

"He only wants you for one thing, and the second he gets, it he'll lose all interest," the nerd says, and he's transparent as fuck.

"You don't know anything about me," I coolly retort, "and you don't get to disrespect Presley like that." I smother a laugh when he puts his chest all up in mine, pretending like he could take me. *As if.* I bench press more than his body weight without breaking a sweat.

"I know a self-righteous prick when I see one," he hisses.

"Desperation is not a good look on you, man. And you reek of it." I grin, because it's comical this guy thinks he's my competition.

"Okay. Enough." Presley pushes in between us, forcing us both back. "This isn't a pissing contest." She smiles at Jimi, but it's full of sympathy, and no dude ever wants to be on the receiving end of one of those smiles.

Crash and burn, asshole. I fix him with a smug smile from behind her back. Sucks to be you, dude.

"I'll see you next week, Jimi."

"Fuck you, Presley," he snaps, pushing past her. "I'm done."

Thank fuck for that. Good riddance to the jerk. "Wow. What a charmer he turned out to be."

Presley presses her lips together, watching his retreating back with a slight frown. "I thought I set him straight last week. He knows I'm not interested in him like that."

I knew she wouldn't be. Call me cocky, but I see the way she looks at me, and that twerp could never match up. "I think he got the memo now."

Reaching for Presley's hand, I wrap my larger palm around her smaller, softer one. A weird fluttery feeling descends in my chest the second her skin makes contact with mine, accompanied by a rake of little shivers cascading up and down my arm. She startles a little, so I'm guessing she felt that jolt of electricity too. Her eyes lower to our conjoined hands as her fingers press more firmly against mine. Her gaze is a mix of confused awe when she lifts her head, and her eyes lock on mine.

Makes two of us, babe. I've no clue what kind of freaky cosmic energy is at work here, but this mad chemistry we share is not unwelcome or unpleasant. We stare at each other, our hands interlocked, and in the depths of her warm brown eyes lies so much hidden meaning and so much potential. Fear threatens to resurface, but I tamp it down, pulling her in next to me. Closing my eyes, I press a soft kiss to her temple, inhaling the vanilla scent wafting from her hair, reveling in the feel of her velvety-soft skin under my lips. "Ready to get out of here?" My voice is thick with longing.

"Yes," she whispers, and when I open my eyes, I'm pleased to see hers are shut too. I hope it means she's committing me to memory in the same way I'm memorizing her.

We walk in silence across the road, turning the block to reach my car. I put the box with her art supplies on the back seat of my BMW X5 before opening the passenger side door for her.

"Nice car," she says, glancing all around as I slide behind the wheel.

"Thanks." The engine purrs as I power her up. "My brother Keven drives one of these, and he recommended it." I glide out into the traffic, casting a quick glance at her. "Are you hungry? Do you want to grab something to eat before your shift?"

"I don't have time."

"We could grab something from a food truck. Are there any on the way?" I'm not familiar with Mattapan because I usually Uber it to the bar and back.

"We could stop at the burrito bar. It's around the block from Ramshackle."

"Okay, perfect." I tap it into my GPS system, and we pull up in front of the silver trailer a few minutes later.

Climbing out of the car, I race around the hood in time to open Presley's door for her.

"Thank you." Her smile seems genuine as I help her out, and I tuck it away on my mental notepad for future reference.

"What's good?" I ask as we survey the menu.

"Everything. The chicken burrito is my favorite though."

We stand in line, and I clear my throat. "Why did you return my gift? Did I buy the wrong things?" I'll admit I know jack shit about art, but the lady in the store said every artist worth their salt wants a Caran d'Ache set.

She shakes her head, and waves of her dark, glossy hair tumble invitingly over her shoulders.

She has fabulous hair.

Plenty I can wrap around my fist, using it to yank her head back as I take her from behind. My dick stirs to life behind my zipper, and I force all thoughts of a naked Presley from my mind before I'm sprouting a full boner. Not gonna lie. I'm dying to get this woman underneath me. But it's more than that. And I don't want to fuck it up by letting my hormones overrule my head.

"It's a perfect gift, Kent. But I can't accept it."

"Why the fuck not?" My brow puckers as we shuffle forward in the line.

"That stuff is super expensive. I can't let you spend that much money on me."

I peer into her eyes, searching for evidence of the truth, and it's blatantly staring back at me. She actually means that.

This might be the moment I truly fall for this woman.

"What if I want to spend it on you and it will hurt me if you continue to refuse it?"

"That doesn't make it right." She tucks her hair behind her ears, and I want to be the one to do that.

I lightly touch her elbow as we move one step closer to the front of the line. "It's a gift, Pres." My eyes flit momentarily to her lush mouth, and I want to kiss her so badly. My dick strains against my zipper again, and I force myself to focus on the conversation, not her tempting as fuck lips. "I saw the way you looked at the box. I know you want it. Accept it. It would make me happy if you do."

She stares at me, her eyes roaming my face, her gaze lingering on my lips a little longer, in a way that pleases me. "Why are you doing all this?" Her breathy, raspy tone unravels me, and my cock is rock solid now.

"You know why. I want to spend time with you." Swallowing a bout of nerves, I put myself on the line. "We have a connection. There's something there, and I want to explore it. I know you think I'm a manwhore, but—"

Her lips tilt in amusement, cutting me off mid-sentence.

Dragging a hand through my hair, I expel air from my mouth. There's no point denying this. The proof is plastered across the web. "Okay, I *am* a manwhore. A reformed one, because I haven't so much as looked at another girl from the minute I met you. I won't pretend I don't want to fuck you, because you're beautiful and sexy, but it's more than that, and I'll do whatever it takes to prove I want this to be different with you."

That might possibly be the longest, most genuine speech I've ever made, and this girl now holds my heart in her hands. As well as my balls, because I'm in scary danger of losing those too.

She opens her mouth to reply when the guy behind the counter shouts, "Next."

I glare at him, because his timing fucking sucks, and I've a sudden desire to swing my fist in his face, but I restrain myself. I order two chicken burritos and two bottles of water, and we take them back to the car.

"This is so good," I say in between mouthfuls of the succulent, spicy chicken wrap.

"Told ya." She smiles before diving in with gusto.

Even her appetite for food turns me on.

I've got serious issues.

She hasn't made any reference to my little speech, and I'm too chicken shit to bring it up, so I say nothing, switching the radio on so we can listen to music as we eat. But it's not awkward. There's a certain level of familiarity with Presley that comes naturally, and I'm relaxed in her company in a way I rarely am with women.

Balling up her wrapper, she shoves it into the paper bag before taking my empty water bottle and wrapper and dumping it inside. Her fingers brush against mine, igniting the same fiery tingles like every time our skin comes into contact. Her touch literally electrifies me, and it's like nothing I've ever experienced.

"Tuesday night," she says, turning in the passenger seat to face me.

"What?" I splutter, confused.

She graces me with a knockout smile. "I'm free Tuesday night."

"You'll go out with me?" I'm sure I'm rocking the whole deer in the headlights look, because I can't believe she's agreed. I thought I'd have to grovel for much longer than this.

Guess I'm just that good at this wooing shit.

I give myself a proverbial pat on the back.

"I will. One date," she cautions.

"And you'll accept my gift," I add, throwing my gaze to the box in the back.

"I will but, Kent." She leans in closer, and I stop breathing. Her mouth is so close to mine it would take nothing to close the gap and slam my lips against hers. But I summon restraint from some long-forgotten place inside me, using all my willpower to focus on her gorgeous eyes. "You don't need to buy me expensive gifts. Little gestures work just as effectively. Like your notes."

"You like them?" I can't contain the grin on my face.

"I do." She's fighting a smile. "I like how it gives me a little insight in to you." Her eyes drift to my mouth, and I know she wants to kiss me as much as I want to kiss her, but I hold back because I won't fuck this up.

"Then I have something else for you," I admit, stretching across her to reach for the glove compartment. My arm brushes across her chest, sending a fresh wave of blood south to my dick. This woman lights a flame inside me every time we touch, and I know when we finally get down and dirty it's going to be fucking explosive.

It's possible I might die of blue balls before then.

Nerves fire at me from all sides as I remove the dog-eared book from the glove compartment. This is a risk, but go big or go home, am I right? I hold the book to my chest. "Do you read?"

"A little. I don't have a huge amount of downtime, and when I do, I usually draw, but I try to read a book or two a month."

"This is one of my favorite books." I run my fingers over the worn cover of *All the Bright Places* by Jennifer Niven. "I discovered it when I was younger and I was going through some stuff. I think the message is powerful." I hand it to her, adding, "I want to know you, but I want you to know me too because I'm not just the things they say about me online. Read it and let me know what you think."

Flipping it over, she reads the description on the back, and I take a few moments to study her.

She's exquisite, but I can tell she doesn't realize it. She doesn't wear much makeup or use a ton of product in her hair. She dresses edgy but always with comfort in mind, and she looks like someone who is content in her skin. I'm dying to know what the ink on her lower arms means and to explore the other tattoos she's hiding underneath her clothes. She looks good in my car, and I know she'll look good in my arms, and I truly, honestly, sincerely want to see where this leads.

Reforming Kent

Because Presley is the first good thing to happen to me in years.
And I really don't want to fuck it all up.

Chapter Eight
Kent

Istop by the toy store on my way to Eva and Kaden's house the following night, picking up the latest princess doll for my niece Milly and a bunch of superhero figures for her brother Matthew. On the spur of the moment, I pick up a bottle of wine and some chocolates for my sister-in-law.

I didn't announce I was dropping by, but I'm expecting Eva to be in because their kids are both under five and I know Kade is out in the city drinking with my other brothers tonight. I got the invite but passed because I know the hot topic of conversation will be Keats and Austen's June wedding, and I want no part of that shit.

After tapping the code into the keypad by the gate, I drive up the winding driveway to my brother's plush family home. The security system will have notified Eva of an impending visitor, so I'm not surprised to see her waiting at the front door for me. I park the car in front of the house and hop out, grabbing the bags from the back seat.

"This is a nice surprise," Eva says, giving me a one-sided hug as I stand awkwardly in her doorway.

"I need to talk to you about something," I admit when she releases me, stepping aside to let me in.

"Kade isn't here." She closes the front door, following me down the hallway and into their open living area.

"I know. I came to talk to you." I shove the bags at her. "Where are the rugrats?"

"Asleep." She places the bags on the large island unit in the kitchen, peering inside. "Oh my God. Milly is going to love you forever for this," she exclaims, removing the box with the doll. "She's been begging us for this, but Kade told her she had to wait until her birthday."

I poke my head in the fridge, grabbing a beer. "Great. Now he'll have extra ammunition to rip me a new one."

Kaden is my eldest brother, and he's been the most vocal about the rift in our family, squarely laying the blame at my door. He doesn't waste any opportunity to berate me, and I'm fucking sick of him sticking his nose where it's not wanted. It's the other reason I came here tonight; I knew there was no chance of running into him.

"Kade worries about you, Kent," Eva says, extracting the wine and the chocolates from the bag. She kisses my cheek, smiling warmly at me. "This was thoughtful. Thank you."

I shrug, not wanting to make a big deal out of it.

I pop the cap on my beer and grab a wine glass from the overhead cupboard for my sister-in-law. She pours a healthy amount of ruby-red wine into the glass, and I arch a brow.

She slaps my arm, laughing. "Stop looking at me like I'm a lush. It's been a tough week."

"Trouble with my brother?" I inquire as we walk into the living area, claiming seats at opposite ends of the gray leather couch.

"Of course not." Her face lights up at the mention of Kaden, and I wonder if Presley will someday look like that when someone mentions me.

I silently scoff. As if I could ever warrant that kind of lovesick affection. I must be short a few brain cells for my mind to have gone there. I'm under no illusions about this thing with Presley. I mean, it's a miracle I feel this way about her because no other woman has ever elicited the same response, and I know that's huge. While there is a strong part of me that wants things to work out with her, I'm self-aware enough to know I will fuck it up because I always do.

I've done a lot of thinking in the last twenty-four hours and hoping and praying I don't fuck things up is a futile strategy. I've got to face the facts. Nothing good ever lasts in my life because I have a self-detonation button I can't help pressing. I *will* fuck things up with her, so I'm better off entering into it with my eyes wide-open. That way, I can enjoy whatever time we have together and when it ends up in ruins at least I'll be expecting it.

"Kent." Eva peers into my face, her expression etched with concern. "Where'd you go?"

"Sorry. I wandered off. What were you saying?"

"Things are great with Kade and the kids, but the stress and pressure of work is getting to both of us. There is always so much to do and not enough hours in the day."

I slouch back in the chair, resting my ankle on my knee as I get comfortable. "Hire more staff, and didn't McConaughey take on more responsibility recently?" I remember Red, his wife, mentioning something about Brad becoming a director or some shit. I tend to tune out when Rachel waxes lyrical about her husband.

Brad is like a surrogate Kennedy, having lived with my family for several years when his family fled overseas. He's best friends with my brother Kyler, and Rachel is Faye's best friend. Both women are from Ireland, but they've been living here for years.

"Brad is our global sales director, and he's doing a lot of the heavy lifting and most of the international travel, but we can't keep pulling him away from Rachel and Elodie. She's not even two, and she needs her daddy."

"Again, hire more staff. The business can afford it, right?" The last I heard, Eva and Kade's online golf business was booming, hence the expansion into Europe.

"I know you're right, but even finding the time to recruit someone is challenging."

"Outsource it to a recruitment agency. I bet Faye could recommend someone." Faye, Kyler's wife, works part-time as head of human resources for my mom's interior design company. Mom's business partner is Brad's mom, and they hold an equal share in the thriving interior design company. Faye shares the HR role with another woman, because she didn't want to go back to working full-time after the twins were born.

Or so Mom says, because I haven't talked to Kyler or Faye much since Ciara and Cathal arrived on the scene. A pang of guilt sweeps through me, and I know I've got to make more of an effort with my family. If they all agreed to not discuss Keats, it would be easier, but my family is a bunch of busybodies, and they won't rest until they have fixed things between me and my triplet.

There's more chance of Kanye being president than things getting resolved with Keaton.

"You're full of good ideas tonight," Eva muses, running the tip of her finger around the top of her wineglass. "We should talk more often."

I roll my eyes, and Eva laughs, kicking off her shoes and tucking her long, slim, olive-toned legs into her chest. My sister-in-law is a beautiful woman, and Kade is a lucky guy because she's also super smart and she has a big heart. All my brothers chose well, but I'm only close with Eva and Selena because none of the others understand me.

From the minute I met Eva, she accepted me for who I am, flaws and all. She never judges. She only ever wants to help. If I didn't think she'd instantly tell my brother, I would confide in her. I've come close once or twice when I've gone through a particularly rough patch, but knowing she'd tell Kade always holds me back.

"So, what's going on with you? How is Harvard Law?"

"It's good. The coursework is intense, but I'm keeping up."

"And how's the love life?"

Only Eva could refer to my "sex life" as a "love life." I smother my snort of hilarity. "That's actually what I want to talk to you about.

I have a date next Tuesday, and I have no idea where to take her." I pin puppy-dog eyes on her. "Help a guy out?"

Her eyes pop wide with excitement. "Who is this girl, and when can I meet her?"

I raise a palm. "Hold your horses. It's one date. It's not like I'm going to marry her."

"This is huge for you. We both know that." Eva's grin is so wide it threatens to split her face. "Tell me all about her."

So, I do. I tell her the little I know about Presley.

"She sounds wonderful, and you clearly like her. I'm excited for you."

I shrug, shifting on the couch, uncomfortable with the direction the conversation is going. "Where should I take her? I've spent all day looking at options, and I can't decide." I exhale heavily.

"From what you've said, Presley doesn't want extravagant gestures, so take her someplace cool, maybe a little off the beaten track. A bar with a good rep for food and a variety of craft beers maybe?"

"She works in a bar, so I want to take her someplace different."

"What about that new restaurant, Moam? The food is supposed to be delicious, and they have a full bar with craft beer and a cocktail menu. Kade and I have been meaning to check it out."

"Check what out?" my brother asks from behind us.

I stifle a frustrated groan. *What the fuck is he doing home this early?*

"Moam," Eva says, setting her wineglass down and standing. She walks to her husband, flings her arms around his neck, and kisses him. It's no chaste peck on the lips either. They are all lips, tongues, and teeth, and there is no denying the passion they share.

A tight pain spreads across my chest as I look away, not wanting to intrude on their private moment.

"What are you doing here?" Kade asks a few minutes later, adjusting himself in his pants.

Fucking gross.

I do not want to see that shit.

Eva removes the laptop bag from Kade's shoulder, helping him slide his coat off as he frowns at me. "I thought you had to study."

"Last-minute change of plans," I lie, leveling him with a challenging look, daring him to push me on this.

"Kent has a date." Eva pipes up, and I fix her with a warning look. "I don't keep things from my husband," she supplies. "Unless you tell me something in complete confidence. I didn't think it was a secret."

I eyeball my brother. "I don't want the others to know. It's only a date. It probably won't go any further." I know my family. They will gush like crazy if they find out I'm dating, and I could do without the familial pressure. It's not like the odds aren't already stacked against me and Presley.

"She must be really good in bed if you want to take her out," Kade says, and Eva thumps him on the arm.

"I haven't even kissed her," I hiss, slamming my beer down on the table before standing. I am fucking sick of the judgment from my family.

"Wow." Kade smiles, and it seems sincere. "You really do like her." He clamps his hand on my shoulder. "Good for you, bro. I hope it works out."

I bob my head, clawing a hand through my hair. "Thanks for the advice, *Evelina*." I hug my sister-in-law. "I'll check that place out."

"I'll walk you out," Kade says, and I count to ten in my head.

"If you're planning on lecturing me, save your breath," I say when I step outside the front door.

"How long are you going to keep this up, Kent?" Kade leans against the side of my SUV, scrubbing a hand along his jaw. Bruising shadows linger in the space underneath his eyes, and he looks tired.

"Just butt out, Kade. I'm sick of everyone getting on my case about it."

"You can't do this forever. He's your brother, Kent. Your triplet, and it's killing him that you won't talk to him. Won't accept him. So what if he's gay? It doesn't change who he is to us. And Austen is a great guy. I think you would really like him if you took the time to get to know him."

"It's not going to happen, man." I kick at the gravel underfoot.

"You can't avoid them forever. And if you're planning to skip out on their wedding, think again." He straightens up. "Man up, Kent. The next time Keats texts you, *reply*. Go talk to him."

"It's not that simple," I say through gritted teeth.

"It really fucking is. You just talk."

"You don't understand. I—" I cut myself off because there's nothing else I can say. I can't do this now—or probably ever. I certainly can't bring this up with Keats a few months before his wedding.

"You're right, I don't. Enlighten me."

I stare at my brother's troubled expression. "I can't."

Disappointment crosses his features as he shakes his head. "Why won't you tell any of us what's wrong? This is just like your teenage years all over again. You've shut down and shut us out, and you might have gotten away with that crap when you were a kid, but you're a fucking adult now, Kent, and it's time to start acting like one."

"Fuck you, Kade." I push at his shoulders. "You're not my father, and you don't know shit about me."

"I know if you don't fix things with Keats before the wedding you're going to regret it."

Chapter Nine
Presley

I check my reflection one final time in the mirror, pleased with the result. The black dress is plain, but it hugs my curves and skims my thigh, and I hope it's sexy in an understated way. I don't want to give Kent the wrong impression. I want to look good without it being an invitation. If he thinks he's getting into my panties tonight, he's got another think coming.

The pile of clothes on my bed illustrates how difficult dressing for this date has been. I don't recall ever being this indecisive when I was dating Lync, and the situation with Chris was entirely different.

I add a colorful choker around my neck before sliding my feet into my knee-length lace-up boots. They have a medium stiletto heel, and I like the confidence I get from the extra few inches in height. Kent is tall so I can wear them and not worry about towering over him. I spritz some perfume on my neck and my wrists and add another layer of deep-purple lipstick to my mouth. Deciding I'm done, I snatch my red leather jacket and head out into the living area to wait for Kent.

A smile crests over my mouth, like it does every time my gaze gravitates to the flowers Kent sent me. I sniff the blooms, but only a lingering scent remains. They have lost their freshness and are starting to wither; however, the flower-pressing kit arrived today, so I plan on spending my day off tomorrow drying and pressing the flowers. When they are ready, I intend to stick them on the drawing I've sketched, and then I'm gonna frame it and hang them on the wall.

It might be overkill, but I think a girl should always remember the first time a guy gave her flowers.

Kent rings the door at exactly eight, and I'm pleasantly surprised at his punctuality. A rush of butterflies invades my tummy, and I'm trembling a little as I grab my purse and head toward the front door.

I draw a brave breath as my fingers curl around the door handle.

Here goes nothing.

Opening the door, I force myself not to react when I get an eyeful of Kent. He looks utterly fuckable in his black designer dress shirt and tight-fitting jeans. His sleeves are rolled to his elbows, highlighting the glorious ink on his arms, and with the way his shirt is stretched across his impressive chest and biceps, I'm going to have a hard time keeping my eyes on his face tonight.

"Liking what you see, Presley baby?" That notorious shit-eating grin comes out to play.

"Meh. I've seen better," I joke, attempting to hide my lust behind humor.

"Well, I haven't. You look fucking hot." His gaze rakes leisurely over my body like a sensual caress, and desire coils low in my belly. He whips a single purple rose out from behind his back, handing it to me. It's set within a small square glass vase, and I've never seen anything like it. "It's an infinity rose," he explains, sounding a little nervous. "The woman in the shop said it would last a year if you leave it in that and don't water it."

Our fingers brush in the exchange, his touch heating me instantly. "It's stunning. Thank you so much."

I leave it on the kitchen counter, set the alarm, and lock the door. Kent lets me walk first, trailing behind me, and I've a sneaky suspicion he's checking out my ass.

"Nice boots," he says when we exit the building.

My lips twitch. "Let me guess, you're imagining me flat on my back, naked except for the boots wrapped around your neck."

"Damn." He adjusts the front of his jeans. "I wasn't before, but I am now."

"Liar," I tease as we approach his car.

"All right. I'll admit it," he says, opening the passenger door for me. "I was imagining something like that, only my vision was dirtier."

I lean against the door. "Now, I'm intrigued. Don't leave a girl hanging."

He moves his face in close to mine, his eyes dipping to my waist. Pressing his mouth to my ear, he says, "My fantasy was similar, except your hips were arched and I was eating you out with your booted thighs squeezing my face."

My panties are instantly drenched, my core pulsing with need. It's been way too long since I was laid, and that acknowledgment sends all kinds of alarm bells ringing. I'm in even more danger with this guy than I thought. Resisting Kent will not be easy. "Holy fuck." I slap a hand across my chest. "I'm sorry I asked."

He saunters off with an arrogant swagger, and I'm grateful for the few seconds to compose myself before he gets behind the wheel.

The waiter escorts us to a table in the corner, offering us some water while he sets the menus in front of us. I've never heard of this place, but that's not strange. On the rare occasions I venture into downtown Boston, it's usually to drink not eat in some fancy-pants restaurant.

The décor is nice with its dark wood tables, velvet-backed chairs, low industrial-type lights, and exposed ceiling, but it's a lot more formal than my usual hangouts, and the crowd seems older too.

I cast a surreptitious glance around as I pretend to peruse the menu, and most of the men are in dress pants and shirts, while the women wear expensive gowns. I shift on my seat, feeling a little out of my comfort zone, but I'm determined to force my concerns aside and enjoy the night.

It's not every day I get taken to a place like this.

I refocus on the menu, and my eyes almost bug out of my head. "I think the waiter gave me the wrong menu," I tell Kent, raising my eyes to look at him. His brows knit together as he glances between his menu and mine. I lower my voice, stretching across the table as I say, "The cheapest entrée is one hundred dollars."

"It's okay. I'm good for it." Kent's tone is dismissive but not arrogantly so. I suppose, if you're him, having grown up in a family as wealthy as the Kennedy family, it's not something you give much thought to.

I want to tell him he doesn't need to spend this kind of money on dinner, but I don't want to insult him either, so I mash my lips together and say nothing.

Across from us, a party of ten is being seated, and I don't miss how several of the women gawk at me, their eyes raking my body, and my ink, with barely concealed derision. Even though my dress is short, it isn't revealing, but to them, I probably look like a hooker. I hold the skinny blonde's gaze for longer than is socially acceptable, but she was rude first, staring at me like she couldn't believe I have the nerve to sit here.

"You got a problem?" Kent asks, stabbing the woman with a dark expression. "Because I've got to say I don't much like the way you're looking at my date."

Her eyes pop wide as she blatantly eye fucks Kent. "You're a Kennedy," she rasps in what she probably thinks is a sultry tone. To me, she sounds like she's got a ten-pack-a-day habit.

"And you're a rude bitch," Kent says, standing. Deliberately turning his back to the woman, he pins his eyes on mine. "Come on. Let's get out of here."

I don't need to be told twice. Grabbing my jacket, I hold my head up high as Kent escorts me from the place with his hand pressed protectively against my lower back.

"Fuck, Presley. I'm sorry about that," he says when we're outside.

"You don't have to apologize. It's not your fault."

He takes my hand, lacing his fingers in mine, as he walks me back toward where he parked the car. "I asked my sister-in-law for advice on where to take you, and she suggested Moam. But Eva and my brother are older, and it's more their kind of place. Definitely not mine."

"Nor mine," I agree. "It's a beautiful place, and I'm sure the food is gorgeous, but I think the one-hundred-and-sixty-dollar steak would stick in my throat. I could buy groceries for two weeks with that."

We pull up in front of his car, and he spins around so he's facing me. "Does my money bother you?"

"It doesn't *bother* me. It's just not something I'm used to, and like I said, I don't need extravagant gifts or meals." I gesture at myself. "This is me. I'm a no-frills kind of gal."

Kent reels me in flush to his body, lightly landing his hands on my hips. "Don't undersell yourself, Presley baby. You're the real deal."

I'm not sure what kind of emotion I'm conveying, but it's enough for him to elaborate.

"I mean it. Most girls are only interested in me because they want sex, money, or celebrity. You want none of those things, and you have no idea how fucking amazing it is to meet someone with no agenda."

"I never thought about that before," I admit, placing my hands on his shoulders. I might as well take advantage of the opportunity while we're pressed up against one another. "That sucks."

"It does." He leans his face in closer, and my heart stutters behind my rib cage. Blood thrums in my ears as his lips press against my cheek. Fiery tingles zip all over my face, and an embarrassing little whimper escapes my mouth.

Kent pulls back, his lips curling in amusement, but he doesn't comment on it because a camera flash goes off in our faces, and he curses under his breath. Opening my door, he urges me inside. I watch through the window as he has a heated exchange with the guy holding the camera. It's a professional camera, strapped around his neck, so I'm guessing this guy is a paparazzo.

"Fucking parasite," Kent hisses, climbing behind the wheel.

"Is everything okay?"

Resting his hands on the wheel, he turns to face me. "That will probably show up online tomorrow. He was fishing for information about you, but I told him nothing."

"Thanks, and don't worry about it. I don't care."

He opens his mouth, then closes it, looking contemplative. Shaking his head, he starts the engine. "So, I know this little Italian place. It's not much to look at, but the food is to die for, and—"

"Sounds perfect," I say, smiling enthusiastically. "Let's go."

"This is more like it," I admit, a half hour later when we're tucked in a cozy little booth at the back of the quaint little Italian place, having just ordered. The room looks like it hasn't had a makeover since the sixties, but the place is clean and warm, and it feels homey. More importantly, I don't feel like I stick out here.

"I should've just taken you here in the first place," Kent says, stretching his arm across the back of the booth behind me.

"Why didn't you?"

"I wanted to impress you."

A grin lets loose on my lips.

"What?"

"I like that you're honest."

"My honesty usually gets me in trouble," he says, placing his hand over the glass as the waiter moves to pour wine in it. "I'm driving," he explains, pushing my glass in the waiter's direction.

"How come?" I ask after the waiter has left.

"I've got a big mouth and little filter, and sometimes I say things to deliberately piss people off."

I burst out laughing. "Shocker right there."

He stares at me with an indecipherable expression, and now it's my turn to ask, "What?"

"You have the most amazing laugh, and your beautiful face just lit up like the Fourth of July. You should do it more often."

I grin. "Why, Kent, that might just be the nicest thing anyone's ever said to me."

"I sincerely hope that's not the case. And if you're relying on me to sweet-talk you, you're in a world of trouble." His blue eyes latch on to mine, and I momentarily forget how to breathe. We're sitting so close our thighs are brushing, and every aspect of his gorgeous face is magnified at this proximity.

"I have a feeling you're too hard on yourself," I say before taking a sip of the crisp, cold white wine.

He shrugs. "Let's not talk about me. Let's talk about you. I'm sure that's infinitely more interesting."

"I beg to differ, but what do you want to know?"

"Tell me about you. Your family. Where you grew up." He drinks from his glass of water as he waits for me to talk.

"Not much to tell. My parents died when I was nine, and I grew up in the foster care system until I aged out at eighteen."

He rubs the back of his neck. "Shit. I'm sorry."

I shrug. "Don't be. It is what it is, and while I don't talk about my childhood much, I have nothing to hide either."

"How did your parents die?"

"Car crash. We were coming home from the movies, and a truck plowed into our car. Mom was killed instantly, and Dad died on the way to the hospital. I was in the back seat, and I escaped with cuts and bruises and a broken left arm."

"That must've been tough to deal with as a kid."

I take a healthy glug of my wine. "It was. I didn't speak for a full year after they died. My social worker sent me to a therapist, and she said I had PTSD."

"How did you overcome that?" he asks, looking genuinely interested.

"Therapy and time and meeting a couple guys in my new home. Connecting with Clay and Chris was a turning point for me."

"They're friends or…"

"Clay is my de facto big brother, and he's looked out for me from the minute I met him. Chris is the same age as me. We were friends for a long time before we became more."

The waiter arrives with our pasta then, and the timing is perfect. I'm not sure I want to talk about my ex on a first date. Especially with the complicated history Chris and I share and the fact I still talk to him, still see him.

Lync hated Chris. Hated he was still a part of my life.

No one understands the bond between us, or how what we went through means we will always share a connection. Even Clay doesn't understand it. He's washed his hands of Chris, and he wants me to do the same, but I can never turn my back on him. Anyone in my life will just have to find a way to deal with it.

"What about you?" I ask, in between bites of mouthwatering creamy fettuccine. "I know what I've read about your family, but what are they really like?"

He chews his food before speaking. "Loud. Nosy. Annoying. Suffocating."

My eyes pop wide. I wasn't expecting him to say that.

"That probably sounds terrible," he adds, tossing his steak and pasta around his plate. "And they're not just that. My family is close, and they're good people, but I've always been on the fringes. I've always felt like I don't fit in."

"That sounds lonely."

"You've no idea," he murmurs, swallowing a mouthful of food.

"Aren't you close with your triplets? There are lots of pictures of you with Keaton and Keanu online."

"We were close growing up, but it's different now." His tense body language suggests there is more to the story, but I don't push him further. "And you really shouldn't believe half the shit you read online."

"I know the media can twist things. I can't imagine how invasive it must be to have outsiders so interested in your family." I pop the last mouthful of fettuccine in my mouth, chewing carefully. "What happened back at the other restaurant happens a lot, I'm guessing?"

He nods. "It's why I usually hang around campus, or attend house parties, or avoid downtown Boston. I fucking hate judgmental assholes and bottom-feeders who try to latch on to me for what they can get." He pushes his empty plate away, angling his body so he's facing me head-on. Our knees are pressed together, and his fingers toy with the ends of my hair as he stares at me. "I should warn you if you continue to be seen with me you will get papped, and they'll want to know about you. They'll dig into your background and—"

I press my fingers to his lips, stalling him. "We'll be careful, and I never see any reporters or paparazzi around Mattapan."

"That's actually how I ended up drinking at Ramshackle," he says, his fingers winding through my hair, eliciting the most pleasurable sensations. I'm fixated on him as he explains. "I was fed up with cameras going off in my face, and I wanted to find someplace where the paps would never even think of going. I was watching the news, and there was a report about a drug-related shooting outside the bar, and it piqued my interest. I conducted some research and ended up in Ramshackle the next night. Haven't looked back since."

"That is the most fucked-up logic I've ever heard," I admit, and my voice betrays my disbelief. "Do you have a death wish or something?"

His hand moves to the nape of my neck, and he draws me in close, pressing his forehead against mine. "Not anymore," he whispers over my mouth, his warm, spicy breath fanning over my lips. "And I think it was fate, because that news report led me to you, and I have zero regrets about that."

Chapter Ten
Presley

"Thank you for a wonderful date," I tell him when we reach my front door. "I enjoyed spending time with you." Butterflies scatter in my chest as I turn to face him, my spine flat against the wooden door.

"I had a good time too," he says, planting his hands on either side of my head and leaning in. "I'd like to do it again." He moves his head closer, his eyes lowering to my mouth for a split second before he rubs his nose playfully against mine. "When is your next night off?"

I don't admit it's tomorrow as that would come across as equal parts desperate and overly enthusiastic. "Sunday," I say in a breathy tone, my body humming at the heat rolling off Kent in waves.

"That's so far away," he murmurs, planting a soft kiss on my cheek.

"You know where to find me in the meantime." I attempt to quell my heaving chest as he trails a line of feather-soft kisses along my face. I'm close to hyperventilating, and he hasn't even gone near my mouth.

"Classes are back this week," he admits, nuzzling his face into my neck. He inhales sharply, and a jolt of liquid lust pulses low in my body. "And exams start next month, so I've got a full schedule. But I'll try to stop by."

He straightens up, pushing off the door, and I instantly miss his closeness. His perplexed eyes probe mine, and he rocks back on his heels. "I don't know what I'm doing here except I like it."

"I like it too." I fist a hand in his shirt, reeling him back in. "Don't first dates usually end with a goodnight kiss?" I arch a brow, attempting to drown out the stampeding butterflies careening around my chest, praying he doesn't notice how my entire body is trembling at having him this near.

"I wouldn't know." His gaze fixes on my mouth. "This is the first date I've ever gone on."

I blink repeatedly, staring at him in shock, trying to find the lie behind those words but only finding truth. "Are you seriously telling me that I'm your first date at age twenty-three?"

"That shocks you?" He places his hands on my hips.

"Yes," I truthfully reply. "How does that even happen?" He is gorgeous and charming and I know he's had girls crawling all over him.

"Never met a girl I wanted to ask out on a date."

My heart swells behind my rib cage. "I'm honored you chose me, and I hope it lived up to your expectation."

He clasps one side of my face in his large palm. "I didn't know what to expect, beyond getting to know you a little more, and it more than lived up to that." His eyes lower to my mouth, and his pupils darken with blatant desire. "I'm giving you that goodnight kiss now," he adds, his voice thick with lust, before his mouth descends upon mine.

Time stops. The world around us no longer exists. There is only the touch of his hand on my face, the feel of his erection pushing against my stomach, and the hypnotic taste of his lips as his mouth moves skillfully against mine.

I drown in him. Opening my mouth willingly for his tongue and grabbing his hips, pulling his body in flush against mine. Holding my face in both his hands, he angles my head, deepening the kiss as his lips and tongue worship my mouth.

Stars explode behind my shuttered eyes, and I'm awash in heavenly sensation, my entire body putty in his expert hands. I run my fingers through his hair, gently rocking my hips against his as his pelvis moves sensually against mine. There is no denying our mutual arousal, but his thrusts aren't forceful. His body moves languidly against mine while he focuses his attention on making love to my mouth.

I am lost in Kent Kennedy, and I never want him to stop doing this.

No man has ever kissed me like this.

Like I'm his world and he'll die if he can't keep tasting me.

I don't know how long we kiss for, but it feels like forever before we finally pull apart, to draw a breath.

His lips are swollen, his hair is messy from my fingers, and his skin is flushed. "Damn." He rubs his thumb along my lower lip. "If all goodnight kisses are like that, I've seriously been missing out."

"You and me both," I croak, my voice heavy with desire.

He kisses me again. Just once. It's infinitely tender, and I swoon beneath him.

"Good night, Presley baby," he whispers into my ear. "Sweet dreams."

I stand at my door for way longer than necessary, touching my lips with a cheesy grin on my face, just staring at the hallway, wondering how I got to this point in my life. Because there's no denying I am attracted to this man. More than that, I need to understand what makes him tick, and there is zero point trying to deny I want him badly because it's the truth. No man has ever claimed my attention so wholeheartedly, and though it's risky, because he doesn't date and I'm not sure he even knows what he wants beyond getting me into his bed, I'm invested now, and I'm not walking away.

I'm floating on a cloud the next day, especially when I receive another delivery of infinity roses. This time, there is a whole bunch of them in a beautiful white and silver box. My giddy grin expands as I read his new note. It simply says, "Welcome to my World," and there's a YouTube link underneath it. I type the link into the browser on my phone, and my heart melts as I listen to Elvis sing. The song is about a man inviting a woman into his heart and how he'll be waiting with open arms.

The hidden message thrills me.

Who knew the bad boy could be such a romantic underneath that cocky exterior?

After a workout in the gym, I spend the rest of the day pressing flowers into my drawing, setting it aside when it's finished. I'll bring it to the custom framing shop on my way to class tomorrow.

Imogen and Kady are coming over for dinner, and I'm in the middle of prepping the lasagna when the doorbell rings. Rubbing my hands on the front of my apron, I head to the door, checking the peephole before I open it.

Chris falls through the door, and I barely catch him in time. Cigarette smoke mixes with alcohol fumes and stale sweat as I hold my ex in my arms. "Jesus, Chris." I grip his upper arms, holding him up off me as I use my foot to close the front door. Tucking his arm around my shoulder, I half-carry, half-drag, him over to my couch, throwing him down flat on his back.

His eyes roll in the back of his head, and he groans as he shifts onto his side. I snatch the trash can in the nick of time, shoving it under his face before he heaves into it. His entire body is shaking, and sweat beads on his brow, plastering strands of his stringy dark hair to his face.

A familiar ache lances across my chest as I watch him puke his guts up. It's mixed with the usual disgust and frustration and anger.

My feelings when it comes to Chris are a complicated mix, and it doesn't get any easier.

He looks worse this time. Thinner than I've ever seen him and so fucking washed-up.

"Sorry, babe," he groans, flopping back down on the couch when he's expelled the liquid contents of his stomach.

"Don't move," I instruct, putting the trash can to one side while I go to the fridge and remove a bottle of water. I hand it to him. "Drink that. I'll be back in a sec."

Taking the trash can into the bathroom, I rinse it out in the sink before running the bath. I grab the box of supplies from the cabinet, placing it in the sink, before setting a large fluffy towel down on top of the closed toilet seat. Then I remove sweats, boxers, and a clean T-shirt from the drawer in my dresser where I keep Chris's things, adding them on top of the towel. I check the temperature of the water before switching the faucets off and moving out into the living room.

Chris is slouched awkwardly against the corner of the couch, drinking the water. I sit beside him, clasping his face in both my hands. "You look like death warmed over."

"Hello to you too." He flashes me a smile, and my heart hurts all over again. That smile used to warm every part of me on lonely nights, and it reminds me of the sweet boy I used to know before his addictions took control, transforming him before my very eyes.

"Where have you been?" I ask, hating how his pupils dilate and roll around his eyes. I'm not surprised. I doubt Chris has many lucid moments these days.

"Around." He shrugs, and I don't push it.

"You scared me," I truthfully admit. It's been eleven weeks since I've seen or heard from him. He usually shows up here more frequently, and this time, I thought it had happened.

That I'd get a knock on the door telling me he was dead.

Relief mixes with frustration and anger in my veins, but I put a leash on it. I know from past experience there is no point even attempting to talk to him when he's high and drunk. The times I've gone there have ended up in an almighty argument, with horrible words spewed on both sides, and I've finally learned my lesson. I'll wait till I've sobered him up and he's eaten and slept, and then I'm going to try to get through to him.

Again.

"Come on." I stand, extending my arm. "Let's get you into the bath."

I help him into the bathroom, putting toothpaste on his toothbrush before curling his hand around it. I add some scented bubble bath to the water in the tub, swirling it with my hand, while he haphazardly cleans his teeth.

I suck in a breath, shutting my nostrils off so I don't ingest the noxious odors bleeding off him in pungent waves. The scent of weed clings to his filthy clothes, and he looks like he hasn't showered in weeks. Dirt clings to his skin as he sheds his outer layers, and I frown at the fading bruises on his chest, wondering what other trouble he's gotten himself into.

"Call me if you need me," I say, keeping my back to him as he gets into the tub.

"Thanks, Pres. I owe you."

I gulp over the lump in my throat, hating how things have turned out for him. That this is what it has come down to. There was a time I thought Chris and I would last the whole distance, and remembering how it all fell apart still guts me every time. Ignoring the tight pain in my chest, I force thoughts of the past aside and focus on the here and now.

Pulling on a pair of latex gloves, I scoop up his clothes and head out to the kitchen. I shove them into a trash bag because there's no way they are salvageable. I'll just pick him up some things from the secondhand store tomorrow.

"I'm really sorry to do this to you, babe, but Chris has just shown up," I tell my bestie, as I fling the trash bag in the dumpster at the back of our triple-decker, with my cell pressed between my ear and my shoulder.

Silence greets me, and I inwardly groan. "Mo."

"It's fine," she says, resignation clear in her tone.

"Order pizza for Kady, and I'll give you the cash tomorrow," I offer, because I hate letting my godchild down.

"You don't have to do that. That's not why I'm upset."

I push through the door, stepping inside the building, taking the steps two at a time. "I know why you're upset." She tells me enough, and I know it comes from a place of concern.

"How long are you going to keep doing this, Pres? He's not your responsibility."

"He has no one, Mo. And I've got to try." Tears prick my eyes as I step out into the hallway that leads to my apartment. "If he dies, and I did nothing, I could never live with myself."

"Have you ever considered you could be part of the problem?" she softly inquires. "Maybe if you weren't there, he'd stop and take a long hard look at himself."

"If I wasn't here, he'd probably be dead already." My tone is clipped, anger seeping through.

Not at her. More for the situation.

I know Mo speaks a lot of truth, but she doesn't get it. She doesn't understand all the ways in which Chris helped me. How inextricably we're connected. She doesn't understand I can't walk away because turning my back on him would be like turning my back on myself.

"Look, I don't want to fight with you. And fuck, you've got the biggest heart, Presley. I just don't want to see you hurt, and you're always so sad after each visit."

"Because it hurts me to see him like this, Mo." I press my forehead into the wall beside my apartment, not wanting to go inside in case Chris overhears this conversation. "For years, he was my salvation. He kept me going at times when I wanted to die. Ignoring him when he needs me would be a shitty way to repay him, and I won't do it. I know you're only concerned, but you've got to drop this before we both say something we regret."

"I'm sorry," she whispers.

"Don't be. I appreciate that you're looking out for me. Order pizza, and tell Kady I'll pick her up after school next Wednesday. We can go to the park. Maybe catch a movie."

"She'll love that. Thanks, Pres." A pregnant pause filters down the line before she says, "Love you."

"Love you, too."

I hang up and enter my apartment, pleased to find Chris dressed, sitting up on the couch, and drying his hair with a towel.

I plaster on a fake smile, dropping down beside him. "You look a little more human now." I tilt his face from side to side. "You could use a shave and a haircut though."

"Could you?" he asks, arching a brow. The wildness in his eyes has calmed a little, but I know whatever he has taken is still lingering in his system.

"Of course." I pat his knee. "Just let me get the lasagna in the oven, and then I'll take care of you." I hand him the remote. "Knock yourself out."

Chris watches TV, sprawled across the couch, while I finish the lasagna, popping it in the oven before fixing a salad and cutting slices of fresh, crusty bread. Then I retrieve the box with his stuff from the bathroom and pull a chair into the middle of the living room, forcing him to sit down.

"Your hair is so long," I acknowledge as I drag the comb through it. It's almost hitting his shoulders.

"You didn't cut it last time, and I don't trust anyone else to do it."

He'd rather spend his money shooting shit in his veins than spend it on a haircut, he means, but I bite my tongue, keeping those thoughts to myself.

I cut his hair, keeping it tight to the nape of his neck and along the sides, and then I shave off his beard, using the electric razor I keep here for him.

He wolfs down two servings of lasagna, and then we watch TV for a couple hours before he falls asleep on the couch. I drape a blanket over him, tucking a pillow under his head, before switching off the lights and creeping out of the living room.

Usually when he shows up, I let him sleep in my bed for the few nights he stays, because God knows where he sleeps most nights, but not this time.

Kent and I are at the start of something good, and it doesn't feel right to let another man into my bed, even if there's nothing remotely sexual about it.

I drift off to sleep with thoughts of Kent swirling through my mind, wondering when I'll see him next.

Chapter Eleven
Kent

"Who pissed in your cornflakes?" Topher asks as I slam my tray down on the table in the cafeteria Friday at lunch.

"Is it anything to do with that photo of you online?" Lance inquires, shoveling pizza into his mouth as I claim the seat beside him.

I want to go back to Tuesday night and beat the shit out of that paparazzo and break his camera into a million pieces so that pic of Presley and me ceases to exist. At least I know why Whitney has been blowing up my phone again. I haven't answered or listened to the hundreds of messages she's left me, deleting them the second they land in my inbox. Going cold turkey with her is the only way I'll get through to her. She needs to understand we are done for good this time.

Perhaps the pic of me and Presley will convince her once and for all. Looking at my lovesick mug in the photo pisses me off now I know I'm being played, but Whitney can be in no doubt this girl means something to me. The way we're pressed against each other, and the look in both our eyes, conveys she is no casual hookup.

"Who's the hottie?" Mitch asks, pulling up the picture on his cell. "You bang her yet?"

"Fuck off with the twenty questions," I snarl, in no mood for an interrogation. I've been severely pissed since I showed up at Presley's place, early yesterday morning, and spotted a guy leaving her apartment.

Fate led me to you.

Blech. I cringe as I recall my words from Tuesday night. *What the fuck was I thinking?* Sending her flowers and notes and obsessing over a goodnight kiss that was hotter than any kiss ever in the history of time.

I was basically turning into Kyler, so I should probably thank the mystery dude for forcing me to wake the fuck up.

Presley is probably laughing her ass off at how stupidly naïve I am. To think I believed her. I believed all of it. But it was obviously a lie, and I'm a fool because I fell for it. *And do you know what's worse?* I still can't get the bitch out of my head. It's like she's taken up permanent residence, and now she's invoking squatter's rights. There's only one way to deal with it, and there's little time to delay. "We hitting one of the frat parties this weekend?" I ask, stabbing a piece of chicken with my fork, imagining it's the mystery dude's head.

"Hell yeah." Toph blatantly eye fucks a curvy redhead as she saunters past our table, swaying her hips and making her interest known.

"Good. I need to get trashed."

Mission accomplished, I think, the following night as I'm sprawled across a couch in the basement of the frat house, my body soaring someplace above me. We were here last night too, and I got totally wasted, spending most of today sleeping before dusting myself off and putting my party hat back on. My limbs sink into the cushions underneath me, and I'm blissfully numbed out.

Presley who?

Fuck that bitch.

"Hey, babe." A girl crawls up my body from the end of the couch, and I can scarcely summon the energy to tilt my head in her direction.

She straddles my lap, grinding on top of me as she leans down, thrusting her ginormous fake tits in my face. "Want me to suck you off?"

"Does a bear shit in the woods?" I joke, rolling my eyes to the ceiling as I pull on my blunt, inhaling the heady fumes, sucking them deep into my lungs.

She wastes no time unbuckling my belt, shimmying my jeans and my boxers down my legs, and lowering her mouth to my cock. She goes to town on me, slobbering and sucking, and...nothing happens. I look down at my limp dick in her mouth, and she stares at me with a frown. "Your technique could use some work," I deadpan, pushing her off. "Go practice on some other poor sucker."

"Asshole," she spits, climbing off me. "Not my problem your cock's dysfunctional. You should get that checked out."

I yank my boxers and jeans back up, shooting daggers at her back. "You should demand a refund from your plastic surgeon," I yell after her. "Those tits made my cock shrivel up and die." Take that, slut.

I puff on my blunt, closing my eyes, willing that bitch Presley Barlow to take a hike.

This is all her fault.

She broke me.

Broke my cock.

I can't even get it up now. Unless I'm in the shower, hand wrapped around my dick, imagining she's on her knees, worshiping my cock like it's the best thing she's ever had in her mouth. And just like that, life returns to my lower regions, and my cock thickens behind the zipper of my jeans.

Fuck. My. Life.

I pop a couple benzos, washing them down with a few tequila shots, and join my buddies at beer pong before I decide it'd be a great idea to pay Presley a visit, to tell her exactly what I think about her cheating skanky ass.

Ramshackle is packed to the rafters when I arrive an hour later. Pushing my way through the crowd, I make it to the counter, edging a couple of girls aside so I can plant myself directly in front of the woman who has taken a machete to my heart.

Presley hasn't noticed me yet because she has her back to me as she makes a couple of cocktails. A "Happy Birthday" banner hangs over the top of the bar, confirming tonight is a special occasion. Glancing over my shoulder, I notice a bunch of balloons and banners spread across a few booths. Someone is celebrating a twenty-first. Music blares from the wall-mounted speakers, and a group of chicks dances in the middle of the room, whooping and hollering, holding beer bottles aloft as they butcher the song, screaming out the lyrics.

I turn back around, my eyes hungrily roaming Presley's tempting form. She's wearing ripped black jeans and a fitted red and black corset top that ties at the back. A tantalizing strip of skin is exposed where the top ends and her low-rise jeans start, and I long to flatten my tongue to her flesh and press a row of kisses along her silky-soft skin. She shakes her hips in tune to the music as she fixes a line of cocktails, and my gaze is glued to the sexy motion. When she turns around, my eyes almost bug out of their sockets. Her gorgeous tits are molded perfectly in the low-cut top, and layers of her thick, dark hair kiss her shoulders in seductive waves.

"Kent. I didn't know you were dropping by." Her face lights up, like I'm her favorite person in the world, and I almost fall for it. Almost.

"Where's your fuck buddy?" I snarl, looking around the bar.

Her brows pucker as she sets the drinks on a tray. "I don't know what you mean."

"Sure, you don't," I slur, grabbing the bar when I feel myself swaying. "If you needed a dicking, I would've gladly volunteered. That skinny dude didn't look like he had it in him." Word vomit pours from my mouth. "For one second, I believed what we had was real, but you fucking played me."

She slides the tray to her blue-haired friend before turning to

Ford. "I need five." She told me they alternate shifts, so I've no clue why he's working as well. Unless they knew it would be busy with the party and it was an all-hands-on-deck scenario.

Presley disappears, and rage boils underneath the surface of my skin. Grabbing the nearest drink, I down it in one go.

"Hey! What the fuck, asshole?" A whiny female voice protests at my side. I swing my gaze on her, and the change in her demeanor is comical. "It's you," she rasps. She wiggles her fingers at me, even though I'm standing right in front of her. "Hi, Kent." She giggles, and the sound is like a dagger slicing through my brain.

Behind her, I spot Presley making her way toward me. I sling my arm around the girl's shoulders, tugging her into my side. "Hey, babe. How about you and me ditch this joint?"

"How about I give you three seconds to get your drunk ass in the back room before I kick you permanently to the curb," Presley snaps, glaring at me.

As if I'm the one in the wrong.

The girl leans in closer to my side, sliding her hand around my back, her palm landing on my ass. I push her away so fast she loses her balance, wobbling on her skyscraper heels before falling. Presley catches her at the last second. "Watch it, Luanne. And stay away from him." She jabs her finger in my direction, and her blatant possessiveness is hot.

Maybe I got it wrong?

I don't know. I'm confused.

Presley grabs my hand, tugging me forward, past the bar, through a door, and into a back room. She roughly shoves me down on a small, lumpy couch before slamming the door shut behind us.

"What the fuck is your problem?" she yells, standing in front of me with her hands on her shapely hips.

"You cheated on me," I hiss. "You fucking bitch," I add because I'm seething again and the drugs and alcohol in my system are messing with my thought process.

She sighs, sitting down beside me, clasping my face in her hands. "You saw Chris. When were you at my place?"

"Yesterday morning. I drove there before classes started because I was hoping to buy you breakfast." Wait, that name rings a bell. I remember her mentioning Chris. "You're sleeping with your ex? How fucking cliché." I slap her hands away.

Her features soften as she shakes her head. "You're such a dumb-ass." She presses her forehead to mine. "Is this why I haven't seen you since Tuesday night?"

"I know I'm no dating expert, but I didn't think I had to specify we were exclusive. I won't fucking share you."

I've shared fuck buddies in the past, and I'm not unaccustomed to threesomes, foursomes, and moresomes, but none of those chicks meant anything to me. Presley is different, and different rules apply. Even the thought of any man putting his hands on her sends me into a jealous rage.

She lifts her head, drilling me with a serious look. "Firstly, we went on *one* date, Kent, and we never discussed dating exclusively or dating at all, and secondly, I didn't have sex with him. Chris is just a friend. It's strictly platonic between us these days. It has been for years."

I bark out a laugh. "You expect me to believe that?" The rooms spins, and I slump to the side of the couch. "Woah."

She straightens me up, staring into my eyes, cursing under her breath. "Are you high right now?"

"As a fucking kite." I grin, and she exhales heavily, not looking pleased at all by my admission.

The door opens, elevating the noise levels to ear-deafening, and Ford pokes his head in, eyeballing Pres as he shouts, "Sorry to break this up, but we're hammered out here. I need you."

"I'll be right there," Presley shouts over her shoulder before returning her focus to me. "You've got this all wrong, Kent, and we need to talk, but now isn't the time."

"I'll wait," I blurt, like a total pussy, because I don't want to go. I lean back along the length of the couch. "I'll just crash until your shift is over."

She chews on the corner of her mouth, looking undecided. "Okay, but don't touch anything. We're not supposed to bring non-staff members back here."

I roll my eyes, looking around at the shithole that is their staff room. "Trust me, I won't touch a thing."

She stares at me for a minute before her shoulders relax. "Fine. Did you have anything to eat?"

I shake my head. "I was passed out for breakfast and lunch, and I had a liquid dinner." I flash her one of my panty-melting grins, but she does *not* look impressed. Two strikes in a row. Not a good result. Three and I might be out. I fix her with my most sincere puppy-dog-eyed expression, hoping to reclaim some ground.

She mutters something under her breath before leaving the room, the noise of the party blasting through my ears when she opens the door.

Presley returns a few minutes later with a plate stacked with chicken tenders, mini burgers, and potato wedges. She places it on the coffee table along with two bottles of water and some silverware. Wrapping my hand around the fork, she pins me with a no-nonsense look. "Eat and drink and then sleep. I'll wake you when it's time to leave."

My body shakes and my stomach lurches as I come to. Nausea churns in my gut, and sweat sticks my shirt to my back. I don't feel so hot. The room swims, and my vision blurs in and out. I can just detect Presley's gorgeous face through the haze. "Hey." My mouth feels like smelly socks married soiled boxer briefs and made a baby in there.

"Thank fuck," Presley says as her features come into clearer focus. "I've been trying to wake you for twenty minutes. It's time to go." She's lucky she was able to wake me at all. Usually when I mix booze with benzos I'm out for the count and nothing or no one can rouse me.

I move to stand, promptly falling back on my butt on the couch. My stomach lurches again, and I wrap an arm around myself, willing the food I devoured earlier to stay the fuck down. I do *not* want to hurl in front of my woman.

My woman.

What the actual fuck?

"I need to get home." I attempt to stand a second time, thrusting my hand out against the wall to steady myself when I sway on my feet.

Presley thrusts a bottle of water at me. "Drink that and give me your cell. I'll call you an Uber."

"I'm not a baby. I can call my own fucking Uber," I snap, removing my cell from the pocket of my jeans, willing my eyes to focus on the screen.

Presley whips the cell from my hand, pressing my thumb down on the screen to unlock it before swiping her fingers across the keypad. "You are so fucking stubborn."

"You're so damn bossy."

"Done." She lifts her head, her troubled eyes examining my face. "I added my number too. Come on. Ford is waiting to lock up. We'll wait for the car outside. The fresh air might do you some good."

She grabs her bag and jacket from a hook by the wall, sliding her arms into the vibrant leather sleeves and crossing her bag around her upper torso. I let her take my hand and lead me outside.

Ford smirks at me, and I flip him the bird. "You still owe me, Kennedy." He points a knowing finger in my face.

"I haven't forgotten, pussy."

He laughs before his expression sobers. "You need a hand, Pres?"

"Nah. This isn't my first rodeo. I've got this."

"What the fuck does that mean?" I ask as she guides me outside.

"That I'm used to babying assholes who insist on abusing their bodies with shit that's no good for them." She glares at me, and I cower a little. "We won't last long if I discover you're addicted to that poison, Kennedy. I won't go through this again."

"I'm not addicted." I scoff at the very thought. "I work hard all week and keep my nose clean, so I let loose on the weekend. It's not a big deal." I wrench my hand from hers. "I don't need a babysitter or a lecture. I get enough of those from my family."

"Don't get your panties in a bunch. I care. Is that so bad?"

"You're really not fucking your ex?" I ask because I need to know the truth.

She moves in closer, hooking her pinkie in mine. "I'm not fucking my ex. For as long as we're dating, I won't fuck anyone else."

"Come home with me," I ask. Her lips purse. "Not for sex," I rush to add though I can't believe those words just left my lips. "Just to sleep. I want to hold you." Grabbing her hips, I pull her in close to me. "I make a mean scrambled eggs, so I'll even throw in breakfast."

"I should really go home," she murmurs.

"Please, Pres." I lose all trace of humor, shielding nothing from her. "You said we need to talk, so let's go back to my place, and we can talk in the morning. I promise I won't lay a finger on you. Scout's honor."

She narrows her eyes. "You were never a boy scout."

"Actually, I was," I correct her. "For one month—until we had our first camping trip and I was caught pissing in the scout leader's bag."

"I think you came out of the womb with a capital T for trouble stamped on your chest."

"I think you're probably right." I circle my hands around her waist as a car pulls up to the sidewalk. "So maybe I do need a chaperone after all? Wanna escort me home?"

Chapter Twelve
Presley

I *must need my head examined,* I think as I grab the key from Kent's hand, fitting it easily in the lock. *What in the world possessed me to agree to spend the night?* I'm not worried about him putting the moves on me because the guy can barely keep his eyes open. He nodded off in the Uber, and he practically sleepwalked his way into the building. But I am worried about getting invested in another guy who has controlling addictions.

Opening the door, I try not to gawk as we step foot inside the plush apartment Kent calls home. This room is a massive open-plan living room with kitchen and dining area at the back. Wall-to-wall windows are covered with luxurious silver-and-blue-striped curtains, and all the furniture is sleek and modern and clearly very expensive. Stairs lead off the right side of the room, and there are a couple of closed doors behind it, leading to other rooms.

"Up here," Kent mumbles, stifling a yawn. I follow him up the stairs to the next level, walking down a long hallway, past another couple of closed doors, and up another flight of stairs to his bedroom. Kent's bedroom occupies the entire floor space up here, and it's bigger than my whole apartment. It's magnificent with stunning views and his own private living room.

"Holy shit," I say as Kent flops down on the bed, face-first. "This is incredible." The curtains are open, highlighting a spectacular view of the city spread out before us. At this late hour, there is only a smattering of lights in the distance.

"Presley baby," Kent mumbles, and I swing back around, walking toward the large king-sized bed.

I round the bed, sitting beside him, brushing strands of dark hair from his brow. "Can I get you anything?"

"Just you," he says, reaching a hand out to cup my face. "I have shirts in my closet. Grab one to sleep in."

I press a kiss to his cheek as I stand. "I'll be right back."

I step into his walk-in closet with my mouth trailing the ground. There are rows and rows of clothes and too many shoes to count. Casual clothes are lined up beside fitted suits and a collection of dress shirts and ties in every imaginable color. A collection of expensive watches and cufflinks sits atop the mahogany dressing table in the center of the room. A row of strip lighting at the top of the mirror above the dresser illuminates the room, highlighting my features in stark contrast to my surroundings. This is a world away from anything I've ever known, and I'm not sure if I fit in here.

My cell vibrates in my pocket, and I remove it, reading the reply to my text.

> Chris: I'm not at your place. Had to head out. I'll see you again soon. Thanks for looking after me. I owe you.

I drop onto the chair in front of the dresser, resting my head in my hands. I was hoping I had gotten through to Chris this time. That he was going to seek help and stay with me until he got clean.

But it's the same tired, worn-out story.

He stayed with me three nights this time. I got to stuff him full of home-cooked food, made sure he slept well, and got him some new clothes and another new cell. I have no idea what he does with his cell phones, but I have a stash of disposables purely for my ex.

I don't bother replying because there is nothing more left to be said. Instead, I offer up a silent prayer someone will look after him until the next time he shows up at my place.

Seeing Kent similarly trashed has messed with my head.

I know what he said, but I also know how alluring addiction is. Just because he keeps sober during the week and only indulges on the weekend doesn't mean he has control over it.

There was a time I might have gone down that slippery slope, but seeing what that shit has done to Chris was my saving grace. Now, I don't touch drugs, and I rarely drink to excess. I haven't worked my butt off since I graduated high school to flush it all away. Having a set goal has helped me avoid falling into the trap a lot of foster kids fall into. I know being around Chris and Clay means I'm still a part of that world, but I never let myself forget that, so I don't get sucked in. I've come too far, worked too hard, to let that happen.

Imogen wishes I would cut them loose because she hates they are my ties to the criminal underbelly and drug culture, but I can't do it. I can't turn my back on the two guys who got me through my teenage years. I care about them. Walking away would be too selfish, and it'd hurt me too.

I stand, yawning as a wave of fatigue washes over me. It's been a long, draining day, and I just want to crash. Finding a pile of T-shirts, I choose a plain white one with an embossed Boss logo and take it out to the bedroom.

Kent is snoring on top of the covers, lying belly down, in only his tight boxers. My eyes travel over the length of him from his feet to his broad shoulders, memorizing his toned legs and powerful thighs, his pert ass, and muscular back. The ink on his arms extends along the top of his back, and it's good work. Whoever did this knows their stuff. The rest of his back is smooth and unblemished. A blank canvas ready for the taking.

I wonder if he'd ever let me ink him? The thought excites me more than it probably should.

My features soften as I focus on his gorgeous face. He looks so much younger in sleep. His long lashes fan across his chiseled cheek, and strands of his dark, silky hair brush against his brow. His full lips are slightly parted, air slipping softly from his mouth.

He is physically beautiful, hiding all the broken, tormented parts on the inside. Perhaps that is why we are drawn to one another. Kent is shielding hidden depths I have barely begun exploring, and he's only started to crack my veneer.

I don't really know why I'm here, and while one part of me feels like a stranger in a foreign land, another part of me feels like this is home. I can't determine which side is more troubling.

I traipse into the bathroom, gently closing the door as I gaze in awe at the opulent room with matching marble features. His and hers sinks rest in front of a large mirror with bright overhead lighting. A massive walk-in-shower is enclosed behind floor-to-ceiling-length glass, and a ginormous freestanding claw-foot bath sits alongside a wide window. At this height, there is no one overlooking the property on either side and no obstruction marring the citywide view.

I slip out of my clothes, knotting my hair in a messy bun on top of my head as I take a quick shower, lathering myself in Kent's body-wash, recognizing the spicy fruity scent as it covers my skin. I towel myself dry and slip on Kent's shirt, sans underwear, because I don't have any clean panties with me and the shirt is long enough to hide my intimate parts anyway. Borrowing one of the toothbrushes I find, I brush my teeth.

Tiptoeing back into the room, I close the curtains and pull the comforter up over Kent before sneaking back downstairs. My mouth is parched, and I want to find some Tylenol because I'm sure Kent will have the mother of all hangovers in the morning.

I pad into the main living area, admiring the beautiful décor, wondering if Kent's interior-designer Mom designed the space because it is truly stunning. I'm too busy ogling the room to notice the man standing behind the island unit, staring at me like I might be an apparition.

I jump, emitting a startled squeak as I slap a hand against my chest.

"I'm sorry," he says in a deep voice that sounds eerily similar to his brother's. "I didn't mean to frighten you."

He's wearing low-hanging pajama pants, a loose white shirt, and a curious expression. I recognize Keanu from pictures online, and I know he co-owns this place with his triplet, but Kent said he is rarely here anymore. Now he and Selena—his wife—have graduated Harvard, they apparently spend most of their time at their house in Wellesley.

"No apology is necessary. Kent didn't tell me you were here. Is Selena with you?"

"She's sleeping," Keanu confirms. "And Kent doesn't know we're here. We had a fundraising event in the city that went on longer than expected, so we decided to crash here rather than making the trip back home."

I walk toward him, conscious of how this must look. Me naked underneath his brother's shirt. "I'm Presley." I smile, holding out my hand. "I've been looking forward to meeting you."

"Keanu. But you obviously know that." He shakes my hand, and a genuine smile spreads across his mouth. He looks so much like Kent it's unnerving. "So, you two are dating now?" he asks.

"To be honest, I'm not really sure what we are," I truthfully admit. "We've been on one date, and we're supposed to be going out again tomorrow night. Things are a little complicated."

"Aren't they always?" The kettle pings behind him. "I was making some peppermint tea. Would you like some?"

"That would be lovely."

He gestures at the table on the left. "Take a seat. I'll bring it over."

I watch as he makes two cups of tea, enchanted by how similar his mannerisms are to Kent's. He's not as broad or as built as his triplet, his leaner muscles a nod to his previous modeling career, and his hair is shorter and cut much tighter at the sides, but he's every bit as hot as Kent.

"You guys got in late," he says, handing me a mug before claiming the seat across from me.

I inhale the minty goodness, briefly closing my eyes as the calming scent swirls around me. "I was working, and Kent showed up. He crashed in the staff room until the bar closed."

"Which bar do you work at?"

"I'm co-manager of a bar in Mattapan called Ramshackle. It's a dive, but the owner is good to work for, and my coworkers are great."

"We'll have to stop by and check it out sometime."

I almost choke on my tea. "I'm not sure that would be a good idea though my boss would probably fire me if he heard me saying that." His brows pucker in confusion as I take a sip of my tea. I grin. "Business has tripled since Kent started showing up. I think every woman in the vicinity has been in there at least once the past couple of months."

He chuckles. "Sounds like my brother."

"He's been making quite the name for himself in Mattapan."

"That's how you two met?" he asks, curling his fingers around his mug.

"He didn't tell you?" I assumed Kent had spoken to his brother because he seemed to understand who I am.

"I haven't spoken to him in a couple weeks. Sel and I were in Italy. We only got back a few days ago, but I know who you are. He told my sister-in-law Eva all about you."

Warmth blossoms in my chest. "Kent mentioned he was closest to Eva and Selena."

Keanu nods. "He is, and Sel will be so happy when I tell her you're here. She's delighted he's met someone."

"It's very early days," I caution. "But I like him, and I think he likes me."

Keanu beams at me. "I look forward to getting to know you better.

Maybe we can all go out to dinner or you and Kent can come to our house one weekend."

"That sounds great."

We finish our tea, and Keanu shows me where the first aid kit is. I grab some Tylenol and two waters from the large fridge, and then we say goodnight, and head to our respective rooms.

Kent is still conked out as I crawl under the covers alongside him. I stare at his beautiful face like a creeper until my eyelids grow heavy, and I eventually fall asleep.

I wake the next morning, pressed up against Kent with my back to his chest and his muscular arm clamped tight around my stomach. The covers are pooled around our waists, and the room is bathed in darkness, the heavy drapes blocking out all light, so I've no clue what time it is.

"Morning, Presley baby," Kent whispers, nuzzling his face in my neck. "Did you sleep okay?"

"Like the dead," I admit, grabbing his arm, biting back a pleasurable moan when his tongue darts out, licking a trail along the side of my neck.

"You smell like me," he murmurs, nibbling on my ear.

"I took a shower last night. I hope that was okay."

He turns me around in his arms, smiling. "Of course. I'm only sorry I wasn't awake to participate."

I swat at his chest. "You passed out pretty much the second you hit the bed."

"Sorry about that."

I trail my fingers through the scruff on his chin and cheeks. "How are you feeling?"

"Like I got run over by a truck, but I'll live." He kisses the tip of my nose. "Thanks for the Tylenol and the water." He kisses my cheek. "And for coming home with me. I like waking up beside you." He leans in to kiss me, and I shuck out of his arms, shrieking. He stares at me like I've grown ten heads.

"I need to brush my teeth and pee." I swing my legs out of the bed. "Hold that thought!"

I race into the bathroom with his hearty chuckles chasing me. I attend to business, drag a comb through my hair, and brush my teeth before crawling back into bed with him.

"You're too cute for words," he says, resting his palm on my hip and pulling me in close. "Come here." His hands wrap around my back, and he holds me flush against his body as his gaze dips to my mouth. Every solid inch of his hard body is pressed against mine, and my panty-less pussy floods with warmth when I feel his thick length prodding my stomach.

"We should talk." I remind him, dragging my lower lip between my teeth.

"We can talk later." His seductive voice sprouts waves of goose bumps along my arms and the back of my neck. "If I don't get to taste you right now, I'm likely to self-combust."

A giggle bursts from my lips, quickly swallowed by his mouth. Circling my arms around his neck, I press my body into his as we kiss, basking in the feel of his skillful mouth gliding against mine. He licks at the seam of my lips, and I open for him, his minty breath fanning across my mouth, confirming he's also brushed his teeth. Our tongues tango, the tempo rising as we grind against one another, and my skin heats like it's on fire. Kent's fingers slide under my shirt, his hand stalling when it reaches my bare ass. "No panties?" he rasps into my mouth.

"I've got nothing on under your shirt," I admit, grazing my teeth along his stubbly jawline.

"Fucking hell. Are you trying to kill me, woman?"

I giggle, placing my palm on his erect cock. "I can take care of that for you." I peer into his eyes, conveying my message. I'm willing to look after his needs, but I'm not fucking him.

Not yet.

I know once we go there I will be completely under his spell, and I'm not ready to hand over that much power yet. Kent's kisses destroy me, in the best way, so I know his cock will ruin me for all others. I need to build up to that in a way I've never had to with any other guy.

"Not until I take care of you first," he says, moving his body until I'm underneath him and he's hovering over me. His fingers pluck at the edge of the shirt. "Can I take this off? Can I look at you?"

"Only if you get naked too." *Because, come on?* I totally want to see what every conquest has been raving about online.

Kent stands, smirking as he pushes his boxers down his legs, kicking them away, standing proudly before me, stroking his impressive erection as it juts out from his body like a weapon that will lay siege to my womb.

I lick my lips, sitting up in the bed, eyes firmly fixed on his as I slowly pull the T-shirt up over my body. I toss it aside, brushing messy strands of hair out of my face as I lie back, letting him drink his fill. "Liking what you see, *baby*?" I tease, running my fingers down the front of my body, casually fondling my breasts.

"Holy fuck, Pres." Kent crawls back over me. "You are a work of art." He leans down, planting a kiss on my flat stomach. "Beautiful." Carefully, he presses down on top of me, keeping himself propped up on his hands so his full body weight isn't resting on me. Bending his head, he kisses me, and there is nothing slow or tender about this kiss. It's hard and demanding and full of everything I'm feeling. "I want to make you come with my fingers and my mouth. Let me?" He stares deep into my eyes, and I drown in the oceanic blue depths of his gaze.

I nod. "I'd like that."

A wicked glint gleams in his eye as he slides down my body, nipping, kissing, and sucking as he goes. He lingers on my breasts, lavishing worship on them, fondling and sucking, his tongue laving the hardened tips until it feels like I might melt into a puddle on his bed.

"Kent," I squirm. "Please."

"Please what, Presley baby?" he asks, grinning as his teeth pluck at my nipple while he watches me through hooded eyes.

"Please fuck me with your mouth and your fingers."

"I love these." He kneads my breasts. "Perfect handfuls."

"I'm glad you approve." I fake pout. "Now get to work on my pussy."

He barks out a laugh. "Bossy in the bedroom too. Noted."

I spread my legs as he positions himself between the apex of my thighs, hissing when his hot mouth licks a line along my slit. He works me over with skill, flattening his tongue against my clit as his fingers push inside me. Then he alternates, plundering my inner walls with his wicked tongue while he rubs my clit with the right amount of pressure.

I shatter, breaking apart as every molecule in my body floats, existing on a new plane. My limbs tremble and my core throbs as fiery after-tremors rip through my sated body. "Hot damn." I prop up on my elbows. "I do *not* want to know how you came to be so good at that."

"No pussy has ever tasted so sweet." He flops down on the bed beside me, grinning.

An unwelcome thought infiltrates my mind. *How many women has he entertained in this bed?* It twists my insides into knots. But all negative thoughts flit away at his next words. "You taste like heaven on my tongue, and it's only fair to warn you I think I'm addicted to you."

I push him flat on his back, straddling his hips. "I think it's fair to say I'm on my way to being addicted to you too."

Chapter Thirteen
Presley

I lower my lips over his hard, thick shaft, keeping my eyes locked on Kent's as I take him deeper into my mouth. A strangled sound rips from his throat, and he jerks his hips as his eyes roll back in his head. I glide my lips up and down his erection, stretching my mouth wide, taking as much of him inside me as I can manage. Curling my hand around the base of his cock, I pump him in time with the movements of my mouth, savoring the first taste of him on my tongue.

I know not every woman enjoys giving head, but I fucking love it. I love having control over my man's pleasure, being in sole charge of bringing him to dizzying heights, and I love watching him come apart in my mouth.

"Fuck, Presley. That feels so damn good," he moans, thrusting his hips forward, in sync with me. With my free hand, I fondle his balls, alternating my attention between them as I suck him faster and deeper. Tears leak from the corners of my eyes and my jaw aches because Kent is big, and his long length is hitting the back of my throat even though I don't have all of him inside.

"Gonna come, baby," he warns, and I suction my lips tighter

around him, signaling I want him to let go in my mouth. He roars out his release a minute later, spilling jets of hot, salty cum down my throat.

"Fucking hell, babe." He lifts me by the upper arms up over his body, slamming his mouth down on mine. "I don't want to know how *you* got so good at that," he murmurs when we eventually stop kissing.

"I enjoy giving head," I admit, shrugging while I press a kiss to the underside of his jaw. "I like blowing *you*."

"I could tell, and it's so freaking hot." He nuzzles his chin in my hair.

I rest my head on his chest as his arm encircles my waist, keeping me pressed in close to his naked body. I swirl my finger through the intricate ink winding along his collarbone. "Does this phoenix mean something?" I ask, examining the stunning design. The wings extend down his arms and join the flames flickering across his upper back. My gaze trails the length of his arms, noting the snakes and daggers and embedded lines of poetry.

Kent remains silent, his lips pressing together, and that gesture tells me every item inked on his skin represents something personal to him.

Something he's not willing to divulge yet.

I drop the subject because I will never force him to admit any of his truths. They should come freely because he trusts me and wants to share another piece of himself with me.

"I'm going to have my own tattoo shop one day," I explain, resting my chin on his chest as I stare into his eyes.

"Yeah?" Interest flares behind his retinas.

I tell him about my plan. How I nearly have enough money saved so I can afford the apprenticeship and the courses.

"Is that what the art class is about?" he asks after I've spilled my guts.

I nod. "Primarily, but I also love drawing. Even if I didn't aspire to be a tattoo artist, I would be doing something creative. It's more than just a job or a passion. It's a way of life for me."

"I'll have my very own personal tattoo artist." He tweaks my nose, grinning at me. My heart rate kicks up at his words and the suggested longevity behind them. "That will be cool."

"I'd love to ink you," I admit.

"Then you shall," he adds, pressing a kiss to the top of my head. "We should get up. I know Keanu wants to have breakfast with us before they head home. He told me he met you in the kitchen last night."

I nod. "He's a nice guy. I couldn't get over how much you look alike." Reluctantly, I extract myself from Kent's warm embrace, swinging my legs out the side of the bed and standing.

Kent climbs out his side, his gaze darkening as he takes in my naked body. "Fuck, you're a sight for sore eyes, Presley baby." He licks his lips. "I think you should sleep in my bed every night."

I bark out a laugh, padding around the bed. "Yeah, I don't think so." My nose scrunches up as I stare at the wrinkled sheets. "I can only imagine how many women have been in that bed." A shiver works its way through me.

"That seriously bothers you?" He scrubs a hand over his jaw as his brows knit together.

"I know you have a past, Kent, and I'm sure it's one we'll frequently run into. I can deal with that, but sleeping in the same bed where you've had orgies and shit..." I make a disgusted face. "Not appealing."

"I'll buy a new one."

"I don't expect you to do that. Maybe you could stay at my place sometime?"

Now it's his turn to make a disgusted face. "And sleep in the same bed where you've fucked other guys?" He tweaks my nose. "Double standards, baby."

"I've had two guys in my bed. How many women have been in yours?" I arch a brow, instantly clamping a hand over his mouth when his lips move to speak. "I don't actually want you to answer that. I really don't need to know." I'm not a naturally jealous person, but even I have my limits.

"I know about Chris, but who was the other guy?" he asks.

"I'll tell you after breakfast. We shouldn't keep Selena and Keanu waiting."

I throw on my ripped skinny jeans and my top from last night, sliding Kent's white shirt on over it because my corset top is not breakfast appropriate, and then I follow Kent downstairs. He's in low-hanging gray sweatpants and a sleeveless white training top that highlights his bulging biceps and the glorious ink on his arms.

When our feet land on the lower level, I lean into his side, pressing my mouth to his ear. "Your arms are the stuff dreams are made of. I could get off just staring at them."

He slams me up against the wall, smashing his lips down on mine and devouring me like *I'm* breakfast. He nips at my earlobe. "Damn, babe. You can't say shit like that and not expect me to strip you bare and fuck you into next week."

"Ahem." A throat clearing has us breaking apart.

"Morning." Keanu grins, holding a mug in one hand as his other arm is wrapped around his wife. Selena is tall and willowy with long blonde hair that falls halfway down her back. She's tucked into Keanu's side, smiling at Kent.

"Morning," I reply, taking a step toward Selena. "It's nice to meet you. I'm Presley."

"Nice to meet you too." Her expression and her voice are soft, confirming her gentle manner. "Keanu was telling me all about you."

"Great," Kent grumbles. "And I suppose you've been all over the family group chat."

"Suck it up, bro." Keanu thumps Kent in the upper arm. "Presley is the first woman to hold your attention. That's big news." His eyes twinkle as he fixes them on me. "Everyone is dying to meet you."

Kent pulls me in front of him, wrapping his arms around my waist. "Everyone can fuck off. I'm not sharing her."

Selena beams, and she looks truly happy for us. I already know I like her. I wasn't sure what to expect because she's a famous model and her tragic backstory is well known, but she seems sweet and shy and down-to-earth. I know she's had it rough and she's been through the wringer dealing with PTSD and other stuff as a result of being a victim of sex trafficking. She clearly has tons of inner strength to have survived such an ordeal and to fight for the life she wants. I admire her even though I don't know her yet.

"Let's make breakfast, and leave the girls to talk," Keanu suggests, pecking his wife on the lips before walking toward us.

Kent squeezes my hand before releasing me from his arms. "Is there anything you don't eat?" he asks, and I shake my head.

"I'll eat pretty much anything."

Keanu returns with two mugs. "Peppermint tea," he explains, setting them down on the coffee table.

The guys walk into the kitchen while we take seats beside one another on the couch. "He's so thoughtful," I supply, glancing in Keanu's direction as I grab one of the mugs.

"He really is," Selena says. "He takes such good care of me. He's an amazing husband."

"I can already see that."

"How long have you and Kent known each other?" she asks, sipping her tea.

"Only a couple weeks though it feels longer."

She nods as if she understands. "Keanu says you manage a bar?"

We chat for a few minutes about my job, my art class, and my hopes of becoming a tattoo artist, and she tells me about her past modeling career and talks animatedly about Moonlight, the support center she is building for victims of sex abuse. I've read all about it and Kent has mentioned it, but hearing her talk passionately about all her plans really brings it to life for me.

"I think what you are doing is incredible," I admit. "And you are so brave to have told your story. I am in awe of you."

Her cheeks redden, and she shrugs casually, like it's no biggie.

"My parents died when I was nine, and I went into the foster care system after that," I tell her. "I saw abuse growing up, and the kind of facility you are building is really needed. I know there are supports currently available, but it's not enough. If I can do anything to help, volunteer or something, I would be happy to do it."

She clasps my hand in hers. "That would be wonderful, and thank you for sharing that with me."

"Breakfast is ready," Kent says, and I jerk my chin up, startled to see him right in front of me. I hadn't heard him approaching. He eyes me with a slight frown, and I wonder where his head is at.

We enjoy a relaxed breakfast with Kent's brother and sister-in-law, and the guys definitely know how to take care of their ladies, cooking up a feast of bacon, eggs, mushrooms, and potatoes.

Kent and I clean up since Keanu and Selena need to get moving. They are supposed to drop by her mother's house before heading back to Wellesley.

We walk them down to their car, and I hang back with Selena. We stop a few feet away from Keanu's SUV, and I'm surprised when Selena pulls me in for a hug. She doesn't seem like a hugger to me.

"I'm so glad to meet you, Presley. I hope I'm not speaking out of turn when I say I really hope I see you again. Kent is different with you, *good* different, and I hope you guys make a go of it."

She glances over her shoulder at where the guys are talking. "Kent can come across like nothing fazes him, but it's not true. Kent is deep and complex, and I'm not sure anyone has really uncovered the man behind the mask." She takes hold of my hands, imploring me with her eyes. "Be patient with him. He's a good man, and I can tell he has feelings for you." She slips a card into my hand. "That's my number and Keanu's. If you ever need to call us, don't hesitate." She glances at the guys again. "We love Kent and want him to be happy." She smiles at me, dropping my hands. "I think you make him happy, Presley, and I hope he makes you happy too."

Chapter Fourteen
Presley

I'm still mulling over her words as we wave them off and head back inside. "What was Selena saying to you?" Kent asks, opening the door for me.

"Just that she hopes we meet again," I fudge. "I really like her. She's such a sweetheart and so strong."

"She is, and she loves my brother good. He was a grumpy motherfucker during the years they were apart. He's much more pleasant to be around now."

I laugh, though I find it hard to believe, because Keanu doesn't seem the type.

"Are you in a rush?" Kent asks when we step back inside the apartment.

"I have nothing planned." I had purposely kept my schedule free today, even though I hadn't heard from Kent, in the hope our date would still go ahead.

"Could we walk and talk? I have a killer headache, and I wouldn't mind some fresh air."

"That sounds good, but I'm not really dressed appropriately." I gesture at myself.

"I can give you one of my hoodies, and Selena won't mind if you borrow some sneakers."

A half hour later, we enter Cambridge Common, walking side by side around the park. It's a busy spot, with plenty of walkers and joggers, and families with small kids making use of the playground.

"Tell me about Chris," Kent says, getting straight to the point.

"I need to tell you about Clay to explain about Chris, so I'll start at the beginning. After my parents died, I was placed in a foster home, but I only lasted a year there. I was in shock and grieving, and I didn't speak the entire year. The foster parents couldn't hack it, so I was placed with the Rinaldis."

Bile collects in my mouth as I think back to a time I'd rather forget. Kent takes my hand, pulling me out of the path of a teenager on a bike. My fingers wrap around Kent's, and I cling to his warmth as I continue telling my story, trying to stick to the facts so I don't terrorize him or scare him off.

"That's where I met Clay. He'd been with them for eighteen months when I arrived. He was five years older than me, and he instantly took me under his wing." I wet my dry lips, skimming over the horrific parts of that experience. "It wasn't a good home. Jean, the mom, was always drunk, and her husband, Jeff, was a creep." That's putting it mildly.

Kent's fingers tighten against mine, and he pulls me over to one of the empty iron benches, making me sit down. "Did he...hurt you?"

"No, but only because Clay stopped him before he could touch me." A shudder whips through me, and I squeeze my eyes shut, warding off memories I've long since buried.

"Is that the truth?" he whispers, and I blink my eyes, shocked to see so much fear and rage pooling in his eyes.

"I'm not lying. Jeff didn't touch me sexually, but he was building up to it, and there were plenty of close calls, where he brushed against my arm or I swore I felt his fingers crawling up my leg, and the way he looked at me." A nasty shiver inches up my spine. "He looked at me the way no grown man should look at a ten-year-old girl."

Kent squeezes my hand again, and his Adam's apple bobs in his throat.

"Anyway, when Jeff made his move, Clay was ready for him, and he protected me. Then he called the social worker, and he got Jeff arrested. Clay and I were rehoused in this bigger home in Roxbury. There were four other foster kids already living there. All boys. Chris was one of them. He was ten, same as me, and we became instant best friends. He became my whole world at thirteen when Clay aged out and he had to leave me behind."

"When did you become more?" Kent asks, staring into my eyes. He's giving me his full attention, listening intently.

"He kissed me at fourteen, and we became boyfriend and girl-friend around that time."

"And they allowed that? Your foster parents?" Kent inquires.

"They didn't seem to care." There were plenty of nights Chris crawled into my bed, and they turned a blind eye, but I'm not admitting that to Kent. He doesn't need to hear those kinds of details.

Kent frowns. "They don't sound great either."

I shrug. "Gerald and Anna were fine. They ensured I had a roof over my head, food in my belly, clothes on my back, and they were strict about school and made me sign up for all kinds of extracurric-ular activities. But it was never like having real parents." I peer into his eyes. "They could never replace my mom and dad. They didn't pretend to love me or really care about where I went or who I was with. They covered the basics, and they weren't unkind to me."

It's hard to properly explain to outsiders that I feel no connection to the people I lived with because they were never true parental figures. They were more like roommates who got paid to let me live with them. Even Clay doesn't get it, and he still gets annoyed when I refuse to tag along on visits.

"Do you see them anymore?" Kent asks, rubbing circles on the back of my wrist with his thumb. I'm not sure he's aware he's doing it, but it's amazingly comforting.

"I drop by to see them every Christmas, but that's only because Clay makes me."

Kent frowns.

"Clay was always closer with them than I was," I continue. "He still visits them once a month. I didn't have a close relationship with them. I was grateful for all they did for me, but they were paid for it, and I never felt like more than a job to them, so no, I don't keep in regular contact."

"How long did you and Chris go out for?"

"From the time I was fourteen until I was nineteen."

Shock splays across his face. "That's a long time."

"We were thrust together by our situation, and it wasn't like a normal boyfriend-girlfriend relationship. We didn't go out on dates or do any of the normal stuff. It's more we were a lifeline for each other." Air expels from my mouth. "It's difficult to explain, but we needed each other, and we got one another through foster care after Clay was gone. After we aged out and moved in together, it all went to shit, and we broke up." And that's as much as I'm prepared to tell him at this juncture.

"And the other guy?"

"I met Lync when I was twenty-two when his piece-of-shit band was hired to play a birthday party at Ramshackle. We dated exclusively for a year until he got a once-in-a-lifetime opportunity to join Ruminate on tour."

Kent frowns. "Should I have heard of them?"

I roll my eyes. "Duh. What rock have you been living under?"

"I'm not big into the music scene," he says, pulling out his cell phone.

"Ruminate is signed to Torment's record label. Please tell me you've heard of Torment?" They are only one of the biggest rock bands in the world.

He shoots me a caustic look. "I know Torment. I met Ryder Stone one time at a charity event I attended with my mom."

"Well, Ryder's younger brother Wilder plays lead guitar for Ruminate, and they're the latest big thing. They opened for Savage Mania on their last world tour, and now they are headlining their own tour, so Lync landed on his feet."

"Why'd you break up with him then?" His gaze flicks between me and his cell phone.

"I didn't want to compete with groupies, and the long-distance thing didn't appeal to me. Besides, I knew it had run its course." Lync is a great guy, but he was never the love of my life.

Kent scowls, glaring at the photo on his screen. "It seems you have a type," he drawls, flashing the pic at me. It's a close-up of Lync on stage. His long dark hair is covering his face, and his head is down, his gaze focused on his fingers as they pluck the strings of his guitar in front of a massive crowd. "Should I lose my muscles, drop fifty pounds, and grow my hair longer?"

I can't keep the smile off my face as I lean in closer, running my fingers through his messy hair. "Please don't. I happen to like you just the way you are. Besides." I rub my thumb across his lower lip. "Neither of my exes lasted the distance, so clearly they *aren't* my type." I press my mouth to his, kissing him quickly.

"But you still see Chris." A muscle pops in his jaw.

"It's complicated with Chris. We've practically grown up together, and he needs me. He's not in a good place."

"What does that mean?"

Air whooshes out of my mouth. "Chris is an addict, Kent, and I'm basically the only person invested in keeping him alive."

We head back to the apartment after I drop that bomb because I'm not comfortable talking about Chris's addiction out in public where anyone could hear us. But I want to have this conversation with Kent because I want to understand where he stands in this regard and whether I have cause to be concerned about his drug and alcohol use.

"You want anything to eat or drink?" Kent asks when we return to his place.

"Just some water, please."

I flop down on the blue velvet couch, untying Selena's sneakers. Kent hands me a bottle of water, claiming the seat beside me. He wolfs down a sandwich, watching me take sips of my water. I pull my knees up to my chest when he's finished, twisting around so I'm facing him.

"How bad is it with Chris, and should I be worried about him around you?" he asks, leaning back in the couch and crossing one ankle over his knee.

"Chris would never hurt me. He never has." Physically-speaking. But I'm not getting into all the ways my involvement with Chris has fucked with my emotional and mental well-being. "And it's bad. He's overdosed three times already. The last time was real touch and go." Tears prick my eyes remembering it. My chest heaves, and I look down at my lap.

"I'm sorry," he says, sounding genuine.

"You'd think I would be used to it by now, but it doesn't get any easier. I want him to get help, but he...he just wants to die." A sob escapes my mouth, and Kent scoots closer, taking my hands in his.

"If you need money for rehab, I can help."

I lift my head, my tears instantly drying. "Why would you offer that? You don't know him."

"I know he's important to you."

I press a hard kiss to his mouth. "Don't let anyone ever tell you you're not a good guy, Kent Kennedy."

"Don't gush too much. I was also thinking he'd be out of your life for at least a few months if he was in rehab, so it wasn't a completely selfless offer."

My lips curve at the corners. I love his honesty. It's refreshing. "It was still a fucking generous offer. One I thank you for, but Chris would never take you up on it. He doesn't want to help himself. I truly think he has a death wish." Pain slices across my chest again. "If he dies, it will devastate me. He and Clay are the closest I have to a family. I can't lose either of them without losing myself."

"I'm not gonna lie, Pres. The fact you're so involved in Chris's life bugs me. One, I think he's a selfish prick for doing this to you. Two, I hate how much you care about him. I think I'm…" He averts his eyes and withdraws his hands from mine. "Fuck." Air expels from his mouth, and his eyes are a mix of bewildered and tortured when he looks at me again. "I think I'm jealous."

My heart melts. This guy has the power to fucking slay me. I crawl into his lap, circling my arms around his neck. "What's going on with us, Kent?" I tip his head back. "What do you want?"

He gulps audibly. "I'm fucked if I know." He looks so stressed trying to figure this out, and he's burrowing a new path to my heart.

I run my fingers through his hair, fighting a smile. "Do you like me and want to spend more time with me?"

He nods without hesitation.

"I like you and want to spend time with you too, so how about this?"

He quirks a brow.

"We agree to casually date. Exclusively. And just see where things go. No expectations. No labels. No pressure. And an agreement that we will always be honest with one another, especially if either of us wants to end this. Would that work?" I ask.

He flashes me that blinding smile of his, and my ovaries swoon. He rubs his nose against mine. "Not just a pretty face."

"Is that a yes?" I whisper over his mouth.

He closes the gap between us, kissing me passionately until I can't remember where he starts and I end. I reposition myself on his lap so I'm straddling him, and we kiss like it's going out of fashion. "I'll take that as an affirmative," I rasp when we finally surface for air.

"You need to be patient with me," he says, mirroring Selena's words.

"Not a problem," I reassure him. "And you'll have to be patient with me. I'm not used to the world you live in. The money. The paparazzi. The celebrity."

"I will do my best to shield you from all that, and you can trust I've got your back." Something close to a grimace washes over his face. "In the interests of honesty, I should bring you up to speed on something."

"Okay."

He lifts me off him, placing me on the seat beside him, threading his fingers through mine. "I need to tell you about Whitney."

Chapter Fifteen
Kent

"**O**kay. I'm listening." Presley gives me her undivided attention, setting her empty bottle of water down on the side table.

I keep a firm hold of her hand, as I begin explaining, because I need to be touching her. There's no way of sugarcoating this, and I'm fearful she'll be disgusted. Afraid this might send her running for the hills. I want to explain this properly so she understands that Whitney is no threat to her. What Presley and I are building far exceeds anything I ever shared with Whit. "Whitney is Faye's half-sister. They have the same dad."

"And Faye is your cousin. The girl who is married to Kyler, right?" she adds, and I feel like giving her a gold star.

Honestly, trying to keep up with who is married to who and which kid belongs to who is becoming problematic in our large and ever-growing family. I nod. "Yeah, that's Faye. Anyway, I met Whitney the same time Faye did. I was fifteen. Whit's a year younger, and we were drawn to one another from the start. Not for the reasons you're probably thinking," I rush to add in case she's reading too much into it. "We're both messed up and self-destructive, and we formed a kind of fucked-up bond."

"I thought you never dated anyone." Her brow puckers and her nose scrunches up. It's adorably cute.

"Whitney and I have never dated." There's no polite way of putting this. "We're casual fuck buddies, who generally sleep together whenever we see one another. It's usually at family events, but there have been a few occasions where I've hooked up with her when I was in New York for the weekend. She lives there," I explain.

"And that's been going on for years?" Her facial expression gives nothing away so I can't tell if she's disgusted or what she's thinking.

"Yeah. On and off. I ended things completely over four years ago because she caught feelings and I didn't feel the same way, but I hit a rocky patch, and we started up again." I'm not proud of how weak I was. And it wasn't fair to Whitney because I see now that I gave her false hope, but I've always been a selfish prick.

"Are you still seeing her now?" Presley withdraws her hand from mine, crossing her arms around her body.

"No. I was with her for the last time the week before I met you. I told her that night that we were done for good. She hasn't taken it well."

"You might not want to hear this, Kent, but you *had* a relationship with that girl. It doesn't matter what label you gave it. She's been a part of your life for years."

I vehemently shake my head. "I didn't. We never went on dates, and we were never exclusive. She's like the female equivalent of me. She fucks around, gets messed up, and I don't care what she claims to feel; she is only clinging to me because I'm familiar, because I understand her, to a point."

"Tell yourself whatever you want, but the truth is, you had a relationship with Whitney, Kent. It might not have been traditional, but you have been with each other on and off for years. That's not insignificant."

"It was fucking sex!" I yell, getting frustrated she's trying to make this into something it's not. "That's all. I don't love her, and she doesn't love me." I know Whitney thinks she does, but she's fucking delusional.

"Can you honestly tell me you don't care for her at all?"

I straighten up as I glare at her because this is not how I saw this conversation going. "It's almost like you want me to love her."

She shakes her head, and waves of her gorgeous glossy hair cascade around her shoulders. "That's not it. I just want you to be honest about what she means to you because I've been truthful with you about Chris."

"That is an entirely different scenario," I scoff.

"Is it though?" She cocks her head to the side, looking contemplative. "Because it sounds to me like circumstances threw you two together and that she was a kind of lifeline for you too."

My initial instinct is to completely deny her claims, but there's a kernel of truth in her words. My tongue darts out, wetting my dry lips, and I wonder why the fuck I thought it was a good idea to raise the subject of Whitney. "Circumstances did throw us together, and there was a codependency there, but that's where the similarities end, Pres."

I rub the back of my neck. "Whitney was an escape. Like a comfort blanket for a brief time," I acknowledge, "but she has never been a lifeline for me. I haven't confided anything of importance to her because that's not who we were to one another. And I do care about her, but only because there is history there. I wouldn't even call her a friend. She's not someone I want in my life. We're toxic for one another." I lean forward, peering deep into her eyes, wanting her to see this truth. "I have never loved her, and she never made me feel the way you do."

She scoots closer on the couch, until our feet touch. "How do I make you feel, Kent?"

"Like I'm walking on water. Like there is light at the end of the tunnel for me. Like I might be worthy of you. Like I could be happy with you. You consume my thoughts, and I just want to be with you because you fill me full of feelings I never thought I'd ever get to experience. We haven't even had sex, and it doesn't matter because I just want to exist with you."

It's official. I have now traded in my man card and turned into Kyler.

I'm so screwed.

She grabs my face and kisses me hard. "I just want to exist with you too," she whispers over my mouth. "Even if the thought terrifies me as much as it excites me."

I wind my fingers into her hair, holding the nape of her neck. "Why are you scared?" I know why I am, and I want to see if it's the same for her.

"Because you have the potential to make me feel so damn much, Kent Kennedy. This feels intense in a way I've never felt with anyone before, and I'm scared you'll hurt me."

"I feel those things too, and I'm shitting myself half the time." I pull her to me, needing to taste her lips. I kiss her softly, drowning in all things Presley, and the same flux of emotions churns inside me, like every time I'm with this woman.

"I've thrown shade at all my brothers for being pussy-whipped," I admit. "Scoffed at their declarations of love and looked down my nose at the idea that it could exist for me. You're challenging my entire belief system, Presley baby, and I'm scared I will let both of us down because that's what I'm good at." I avert my eyes, not able to look at her when the truth of those words seeps from every pore.

"Kent." She holds my face tighter, forcing my gaze to hers. "We've both been shaped, in different ways, by our past experiences, but that doesn't mean we're doomed to fail. Being aware of our pitfalls means we can work to avoid them. All I ask is that you try and that you don't deliberately set out to hurt me, and I will promise you the same."

"You are too fucking good for me, you know that?" I press my forehead to hers. "You are so beautiful, and smart, and compassionate, and strong, and I want to be worthy of you. I really fucking do."

"I could say those same things about you, and it kills me to hear you speaking about yourself like that. I've already seen that you are more than the person you are portrayed to be. More than the person you think you have to be." Her eyes stab mine with fierce determination. "Give me your truths, Kent. Even if those truths hurt. At least it will be real."

"I will try." That is as much as I can promise right now. "And the last thing I want to do is hurt you. This feels like the start of something special, and I promise I will do everything in my power not to fuck it up."

She takes my hand, pressing a kiss to my palm. "That is all I can ask of you." She rests her head on my chest, and my arms automatically go around her. I close my eyes, praying to a higher power to not let me screw this up. "Kent." I glance down, and she's looking up at me, her big brown eyes swimming in possibility. "I need to know about the drugs and the booze, and I need you to be honest with me."

Every muscle in my body locks up, and she straightens up, feeling it. "What do you want to know?"

"Be honest with me. Do you have a problem?"

I understand why she's asking. She's clearly been through the wringer with Chris, and I owe her the complete truth. "There were a few years during my teens when I had a problem. When I consciously got high and drunk and I pulled all kinds of shit. Got into trouble with the law. Put my parents through hell. It's a miracle I graduated high school and got into Harvard, but I did, and things changed for me there."

"In what way?"

"I met someone who helped me realize I was throwing my life away. She was so strong and so brave, and she forced me to take a long hard look at myself. I chose to take back control and start living my life the way I wanted to live it. It was then I decided I was going to pursue a career in law, and I stopped a lot of the dysfunctional behaviors."

"Yet you still do shit on the weekends. Why?"

"I guess old habits die hard, and I...I was so lonely." I peer deep into her eyes. "Until I met you, and now I have a reason to not do that anymore."

Tears well in her eyes. "Please don't do it for me." She shakes her head, and I want to remove that look of desperate sadness from her eyes. "Do it for yourself, because that's the only way it will be meaningful."

"I get why you're worried. You don't need a Chris two point oh, and I promise I don't have a problem. It's recreational, and I'll stop."

She plants her hands on my shoulders. "Just don't lie to me about it, Kent. No matter how bad it gets, promise me you will come to me and you will be truthful."

"I can do that. I promise." I rub my nose against hers. "I've never had anyone who cared enough to want to know."

Surprise splays across her face. "With how close your family is, I very much doubt that."

I shrug, casting my eyes away. "I told you I am on the outskirts, and they've all had their own shit to deal with. None of them have ever known how to deal with me."

She slings her arm around my neck. "Well, I'm here for you now. And I think that's enough of the heavy." She pecks my lips. "Just one last thing. How do you plan to handle the Whitney situation? She's going to freak when she finds out about me."

"She already is." I pull her onto my lap. "She saw that picture of us online, and she's been blowing up my phone every day."

"You haven't spoken to her?" I shake my head, and she purses her lips. "You need to tell her, Kent. You owe her that much, and if I'm going to be in your life, I need you to be honest with her so I'm not ambushed."

We spend the rest of the day in my apartment, just talking, discussing my favorite book—which she took the time to read— watching back-to-back movies, and making out like we're teenagers again. Instead of going out, I order takeout, and then I drive Presley home later. I begged her to stay again, but she has to be at the bar early to open up, and I have an eight-a.m. class, so it's not possible.

Her comment about my bed is playing on my mind, and I wonder if that's the real reason she didn't stay. I want her to be comfortable here, so she'll stay over as often as she can, which means the bed has got to go. The second I get home from dropping her off, I order a new one, trying not to reflect on how Kyler-like the gesture is.

We don't see enough of one another in the next couple of weeks. Between my classes, extra tutorials, and studying for my exams— which start in three weeks—I have little free time, but I sneak in opportunities to see Pres whenever I can.

Presley has a full schedule too with alternating day and night shifts at the bar and her art class, which means finding time for dates is challenging. She is off every Wednesday, so it becomes our official date night, and we've grabbed dinner and a movie both times. The first weekend, she worked the day shifts, and I collected her after I was finished at the library both days, taking her back to my place where we stayed holed up on the couch, watching TV, and eating takeout before retreating to bed.

We still haven't fucked, and I know she's purposely holding back, but I won't push her. It makes the expectation all that much sweeter, and I'm enjoying getting to know her intimately, understanding all the other ways in which I can make her body sing.

This weekend, Pres is on nights, which sucks, but I cram in extra studying so I'm not tempted to go partying with the guys.

It's Sunday night, and I'm perched at the counter in Ramshackle, waiting for Presley's shift to end, when my phone rings. I'm tempted to send Mom to my voicemail, but she's tenacious, and she'll just keep calling. I gesture at my phone to Presley as I walk outside to take the call.

"Mom. What's up?" I ask, walking away from Bugger because that dude is nosy as fuck.

"Kent. At last. Honestly, one would swear you were living on Mars it's that difficult to get a hold of you."

"I'm busy, Mom." I stop at the corner, tucking myself against the wall.

"So I've heard." I can almost feel her smile.

I grunt. "Keanu told you about Presley."

"He did, and I'm happy for you. That's why I'm calling. I would like to invite her to Easter dinner."

"She's got plans," I automatically reply because I feel the need to keep her away from my family. It's not that my family is horrible, but they're a lot to take on. Besides, I've no clue how I'd explain the Keaton-Austen situation without coming across like a total douchebag.

"What plans? Selena said she's an orphan and she isn't close to her foster parents."

"She's having dinner with her friends," I lie though it's possibly the truth. We haven't discussed next weekend, but we need to.

"Send me her number," Mom says, using that confrontational tone she deploys when she's determined to get her own way.

"Mom." I enunciate the word. "Just drop it. I'll bring her home some other time."

"I want to extend the invite, Kent. If she declines because she has other plans, that is fine, but I want her to know she is welcome at your home any time."

"I'll relay the message," I lie.

"Nice try." Mom is pouting. I can visualize her in my head. "But I don't believe you. Text me her number or I'll call Keven to retrieve it for me."

"You don't play fair."

"I've never pretended to be an angel."

I roll my eyes even though she can't see me. "I'll invite her, and if she says no, I'll get her to call you to explain." There is no other way around it. Mom will not surrender until I do as she wants.

"Excellent. Now, about you and Keaton."

"Mom, don't." I grind my teeth to my molars. "That has nothing to do with you or Dad. Just leave it be."

"It's been over two years, Kent! And he's getting married in June. I expect you to have patched up your differences by then. It's time, Kent. This isn't going on any longer. We miss you, and I want everyone to get along again. Please, honey. Please try for me."

I know I can't avoid it forever, and maybe I can do this if Presley is with me. Maybe she'll give me the strength I need to put it behind me and make amends with my brother. I do miss Keaton.

"I'll try." It's as much as I can promise.

"Thank you, honey."

"Will Whitney be at Easter dinner?" I ask because I'll need to warn Presley if she plans on coming.

"Not this year. It's their mom's turn to have them for Easter dinner, so it will just be Adam joining us."

Relief threads through me. That makes it easier. "Okay. Let me go talk to Presley."

"Goodbye, love. See you next weekend."

I hang up, pushing off the wall when a familiar face slips out from the shadows.

"Kennedy."

"Jet."

"You keeping a low profile or are you buying someplace else?" he asks.

"I'm cutting back." I haven't popped anything since Presley and I had our chat, but I'm still smoking weed on the weekend. She doesn't appear to mind that.

Jet barks out a laugh. "Whatever you say, man."

"I'll take some weed." My supply is running low. "And some pills," I add, knowing I will need something stronger to take the edge off next weekend.

We conduct our business and part ways, and I head back into the bar to ask Presley if she wants to have Easter Sunday dinner at Chez Kennedy.

Chapter Sixteen
Kent

"**S**o, this is how the other half lives, huh?" Presley says as we drive up the winding driveway toward my family home on Easter Sunday morning.

"This was normal to me growing up. We went to a private school, and all the kids were wealthy."

"Are you sure I'm dressed okay?" she asks, twitching in her seat. It's unusual to see Presley rattled since she's always so self-assured, but she's definitely nervous. She's been peppering me with questions about my family the entire journey from Boston.

"Baby. You look gorgeous." I slide my hand across the console, squeezing her bare thigh. She's wearing a figure-hugging black dress with a gold stripe at the collar and the hem and long sleeves that flare at the end. The dress stops mid-thigh, and she is sexy and elegant and wholly fuckable. She's wearing sky-high stilettos that accentuate her slim legs, and I'm having a hard time stopping my dick from jumping out of my pants and finding a home in her warm pussy. "Stop worrying. My family isn't judgmental like that. Mom is going to take one look at you and proclaim you beautiful."

It's the truth. Presley is stunning, and I'm bowled over by her effortless beauty. Her hair is down in soft waves, and though she's wearing more makeup today than she normally wears, there is no disguising her natural beauty. Her full lips are painted in a warm peachy color, and her high cheekbones are accentuated with a subtle blush. Smoky eyeshadow behind thick black lashes makes her big brown eyes seem even bigger.

"I don't want to let you down. I know this is a big deal for you," she says, squeezing my fingers.

I stop the car to the left of the front door, put it in park, and kill the engine. Leaning over the console, I kiss my girl. "That's an impossibility. You could never let me down. Thank you for coming with me." I'm glad she is here, and I'm determined to be a model boyfriend.

"Thank you for wanting me here." She runs her fingers through my hair. "By the way, you look gorgeous all dressed up." I'm wearing dress pants and a fitted black dress shirt because Mom expects all of us to make an effort for the big family occasions.

"Stop stealing my lines." I kiss her softly.

"Before we go in," she says, rummaging in her bag. "I want to give you this."

"What is it?" I ask, taking the silver-wrapped square package from her hand.

"Open it and see." She smiles, pulls her bottom lip between her teeth, and watches me tear at the wrapping.

I stare at the picture while my stomach turns cartwheels and my heart beats to a new rhythm. She has framed the picture of us that was online. It's the only one the paparazzi scum has managed to take as we've been discreet anytime we've gone out since.

"I made the frame," she says, sounding nervous. "And I have a matching one by my bed. I thought you'd like a copy."

"I love it." My ecstatic smile is genuine. "It's a good picture of us." I love the way we are looking at one another in this shot. Like we exist only for each other. And it was our very first date, proving the connection and the chemistry has been there from the very start.

"I know it's not much, but I wanted to do something for you because you are always showering me with flowers and gifts."

"I like spoiling you," I admit, as the front door opens. I was wondering how long it would take Mom to make an appearance. She's not known for her patience.

"The firing squad has arrived," I joke, jerking my head in the direction of my parents.

"Stop that." She nudges me in the ribs. "Your mom was lovely on the phone, and Selena loves her to bits. You make her sound like an ogre when I know that's not the truth."

"Stay there," I tell her, deliberately not responding to her statements. "I'll get your door." I climb out of the car, nodding in my parents' direction as I round the hood and open Presley's door for her. Placing my hands on her hips, I lift her down, grasping her hand firmly as she grabs her bag and the large wrapped present she brought for my parents. I told her she didn't need to bring anything, but she insisted.

After tucking the present under one arm, I hold her hand as I guide her toward my family home.

"Darling." Mom steps forward, kissing me on both cheeks. "It's so good to have you home." She turns her attention to Presley, beaming at her. "And you must be Presley." She pulls Pres forward, hugging her without invitation. "We are so happy to have you here. Thank you for joining us."

"The pleasure is all mine. Thank you for the invite."

"James." Mom yanks Dad forward. "Come say hi to Presley. Isn't she stunning?"

I smirk as Presley's cheeks flush. She'll soon get used to my crazy-ass family.

"That she is. Our sons are all lucky bastards." Dad takes Presley's hand, raising it to his lips for a kiss. "Welcome, Presley. I've got to admit I'm intrigued to meet the woman who's managed to tame our Kent."

I scowl at my dad, flipping him the bird behind Presley's back.

"I haven't tamed Kent," Presley says, squeezing my hand. "Nor would I want to. I like him just the way he is."

Mom positively glows, and Pres really couldn't have said anything more perfect. "I love her already," Mom tells me, not even attempting to hide that comment from my girlfriend. "Come on in. Most of the others are inside."

"This is from Pres," I tell Mom, thrusting the present at her.

"You didn't need to do this," Mom says, taking the large package. "But thank you. It's most thoughtful."

"I made it myself," Presley says, and I arch a brow. She wouldn't tell me what it was. "I hope you like it."

"Presley is an amazing artist," I tell my parents.

"Then I can't wait to see what this is."

I deliberately hold Presley back, letting my parents walk ahead. "I didn't mention that things are strained between me and Keaton because it's complicated," I say, only being half truthful. I've had plenty of opportunities to tell her about the rift with my brother, but I've purposely held back because I promised I wouldn't lie to her and I'm not ready to tell her the real reason we're not talking. "I'm just mentioning it in case things get tense."

She frowns a little. "Okay."

"Oh, my word," Mom exclaims from the living room just as we enter the large space. My nephew Hewson is helping her remove the wrapping from Presley's present, eagerly tearing at the silver paper, throwing it on the ground. At seven—eight next month—Lana and Kalvin's firstborn is the eldest grandchild, and Mom spoils him rotten. "This is exquisite, Presley."

Every head in the room turns in our direction, and I feel for my girl. She clings to my hand so tight I wonder if any blood flow can get through.

"I'm glad you think so." She holds her head up, smothering her nerves, and warmth spreads across my chest. I love how much of a fighter she is. I know this is stretching her out of her comfort zone, and the fact she's willing to do this for me blows my mind. I must have done something right in my messed-up life to deserve a woman like her.

Mom holds the white-framed glass box aloft, and my brothers and sisters-in-law all huddle around, oohing and ahhing. It's striking. Presley has drawn a phoenix—similar to the one inked on my skin—and filled it in with red, yellow, and gold dried flowers.

"Are these pressed flowers?" Mom asks.

"Yes. I've been pressing all the flowers Kent sends me and making art with them. I don't like throwing anything away, especially something so pretty."

My nephew Cathal wriggles in Kyler's arms as my brother turns to face us with a big smug smirk on his face. "Kent has been sending you flowers, huh?"

"Yes." Presley's brows knit together as she glances between me and my brother, unsure if she's said something wrong.

"How romantic," Kalvin adds, rubbing a hand across his chest. "How long have you two been dating again?" he asks, turning the full extent of his charm on Presley.

"A few weeks," she confirms.

"And you're pussy-whipped already." Kalvin slaps me on the back. "Hah. Payback is a bitch, bro." He rubs his hands in glee. "This dinner just got infinitely more entertaining." He slides his arm around Presley's shoulder. "I want to hear everything."

Presley laughs, and I know she gets it because I told her I gave my brothers crap for years.

"Fuck off," I hiss, yanking Presley away from him. "Go paw at your own woman."

A chorus of chuckles rings out around the room.

"Pay up," Keven says, eyeballing Kaden. Cheryl—Kev's wife—rolls her eyes. Those two are always betting on ridiculous shit, and the rest of my idiot brothers usually wade in too. It's family tradition at this stage.

"You owe me," Kade says, drilling me with a look as he slaps a hundred-dollar bill into Kev's palm.

"I owe you shit."

"Kent!" Faye shrieks, blocking Ciara's ears. "Watch your language!" Ciara and Cathal are Ky and Faye's boisterous twins. I haven't seen them in ages, and they've gotten much bigger. They turn two next month, and it's hard to believe. All the kids are growing up so fast.

"You do know you have zero chance of keeping little ears protected from cussing in this house, right?" Lana says, rubbing chocolate off her three-year-old daughter Hayley's mouth.

"You're the dumbass who made that stupid bet," Keaton says to Kade. "I told you Kent would be the most romantic one as soon as he found the right girl." He smiles at me, and I grind my teeth.

I know he means well, and it's his way of extending an olive branch, but every time I look at him with Austen, animosity flares. Pressing my lips tight, I contain the snarl forming on my tongue. Tension filters into the air, and my instinct is to grab Presley, turn on my heels, and hightail it back to Boston.

"You look so much like Kent and Keanu," Presley says, smiling at Keaton as she attempts to cut through the strained atmosphere.

"I used to think that when I first moved here," Faye says, letting Ciara down so she can run off with the other kids. "But once you get to know the triplets, you'll see the differences." She walks to Presley, thrusting out her hand. "I'm Faye. Nice to meet you."

That sets off a round of introductions as each of my brothers and their girls formally says hi.

"Where's Red and Brad?" I inquire not seeing Kyler's best buddy and his wife or their daughter, Elodie.

"They're in Ireland," Kyler says. "Brad's been based in the UK for the past few weeks, so it made sense for them to celebrate Easter with Rachel's dad."

"Ah, great. Our last guest has arrived," Mom says as a sleek silver BMW pulls up outside the living room window.

My heart drops to my feet when two car doors open. I curse under my breath at the sight of Whitney's long purple hair and the predictable scowl on her face. I spin around, pinning a fierce look at Mom. "I thought you said Adam was coming alone?"

Everyone trades wary expressions.

"Whitney is supposed to be at her mom's," Faye says, responding before Mom can. She sends me an apologetic look that is of fuck all use to me.

"We can leave," I tell Presley, because I won't subject her to this shitshow.

"It's okay," she says, reassuring me with her eyes. "I can be in the same room as your ex if she's okay with me."

A collective groan rings out because the rest of us knows the truth —there is no time in existence, either now or in the future, where Whitney will *ever* be okay with Presley.

"Whitney will be on her best behavior," Mom says, patting Presley's arms. "I'll make sure of it. Don't worry about a thing."

Mom storms out of the living room, dragging Dad with her.

"I'd love to be a fly on the wall for that conversation," Kyler says, grinning.

Faye elbows him. "Don't be mean. She can't help how she feels."

"She can help how she acts though," Kyler murmurs, and isn't that the truth.

I know Faye wants to see the good in her half-sister and she tries not to take sides, but Whitney acts like an immature spoiled brat a lot of the time, and it's one of the reasons why things would never have gotten serious between us. She drives me insane with her whining, and it's why I can only tolerate her in short spurts. I know this makes me sound like a prick, and it's not like I haven't had my immature bratty moments, but I'm moving forward, where Whitney seems stuck in her rebellious teenage phase.

Faye walks toward us, leveling Pres with a direct look. "My sister can be a real bitch, and she's possessive about Kent even though he's told her repeatedly where they stand. I'm not as delusional as Alex. She'll be mean, but let it float over your head. It's nothing personal."

"Wow. Make my girl feel at ease, why don't ya." I wrap my arm more protectively around Presley, working hard not to glare at Faye. If I glare at Faye, Kyler's claws will come out, and before you know it, we'll be fighting. I'm determined to take the moral high ground today, because I don't want Presley to be uncomfortable.

Or any more uncomfortable than she's about to be.

"It's okay," Presley reassures me, sliding her arm around my back, clutching my waist. "I appreciate the warning." She smiles at Faye. "I'll try to bite my tongue."

"No tongue biting is allowed," Kalvin says, practically frothing at the mouth. "Give her hell, Presley."

"Ignore him," his wife, Lana, says. "We all do."

Eva sidles up next to us with Matthew cradled in her arms. He's sick with a chest infection and on antibiotics that make him sleepy. "Make sure you are sitting beside us at the table. I'll act as a buffer."

"She's really that bad?" Presley asks.

"She can be," Eva confirms, grimacing as she looks over our shoulders.

"I need to speak to you!" Whitney roars, storming into the room like a raging tornado, making a beeline for me.

I turn around, with my arm still around Presley, bracing myself for it.

"Whitney." Adam catches up to her, whispering furiously in her ear.

Steam practically billows out of her ears as she listens to whatever her dad is saying, and her nostrils flare with unconcealed anger. "Fine." She stomps her foot, folding her arms around herself as she shoots daggers at Presley. "It can wait till after dinner." She moves forward, encroaching on our personal space, jabbing her finger in my chest. "But we *are* talking."

"There is nothing left to be said." I called her after I talked to Presley, explaining I was dating and reiterating there was nothing between her and me anymore, nor would there ever be. But she wouldn't be Whitney if she didn't ignore me and she wasn't hell-bent on causing trouble.

It'll be a miracle if we survive this dinner unscathed.

"Trust me, there is plenty." Her derisory gaze rakes up and down Presley in a blatantly hostile manner.

Presley extends her hand. "I'm Presley. Kent has told me about you. I'm glad to finally meet you."

Whitney looks at Presley's hand like it's diseased. Planting her hands on her hips, she eyeballs my girlfriend with a devilish glint in her eye. "Well, he's told me nothing about you, and I've zero desire to meet you or know you, so let's quit with the pretense."

"Oh boy." Kalvin chuckles, and Lana swats him in the chest.

I lean into Whitney's face, nostrils flaring. "Don't fucking lie. I called you and told you I was dating Presley, and if you can't be civil to her, you and I have a big fucking problem."

"Oh, whatever." Whitney throws her hair over her shoulders. "Like I give a fuck."

"Dinner's served!" Mom hollers, desperation laced through her tone. She knows, as well as the rest of us, that dinner is now effectively ruined.

"I'm sorry about this," I whisper to Presley as I lead her into the dining room. "We can still leave."

"She doesn't scare me, and I'm not running off."

I kiss her quick, squeezing her waist. When I turn my head around, Whitney is staring at me with hurt in her eyes. Thank fuck I smoked a joint before I came here and that I have some pills tucked into the back pocket of my pants. I have a feeling I'm going to need them before the day is out.

We take our seats for dinner, and Faye and Kyler sit at the opposite end of the table, meaning Whitney is forced to sit there beside her dad and her sister. However, she's on the other side of the table, meaning she can still glare at us, and she hasn't stopped with the poisonous looks from the second we sat down. I try to concentrate on the conversation around us, but it's awkward because I'm conscious of Whitney slinging daggers at Presley in between guzzling wine. Having Austen and Keaton mooning at one another across the way has my nerves on edge too, and I just wish time would fast-forward so it's over and we can leave.

"I don't get it," Whitney pipes up just as the dinner plates are being cleared away. She's already slurring her words, which isn't a good sign. I immediately tense, preparing myself for it. She stares at me, hurt and anger etched upon her face. "She's not even that pretty, and what lame-ass parents name their kid after Elvis Presley."

"For your information," Presley says, eyeballing Whitney. "My parents died in a car crash when I was nine, and Mom called me Presley because she thought the name was pretty. It had nothing to do with Elvis."

I'm embarrassed I never thought to ask her that, and now my Elvis notes seem corny as fuck, but Pres seems to appreciate them.

"You're one to talk," I snap, all out of patience. I take Presley's hand on top of the table, ensuring Whitney sees me doing it. "Your mom named you after Whitney fucking Houston."

"What the fuck does she have that I don't?" Whitney shrieks, standing quickly, knocking her chair over. "I have loved you since I was fourteen, Kent! First, you fuck Keaton's Melissa, and now you shack up with that gold-digging whore, and I have never done anything to deserve being treated like this!" She stalks toward us, and Adam rises, but Faye stalls him, shaking her head. Faye exchanges a look with Kyler before standing, trailing after her sister.

Tears stream down Whitney's face as she stands behind Austen and Keaton, staring dejectedly at me. I can't find it in me to feel compassion, not after she just blabbed about Melissa and insulted my girlfriend again. And I have always, *always*, been honest and up front with her. She knows it was only ever sex for me because I spelled that out clearly.

"Why are you doing this, Kent? You *can't* do this. I won't let you." Steely determination ghosts over her eyes.

"I'm fucking blue in the face telling you I don't have those feelings for you."

"And you do for her?" she screams, shucking Faye away when she tries to reach for her.

"Yeah, I do." I'm not going to lie to her face. She's the one who decided to do this in front of an audience. "It's serious between Presley and me. Rant and rave all you fucking want, Whit, but we're done."

"Well, it doesn't matter, because you're stuck with me now, whether you like it or not." Swiping at her tears, she fixes me with a smug look before curling her lips in Presley's direction, slanting her with a gloating look that turns the blood in my veins to ice.

Panic presses down on my chest, and I'm almost afraid to ask the question, but if I don't, someone else will. "What the fuck are you talking about?"

She grins, tilting her head to the side. "I'm pregnant, and it's yours."

Chapter Seventeen
Presley

Initial silence greets Whitney's declaration, and you could hear a pin drop in the room. Wide-eyed shell-shocked faces stare in our direction, and it appears everyone is dumbstruck.

Inside, I'm slowly disintegrating.

"You're lying," Kent hisses.

"I'm not." Whitney grabs something from the pocket of her jeans, flinging it at Kent. The white and blue stick lands face up in front of us on the table, the word pregnant clearly visible in the digital display. My lungs compress, and my chest heaves. Beside me, Kent is a grenade ready to explode.

He jumps up, straining across the table, glaring at Whitney with his fists clenched at his sides. "All that proves is you let some other dumbass fuck you bare. I always use condoms. *Always*." He jabs his finger in her direction. "You're not pinning this on me," he seethes.

"There's been no one but you since that weekend at the beginning of March." Whitney's lower lip wobbles, and she bursts out crying. "I'm six weeks pregnant. This baby is yours."

The pain in my heart is so intense it's as if a million tiny pinpricks have been pushed into the organ all at once. Eva grabs my hand, squeezing tight, and I look at her, no doubt mirroring the anguish clear in her eyes.

"Bullshit," Kent roars. "This is fucking bullshit." He slams his fist down, and the table rattles.

"You fucking asshole! Don't you dare speak to my daughter like that!" Adam jumps up, racing around the table, his eyes like laser beams shooting fiery rays at Kent as he advances. A muscle pops in Kent's jaw as he crosses his arms, jutting his chin up defiantly as Adam reaches him.

Adam is fast for an old dude, thrusting his arm out, hitting Kent square on the jaw. Faye screams at her dad to stop, but he's lost to his anger, raising his fist again. Kent has youth, strength, and rage on his side, and he recovers fast, retaliating with a firm punch to Adam's nose.

Shouts ring out around the room, and chairs screech as some of the others stand.

Adam roars, briefly touching the blood pumping from his nose, before he fists Kent's shirt, ready to inflict more damage.

Kaden intervenes, tugging him back while James similarly restrains Kent. Keanu appears at Kent's side, folding his arms and leveling a glare at Adam. Across the table, Keaton looks upset as his gaze flickers between Whitney, Kent, and me. Austen has his arm around the back of Keaton's chair, squeezing his shoulder.

A distraught-looking Faye is consoling an upset Whitney, running a hand up and down her back while her sister sobs into her shoulder.

"Get the fuck off me!" Kent roars, wriggling in his dad's arms.

Keven approaches, planting himself in front of Kent. "You need to calm down."

"Don't fucking tell me what to do! This is fucking bullshit, and everyone knows it."

"For once in your life, man up and accept responsibility for your actions," Adam yells, still spitting fire.

"Excuse me?" Keanu narrows his eyes at Adam. "Who the hell do you think you are saying that to my brother?"

"Stop this right now." Alex positions herself in between the men, her gaze bouncing between her son and Whitney and Faye's father. "I know you're upset, Adam, but you have no right to hit my son, and if you won't calm down, you must leave." She doesn't wait for his reply, refocusing her attention on Kent. "Please calm down. We need to sit down and discuss this like adults."

"There is nothing to discuss," Kent barks. "It's not fucking mine."

"Kent." James levels him with a stern look, refusing to let him go. "That kind of talk isn't helping, and whether this baby is yours or not doesn't change the fact Whitney is pregnant and this stress isn't good for her."

"Neither is drinking her fucking body weight in wine!" Kent yells. "Or are we just going to pretend she's not fucking drunk."

"Stop cursing," Alex snaps, rubbing her temples. Thank God the kids are outside on the playground with the sitter and not here to witness this. "And stop shouting," she adds, deliberately lowering her tone.

"Kent is right," Faye says, holding Whitney by the upper arms, fixing her with an unhappy scowl. "What were you thinking?"

"I'm thinking he knocked me up and now he wants to play happy family with that gold-digging slut!" Her tears miraculously dry up as she sends daggers in my direction.

I want to tell her to fuck off. That I'm no gold digger or slut, but I seal my lips because this isn't the time or place. Right now, I wish I had a time machine so I could go back to last week and never agree to come here today.

Alex drills a look at Adam, clearly wanting him to intervene, to call his daughter out on her disgusting behavior, but he says nothing. Does nothing, and I have zero respect for the man.

Memories float to the surface of my brain, and I squeeze my eyes shut, begging them to go away. This is too raw. Too real. And I haven't even told Kent yet.

"There's only one slut around here, and it's not Presley," Kent says, his voice composed but lethal.

Adam roars again, bucking against Kaden as he lunges for Kent, ready to kill him if the expression on his face is any indication.

"Okay. That is enough," Kyler yells, getting up and stalking toward this end of the table. He stops in front of Whitney. "Grow up and stop acting like a brat. Presley has done nothing to you, and you will not insult her again." He looks at his wife. "Please take Whitney to the game room. I'll escort Kent when he's ready." He kisses Faye's temple, and they exchange an intimate look. Faye nods before ushering her sister out of the room but not before Whitney levels me with one final sneer.

"Kent." Kyler walks around to his brother. "I know you're pissed, but the only way we're going to get to the bottom of this is to talk to Whitney. Whether you want to accept it or not, you have been sleeping with that girl for years, and if she says it's your baby, you need to at least hear what she has to say."

"It's not mine," Kent insists, wresting his arm from his dad's hand. "It can't be."

Kalvin comes around the table to join the rest of his brothers, all of them now protectively flanking Kent. The only one still sitting is Keaton, and I can tell he's upset by that. He looks conflicted, and I'm guessing that's down to whatever disagreement exists between him and Kent.

Looking at the wall of men surrounding Kent and their fierce expressions, it's hard to understand Kent's comment about being on the fringes. All I see is a family ready to do whatever is necessary to protect one of their own, and I'm glad they have stepped up for him because Kent needs this.

Kyler shoots me an apologetic look before eyeballing his brother. "I know you don't want it to be yours, but you've got to consider the fact that it could be. Unless you're saying you haven't had sex with her recently?"

Kent's jaw flexes, and the skin on his knuckles bleaches white with how tight he's clenching his fists.

"Kyler is right," I say, rising to my feet as I attempt to emerge from the numbed wall I've retreated behind. "You need to talk to her."

His Adam's apple bobs in his throat. "It's not mine, Pres," he whispers, collapsing against me.

His entire body is a mass of solid stress, and I wrap my arms around him, offering what little comfort I'm capable of offering when I'm shattering on the inside. "Don't go in there all guns blazing. Just listen to what she has to say," I suggest.

"Presley is right," Alex adds in a soft voice. "And there are ways to prove paternity even while the baby is in the womb."

Adam hisses, and I'm close to swinging my fists at him myself. He's a fucking asshole for the way he's treating Kent. I get he's worried for his daughter, and it's blatantly obvious he doesn't like Kent, but throwing shade when he isn't privy to all the facts is dumb and spiteful.

"I don't like the insinuation that my daughter is lying." Adam pulls away from Kaden, removing a handkerchief from his pocket, using it to stem the blood flow trickling from his nose. "I know what you all think of Whitney," he adds, glancing at everyone around the table. "And I know she's got her issues, but my daughter would never lie about something like this." He fixes Kent with the full extent of his hatred, and I hold Kent tighter, instinctively needing to protect him from this. "I have warned you, time and time again, to stay away from her. You have never been any good for her, and I blame you for the way she is. You have selfishly toyed with her feelings with no regard for how it's destroyed her."

"You can't pin that on Kent," Eva says, working hard to maintain a neutral expression. "He has always been honest with Whitney. You're being unfair."

"I think that's enough, Adam," James says in a clipped tone. A muscle clenches in his jaw. "There's little to be gained from assigning blame at this point."

Adam snorts. "Of course, you'd think that. Like father, like son," he sneers. I've no idea what he's referring to, but judging by the shocked gasps and furious expressions from the rest of the family, I'm guessing he's referencing something horrible from the past.

"Okay, Adam." Kyler grips his father-in-law by the shoulders, looking like he wants to knock some sense into him. "You're going to shut up now before you say something you can't ever take back."

"It's already too late," Alex says. Sorrow is etched on her beautiful face as she shakes her head. "We have welcomed you into our home countless times over the years. We considered you a friend, and this is what you really think?"

"I think you've forgotten what a delinquent your son is in your haste to paint my daughter as the villain of the story," he says, clearly unwilling to let go of his anger.

"How dare you!" Alex's hands shake with rage. "That was in the past, and Kent has worked hard to turn his life around. He's studying to be a lawyer for Christ's sake! I won't have you taking this out on him, and we don't even know the facts yet."

"I know a leopard doesn't change his spots," Adam growls, and I narrow my eyes to slits as I glare at him. I run my hand up and down Kent's back in what I hope is a reassuring gesture.

"He was a troubled kid," Kyler says. "So was Whitney. So were lots of teens, but that has no bearing on this. Think of Faye," he adds. "Think of how much this is going to hurt her. You need to stop throwing accusations around and just focus on being there for both your daughters. That's what you should be doing instead of insulting my family."

Adam wets his lips, and his chest heaves. His shoulders slump, and no one says anything for a few beats.

Kent pulls me around in front of him, pulling me in flush against his chest, and I circle my arms around his back, resting my head on his chest. He holds me close, like he might need my touch to ground him.

"You're right, Kyler. I'm sorry. Forgive me, Alex." Adam looks at Kent's mom and then his dad. "I apologize, James."

James exhales heavily, scrubbing a hand across his chin. "Our kids need us. That's all that should matter now."

It hasn't gone unnoticed that his lackluster apology didn't extend to Kent. Or that neither Alex or James has accepted it. I'll be very surprised if their friendship remains intact after this.

"Wow. The world truly has gone to hell in a handbasket," Kalvin says in a light tone, attempting to break up the tense atmosphere. "This day shall forever be known as the day Kyler Kennedy put the oldies in their corner. Nice one, bro."

Kyler rolls his eyes. "Shut. Up." His lips twitch. "Idiot," he murmurs under his breath, but the hint of a smile has broken through.

"Pres." Kent brushes my hair off my shoulder. "I'm going to go speak to her, and then we can leave. Okay?"

I nod, plastering a reassuring smile on my face. "Don't worry about me. I'll be fine here." He kisses me softly even though it'll probably aggravate Adam, but fuck that asshole. He is way out of line. I get he's upset and worried about his daughter, but that does not give him the right to say and do the things he has said and done. Kent kisses me once more, and I know it's his way of conveying it'll be all right, even if we both know that's not true.

If Whitney is pregnant with Kent's kid, this will change everything.

Kent exits the living room with Adam, James, Alex, and Kyler, leaving an awkward tension behind. I sit back down beside Eva, wishing the ground would open and swallow me.

"Just another typical family dinner Chez Kennedy," Keven drawls, leaning back in his chair, his expression devoid of humor.

"We definitely give the Kardashians a run for their money," Keaton adds. While he sounds casual, he's wearing a worried frown, and I can tell he's concerned for his brother.

They all are.

"Here." Cheryl hands me a fresh glass of wine. "You could probably use that. I know I would."

"Thanks." I take a healthy glug of the crisp white wine, but I barely taste it as it glides down my aching throat.

"I'm with Kent," Kalvin says. "Whitney's a conniving little bitch. I think she's lying."

"We don't know that for sure," Kaden says.

"It fits her MO," Keanu says. "She'll do anything to cling to him. I wouldn't put anything past Whitney."

"She's as big a whore as Kent is," Kalvin says. "There's a strong possibility she was fucking others at the same time she fucked him."

"Jesus Christ, Stinky." Lana elbows her husband in the ribs. "Show some tact." She jerks her head in my direction.

"It's okay," I say even though it's not. Implying my boyfriend is a whore suggests he's fucking other women besides me, which I know he isn't, and his brother shouldn't be spouting shit like that. "Kent has told me about his past, and I know about him and Whitney."

"I apologize, Presley," Kalvin says, looking contrite. "That was disrespectful. I only meant to suggest that Kent is probably one of any number."

Lana shakes her head before snatching her glass, guzzling wine like Whitney was earlier.

Remembering how she was knocking back glass after glass makes me sick. *How can she be so irresponsible?* So negligent of the life growing inside her. I swallow another large mouthful of wine, willing the knots in my stomach to unravel because I don't know how much longer I can sit here and pretend like I'm dealing with this.

"I'm going to check on the kids," Eva says, tapping my arm. "Would you like to come with me?"

I latch on to the lifeline she's throwing me. "Sure." Eva turns to her husband. "Can you check on Matthew? He's asleep in your old room. Just make sure he's not burning up again."

"Of course." Kaden kisses her before shooting me a pitying look I hate.

Selena stands as I walk by, reaching for me. "He's going to need you no matter how this plays out," she whispers. "And we'll be here for both of you." Her eyes search mine, and her features soften. "It will be okay. I know it might not seem like that now, but we'll all help you through it."

Keanu stands, hugging me. "Hang in there, Presley."

Their kindness almost undoes me, but I soldier on, walking with Eva outside to the impressive rear garden. They have a large fenced-in pool, various sporting areas and courts, a massive forested area at the very back of the property, and a vast children's playground with swings, slides, climbing frames, and various other little people activities. The five kids are being supervised by an older woman who smiles at us as we approach.

"Mommy." Milly comes bounding toward Eva, flinging herself into her arms, her brown curls bouncing up and down. "Where's Matty?"

"Still sleeping." Eva lifts her up, and her small legs wrap around her mom.

"Presley." Milly's blue eyes are big and clear as she smiles shyly at me. "Are you going to marry Uncle Kent?"

For once, I'm speechless.

"Hey, you little busybody." Eva tweaks her nose, and she giggles. "That's private."

She pouts, and the cutest little frown appears between her brows. "Whitney used to say she was gonna marry Uncle Kent, but now Uncle Kent likes Presley, so does that mean he's gonna marry Whitney or Presley? I'm cu-fused."

Eva grimaces, mouthing "sorry" at me.

"That's grown-up stuff," Eva says, placing her daughter back down on the ground. "And not something you should be talking about. Go back and play with your cousins."

"'Kay." She runs off before changing her mind, doing a fast U-turn, and barreling in my direction. She throws herself at my legs, wrapping her skinny arms around my limbs. "I like you the mostest,

Presley. And you're so pretty. I'm gonna ask the fairy queen to make Uncle Kent marry you."

I'm all choked up, and I can't even acknowledge the child before she runs off to join her cousins.

"I'm sorry about that. She's—" Eva stops talking, her eyes creasing at the corners. "Oh, Presley. Please don't cry. She doesn't know what she's saying." She scans my face with concern, and I realize silent tears are rolling down my face.

I swipe at the dampness on my cheeks, and I can scarcely force words from my throat. "It's okay, and I'm fine," I lie because I'm the furthest from fine a person can be.

I need to get out of here.

Right now.

"I just need to use the bathroom."

"Of course." Her voice is gentle, her expression understanding. "The closest one is at the back of the entryway. Just walk through that door there." She points at a door at the very back of the patio area. "Keep straight until you hit the lobby. The bathroom is on the right."

I follow her directions, easily finding the bathroom, but I bypass it, heading straight for the front door. I slip outside, closing the door carefully behind me so I don't make any noise.

I give no consideration to how I will get back to Boston. All I know is I need to get out of this house and never look back.

Chapter Eighteen
Presley

Tears stream down my face as I walk the long driveway, having given up fighting the memories assaulting my mind. I don't indulge them often, because it's too painful, but I'm powerless to deny them now. Seeing pregnant women or mothers with young babies is always hard for me, but knowing the guy I'm falling for may be having a baby with someone else is an entirely different level of pain.

A car draws up alongside me. The passenger side window lowers, and Keaton sticks his head out. "Get in. We'll drive you home."

I don't bother protesting, opening the back door and climbing inside the luxury SUV. "Thank you," I whisper.

Austen shoots me a sympathetic smile through the mirror as Keaton hands me my purse. "Can I sit beside you?" he asks, looking at me through the gap in the two front seats.

"I'm okay," I sniffle, brushing my tears away.

"I don't think you are." His eyes are compassionate.

"No, I'm not." I offer him a sad smile.

"Do you want to talk about it?" he asks as Austen puts the car into gear, driving slowly toward the front gate.

"Not really."

Austen places a hand on Keaton's knee, subtly shaking his head.

"Okay. We don't have to talk about that." Keaton puts the radio on, keeping it low. "Selena says you have plans to be a tattoo artist," he adds. "Is that true?"

I'm grateful for the subject change, and the distraction, so I tell him about my plans. Austen smiles at me through the mirror as he drives, heading out onto the highway.

"Did Sel tell you Austen is training to be a professional tattoo artist in his spare time?" Keaton inquires.

I shake my head, my eyes popping wide. "She didn't mention it." I glance at Keaton's fiancé. "When do you even find the time?" Austen is a professional football player and the current wide receiver for the Baltimore Ravens. Keaton has his own successful cooking show, which streams online, called *The Queer Kitchen Revolution*.

"I won't when the season starts back, so I'm trying to fit in as many training hours as I can now," Austen replies.

"He's always drawing," Keaton confirms, beaming proudly.

"Me too," I admit.

"He designed and inked this." Keaton rolls up his shirt, showing me the exquisite steering wheel and anchor tattoo on his arm.

I lean in closer to inspect it. "Get out. That is fucking incredible. Something tells me you don't need much training."

"I still have a lot to learn, but I took my time doing that," Austen says. "I didn't want to fuck up my fiancé's arm. Especially when I'll be looking at it for the rest of my life," he adds, grinning at Keaton.

"You couldn't fuck it up." Keaton places his hand on top of Austen's over the stick shift. "That's a virtual impossibility." Austen takes his eyes off the road for a few seconds, and they share an intense look that is wholly intimate. The love between them is completely obvious, and it's a thing of beauty.

All of Kent's brothers seem crazy in love with their partners, and the way his parents are with one another is super sweet too. I can't help wondering how Kent became so closed off to the idea of love when he's surrounded with nothing but good examples.

"I'd like to see your work sometime," Austen says, and I snap out of my thoughts, realizing they are staring at me.

"I can bring my sketchpad next time."

If there is a next time, because everything is up in the air.

"That will probably be our wedding," Keaton says.

Kent hasn't mentioned one word to me about their upcoming wedding, which, now that I think about it, is really strange.

"Congrats on your engagement. I remember reading about it online."

"Thanks." Keaton's grin is wide and proud. "We can't wait."

"Where are you planning on having it?"

"Initially, we were thinking of going abroad, but planning an overseas wedding in three months is a tall order. One even Bridezilla wasn't keen to take on."

"Bridezilla?" I quirk a brow.

"Alex." Austen flashes me a blinding smile, and I can totally see how Keaton fell for this guy.

"Mom loves planning shit," Keaton explains. "But she gave an Italian wedding the thumbs-down unless we wanted to postpone it to next year."

"Which we don't," Austen cuts in. "Because we just want to be married. It doesn't really matter where we do it as long as the people we care about are with us."

Keaton darts forward and pecks him quickly on the lips before he sits back in his seat, smiling at me. "So, we're having it in this gorgeous castle resort and spa, nestled in the Green Mountains in Vermont. We've rented out the entire place so we have complete privacy."

"It sounds fantastic."

"It will be, and we hope to see you there."

We chat casually about all manner of things the rest of the journey, and by the time we reach the triple-decker I call home, I am a die-hard Austen and Keaton fan. It helps that they've distracted me from the anguished thoughts in my head, but there will be no stopping the onslaught once I reach my apartment.

"Thank you so much for the ride," I tell Austen, grabbing my purse.

"Anytime, Presley."

Keaton opens my car door, taking my hand as I climb out. If the triplets are any gauge, all the Kennedy men have exemplary manners. "Thank you, Keaton."

He closes the door, keeping my hand in his. "I don't know if Kent has explained that we're not talking."

"He briefly mentioned it at the house."

Keaton's lips turn down. "And he didn't even mention the wedding to you, did he?"

I shake my head. "He didn't, but he's not really the type to plan far ahead. He only mentioned Easter dinner to me last week."

Keaton drags a hand through his hair. "I don't want to speak out of turn, but we haven't spoken in a long time, and I miss him. I was really hoping to clear the air before the wedding, but this situation with Whitney has thrown a wrench in the works. And I'm worried about how this will affect him."

"You think the baby is his?"

"I don't want to speculate, and neither should you until we find out for sure, but either way, this has the potential to derail Kent. He seemed so happy today. At least, until the She-Devil arrived." He shoves his hands deep in his pockets, staring me straight in the face. "I have no right to ask anything of you, Presley, and I can tell this has been upsetting, but don't give up on him. I know my brother, and he cares about you. It's blatantly obvious. Don't let Whitney come between you, because I've no doubt that's her plan."

I wave them off with a heavy heart before heading inside.

The second I switch off the alarm and close my door, I give in to the grief devouring me from the inside, crumpling to the floor and sobbing as images of my tiny little daughter flash before my eyes, and it's as if I'm losing her all over again.

Pounding on my front door rouses me from sleep, and I lift my head from my pillow, dragging my drunk ass out of bed. The room spins as I stand, and I take a few moments to steady myself before heading to the front door to let Kent in.

I've been expecting him.

I swing the door open, stepping aside so he can enter.

He looks like shit. His hair is sticking up everywhere, like he's been pulling fistfuls of it for hours. His eyes are red-rimmed, and the scent of Mary J clings to his wrinkled clothes. A purplish bruise mars his left cheek, and there's a small swelling on his right cheekbone.

Catching sight of my reflection in the mirror, I realize I'm in no position to judge. I'm still wearing the dress I wore to dinner, and it's creased to fuck. My hair is wild, my usual smooth waves tangled in knots. Mascara stains have dried on my face, and I'm sporting a classic case of panda eyes.

"You left," he says, pinning me with a pained gaze.

"I couldn't stay there." I walk to the kitchen, groaning when I open the fridge door and the bright light stabs me through the eyes. I extract two waters, handing one to him.

"Were you crying?" he asks, inspecting my face.

I nod.

"Come here." He opens his arms, walking toward me, and I sink into his embrace. Closing my eyes, I bury my face in his shirt, clutching him for dear life. "I'm sorry," he whispers. "That's not how I wanted today to go."

I snort because way to state the obvious. He presses kisses into my hair, and I sober up real fast. Looking up at him, I ask, "Is the baby yours?"

A vein pops in his neck, his jaw tightens, and anger blazes in his eyes. "She says it is."

"But you don't believe her."

"I don't." Taking my hand, he guides me into the living room. We sit side by side on the couch. He drags a hand through his hair, rubbing at his eyes. "We've grown up in the public eye, and one thing Dad drilled into us was there will always be people who try to take advantage of us. Girls who will try to trap us with pregnancy, so we've always been careful. Especially me, because I'm usually trashed when I have sex, so I've trained myself to always, always, always wear a condom." He taps the side of his head. "It's ingrained in me, and I have never, ever, fucked Whitney without one."

"That doesn't mean she couldn't get pregnant. It could have broken—"

"Or she could have tampered with it," he finishes for me, pointing at the swelling on his right cheekbone. "When I made that suggestion, Adam got another punch in."

"That man is a delusional jackass, and I can't believe he hit you again. It's so wrong." I'm aggrieved on his behalf.

A smirk ghosts over his mouth. "Don't worry. Dad lost it, and he punched him. I think his nose might be broken."

"It would serve him right." I have zero sympathy—except for Faye. She is trapped in the middle, and it was obvious she was upset earlier.

"Mom made them leave after that, and I don't think either of them will be welcome in our house again."

"I wouldn't want them back in my home." I wet my dry lips, asking the all-important question. "What are you going to do?" I knot my hands in my lap, wishing I had the half-empty bottle of tequila lying on my bed beside me.

"I want her to do a paternity test. I Googled it, and there are three different tests you can get done while the baby is in the womb. She would only have to wait a few weeks to take one, but she's refusing, citing risk to the baby."

"Now she cares about her child," I mumble, still furious with her drinking at dinner.

"Mom tried to talk her into agreeing to meet with a specialist to run through her options. There is a noninvasive procedure that poses no risk to the baby, but she's insisting it's her choice and she doesn't want to do it."

"Because she knows it's not yours?" I peer into his eyes.

He exhales heavily. "Or she wants to make me sweat for another thirty-four weeks. Whitney has a real nasty streak, and this is her way of punishing me for you. I want to believe it's because the baby isn't mine, but the honest truth is it could be. She had a report from her doctor and an ultrasound pic, and the time line stacks up."

Air flees his mouth in shaky spurts, and he hangs his head. Stress seeps from every pore, and I wish I could wipe it all away. The air is heavy with so many unspoken words, and he still doesn't know of my internal torment.

"So, what now?" I ask when I can no longer stand the silence.

He lifts his head, stabbing me with his penetrating gaze. His eyes plead with me for understanding. "I can't abandon her when there's a chance the baby is mine. You saw what she was like today. If that's my kid, I can't risk her going completely off the rails. I'll need to be with her every step of the way."

That shouldn't be necessary, but I expect Whitney will milk every situation until she has driven Kent insane. "And if it turns out the baby isn't yours?"

"Then I'll fucking throttle her with my bare hands," he hisses.

I gulp over the messy ball of emotion in my throat. "Okay. I understand." I stand, offering him a shaky smile. "I'll see you out."

"Sit the fuck back down, Pres." His tone and his expression brook no argument, so I plop back down.

Pursing my lips, I look anywhere but at him. His fingers brush against my chin, sending delicious tremors skating across my face, and I automatically lean into his touch, craving his comfort. He tilts my head around so I'm looking directly into his eyes. "I know it won't be easy." He barks out a bitter laugh. "Fuck, that's the understatement of the century. She will go out of her way to cause problems for us." All humor fades from his face. "I know it'll be tough, but I can't lose you. I *won't* lose you. Not when we're only just beginning. Not when I know how great we can be. Not when I need you," he adds, whispering the last part.

"But you need to be with her," I say in a voice devoid of emotion. It's not like I haven't come to the same conclusion for similar yet different reasons.

"Only as a co-parent. I haven't changed my mind, and I made it very clear that I will support her during the pregnancy, but I will not be her fuck buddy or her boyfriend or her fiancé. I told her there is no future for us except where the child is concerned."

"What exactly are you saying?"

His big blue eyes penetrate mine, stabbing deep, like he wants to imprint these words on my brain. "This doesn't have to change anything between you and me. I know it will be stressful, but we can get through it, and maybe she'll back down when she sees how serious I am about you."

I deliberately ignore his comment. The truth is, this changes everything for me. "You're accepting this a lot easier than I expected," I truthfully say because he was so angry earlier and now he seems resigned to the fact.

His lips tug up at the corner. "Full disclosure. I'm high as a fucking fairy. And before you go off on me, it's the only way I could calm down. My heart was going crazy, and I thought I might actually have a coronary." He drops my face, resting his head in his hands. "I'm not ready to be a father, Pres. I can barely take care of myself. What fucking good would I be to a child?" He lifts his head, looking sideways at me. "Am I a bad person for praying that the kid isn't mine?"

The tortured look in his eyes twists my insides into knots, and I cup the side of his face. "No, Kent. That just makes you human."

His Adam's apple jumps in his throat, and I scoot in closer, circling my arms around him. "I'm sorry she is doing this to you and I'm sorry for what I'm about to say because I want to be there for you, Kent. I truly do. But I can't." Pain presses down on my chest, making breathing difficult.

"Why not?" he asks, his spine stiffening underneath me.

I slide away from him, needing space before I admit this. "Because it's too painful for me." I stand, pacing the floor. "Because it will be a constant reminder of what I've lost."

He climbs to his feet, scrutinizing my face. "What don't I know?"

Tears roll unbidden down my face. "I had a baby," I whisper. "When I was nineteen."

"What?" Shock splays across his face as he stares at me.

"She died," I admit over a sob. "Tillie died in my arms, and I've never gotten over it. Or the fact I might not be able to have any more kids." I swipe at my tears. "So, don't you see? I can't stand by your side while you support some other woman who could be pregnant with your kid. And I can't tell you to let her go through this alone either, because I might never be able to give you any babies and I won't deprive you of the experience, because to do so would only ruin us in the long-term anyway."

Chapter Nineteen
Kent

It takes me a few moments to recover from the initial shock of her confession. The booze and drugs in my system aren't helping either. But I'm not losing Presley over this. I can't. I need her like I need air to breathe. "What happened to Tillie?" I ask, needing to understand so I can talk her out of her objections.

She sniffs, dropping to the floor, sitting cross-legged in front of me. I slide off the couch, adopting the same pose, urging her to explain with my eyes.

"I got pregnant by accident," she says, staring off into space. "And I was fucking terrified because Chris and I had only been living on our own for eight months and things were already bad." She looks down at the floor, knotting and unknotting her hands. "He was either high or drunk most of the time, and he'd just been fired from his job."

When she lifts her head, her eyes are flooded with tears, and I want to pull her into my arms, but I'm afraid to touch her because I've never seen her this fragile and I don't know what to do. "The pregnancy was stressful even though Rafe, my boss, was really great, and Ford and Imogen were amazing. Chris regularly failed to show up for my appointments, so Mo came to every single one." Her smile is sad. "Kady was only five then, and it wasn't easy for Mo to get a sitter, but she never missed a single appointment. She was my rock."

Tears roll down her face, and I lean forward, brushing them away with my thumbs.

"I went into early labor at twenty-four weeks. The usual odds for babies born that early is fifty-fifty, but Tillie had a congenital heart defect that lessened her chances." A sob splinters the air, and pain radiates across my chest. "She lived for three days." Her eyes are swimming in tears. "I have never prayed as hard as I prayed those three days, but it was all in vain. She took her last little breath in my arms. Chris was with me, and whatever shreds of humanity he was clinging to died that day as well. That was the day I lost both of them."

She sniffs, wiping the tears on her cheeks with the sleeve of her wrinkled dress. When she stares at me, it's like she's staring right through me. "We had nothing to say to one another after that. We buried our daughter, and he moved out the next day. I didn't see him for over a year, and at first, I refused to have anything to do with him because he fucking left me to deal with the fallout by myself."

Anger replaces her tears. "I was a total mess. I threw myself into work, taking every available shift, just so I wouldn't think about it. I wouldn't talk about Tillie or Chris, and I still haven't processed it all." Tears flood her eyes again, and I can barely breathe over the agony pressing down on my chest.

"It still hurts, Kent." She slaps a hand over her chest, right where her heart is. "I still can't look at babies without remembering how I lost mine. Tillie would've been six now, and anytime I see kids of a similar age, it guts me all over again." She buries her face in her hands, and her entire body heaves as she sobs, propelling me into action.

I crawl to her side, pulling her onto my lap, wrapping my arms around her, holding her tight, wishing I could absorb some of her pain. "I'm so sorry, baby." I dust kisses into her hair. "I'm so fucking sorry that happened to you."

"Worst of all is the knowledge I might never be able to conceive again," she adds, fisting my shirt, her words slightly muffled. "They discovered a tumor on one of my fallopian tubes. That type of cancer is rare, especially in young women. They removed the damaged tube, and while they've said it's not impossible to get pregnant, it's going to be harder. Plus, I had to have other treatment to ensure the cancer was gone, and that could've affected my fertility."

"It doesn't mean it won't happen," I say, brushing hair out of her face. "And we can hire the best specialists and get the best advice when the time comes."

I can't believe we're talking about this and I'm not freaking the fuck out. Thank you, Mary J.

"Nothing is guaranteed, and I don't know if I could cope with the stress. In my head, the two things are connected. I don't know if I'll ever be mentally able for another pregnancy."

"Did the doctors say the cancer caused you to go into early labor?" I softly ask.

"They said it's unlikely, but they couldn't rule it out either." She rests her head on my shoulder, slumping against me in defeat.

"We don't need to worry about that now." I attempt to reassure her. "And there are other things we can do if you can't get pregnant."

"You say that now, but you don't know how you'll feel in the future."

"Honestly, Pres. I've never been too sure whether I wanted kids at all," I truthfully admit.

"Why not?" she asks, peering up at me with her big tear-filled eyes.

I shrug, not wanting to get into it. "I have my reasons."

"Well, you might not have any choice in the matter now," she says in a cold tone.

Anger bubbles under the surface of my skin because Presley could be right. If this baby is mine, I'm a dad whether I want to be or not. I could never leave any child of mine to grow up without a father, so if it's true, I guess I'll have to man up and grow up.

"No," I agree. "But there is a choice when it comes to us, and I want you with me, Presley. This hasn't altered how I feel about you. You're too important to me. And think about it. If this baby is mine, you can help me raise him or her."

She goes rigid in my arms before pushing me away, scooting back like I've just shot her. "Have you not heard a word I just said?" she yells.

"Of course, I have. But this might help. And if you want to talk to a grief counselor, I can pay for it or—"

She hops up, and more tears flow down her face. "Get out." She points at the door. "Get out and stay out, Kent. You can't offer me some other woman's baby like that will paper over the cracks in my heart. My daughter cannot be replaced with someone else's child!" she screams in between crying.

I scramble to my feet, moving cautiously toward her. "I didn't mean to imply you could. I just—"

"It doesn't matter, Kent." She rubs at her eyes. "I can't do this. I can't do this with you anymore. I'm sorry, but this is where we draw the line."

"Presley, please. I know my life is a train wreck right now, and you're upset with good reason. I'll give you some time to think about it, but please don't push me away." This girl is all I'm holding on to right now, and if I lose her, I will lose my shit.

"I can't be there for you, Kent. I wish I could, but I just can't go through all this again. I can't relive the memories because it will kill me."

"So, that's it, huh?" I fold my arms, letting anger replace the panic and fear flowing through my veins. "You're gonna cut me loose just like that." I close the gap between us, leaning into her gorgeous face, hating that I ever met her. "I don't know if it's my baby, and you won't even wait for paternity to be determined."

"You said she won't have the test!" she screeches.

"I can go to court and make her," I bark. "And I would've done that for you if that's what you needed." I shove past her, feeling way too much, and I know if I stay here any longer I will say something I really regret. "But you've just tossed me aside like I never fucking mattered." I stalk toward the door with Presley hot on my heels.

"That's not true. Of course, you matter!"

I yank the door open, almost pulling it off the hinges. I spin around to face her. "It's okay, Presley. You're off the hook. Your conscience is clear. It's not like this is unexpected. You're exactly like everyone else in my life who proclaims to care about me—fucking absent when I need you the most."

Chapter Twenty
Kent

A sharp buzzing sound reverberates in my ear, and I grab a cushion from the floor, covering my head to block out the noise. My phone vibrates on the coffee table, shuddering along the glass with each successive ring, while the buzzing sound grows louder, drilling painful holes in my skull.

"Fuck off!" I yell, burying my face in the couch while holding the cushion tight over my head in the hope the noise will disappear.

But it doesn't, and it's like the two sounds are in sync, buzzing and vibrating in an annoying rhythm that has me throwing my cell across the room in a rage.

Two seconds later, a massive thud has me bolting from the couch in fright. Swaying on my feet, I turn around, my eyes popping wide when I spot the open front door, hanging off one of the hinges. A huge chunk is missing from the other side of the door frame, and the chain is broken in half, scattered across the floor. "What the actual fuck?" I stare at Keanu and Keven as they enter the apartment, making a beeline for me.

"Jesus Christ, Kent." Keanu's gaze rakes me from head to toe, his nose scrunching in distaste, while Kev looks around the messy living room with a neutral expression.

"You stink to the high heavens," Keven says, holding his cell to his ear. "Hey, Eugene. It's Keven Kennedy. I need a favor."

I tune my older brother out, still staring at the door in shock. "I can't believe you kicked the fucking door in."

"What the hell do you expect, Kent?" Keanu plows his hands through his hair, and judging from the way it's sticking up in all directions I'd say he's been doing that for a while. "You don't show up for class, you chained the fucking door from the inside on purpose so we couldn't get in. And you haven't answered your phone to anyone in days." Tears prick his eyes as he clasps my shoulders. "We didn't know if you were even alive."

I scoff, pushing his hands off. "Don't be so melodramatic. As if I'd off myself because of that slut."

A scowl paints his face, and I know what he's thinking.

"Whitney!" I yell. "I meant Whitney. I might be fucking fuming at Presley for dumping me, but I'd never call her a slut."

I've called her plenty of other unmentionables while I've locked myself away in my apartment with copious bottles of JD and a variety of narcotics for company, but he doesn't need to know that.

"Get your smelly ass in the shower," Kev says, shoving me toward the stairs.

"Fuck you." I swing back around, almost tripping over the trash underfoot, grabbing the half-empty bottle of whiskey off the floor and plonking my smelly ass back on the couch. "This is my place, and you don't get to boss me around."

Kev smirks, crossing his arms as he levels me with a smug look. "Fine. Ignore us. We're the only people standing between you and Mom and Dad." He jerks his head at Keanu. "Come on. Let the rents deal with his sorry ass."

I huff out an exasperated sigh. "Motherfucking assholes." I take a healthy glug of whiskey, relishing the burn as it glides down my throat. I stagger to my feet, and the room spins, along with my empty stomach. "Keep your pants on. I'll get in the shower." I'd rather face Kev and Keanu over Mom and Dad any day.

If Mom sees the state of me and this place, she'll whisk me back to Wellesley and put me under house arrest until I've gone cold turkey and come to my senses. The very last thing I want or need is a clear head because then I'll have to think about all the shit in my life.

Like the fact Whitney has been blowing up my phone every hour of every day, leaving tearful, whiny, pleading messages interspersed with hateful, angry tirades about how she loathes my guts and she's going to fucking ruin my relationship.

News flash, slut: You already did. You stupid cunt.

I might've actually texted that to her. Or perhaps I imagined it. I don't really give a fuck either way.

"Go, Kent." Keanu pries the bottle from my fingers, forcing me upstairs. "And shave while you're at it. You look like Bear Grylls after a three-week expedition in the wild."

Slight exaggeration, but whatever.

When I return after a long soak in the tub and a quick tidying of my stubble, I discover my brothers have been busy cleaning up the place. Some old dude with a beer gut is fixing the front door and replacing the chain. Selena is in front of the stove, cooking something. My stomach growls loudly as tempting smells waft through the apartment, reminding me it's been a while since I ate anything substantial.

Selena glances over her shoulder, as I pad toward her, inspecting my face with blatant concern.

"Hey, Sel." I bend down, kissing her cheek. "What's cooking?"

"Keats' chicken parmigiana. I made salad too."

And, she just had to mention my estranged brother, but I smother my scowl of annoyance because this is Selena and I'm incapable of being mean to this girl. "I'm starving." I rub a hand across my flat stomach. "When will it be ready?"

"Twenty minutes." Putting a lid on the pot, she turns around, gently wrapping her arms around me. A lump the size of a bus wedges in my throat.

Hugging others doesn't come naturally to my sister-in-law because of her past experiences, so to be on the receiving end of one makes me feel special. Keanu watches as he wipes down the table, and I know if I make one wrong move with his wife he'll tear me a new asshole.

"I'm okay," I croak, timidly patting her back. I am genuinely *that* scared of my brother, and he's not even the most territorial of the Kennedys. That accolade belongs to Kyler, but most of my brothers would give him a run for his money.

"No, you're not." She releases me, tilting her head to the side as she examines every millimeter of my face. "Level with me. What have you taken?"

"What haven't I taken is probably an easier question to answer." I shrug, downplaying it.

"I hate seeing you like this. What can I do to help?"

"Make the baby not be mine," I blurt. *And get me my girl back,* I add in my head.

"You don't know that it is," Keanu says, approaching with a knotted trash bag. "Mom's been talking to Dan Evans. Whitney will have to take a paternity test while pregnant. There's no way she can avoid it."

"She'll dig her heels in and force you to go the legal route. I'm not saying you shouldn't do it, but dragging her through the courts will upset Faye," Keven says, appearing behind Keanu. I'm not sure where he was or what he was doing.

"Faye is talking to her," Selena says. "She will get her to agree."

I harrumph. "Whitney doesn't listen to a word Faye says. If anything, that will only make her more determined to hold out." Faye has always wanted a sister, so she makes allowances for Whitney. Far too many, if you ask me, because Whitney can be a real bitch to her sometimes.

"Irrespective of how it goes down, you need to pull yourself together. Don't throw everything you've worked for away," Keanu says, clamping a hand on my shoulder. "Your exams start in ten days,

Kent. Don't let Whitney ruin your legal career before it's even begun."

"All right! Enough with the lecture, Mom."

"We care about you," Selena says. "And you've had us worried sick." She chews on the corner of her mouth as Kev walks over to talk to the man at the door.

"I didn't mean to worry anyone. I just wanted to blot it all out."

"I get it, man." Keanu leans back against the counter, folding his arms as Selena returns to check on dinner. "But you can't shut us out. You can't shut *me* out. I'm your brother. When you hurt, I hurt."

"Christ." I scrub a hand over the thin layer of scruff on my chin and cheeks. "Enough with the emotional blackmail. I get it. I fucked up. Again."

"Have you heard from Presley?"

My lips thin as I shake my head. "She's washed her hands of me."

"She just needs time to process. Give her a little space."

He doesn't understand because I haven't told anyone in my family what Presley confided in me. As mad as I am at her, I wouldn't do that. It's not my story to share. "That won't matter. She can't handle the situation, and she won't even try."

I think that's the hardest pill to swallow. That I'm not worthy of even the smallest effort. I guess everything I thought I knew about her was wrong. And the thing that pisses me off the most is how she let that degenerate junkie ex, Chris, back into her life after he abandoned her when she needed him. Yet she enables him and picks up the pieces every time he flits in and out of her life. She can support him after he failed her, yet she won't even try for me, and that speaks volumes.

"The prodigal son returns," Mitch singsongs the following day when I show up in the dining hall.

I flip him the bird. "Miss me, honey?"

"So damn much." He slaps a hand over his chest, feigning emotion.

"Where the hell were you?" Lance asks, shoving his empty plate aside.

"Dealing with some family shit." I take a bite out of my burger, hoping my full mouth will shut him up.

"What family shit?" Toph asks, leaning back in his chair.

I eyeball him as I slowly chew my food, making it clear the subject is off-limits.

I'm not close enough to the guys to tell them anything serious about me. We hang out in classes and party together, and that's the extent of our friendship.

I'm not about to change the natural order of things when it has always worked perfectly. "Tell me what I missed," I say when I finish my burger, pulling out my phone to take notes.

I spend the weekend and the following days poring over my books, throwing myself into studying so I don't think about all the crap in my head. I still haven't heard from Presley, and I can't lie to myself—I was clinging to a sliver of hope, but that's pretty much withered and died now. I veer between anger and hurt, and I'm so fucking tempted to call her or just show up at the bar, but my stubborn pride won't let me.

She needs to come running to me, not the other way around.

I miss her like crazy, which is nuts. *How is it she dug her way into my life so fully in such a short period of time?* I have never believed in love, never expected to find someone I cared about, yet with her it was so natural I didn't even realize it was happening. *Is that how it's supposed to be when you find your person? Is she that for me? Or am I just sick of the endless random fucks and lonely nights and she came along at the right moment?*

I don't know. And it doesn't matter now. Because she showed her true colors in the end.

Even though Selena and Keanu have stayed here every night this week, I'm back to my miserable, lonely existence, and my body craves release from this torture. If it wasn't for Selena, I'd be drowning my sorrows and numbing my pain, but I don't want to see that same pity in her eyes. So, I'm trying to be strong, and apart from the occasional beer, and a nightly joint I permit myself to smoke, I'm abstaining.

We're eating takeout Thursday night when Keanu's cell rings repeatedly. Swiping his finger across the screen, he frowns, sighing loudly.

"Who is it?" Selena asks, placing another serving of salad on her plate.

"Whitney." He glances at me.

"Why the fuck is she calling you?"

He levels me with a knowing look. "Probably because you've turned your cell off, making it obvious you're ignoring her. You've got to speak to her sometime."

"I'll speak to her when she agrees to take the paternity test." So far, Faye has had zero success convincing her stubborn-ass sister to voluntarily agree. I've already told Mom if she doesn't agree by next week to file the paperwork. I've got exams coming up and an interview with a family law firm in Boston for a summer internship. I do not need this shit messing things up for me any more than it already has.

Keanu presses play on his phone, turning the speaker on so we can all listen to Whitney's message.

"Keanu," she sobs. "Why won't he talk to me? How can he do this to me?" she adds, slurring her words. "If he doesn't care about me, maybe he'll care about his baby," she screeches as her pain transfers to anger. "For every day he refuses to speak to me, I'm getting drunk. And if that doesn't work, I'll sell my story to the media." She hiccups, and my hands ball into fists as rage pummels me from all sides. "I can already see the headline. Cruel Kennedy asshole abandons his baby momma in favor of gold-digging whore."

I jump up, and my chair slams to the ground as I grab fistfuls of my hair, pacing the floor like a deranged lunatic. The next time Whitney calls Presley that, I will wring her fucking neck, pregnant or not. Keanu shuts the message off when the doorbell chimes. I stalk off, yanking it open with force.

"What's happened now?" Kyler asks, sighing heavily as he takes in the murderous rage on my face.

"Play it," I yell at Keanu as Kyler brushes past me, and I slam the door shut.

Kyler dumps an overnight bag on the floor and stands still, a look of stoic resignation on his face as he listens to Whitney's threat. "We need to take control of this situation," he says, after the message ends with Whitney's cackling, drunken laughter. "It's why I dropped by."

"How?" I wave my hands in the air. "She won't agree to the test, and apart from going the legal route and ignoring her, I don't see what else I can do."

"We can't let her go to the press," Keanu says. "If this gets out, it'll be a fucking goat rodeo."

We all stare at him, and he smirks.

"Bro, no one uses that word anymore." My brother is fucking weird.

"I'm claiming it," Keanu says, grinning. "It's more inventive than shitshow or train wreck, and I like to be original."

I glance at Selena. "I don't know how you put up with him."

Kyler points at me. "We're flying to New York tomorrow," he says, ignoring our banter and refocusing the conversation.

Thank fuck tomorrow is an optional day, because I barely managed to sweet-talk my way out of last week's poor attendance. They take that shit seriously at Harvard Law, and I can't afford to miss any more days. I was planning on attending my study group tomorrow afternoon, but I can study on the plane instead.

"Dad booked Michael to take us since he has some golf thing he can't get out of. I'm staying here tonight, and we can travel to the airport together in the morning."

"Why are you staying here?" I ask, cocking my head to one side. Kyler never voluntarily leaves his wife and children, and it's not like he couldn't just drive to the airport from Wellesley.

He rubs the back of his head. "Faye doesn't approve of my plan, and we had a massive argument."

"You shouldn't be the one to do this," I tell him.

"I'll go with Kent," Keanu offers. "It's not fair to put you and Faye in the middle of this."

"We're already in the middle, and things are fucked thanks to my dumbass father-in-law."

"Mom's not budging?" Keanu says, and I arch a brow.

"She told Adam he's no longer welcome at the house," Kyler explains, and warmth blooms in my chest. It's a strange feeling. One I'm not accustomed to, because Mom's go-to reaction to me is to instantly assume I'm guilty of whatever I'm being accused of. Yet she didn't hesitate to defend me at Easter dinner, and she's standing her ground. A messy ball of emotion clogs the back of my throat.

"She is furious over how Adam treated you," Kyler continues, staring me straight in the eye, "and the fact he won't force Whitney to have the test. Can't say I disagree though I've held back on voicing those opinions to my wife. Faye is disappointed with her dad but making excuses for him 'cause he's all cut up over his breakup with Callie."

"That's no excuse to take it out on Kent," Selena says, clearing away the half-eaten dinner plates.

"I agree, and so does Faye, but she's trying not to choose sides."

"I don't want to cause trouble in your marriage," I say, wetting my dry lips.

"This isn't your fault, and the best way of resolving this is to talk face to face with my sister-in-law. This whole thing is fishy, and I'm sick of Whitney manipulating Faye. She's a self-centered little bitch who only ever thinks of herself. The only time she calls Faye is when she needs something, and she has made no effort with the twins."

I avert my eyes because I've made little effort with them either. Something I promise myself I will rectify once I handle this situation. "How is this going to work?" I ask, pushing my remorse aside to deal with another day.

"We'll show up at NYU and give her no choice but to speak to us. She isn't the only one who can make threats. If she goes to the press, we'll release that voice message. If she refuses to volunteer for the test, we'll provide it to the court and petition for full custody of the child once he or she is born. Provided he's yours," he adds. "Once it goes legal, there is no way of keeping it out of the public eye. Her reputation will be in tatters. She'll fucking agree. She's too self-obsessed not to."

"Damn." Keanu whistles under his breath. "Faye will divorce you if you do that," he jokes.

"Faye will be fucking pissed at Whitney when she hears that message, and she'll come around to my way of thinking once she calms down. I can't stand by and watch Whitney hurt my wife and my brother any longer. This is being dealt with now."

"Thank you." It feels good to have my brother step in and help me to take back control.

He pulls me into a hug, slapping me on the back. "No thanks are necessary, man. You're my brother, and I'll always have your back."

Chapter Twenty-One
Kent

"**A**re you sure this is the right location?" I ask Kyler as we head up another flight of stairs in NYU toward the offices.

"You doubt your FBI-agent brother?" He quirks a brow, stepping sideways to let a girl pass. She does a double take, staring at both of us with her jaw trailing the ground.

"Move along. Nothing to see here." I growl at her, and she scurries off.

Kyler chuckles. "Charming as ever."

"Fuck off." I flip him the bird. "I hate being objectified."

He stares at me like I'm an imposter wearing his brother's skin. "Since when?"

"Since always. Why the hell do you think I never went back for seconds?"

"You did with Presley."

"Are you looking for me to hit you?" I snarl, stomping past him down the hallway.

He catches up to me. "I wasn't implying what you think I'm

implying. Presley is the only woman you've deemed worthy of spending time with, and you're just giving up."

I shove him into the wall. "You don't know what the fuck you're talking about, and I can't do this now." I let him go, breathing heavily.

"I'm sorry. My timing is shit, but we *are* talking about this on the plane ride home."

"Oh joy. Something to look forward to," I deadpan, looking at the locator app on my screen and following it to a closed mahogany door.

Professor Lemmings is written in big gold letters on a plaque on the door.

"Is Kev sure this is right? I thought her schedule said she had German class now?" Whitney is studying languages with business, but it's a miracle she's made it to senior year, because she's the least academic person I know.

"This is the right place." Kyler frowns, jerking his head toward the room as my hand lifts to knock. He shakes his head, pressing his ear flush to the door. His eyes widen in shock.

"What?"

"Shush. Listen."

I press my ear to the door, not hearing anything at first. I wait, and then I hear it—groaning and the sound of wood creaking. Kyler and I exchange a look as I attempt to quietly open the door, but it's, predictably, locked. Holding up one finger, I remove my wallet and extract one of my cards. I hand him my cell, and he knows what to do. I'm extra careful as I slide the card along the side of the door, pressing it gently against the lock a few times before it gives way with a subtle click. The noise from inside has increased, so I doubt they are aware we're about to break up their little party.

We work in tandem, and I swing the door open as Kyler presses record on my cell phone.

Whitney is draped across the professor's desk with her skirt bunched at her waist, ass in the air, and her hands gripping the edge of the table. A tall dark-haired man—the professor, I assume—is slamming his dick into her pussy, his pants pooled at his feet, completely oblivious to the fact he has an audience.

What a tool.

Lucky for us.

I glance at Kyler, ensuring he's got the footage, before I walk toward them. "Well, well, well. What do we have here?"

Whitney shrieks, and the professor pulls out, turning around to glare at us, his small dick jutting out, coated in her juices. "Who the hell are you, and how did you get in here? I locked that door."

The door slams shut as Kyler walks to my side.

"I'm sure you did," I say, smirking as I cross my arms and eyeball him. He looks young for a professor. Maybe he's a prodigy like Eva or he's one of those dudes who looks younger than he is.

Whitney pulls her panties up and fixes her skirt, her wide-eyed expression betraying her shock and her panic. I can almost see the wheels turning in her head as she grapples with some excuse.

"Is he the father?" I ask, drilling her with a "don't mess with me" look.

"What?" The dude pulls up his pants, swinging his gaze around to Whitney. "You're *pregnant?*" Horror creeps over his face.

"How long have you two been bumping uglies?" Kyler asks, discreetly holding my cell behind his back. It's still recording.

"That's none of your fucking business, and you need to leave," the douche says, tucking his shirt into his pants and buckling his belt.

I prod him in the chest with my finger. "That's where you're wrong, Professor. She's trying to pin the blame on me, and I'm not leaving this fucking office until I get the truth."

"It can't be mine," he blurts. "That's the first time we've screwed."

Hurt flares in Whitney's eyes, and that gives the game away.

Kyler notices it too. He steps forward, putting himself all up in the guy's face. Kyler has at least three or four inches in height on him and a well-rehearsed mean face. He's intimidating as fuck when he needs to be. "I'll give you one opportunity to come clean before I call my FBI-agent brother and tell him to hack into your office computer, your home computer, your cell, and unearth all your little secrets." He shoves his chest. "Tell me, is Whitney the only student you're banging, or are there more?"

He's not fast enough to conceal his alarm, and I know we've hit the jackpot.

"How many students are you fucking?" I ask. "How many others have you knocked up?"

Whitney's panic has transformed into full-blown rage like I knew it would.

"You're fucking other students?" she screeches, stalking toward him and pushing him in the chest. "You told me you loved me!"

"I do love you, baby, but you know I'm married. This was never going to be a permanent thing."

"Why do you think I lied and said he was the father?" she screams, waving her hands in my direction.

About a hundred layers of stress instantly lift from my shoulders. I feel like fist punching the air, but I pause the celebration, wanting to see how this plays out.

"I did it to protect you," she sobs, her palms flattening on his chest. "Because I love you, and I know you can't leave her. This way we still could've been together. We could've made it work."

She is even more delusional than I thought. *What kind of twisted logic is that?* No wonder she tried to pawn it off as my kid. Deep down, she knows this guy won't be there for her. I'm a lot of things, but if this baby was mine, I would've made sure she was looked after and that neither of them wanted for anything.

To think she has the nerve to call Presley a gold-digging slut.

He lowers her hands and takes a step back. "It can't be mine. I always use a condom," he says. "You're not pinning this on me either." He narrows his eyes at her. "I know you've fucked half the football team, because they trade stories about you, and my TA said he screwed you two weeks ago."

"Only because you were ignoring me!" Whitney hisses, shoving his shoulders. "I needed to reclaim your attention, and it worked." A sneer curls the corners of her lips.

"The point is, you're a slut," he explains, "and the father could be any number of guys."

"The baby is yours!" Her lower lip wobbles, and I think reality is finally sinking in. "I'm twelve weeks pregnant, and the only guy I was fucking in February was you."

"You're a real piece of work, Whit." I shake my head. "I can't believe you tried to fuck up my life like this."

"You fucking deserved it for the way you've toyed with my emotions for years." Her smile turns malicious. "Payback is a bitch, and Presley will thank me one day for doing her a favor. You're a fucking loser, Kent. A washed-up good-for-nothing player who thinks his shit doesn't stink. Well, guess what, asshole. It does, and you're a—"

"That is enough, Whitney!" Kyler roars. "You will not fucking insult my brother ever again." Kyler forcibly calms down before looking at me. "You should go. I can handle it from here."

"I'll wait for you." It's the least I can do when he's come all this way to help me.

He shakes his head. "I need to deal with this, and I'll be a while." Taking my arm, he pulls me toward the door. We step outside into the hallway as Whitney and the professor start arguing. "Take the jet back home. Call Faye, and tell her what's happened. She'll want to be here. Then call Keven, and get him to hack into that asshole's stuff. I need evidence to bury the bastard. If he thinks he can shirk his responsibilities when it comes to that baby, he can think again. Better update Mom and Dad too."

"What are you going to do?" I ask, taking my cell from him and slipping it in the pocket of my jeans.

"I'm calling Adam, and we're going to deal with that asshole." He clamps his hand on my shoulder, grinning. "You're off the hook, bro."

"I am so fucking relieved."

He pulls me into a hug, slapping me on the back. "Me too, little brother. None of us wanted you to be tied to Whitney for life like this."

I cling to him, feeling surprisingly emotional. In fact, my emotions are running riot, veering all over the place. "Tell me about it."

"Maybe now you can make things right with Presley."

Shucking out of his embrace, I shrug because it's not as cut and dry as that. "She walked away, Ky. She had her reasons, but she still didn't try."

"If you care for her, don't let this come between you. I don't know what went down or what her reasons were, but we all say things in the heat of the moment, and maybe she regrets it or she's holding back because she thinks stepping aside was the right thing to do. You won't know unless you talk to her."

"Maybe." If I'm being honest, my inclination is to rush to Presley to tell her it's okay, but she hurt me, and do I really want the hassle of being in a relationship with a girl who runs at the first sign of trouble?

I never had to deal with this shit when I was casually fucking around, and I'm not sure I'm cut out for it. The past twelve days have been sheer hell.

"I better call Adam," Ky says. "And get back in there before they kill each other," he adds when the shouting escalates to ear-piercing levels.

"Thanks, man." I swallow back a lump. "I owe you."

"Sign up for some babysitting stints and we'll call it even," he says with a grin as he stabs buttons on his cell.

"Just tell me when and where," I call out before walking off, feeling like a one-hundred-pound weight has just been lifted from my shoulders.

Chapter Twenty-Two
Presley

Drawing a brave breath, I raise my hand and rap twice on the door. It swings open a minute later, revealing a different Kennedy brother.

"Hey, Presley." Surprise splays across Keanu's face, and my stomach takes a nosedive.

I wasn't expecting anyone else to be here on a Friday evening, and I'm not so sure this is a good idea now. Maybe I should have called Kent in advance and arranged to meet him at an agreed time. But I'm here now, standing in front of Kent's brother like a dummy. "Hi, Keanu. Is Kent here?"

"He's not, but he should be home soon. Come in and wait for him." He steps back, ushering me inside.

"Presley." Selena walks toward me with a welcoming smile. "It's good to see you."

I don't feel like I can walk away now without seeming rude, so I step inside, and Keanu closes the door behind me.

"How are you?" Selena asks, holding her hand out for my jacket.

I shuck out of it, giving it to her. Keanu promptly plucks it from his wife's hands, walking to the coat stand in the far corner to hang it up.

"I'm okay. How have you been?"

"Busy," she says, guiding me to the velvet couch.

"Can I get you something to drink, Presley?" Keanu asks. "Tea, coffee, water, wine, beer?"

"Peppermint tea would be great."

He flashes me a big smile. "Coming right up." He leans down, kissing his wife softly on the lips. "You want some too, love?"

"Please." She stares into his face, and they share an intense look which makes me feel like an intruder.

I avert my eyes until I hear Keanu walking off. I smile at Selena, unsure what to say. *What must they think of me after the way I abandoned Kent?* I'm so ashamed of the way I treated him and how I basically kicked him out of my place. "You must think I'm terrible," I say because there's no point pussyfooting around the elephant in the room.

"Not at all." She shakes her head.

"I shouldn't have reacted how I did, but it was an emotional day, and it brought everything back from the past."

Her brows knit together.

"He didn't tell you?" Disbelief threads through my tone. I felt for sure he would have told Selena and Keanu or Eva what went down. The fact he didn't only makes me appreciate him more.

"All Kent said is you broke things off with him and he didn't want to talk about it."

Keanu returns with our tea. After handing both of us a mug, he claims a seat on the couch across from us, sipping from a beer.

"I lost a baby," I say because I want to try to explain it to them. I'm grateful Kent kept my confidence, but I'm here to grovel, to ask him to give us another chance, and I could use some supporters on my side because something tells me Kent will not make it easy for me. Nor should he. I let him down when he needed me, and I can only imagine how difficult these past couple weeks have been.

"I'm so sorry." Selena pats my arm.

"It was six years ago, but I never processed the pain. I buried it deep and denied myself the time to properly grieve. That day, Whitney's announcement brought it all to the surface again, and I couldn't handle it." I pause to drink the tea, needing time to let the pain in my chest settle. "Kent needed me to support him, and all I could feel was my own pain. I pushed him away when I should have pulled him close."

"You're here now," Keanu says, sitting up straighter.

"And he'll forgive you," Selena adds with more confidence than I feel.

The front door opens, and I stiffen. Blood rushes to my head as nervous adrenaline sweeps through me. I glance over my shoulder to where Kent has stalled in the doorway. My heart pounds behind my rib cage as I drink him in. It feels like months, not twelve days, since I've seen him.

He looks tired and shocked to see me here but so damn good. I've missed his devilish blue eyes and his flirtatious smile and the feel of his stubble underneath my fingers. I've missed his dry humor, his cheesy notes, his infectious smile, and his drugging kisses. I've missed seeing him studying at the bar or waiting outside work to drive me home.

I've just missed him.

Period.

Way more than I ever thought it was possible to miss another soul.

Putting my drink down I stand, and turn around, trying to ignore the jangling nerves churning in my gut. "Hi."

"What are you doing here?" he asks, closing the door and walking toward us. His expression is giving nothing away, so I can't tell if he's happy to see me or not.

"I came to see you. I was hoping we could talk."

"We didn't call her. Presley is here of her own accord," Selena says, and her words confuse me a little. *Why would they have called me?*

"We're going for a walk," Keanu adds, already standing and towing Selena toward the door.

"Good luck" she mouths before they exit the apartment.

Silence engulfs the room as Kent and I stare at one another. I clear my throat, preparing to eat humble pie. "I missed you so much," I whisper.

My words propel him into motion, and my heart skips a beat when I think he's coming for me. But he bypasses me, sitting down on the other couch in the seat his triplet just vacated. "Yet you never called or texted. For twelve fucking days."

I sit down on the edge of the couch, leaning forward with my elbows on my knees. "I wanted to," I truthfully admit.

He scoffs. "You never struck me as the type of girl to not go after what she wants, so if that was true, it wouldn't have taken you this long to show up here." He grabs the beer his brother was drinking, knocking back a mouthful.

I wet my dry lips, picking up my mug, purely to have something to occupy my hands. "I was upset the first couple of days," I begin explaining. "Trapped in the past, reliving my pain as if it had only just happened. Then I tortured myself with images of you and Whitney with your baby. Then I realized I'd made a terrible mistake in pushing you away. I let you down when you needed me the most, and I was so ashamed. I worried about you every day, and I went to pick up the phone hundreds of times, but I convinced myself it was better like this. That I would only get in the way."

"What changed your mind?" His eyes remain glued to my face as he drinks, but he's wearing a mask, giving me nothing, and I deserve it.

"I spoke to Mo. We talked it through, and I realized I need to get a handle on my grief so it doesn't derail my future. I can't go through life getting upset every time I see a baby or little girls the same age as Tillie. And something you said stuck with me, so I found a therapist who specializes in this kind of trauma, and I have an appointment next week."

"That's good, Presley, and I hope it helps, but it still doesn't explain why you're here." A muscle ticks in his jaw, and heat flares behind his eyes.

"I'm here because I made a big mistake, and I regret how I treated you and the things I said." Moisture pools in my eyes, and I stare at him, shielding nothing, wanting him to see everything I'm feeling. "I was scared, Kent, and I'm still scared, but I'm willing to try for you because I don't want to lose you. Please give me another chance. Let me prove to you that I can support you through this."

I pause briefly, summoning hidden strength so I don't lose my nerve. "I can't promise I won't have moments when I'm overwhelmed or it hurts, but I promise I will never take that emotion out on you again. I want to be with you. You make me happy, and I know we can be so good. Whatever goes down, we can handle it together. And if it's your baby, I would be honored to stand by your side as you navigate parenthood."

It won't be easy, because Whitney will see to it, but she's not taking away the first good thing to happen to me in years just because she's a mean, spiteful little bitch.

Very slowly, Kent sets his beer down on the coffee table, never taking his eyes off mine. His expression is guarded again, and I can't tell if my words have been enough. He clears his throat. "Come here." He wiggles his fingers in a come hither gesture.

Setting my tea down, I walk over to him, my calm exterior disguising my shaky insides, and stand between his legs.

In a fluid move, he pulls me down on his lap, circling his strong arms around me. My heart threatens to escape my chest it's beating so hard and so fast. I peer into his stunning blue eyes, relieved when I see emotion gazing back at me. "You hurt me," he says, his voice gruff and deep.

"I know, and I'm so sorry."

He presses one long finger to my lips, shushing me. "More than that, you disappointed me." He places his hands gently on my hips, but I still feel the warmth from his fingers searing through my shirt.

I nod, because I accept I have disappointed him. I have disappointed myself.

"You have always been so fucking strong, Pres. So confident and self-assured, like nothing would ever faze you. When you kicked me out that night, I was upset, and then anger set in because you tossed me aside so fast. I kept thinking of how Chris let you down and yet you stood by him."

Tentatively, I rest my hands on his shoulders, staring straight into his eyes as I admit this truth. "The situation with Chris is complex, Kent, and it's tied up in so much guilt and grief. I told you I didn't see him for a year, and when he came back, in the state he was in, I couldn't turn him away. I couldn't let him sleep on the streets even though I was fucking livid with him. I can see how you would think what you were thinking, but it's not the same." I chew on the inside of my mouth before I admit this next truth. "Mo has wanted me to cut ties with Chris for years. She thinks I enable him and it's my grief talking, and I...I think she's right."

"I don't want to talk about your ex," he says in a clipped tone.

"Kent." I cup one side of his face. "Neither do I except I need to say this last thing." My chest heaves as I prepare to lay myself at his feet. "I'm falling for you, Kent. Like seriously falling in a way I have never fallen before." I drill my eyes into his. "I never felt this way about Chris. Not even close to it, and there is no competition in my eyes. If it comes down to it and you need me to choose, I will always choose you."

He can't know how big that declaration is, because everything I just said is true. "I feel a responsibility toward Chris," I add, "because of our past and he was Tillie's father. Her death was the final nail. It was at that point he lost his will to live. I know I'm the only person alive who cares what happens to him, and that is the reason I haven't abandoned him, but if you need me to do it, I will do it for you."

Taking my hand, he presses a tender kiss to the inside of my wrist. "I would never force you to make a decision like that. I can't say I like the guy wandering in and out of your life, but I get that he's not a threat to what you and I have, and if you are truly all he has, then you can't abandon him."

That's what I've been telling myself all these years, but how long can I continue being Chris's crutch? At some point, I am going to get married and hopefully have a family, and I can't still be propping Chris up. "I've done a lot of deep thinking since we broke up," I admit. "And come to a lot of realizations. I'm still working through them, but I'm determined to make positive changes in my life." Steely determination resonates in my tone.

Kent smiles, threading his fingers in mine. "There she is. My little spitfire."

"Can you ever forgive me?"

"I already have," he automatically replies.

My mouth hangs open in shock, and he chuckles. "You should see the look on your face." All humor fades, and his expression turns serious. "I was in New York today, and on the way home on the plane, instead of studying, like I should've been doing, all I could think about was you, and I came to some realizations of my own."

I assume being in New York has something to do with Whitney, and I wonder where things are with the situation. But I don't ask him. Not yet. Not until we've aired everything else we need to air. "What realizations?" I ask.

"I think I was being unfair to you."

"You weren't. Not at all. You—"

He clamps his hand over my mouth, pinning me with a cautionary look that raises all the tiny hairs on my arms in delicious anticipation. "Let me finish. Unless you want me to put you over my lap and spank that naughty ass." I arch a brow, and he chuckles. "You'd like that."

I squirm on his lap, my panties instantly damp. "So fucking much, but we need to finish talking."

"As I was saying before I was so rudely interrupted," he continues, warning me with his eyes to keep my mouth shut, "I had you on a pedestal because you are so perfect to me, but I forgot that even perfection has flaws, and I can't expect you to be strong in every situation, nor should I want you to. Because your vulnerability is beautiful to me too, and I only ever want you to be yourself."

"What exactly are you saying?"

"That it's okay. I understand, and we always lash out at those we are the closest to. Doesn't make it right, but it happens." He sighs, and his tongue darts out, licking his delectable bottom lip, and I can't believe I'm jealous of his tongue.

Geez, I've got it bad.

"I have pulled my fair share of shit over the years, and my parents have always forgiven me. I'd be a lame-ass pitiful excuse of a boyfriend if I didn't forgive you. Especially when you've come here and laid your heart on the line." He winds his hands in my hair, tilting my face up. "And especially when I fucking missed you so bad."

"You did?" Hope soars in my chest.

"I did, baby." He rubs his nose against mine. "It was shocking. I turned into this pathetic heartsick bastard who could barely drag his ass off this couch. Don't tell my brothers, but I think I was actually worse than them when they were going through crap with their girls."

I giggle, and for the first time in almost two weeks, my chest feels lighter. "Will we be okay?"

"Do you promise not to push me away again? Because I'm bound to fuck up or other shit will get thrown at us, and I need to know you're with me, baby. That you won't run away at the first sign of trouble. I need to trust that what we feel for each other is more than something casual that can be discarded easily when the going gets tough."

"I promise I'm in this for the long haul, Kent." I pause to draw a breath. Now is the time to ask it. "What is happening with Whitney? Is the baby yours?"

"Nope." He shakes his head, and his relieved smile tells me everything I need to know. "Thank fuck."

The weight on my chest leaves, but anger simmers in my veins. "That conniving bitch lied to you." I'm seething for him and for me.

"She did, but she's out of my life for good now. You won't have to worry about seeing her ever again."

"And you won't have to worry about me failing you ever again. I made a mistake, but it's one I won't make again because I need you as much as you need me. More than that, I want you in my life because you brighten up my entire world, and I'm sick of living in the dark."

He brushes his lips against mine, too fast for me to latch on. When he eases back, he's smirking. "That was really fucking cheesy, and I'm not sure what it says about me, but I fucking love it."

I roll my eyes, repositioning myself so I'm straddling him. "We both know you love a bit of cheese." I nip at his earlobe, rejoicing when I feel him hardening underneath me. "And I wouldn't want you any other way."

Chapter Twenty-Three
Presley

I'm not sure who moves first, or maybe we both move at the same time, but our lips collide in an earth-shattering kiss I feel from the top of my head to the tips of my toes. Pressing my body against his, I grind my hips against his erection as we devour one another in a mad frenzy of lips, tongues, and teeth. Kent licks the inside of my mouth, and the most primitive groan escapes my throat. Every part of my body is humming with raw desire, and I clutch at him, grabbing fistfuls of his hair as I rock against him, desperate and needy.

"Kent," I rasp into his mouth. "I need you."

I drive my hips into his, and he hisses as my jeans-clad cunt presses into his hard cock.

"What exactly do you need, Presley baby?" His hands glide under my shirt, and his fingers move lightning fast, cupping my breasts through my lacy bra.

"You. I need you." I thrust my tits into his hands as he roughly fondles my flesh.

He tugs at my ear, and a whimper flies from my mouth. "Gonna need you to be more specific, babe."

"Fuck me!" I all but yell. "I need you to fuck me." We haven't gone there yet because I've been purposely holding back. But not anymore. Kent doesn't need to prove anything to me, and I'm ready to take this risk with him. Nothing has ever felt so right, and I want to give him every part of me, consequences be damned.

His hands stall on my boobs, and he tilts his head back, peering into my eyes. "Are you sure?"

"Yeah." I press a hard kiss to his lips. "I'm done wasting time. Take me to your bed, and make me yours."

We race up the two flights of stairs to his master suite, and I slam to a halt when I get a look at the new addition to the room. "You got a new bed," I whisper, walking toward the gigantic four-poster bed like I'm on autopilot. My fingers toy with the sheer white gossamer curtains as he comes up behind me, pressing his chest to my back.

His hands land on my stomach in a possessive hold. "Do you like it?" he asks, brushing my hair aside with his nose, planting a trail of feather-soft kisses along my neck.

"I fucking love it." I turn to face him, flinging my arms around his neck, peppering his mouth with kisses. "What are you doing to me, Kent Kennedy?" I drag his lower lip between my teeth, softly biting on the plump flesh. "You have this amazingly sweet romantic side I am completely addicted to."

Grabbing my ass, he lifts me up, and my legs automatically wrap around his waist. "That's all for you, baby. No one else gets that side of me. Only you."

Tears prick my eyes, and emotion clogs my throat, and I realize something else.

I'm in love with him.

With every part he has deemed to show me—and the parts he hasn't as well.

I want to tell him because my heart is fit to burst, but I'm afraid of scaring him, so I keep the words trapped inside. For now. Instead, I let my hormones win because if he doesn't fuck me now I might just die.

Kent throws me down on the bed, and I fist a hand in his shirt, yanking him down on top of me. Our mouths fuse as we writhe against one another, still fully clothed, and I can't get enough of him. Every molecule in my body is on fire, and he's the only one who can extinguish the flames. I tug at his shirt, rolling it up his body, and he sits up, one leg on either side of me, as he pulls it over his head and throws it on the floor.

He makes quick work of unbuttoning my shirt, exposing my bra-clad upper torso. In next to no time, my bra and shirt join his shirt on the ground and he's leaning over me, tracing a path with his lips from my neck down along my collarbone and to the swells of my breasts.

He cups one boob in his large hand, kneading my sensitive flesh, while his mouth closes over the nipple of my other breast. He sucks hard, lightly grazing his teeth over the puckered bud, and my hips arch off the bed of their own volition. He tweaks my other nipple while his tongue does all kinds of wicked things to this one, and then he alternates, lavishing both breasts with attention until it feels like I could come just from this.

But I want more.

Need more.

It's been so long since I've had sex, and I need to feel this man moving inside me.

"Kent!" I hiss, shoving at his head. "Stop torturing me. I need your cock."

He chuckles, releasing my tit with a popping sound. Hovering over me, he fixes me with that trademark shit-eating grin of his. "My foreplay is torture to you?" he teases, brushing his thumb against my mouth.

"It is when I'm desperate and needy and so fucking wet I'm likely to drown."

He chuckles, sliding his body down along mine, worshiping my overheated flesh with his fingers and his mouth. He pops the button of my jeans, and his eyes stay latched on mine as he tugs the denim down to my hips, pushes my lace thong to one side, and thrusts two fingers inside me. "Perfect," he murmurs, extracting his wet fingers and pushing them in his mouth. "So damn perfect," he adds, making a meal out of licking my juices from his fingers.

My chest heaves and my core aches with need as I watch him fully remove my jeans and underwear before shedding his own jeans and boxers. He walks to the bedside table and retrieves some condoms and lube from the drawer, tossing them beside me on the bed.

Grabbing his hips, I pull him toward me as I sit up, my mouth at the perfect angle to suck his big cock. I don't wait for permission, holding on to his hips as I lower my mouth over his perfection.

Kent has the biggest, most beautiful cock I've ever seen. The flesh is warm and velvety-soft, and he's long and thick as he slowly thrusts into my mouth. I stretch my lips wide, wanting to take as much of him as I can. Keeping one hand on his hip, I use my free hand to play with his balls, loving the weight and feel of them in my palm.

Abruptly, he pulls out, pushing my chest, forcing me to lie flat on my back, sideways across the bed. Dropping to his knees, he spreads my thighs wide, pulling me a little closer to the edge of the bed, before he dives in. His wicked tongue and fingers go to town on my pussy and my clit, and he brings me to an orgasm in record time.

I'm still coming down from the euphoric high when he repositions me on the bed, placing me in the middle with my head propped on several pillows. Kneeling between my thighs, he rolls a condom on before pushing his fingers inside me, scooping up my cum, and using it to coat his condom-covered shaft.

It's the hottest fucking thing I've ever seen, and a fresh wave of lust washes over me. I part my legs wider, inviting him in with blatant "fuck me" eyes, and he stops torturing me, driving inside me in one smooth, hard thrust.

I cry out as he fills me, stretching me like never before, and I close my eyes, absorbing the fullness and the feel of him conquering every part of my being, loving how incredible it feels to have him inside me.

"Open your pretty eyes, baby. I want to see you."

My eyes open, and he leans down, keeping his dick immobile inside my pussy as his dark, heated gaze inspects every inch of my face. Then he kisses me. Dusting unhurried, worshipful kisses on my mouth like time has ceased to hold any meaning. As if time is infinite —like his kisses. He hasn't moved inside me yet, and there is something wholly reverential about being connected to him like this that has nothing to do with carnal desire. His kisses and the feel of him inside me is infinitely tender and one of the most intimate moments of my life.

"Presley, baby." His voice is swollen with emotion as he plants soft kisses on my cheeks, staring deep into my eyes, letting me know he feels the magnitude of this moment too. "I need you to know you are everything to me."

A single tear leaks out of the corner of my eye. My heart is an enlarged, pounding, throbbing, *aching* mass of emotion in my chest. An organ that now beats for him and only him. "You are everything to me too, Kent. Absolutely everything."

"I like hearing that," he whispers, collecting my tear with the tip of his finger. He brings his finger to his mouth, tasting my emotion. "And as much as I want to take my sweet time with you, my balls are about to explode. I need to fuck you hard and fast, baby."

"You won't hear me complaining." I lift my hips, and we groan in unison. "Fuck me hard and fast, Kent. Destroy me for all other men."

He needs no further invitation. His lips crash upon mine as he moves, driving his dick inside me before pulling back out and slamming into me again. I writhe and scream as he pounds into me with a ferociousness I adore. Angling my hips, I thrust up to meet his movements, locking my ankles behind his back.

He rocks into me, over and over, pushing his cock as far as it will go, until it feels like he's impaling my womb, and I can't get enough. My fingers toy with the wiry curls of hair above his dick while his fingers yank and pull on my nipples. Sweat glides down his gorgeous chest, and his abs flex and roll as he thrusts inside my body.

Little beads of sweat plaster strands of hair to my brow as Kent fucks me into the bed like a man possessed. My climax crashes over me out of nowhere, and I shout out his name as the most intense orgasm seizes control of my body.

Kent picks up his pace, fucking me even harder, and my upper body jostles, my tits jiggling, as he grips my hips, dragging my legs over his shoulders, and slams into me a couple of more times. It's rough and raw and hot as hell.

He yells, his body tensing as he reaches his peak, and I can feel him spilling into the condom inside me as I watch the blissful, fierce look of contentment spread across his face.

Tossing the used condom on the floor, he collapses on top of me. I wrap my legs around his waist, holding his face to my chest, dotting kisses all over his dark hair. "That was amazing, Kent," I whisper. "So damn hot."

He grips my side, snuggling in closer to my chest. "I've got that dirty, dirty feeling."

"What?" I splutter, wondering if amazing sex nukes a few brain cells.

He chuckles, lifting his head up, singing an unfamiliar song. His voice is deep and harmonious, and I'm enchanted by this man. It doesn't take me long to connect the dots, and I grin as he serenades me in a really bad impersonation of Elvis. It's not that he can't sing; it's that he doesn't sound even remotely like The King. He falters after a few lines, slanting me a cute lopsided smile. "That's all I can remember of that one."

"You've been memorizing Elvis song lyrics?" I ask, running my hands along the corded muscle of his shoulders.

"I'm nothing if not thorough in my research," he jokes, slanting his head to the side as his palm covers my breast.

"You're such a dork." I playfully shove him, and he rolls us until I'm seated strategically on top of him. His cock is already rock hard again, and my pussy floods with desire.

"Yeah," he agrees, grabbing my hips and grinding his unsheathed dick against me. Sensation rockets through me at the feel of him just rubbing against my folds. "But I'm *your* dork."

Leaning down, I plaster my chest to his and kiss him softly. "Promise?"

"For as long as you'll have me," he says, brushing hair back out of my face.

Forever then. I think it, but that's not what I say. "I'm going nowhere, Kent."

He stares into my eyes, and I get lost in the most beautiful ocean, completely hypnotized by the clear blue crystal depths peering back at me. "Move in with me," he says with no hint of hesitation.

My eyes pop wide, and I sit up. "What?"

"You heard me."

"We only just got back together."

"So what?" He plays with the ends of my hair. "I want you in my life, Presley. We both have busy schedules, and we don't live close to one another. You know it makes sense."

For him, maybe. If I move in here, I'm facing a long commute to work each day, which is not practical. And, as much as my heart is currently doing somersaults at the idea, it's too soon. I'm not ready to give up my independence even if there's a part of me urging myself to throw caution to the wind. "It's too soon, Kent," I say, trying to let him down gently.

Disappointment flares in his eyes, but he quickly hides it. "Just think about it." His hands land on my ass, and he kneads my ass cheeks.

"I'll think about it, but I'm not promising anything."

Stretching up, he rubs his nose against mine. "You know I love a good challenge."

I roll my eyes, knowing I've just thrown down the gauntlet.

"And I'm a persistent fucker when I want something," he adds, grasping both sides of my face. "And I want you in my bed every night and every morning." He flashes me a confident smile. "I'm not going to stop asking until you say yes."

"What happened to letting me think about it?" I narrow my eyes at him.

He smirks. "I've changed my mind." He tweaks my nose. "Sometimes, we don't know what's best for us until someone points it out, and on this occasion, that someone is going to be me."

Chapter Twenty-Four
Kent

It's been more than two weeks since Presley and I got back together, and I ask her to move in with me every single day, but she's still saying no. She has outlined her reasons, and I understand the commute is a big concern because it's not so easy to move between her job and my house on public transportation.

Which is why I'm presently outside Ramshackle, waiting for my girl to finish her shift so I can show her the car I bought her. I fully expect her to be mad, but she can suck it up because this removes a big obstacle, and I'm confident she'll see that once she's calmed down.

When she doesn't appear after a few minutes, I lock the car and saunter inside, winking at Bugger as I shove past him. Dude still doesn't like me much—unless I'm flashing him hundred-dollar bills, and then I'm his best buddy.

I walk across the empty bar, frowning when I don't spot my baby.

"Relax," her friend Imogen says, noticing my frown. "She's in the back getting her stuff." She finishes wiping down the counter before straightening up, folding her arms across her chest, and leveling me with an unfathomable look. "She told me you asked her to move in."

"I did. Several times. Daily." I pull myself up onto a stool as I wait. "Did she also tell you she's the most stubborn woman this side of the Atlantic?"

Imogen shakes her head. "It's not stubbornness. It's called protecting her heart."

"Her heart is safe in my hands. I promise."

She cocks her head to the side. "You mean that."

"I do."

A genuine smile crawls over her face. "I'm glad to hear it because that girl has been through enough heartbreak."

"I agree, and I've no intention of adding to it." There's still a small flicker of fear at the back of my mind that says I'll find a way of fucking it up, that this is too good to be true, but I ignore those thoughts, refusing to let them derail me.

"Good. By the way, thank you for last weekend with Kady. She had a great time."

"She's a good kid." Presley had agreed to watch Kady last Sunday afternoon, so we hit the park and a pizza place before heading back to Presley's apartment to watch some cheesy teen movie on Netflix.

"Also, Ford said to tell you thanks for the purse. Michelle loved it."

"I owed him."

"For what?" Presley asks, emerging from the staff room with her bag on her back and a suspicious look on her face.

"He helped me with some stuff, and in exchange, I got a Miranda Fanning purse for his girlfriend from Red." Red, aka Rachel—Brad's wife and Faye's bestie—works for one of the hottest designer brands in New York. It pays to have contacts in the right places.

"What stuff?" she asks, planting her hands on her hips, letting me know she won't let this go.

"Ford was the one who gave me your cell phone number and your address, and he might have informed me you liked pumpkin spice lattes and suggested which flowers to buy." Honestly, I'm surprised she hasn't figured it out for herself by now.

"That little shit. I'm going to kick his disloyal ass."

Mo laughs, accepting the bag Presley hands her. "Considering where you've ended up, I think you should be thanking him for interfering."

"I second that opinion," I say, slinging my arm around Presley's shoulders when she comes out from behind the counter. "Remind me to thank him when I see him next."

I stand by the door as they switch off the lights and Presley sets the alarm. We walk outside, and Bugger secures the roll-down security gates behind us, locking up and walking off without a word. He's a strange dude but good at his job, and I have peace of mind knowing he's protecting my woman while she works.

Presley frowns, glancing up and down the quiet street. "Where's your SUV?"

"At home." I lean against the side of the shiny new Lexus SUV, sporting a cocky grin.

Her mouth opens and closes as I dangle the keys in her direction. "What's going on, Kent?"

Pushing off the car, I take her hand, placing the keys in her palm. "You can drive us tonight." I turn around, gesturing at the sleek black car. "In your new car."

"No freaking way." Imogen's eyes are out on stilts as they roam over the car. "You bought her a car?" she shrieks.

"What the hell, Kent?" Presley whispers, shock splayed across her gorgeous face.

I drag her toward it. "C'mon, babe. It won't bite."

"No." She digs in her heels, literally and figuratively.

"You don't like it?" I ask, playing along.

"I can't accept this," she splutters, thrusting the keys at my chest.

"Sure, you can. I'm your boyfriend. I'm allowed to buy you gifts."

Her eyes widen as her gaze flits between me and the car. Her hand is still scrunched against my chest, the keys digging into my flesh through my shirt. "Flowers or pencils or buying me dinner is fine. But this is too much, Kent. I can't, *I won't*, accept it."

"I'll take it if you don't want it," Imogen jokes.

"Baby." I grasp her face in my hands, knowing what she needs to hear to stop fighting this. "This is for me as much as for you. I worry about you walking home from here at all hours of the morning. Not being able to pick you up has killed me, and I don't sleep properly not knowing if you're safe." I've had exams all week, which means early starts, so I haven't been able to pick her up after work like usual.

"You've only got two exams left," she protests.

"Then I'll be starting my internship, and I'll need to be in the office early to make a good impression. I won't be able to get you during the week."

Dan Evans gave me a glowing reference, which secured me an interview with the biggest family law firm in Boston. I already know I want to specialize in family law, specifically in helping protect kids' rights and fighting for justice for kids the system has failed, so getting experience during my summer breaks will go a long way toward helping get my career off the ground.

I felt like the interview went well, but this is one occasion where my family name and my reputation are more of a hindrance than a help, so I was pleasantly surprised when they reached out to offer me one of the summer intern positions. I accepted on the spot, and I start next week.

I peck her lips softly. "Please, babe. Just accept the car. If it makes you feel better, you can treat it like a loan." Everything is in her name already, but she doesn't need to be aware of that.

"You're crazy," she says, her gaze lingering on the car, and I know I've got her.

Step one of my "get Presley to move in" plan is in the bag.

"As a bag of cats," I agree, nudging her toward the car. "Get in, Presley baby. Slide behind that wheel and tell me you don't love it."

"I still can't believe you got me a car," she says an hour later when we're in my bedroom, getting undressed for bed. "Or that you talked me into staying here tonight. It makes no sense for me to be here when you'll be gone all day."

I come up behind her, wrapping my arms around her naked waist. "It makes sense because I always sleep better when you are in my arms." True fact. In general, my nightmares have been less regular since Presley entered my life, and I have the best sleep when she's by my side. There is also another reason, one she'll be aware of tomorrow, and I hope that step two in my plan will seal the deal.

"I'm turning into one of those pathetic bitches who lets her boyfriend walk all over her, aren't I?" she asks, turning in my arms.

"If that's true, then I'm one of those pathetic bastards who wants to give his girl the world and will stop at nothing to make her happy."

"We can be pathetic together." She graces me with the biggest smile.

My heart thuds behind my rib cage because I am such a goner for this girl. One smile, one touch, one secret look, and I'm a mushy pile of goo on the ground. "Can we be *horny* together too?" I murmur, dragging my teeth down the column of her gorgeous neck. "Because my dick has been hard from the instant you climbed behind that wheel."

I'm glad Presley knew how to drive, because I'm the idiot who didn't think to check. Clay taught her and Chris to drive, apparently, but she's never had her own car. She was a little hesitant and a lot slow at first while driving Imogen home, but she gained confidence, getting into the swing of things after that, and we coasted all the way to Cambridge.

"I can get behind that plan." A naughty glint glimmers in her eye as she pops the button on my jeans and her hand dives beneath my boxers. "Because I've been wet from the instant my crazy-ass boyfriend gave me a car."

Grabbing the backs of her thighs, I lift her up my body, stalking to the bed and throwing her down. "Strip, and get on all fours," I command, shoving my jeans and boxers down my legs and stroking my throbbing cock. I kick my clothes away, grab a condom from the nightstand, and roll it on as I watch Presley remove the last of her clothes.

She gets into position, looking over her shoulder, as I kneel behind her. I plunge two fingers into her pussy, finding her warm and waiting, like always. My palm comes down across her ass in a firm smack, and she moans. The sound of it has precum leaking from my crown, and I'm not into teasing either of us tonight. I slap her ass a couple more times, pleased when slick liquid drips from her cunt, confirming how much she loves this.

Sex with Presley is out of this world, and I can't get enough.

Grabbing the base of my cock, I position myself at her entrance and thrust inside her.

Presley screams while I fuck her hard. As I pound inside her, feeling her tight walls hug my cock, I know I want to keep on doing this for as long as she's willing to let me. Because nothing has ever felt this good—or this right.

I wake the next morning to the sound of my alarm, automatically rolling over in the bed to snuggle my woman, only to find the bed empty and the sheets cold. "What the fuck?" I sit up, rubbing sleep from my eyes and fighting a yawn. It's a little after eight, but we only fell asleep sometime around three, so there is no reason Presley should be up already.

I take a piss and brush my teeth before pulling a pair of sweats on and wandering downstairs in search of my missing woman.

Delicious scents reach me when I step foot on the last stair, making my tummy rumble and my nostrils twitch with longing. Selena and Keanu returned to Wellesley last week, content now Presley and I are back on track, so I know the only one cooking can be my girl. Knowing she got up to cook for me, before I leave to take my exam, only makes me adore her more.

I pad through the living room, my heart beating to a new rhythm when I spot Presley at the stove, wearing my shirt—*just* my shirt—and dancing to whatever song is playing in her ears.

I creep up behind her, sliding my arms around her waist, chuckling when she screams in fright. She yanks my AirPods from her ears, digging her elbow back into my stomach. "Oh my fucking God, Kent! You just gave me a heart attack!" she screeches, rubbing a hand along her chest, and I smirk.

"Now you know what it feels like to wake up and discover you're not there."

She prods her finger in my chest. "You're not going to sweet-talk your way out of this one. Seriously, don't creep up on me like that. It's...creepy."

I grab her shirt, reeling her into my arms. "Sorry for scaring you." I rub my nose against hers, fighting a smile.

"No, you're not." She fake pouts.

Sliding my hand up under her shirt, I flatten my palm against her ass. "I could get used to this."

She arches a brow in question.

"You wearing my clothes, in my kitchen, *our* kitchen, sharing breakfast"—I back her up against the counter—"going about our day and then meeting back here for dinner before crawling into bed and fucking all night long." I dot kisses all over her beautiful face, and my dick thickens behind my sweats.

"I know what you're doing, and it won't work. You can't pressure me." She gently pushes my shoulders. "I'll spend some extra nights here now I have the car, but please don't pressure me into moving in until I'm ready."

I take a step back, adjusting myself in my sweatpants, sighing while I try to summon patience from somewhere. "I'll try to be patient, but it's not really my thing."

"You don't say," she teases, leaning in to kiss me. "You're something else, Kent Kennedy," she murmurs against my lips.

"Too much to handle?" I ask, only half-teasing as nerves fire at me.

"Never." She kisses me again, pouring reassurance down my throat. "Just ease off a little. Okay?"

Reluctantly, I nod.

"Good. Now breakfast isn't quite ready, so go grab a shower and get fully dressed, and I'll plate it up when you come back."

Like a good little soldier, I do as she says. When I return, she has the table set with plates full of bacon, two different types of eggs, hash browns, mushrooms, potatoes, and toast. She pours coffee into two mugs, gesturing me to sit down.

"Wow. This looks amazing. You didn't need to go to this much trouble. I could've grabbed something at the dining hall."

"I know." She cups my cheek. "But I wanted to cook you breakfast before your exam, and I made lunch for you and the guys." I look over my shoulder, spotting four paper bags on the counter.

"You're spoiling me." I pull her in for a passionate kiss.

"Not as much as you spoil me," she murmurs over my lips. She pushes me away a couple of minutes later. "Eat before it goes cold."

After breakfast, I drag her upstairs, stopping outside the guest bedroom before turning around to face her. "So, I did a thing." I rub the back of my neck, a sudden attack of nerves twisting my stomach into knots. "Please don't see this as pressure," I say even though it is totally part of my devious plan to get her to move in with me. "I wanted to give you this. For your art." I turn the handle on the door, opening it and stepping aside to let her enter.

She walks into the room as if in a daze, her head spinning left and right as she struggles to take it all in.

"Mom helped me," I explain. "She came here a few days while I was taking exams and oversaw the remodel." Presley is always drawing or doing something crafty, and the idea came to me one night last week when I watched her make a new pressed-flower picture in her tiny kitchen. She deserves to have her own space where she can draw, paint, or create whatever art she wants, so I've transformed the unused guest room into an art studio for her.

We replaced the smaller window at the back with two much larger windows, opening up the room so it's brighter and Presley has a gorgeous view of the beautiful city in the distance. A long counter with a deep sink runs the length of the room on the other side with various shelves overhead and cupboards underneath. On the other side is a drafting table and chair, but other than that, the room is largely empty. The walls are completely bare so she can create a mural, hang her artwork, or tack things to it.

Mom knows a guy who makes handcrafted easels, so I bought a few in different sizes along with canvases, sketch pads, paints, pencils, and a whole heap of other things the girl in the art store suggested. I even purchased a tattoo kit, so she can practice, with a machine, bottles of ink, cups, assorted tips and needles, and raw leather to ink on. I have a feeling, with a space to call her own, Presley will discover other arty things she likes.

"I didn't want to add too much because it's your space and you can decorate it however you want, so if you need anything added, just let me know and I can get the workmen to come back," I say, shoving my hands in my jeans pockets.

"Kent." She spins around on her heels, staring at me through glassy eyes. "You did all this for me?"

I nod because who the fuck else would I do it for?

"Oh my God." Her lower lip wobbles as she races toward me, flinging herself into my arms. "I don't know what to say." She's full-on crying now, and I'm starting to worry.

"Babe," I croak out over the lump in my throat. "These are happy tears, right?"

"Yes." She laughs, brushing at the dampness on her cheeks. "I'm so happy right now my heart feels like it could burst." She kisses me hard on the lips. "How did I get so lucky to meet you?" She peppers my face with kisses. "How are you so perfect for me?"

"Stop stealing all my lines," I quip, unused to such blatant displays of emotion.

She straightens up, peering adoringly at my face, and my heart might as well just leap out of my chest and into her hand because this woman owns me. Body, heart, and soul. The realization I love her almost knocks me off my feet. *How the fuck did this happen, and why aren't I more freaked out?*

"Kent." She holds my face, bringing me back into the moment. "Thank you. This is incredible. I don't know what more to say."

"Say you'll be here when I get home."

"I'll be here. Wild horses couldn't drag me away."

I wrap my arms around her, holding her tight, wanting to bottle this feeling, so I can always feel it, because Presley makes me feel whole in a way I have never felt in my life, and I never want to lose her.

Chapter Twenty-Five
Kent

Another couple of weeks pass, and Presley still won't agree to move in permanently even though she is here at least half the week.

I've started my internship, and it's going well so far. There are six other summer interns, and four of them are okay. The exceptions are Tracy—because she seems determined to dig her claws into me even though I've told her repeatedly I have a serious girlfriend—and Rory, who hates my guts purely because of my last name.

Whatever.

I'm keeping out of intern drama, focusing on the work because I want to make an impression, and doing my best to ignore all distractions.

"Babe," I call out, entering our bedroom. "Are you ready yet? We need to leave, or we'll be late." I watch in amusement as Presley struggles to get into her skinny ripped jeans, grimacing as she slowly tugs the denim up her long legs, the action looking almost painful.

"We have to stop eating out," she huffs when she finally gets them on. "Or I won't fit into any of my clothes."

I stride toward her, pulling her into my arms, pinning her with a wolfish grin. "You're perfect, and any extra calories you consume we more than work off in the bedroom or the gym."

I can't keep my hands off my woman, and the feeling seems mutual. Having sex on tap is definitely an added benefit of having a steady girlfriend, but there are so many other things I love about being in a committed relationship—like how those dark parts within me have retreated, pushed down by the happiness that now exudes from my every pore. Or how amazing it is to just *exist* with my girlfriend. You can't put a price on having someone to call when there are highs and lows. When something good happens, Presley is the first person I want to tell. Similarly, she's the only one I want to lean on when things are shitty and I'm having a bad day.

Presley has altered my world in immeasurable, indefinable ways, and we've only just begun.

"I have only been to the gym twice this week," she grumbles, gripping my waist. "It's not cutting it."

The gym I use isn't a part of the Harvard campus, but it's situated right beside my college, so I was able to sign Presley up for a membership. When our schedules permit it, we work out together. Toph and Mitch are members there too, and they ripped me a new one when they spotted us working out together the first time. Let's just say my friends can't believe my transformation from asshole bad boy to dedicated boyfriend, and they never waste an opportunity to remind me I'm pussy-whipped. Presley isn't sure what to make of the guys, and it's just as well I'm not that close to them.

I nip at her earlobe. "Guess we'll just have to have more sex."

She rolls her eyes, gently pushing me away. She plops down on the edge of the bed to pull her boots on. "If we have any more sex, we will never leave this bed."

I throw myself down on the bed beside her, the motion jostling her as she shoves her feet into her boots. "I have zero issues with that." I flash her a cheeky smile, reaching out to thread my fingers in her hair because I need to touch some part of her. Whenever she's close, I *have* to touch her. It's like a compulsion I can't ignore.

"You're such a guy," she says, standing and walking into the bathroom.

I follow her, cupping my crotch and smirking as I say, "Last time I checked."

She snorts, shaking her head, trying to fight a smile. I lean against the door frame, watching as she stands in front of the mirror to apply makeup to her bare face. "You have to be on your best behavior around the twins."

"They will most likely be asleep, and they're not here now." My eyes drink her in and my cock springs to life behind my zipper. "You look good enough to eat." I drop to my knees behind her, biting the inside of her thigh through her jeans.

She shrieks, glancing over her shoulder at me, not sure if she should be amused or annoyed. "You have a one-track mind."

I nuzzle my face in her ass, nipping playfully at her cheeks. "With you, always."

"I thought we were going to be late?" She drills me with a smug look.

Exhaling heavily, I climb to my feet, hating that she's right. Sliding my arm around her waist, I rest my chin on her shoulder, staring at her through the mirror. "Always raining on my parade."

She giggles, and I adore how her entire face just lights up. She is so beautiful, breathtakingly so, but it's her inner beauty that really shines through, making her stand out above the crowd.

Is it cheesy to say she just glows?

Because she fucking does.

I stare at her like a lovesick teenager. I still haven't plucked up the courage to tell her I love her, but I hope she knows by the way I look at her and the things I do to show her in other ways.

She turns to face me, her eyes wide and full of love, opening and closing her mouth as if she was going to say something but thought better of it.

"What is it?" I ask, pressing my body in closer to hers.

"You rock my world, Kent Kennedy. I hope you know that."

My heart races around my chest, like anytime she hints at her feelings for me. "The feeling is definitely mutual," I reply, kissing her softly.

She sways in my arms, and a wave of contentment sweeps over me. I never thought I could feel like this. That I'd ever get to share anything even close to this with a woman. My life has done a complete one-eighty, and that should terrify the shit out of me, but the only scary part of it is the fear of losing her. Those kinds of thoughts cause me to break out in a sweat.

"We need to go," she says, breaking our kiss and yanking me out of my head. She thrusts a makeup bag at my chest. "Put that in the overnight bag, please." I nod, pecking her lips one final time before walking back into the bedroom and packing the small pink bag in my black duffel. Then I zip it up and carry it downstairs to wait for her.

"Thank you so much for this," Kyler says, opening the door to us thirty minutes later.

"No problem, man." I slap my brother on the back as Presley steps into his house, carrying the bag with toys and candy. "I owe you."

Kyler closes the door after me, holding me back as Faye takes Presley by the arm and leads her into the main living area. "Hold up a sec," my older brother says. "I thought you should know the paternity test has confirmed Professor Douchebag knocked Whitney up."

There wasn't any doubt in my mind after the way she reacted that day in his office. I haven't asked anyone about her since, already done with it and her. Whitney no longer occupies any space in my head, and my head's in a better place for it. "Is he going to support her?"

"He has no choice," Kyler says, his expression grim. "Adam is making sure of it."

Bile collects in my mouth at the mention of that asshole. He's probably so relieved that the baby isn't mine he's welcomed the douche with open arms. "I'm guessing he didn't throw punches in *his* face," I say, my bitter tone betraying my venom.

"No, but he did way worse. He registered a formal complaint to the NYU board and got him fired. Then he paid a visit to his wife. Keven found evidence he was having several affairs with different students. His wife has filed for divorce, and no college will go near him."

"Adam's a vindictive prick," I hiss. "Not saying the douche didn't have it coming, but when is Adam going to accept that Whitney is a grown-up and responsible for her own actions?" And how is the douche supposed to pay child support with no job and no income?

Kyler scrubs a hand over his jaw as the sound of conversation filters out into the hall. "I think he harbors huge guilt over his marriage breakup, and he blames that for Whitney's behavior, so he's overcompensating now."

I shrug. "Nothing to do with me anymore, and if anything good has come out of this, it's that I won't have to face either of them again."

"Faye's really broken up over all of this," Ky admits, sighing as he leans back against the wall.

"I'm sorry," I say because I know it's hard for her. Faye and I might not have always seen eye to eye, usually over Whitney, but I don't wish this on her.

"She's really worried about Whitney," he adds.

"I am." Faye appears in the hallway, her heels clicking on the polished hardwood floors. "But Kent doesn't need to hear that." In a surprising move, she wraps her arms around me, hugging me tight. "I'm sorry she did that to you, Kent. I'm disgusted she tried to sabotage your relationship and pin the blame on you." She eases back, dropping her arms to her sides. "I just told Presley the same thing because I would hate her to think I condoned it, and I don't want her to feel uncomfortable in my presence." She eyeballs me, and I see nothing but the truth in her gaze. "I'm glad you guys have patched things up. I really like her."

"Me too."

She smiles as Kyler circles his arms around her waist from behind. "I'd like it if you and I could start over," she adds. "Whitney has always come between us, and it wasn't right."

I shrug, because I understand anything she said was said out of protection for her sister. I might not have understood it at the time, and I gave her hell for it, but I get it now. "It's water under the bridge now."

"Come on, sweetheart." Kyler takes his wife's hand. "Rick has already texted me to say they are en route to the restaurant."

"Enjoy your dinner, and don't worry about anything. We've got this," I say with more confidence than I feel. This is my first time babysitting the twins, but I've got my secret weapon with me—my girlfriend. Presley is a natural with kids, so we will manage.

"We won't be late," Faye says. "Ciara was a bit fussy earlier, and I suspect she might be coming down with something, so I don't want to stay away too long."

Faye brings new meaning to overprotective, but I'd never fault her for that.

I wave them off and walk into the living room to join my girlfriend.

"Well, that was uneventful," Presley admits three hours later as we are pulling out of Kyler and Faye's driveway. The kids were already asleep, and they didn't stir the whole time. We watched TV and made out like teenagers, and it was fun.

"I'm not sure I can say the same for our next destination," I admit, taking the turn that leads to my parents' house.

"You think your Mom has ulterior motives in asking us to stay?"

"One hundred percent."

Mom called during the week when she heard we were babysitting Cathal and Ciara, asking us to stay over so we could join her and Dad for lunch on Saturday. I instantly smelled a rat because it's only three weeks until Keaton's wedding and no one has said one word to me so far, which is not like my family. "I'm sensing it's an ambush."

Presley clears her throat, glancing at me from the passenger seat. "You think she wants to talk to you about the wedding?"

I nod, turning into the entranceway to my family home. I punch in the code on the keypad, and the gates slowly open.

"And you're still not talking to Keaton?" she softly inquires. We haven't discussed it in the weeks since we got back together, although she knows we aren't talking, and after bigmouth Whitney let the cat out of the bag at Easter dinner, now she thinks she knows why. But that's only part of the truth.

"Do you want to tell me why?" Her big brown eyes are earnest as she asks the question.

I swing the car into the parking garage, drive into an empty space, and kill the engine. Forcing myself to look at her, I admit the only part of the truth I'm capable of admitting right now. "I slept with his ex-girlfriend."

She nods because she knew that bit. "Why?"

My leg jerks up and down as I fudge my reply. "I did it deliberately to hurt him. But also to show him that she had an agenda. I'd suspected it for years, and he refused to see it. She would have continued to hang on to him, and I helped him to get rid of her for good."

It's true I helped expose her true nature, but it's not the main reason I had sex with Melissa the night of our twenty-first birthday. I was hurting, and I wanted Keats to hurt too. I'm not proud of my behavior or the things I said to him, but it's all tied up with that dark, twisted space inside me, and I couldn't help how I reacted.

Her brow puckers. "Why would you deliberately hurt Keaton?"

"It's complicated, Pres, and I'm not up to explaining it right now."

She looks like she's considering arguing with me, but whatever she reads on my face convinces her to let it go. At least for now. "What was her agenda?"

I take her hands in mine, needing to touch her. "She's a gold-digging bitch who was only after his money. Keats started going out with Melissa when he was fifteen. Before she got with him, she hit on me, but I turned her down." Even though that was a very bad period in my life, and I was fucking any female with a pulse those days, my instincts always screamed at me to steer clear of that girl. "Then one day she shows up on Keaton's arm, and he's parading her around as his girlfriend, and I didn't trust it. Didn't trust her."

"Why didn't you tell Keaton?"

"I did, but he didn't want to know. I think he thought I was jealous." My brows knit together as something new occurs to me. The day Keaton came out, I was consumed with dark thoughts and the things he said barely registered in my brain, but I still remember some of his words. "Or he just didn't care because he was confused about his sexuality and he thought having a girlfriend would cure him or something."

"I understand why that would've caused issues in your relationship with Keaton at the time, but why now? He's getting married, and it's not like you ever dated Melissa, so I fail to see why you aren't speaking to him?"

I withdraw my hands and avert my eyes. My chest heaves as intense pressure sits on my chest. I squeeze my eyes shut, forcing the images away. "There is more to it," I admit through gritted teeth.

"This is the complicated part?" Presley's voice is soft and her touch tender as she tilts my face around, making me look at her.

My eyes open, and I stare at the woman I love, wishing I could tell her, *wanting* to tell her, but I have never uttered those words to another soul, and I don't know how to say it.

What if she doesn't want me anymore?

Or she thinks I'm less of a man?

The usual self-doubts resurface in my head like they do anytime I think of that night or anytime I'm forced to face the fact my brother is gay and planning to marry a man.

"I can't say it," I whisper, dropping my eyes again, hating how weak I am.

"Can't or won't?" she asks in a gentle tone.

I lift my eyes to her concerned ones. "Can't," I croak. I lace my fingers in her free hand. "I want to confide in you, Presley. Please believe me, but I can't. Not yet."

"You know you can tell me anything, Kent, and it won't change the way I feel about you."

"You say that now, but—" I cut myself off, unable to continue. Blood thrums in my ears and rushes through my veins, and my knee jerks off the floor. I squeeze my eyes shut again, batting at the horror replaying behind my closed eyes.

"It's okay, Kent." Presley's reassuring tone and comforting touch reaches behind the terror, rescuing me from the dark hole. "Open your eyes, honey. Please, Kent. Open them for me."

Pain stings the backs of my damp eyes when I find the courage to open them. "I'm sorry."

She shakes her head, cupping my face. "Don't apologize. There's no need." She leans over, stretching across the console to plant a soft kiss on my lips. "Whatever it is, just know I am here for you. Whenever you want to talk about it, I will listen. And whatever you need me to do, I will do it, because there is nothing I won't do for the man I love."

My heart stutters in my chest, and I swear I stop breathing. My eyes lock on hers. "What did you say?" I whisper, unconvinced I didn't just imagine it.

She kisses me again, but I'm so shocked I don't even move my lips. She pulls back, smiling shyly. "I love you, Kent. I love you so much."

"I love you too," I say, snapping out of it. Pulling her over the console, I situate her on my lap. Sweeping hair off her shoulders, I let loose a massive grin, and the lingering darkness that threatens to resurface has been obliterated by her words. I bask in the warmth of her love as she smiles at me. "I've wanted to tell you, but I was scared," I admit.

"Me too." She nods, hugging me, and I wrap my arms around her back, never wanting to let her go. "I wasn't afraid you wouldn't say it back," she explains in my ear. "Because you show me you love me in so many different ways."

I ease back, looking into her face. "It's scary because now you hold my heart in your hand," I say, "and you want to cherish it, but you're terrified you'll do the opposite." At least, that's how I feel.

She shakes her head with tears in her eyes. "I'm holding your heart, Kent, and I will always cherish it and protect it, and I trust you to do the same with me. You and me is not what scares me. It's everything outside of our control that does. We have this amazing love that burns bright, and I don't want anything to extinguish it. But my life experiences have taught me to be guarded because everyone I love has been taken from me by external factors I couldn't control, and that is the scariest fucking feeling in the world."

Chapter Twenty-Six
Presley

Kent was right, I think as the doorbell chimes the next afternoon. Lunch *is* an ambush. "Mom," Kent growls. "What have you done?"

"What needed to be done," Alex calmly replies, folding her hands on the table in front of her. A lavish spread of sandwiches, wraps, salad, breads, and cakes lies on top of the long table, and I knew there was far too much food for just the four of us. "You need to speak to Keaton and clear the air before his wedding. He's hurting, and I know you love your brother and you can't be happy with the way things are either."

Kent rubs a hand along the back of his neck in an obvious tell.

I'm worried about him.

Whatever this thing is between him and Keaton must be serious because he was visibly upset in the car last night, and I'm attributing his nightmare last night to it. It's only the second time Kent has woken up in the middle of the night, shouting and thrashing, with sweat beaded on his brow and rolling down his back.

The first time it happened, when I asked him about it, he said he used to get a lot of nightmares as a kid and he still had the occasional one. I accepted that explanation without question, but now I'm wondering if there isn't more to it. I haven't forgotten the panic attack he had in the bar either, and I'm wondering if it's all connected.

Sliding my hand under the table, I lace my fingers through his and squeeze, letting him know I'm here for him. He grabs my hand with both of his, clinging to me like I'm his lifeline, and my heart floods with love for this man.

Our mutual confessions of love make me feel like I could climb mountains. Like we can overcome any obstacles in our path, but I'm not a vulnerable little kid or a naïve teenager anymore, and I know it's not that simple. Having found something this precious means it will hurt all the more if I lose it, and I make a silent promise to myself to do everything in my power to protect our love, to always prioritize my needs and Kent's needs, to let nothing come between us.

Keaton and Austen step into the dining room, and a muscle pops in Kent's jaw. Tension bleeds into the air.

"Hey, Mom, Dad, Presley, Kent." Keaton drops his jacket on the back of a chair across the table from us, before sitting down.

"Hey, everyone," Austen adds, claiming the empty seat beside his fiancé.

Alex, James, and I return their greeting while Kent quietly decomposes. His leg shakes underneath our conjoined hands, and his back is rigidly stiff.

"Let's just get this done," he says through gritted teeth, leveling his brother with a dark look.

James clears his throat. "We're going to have our lunch in the sunroom so you kids can talk in private."

Alex puts plates and cups on a tray, handing it to James. Drawing her shoulders back, she clasps her hands in front of her body, preparing to lay down the law. "We love you all, and I know whatever it is you will get through this." Her gaze bounces between her two sons. "The three of you were so close growing up," she continues, obviously including Keanu in her comment. "It was a joy to watch. You instinctively always knew where each other was, and you defended one another when anyone said or did anything nasty. You three were a solid team, and you always, *always*, had each other's backs. I don't know where it went wrong or why, but you need to remember who you are to one another because you have always been more than just brothers." Tears pool in her eyes and it's obvious how much their separation has hurt her. "Please make this right, because it's breaking my heart."

James sets the tray down, circling his arm around Alex, holding her to his chest while she sobs as he leads her out of the room. Austen stands, taking the tray and following them out.

"Do you want to speak alone?" Keaton asks Kent.

Kent shakes his head. "I don't keep secrets from Presley."

Keaton smiles. "Like I don't keep secrets from Austen."

Kent's mouth curls into a snarl, and I plead with my eyes, begging him to at least try.

"Would you like tea or coffee?" I ask Keaton while we wait for Austen to return.

"Coffee, please," he says, pushing two cups toward me. I fill both with coffee from the silver pot as Keaton fills his plate and Austen's plate with food.

"Is she okay?" Keaton asks when Austen reenters the room.

He nods, sitting down beside Keaton, placing his arm along the back of his fiancé's chair. "She's fine."

I squeeze Kent's hand in reassurance.

"What is it you want to say?" Kent asks, his voice gruff.

"Have you been getting my texts?" Keats asks, and I mask my surprise. I had no idea Keaton had been texting Kent because he never said one word to me about it.

"I have."

"So, you know I love you and I forgive you."

Wow. That could not be easy to say. My respect for Keaton has magnified ten-fold.

Austen's face is a mask of neutral calmness, but from the way he's drilling his eyes into Kent, I know he believes Kent is at fault and he's expecting a grand gesture. One I'm not sure Kent is in a place to deliver.

"How can you?" Kent asks, looking down at the table rather than at his brother. "I have done nothing to earn your forgiveness."

"You're my triplet. You're a part of my soul, and I'm done missing you. Whatever it is, we can overcome it together."

Kent's Adam's apple bobs in his throat.

"Can you not even look at me now, Kent?" Keaton asks, and his pain is clear to see.

Kent lifts his head, staring at his brother, and I can tell it hurts him to do it. "If this was just about missing you, we'd have been speaking ages ago," Kent admits, and I rub soothing circles on the back of his wrist, urging him to continue.

Austen's gaze flicks to mine, and we exchange a silent communication. I can tell this is as hard for him as it is for me.

Neither of us understands it, but we don't have to understand it to support our partners.

I have only met Keaton and Austen one time, but the love they share is unbreakable and undeniable. There is no doubt in my mind Austen would move mountains to make Keaton happy like I would do for Kent. Austen subtly nods at me, and I return it, both of us confirming we will do whatever we can to help make this right—even if we haven't spoken the words out loud and even if we don't fully understand it.

Keaton leans his elbows on the table, straining toward his brother. "What is it about?"

Kent shakes and his eyes narrow as he struggles to hold on to his control. Snaking my arms around his trembling body, I hold him close, whispering assurances in his ear.

Tears pool in Keaton's eyes. "Did something happen to you, Kent?"

Kent goes rigidly still, and you could hear a pin drop in the room.

"Because it's the only thing that seems plausible," Keaton continues. A tear rolls down his face, and Austen circles his arm around

Keaton's shoulders, moving in closer to his side. "I have thought about this over and over, and I don't believe you're homophobic. I can't accept you hate me because I'm gay. It just doesn't make sense."

Kent shucks out of my arms, climbing to his feet. "Don't." He shakes his head repeatedly, jabbing his finger in the air, waving it in his brother's direction "Don't conjure up stuff to explain this." He starts pacing the room, and I can almost see the demons sitting on his shoulders, clinging to his back, whispering ugly truths in his ear, imploring him to lash out. I won't let them take Kent from me or make things worse with his brother.

So, I get up, cross to my boyfriend, and pull him into my arms. Over his shoulder, I gently plead with Keaton to drop this. Whatever it is, Kent is not ready to discuss it. *Who knows if he ever will be?*

"It's okay." Keaton stands, coming over to us. "I didn't come here to upset you."

"Why did you come here?" Kent asks, lifting his head from my shoulder. He repositions us, moving me so I am pressed against his side but still a little in front of him, slightly blocking his body. His arms go around me, and I hold on to him, making sure he knows I am here and he can lean on me.

"To ask you to be my best man at the wedding."

Silence descends on the room. Kent stares at his brother in shock. Austen comes up alongside Keaton, linking his fingers through his. "Why would you want *me* to be your best man?" Kent splutters.

"Because you're my triplet! Because you've been there for me through every other major event in my life and I need you to stand at my side while I marry the man of my dreams! I only want you and Keanu. The others understand. And Austen is just having his brother, Orwell, and his friend Colton as his best men." The words burst from his lips in a nervous rush.

Poor Keaton.

He's terrified Kent will turn him down.

To be honest, so am I.

Kent can barely look his brother in the eye, and though we don't understand the reasons, he's not accepting of Keaton marrying Austen. My heart breaks for them. I understand why Keaton wants Kent to be there, even if he doesn't support the marriage, but it isn't right. Or maybe Keaton knows, deep down, that Kent does support him, that it's not personal, and Keaton is selfless enough to look beyond the exterior hate, because he just wants his brother at his side.

"Keats," Kent croaks, and pain twists in my gut when tears run freely down his face. "I want to be there for you, I do, but I...I don't know that I can."

Keaton steps closer, cautiously placing his hand on Kent's shoulder. "I won't force you to do it. You don't even need to give me an answer today, but please say you'll think about it. I don't want to look back on my wedding and feel sad because my brother wasn't by my side. I don't want *you* to look back and regret that you didn't do it." Keaton's shoulders slump. "Just think about it. Please."

Austen steps up behind Keaton, placing his hand on his hip, holding him close. Emotion-filled energy swirls around us as Kent grips me tighter. More tears fall from his eyes when he says, "I don't know how you can want me there. Not after how I've treated you."

"It doesn't matter," he says, when we all know it does. Keaton has the biggest heart, and I have a sudden urge to hug him because he's cut his heart open and he's laying it at Kent's feet. He is prepared to do whatever it takes to have his brother by his side when he marries the love of his life, even accept his hidden truths if it means he gets his brother back.

"It does, brother," Kent says, staring his brother in the face. For the first time, he doesn't look away, eyeballing Keaton with less obvious conflict. I know the turmoil is still there, coiling under the surface, because there is no way you can overcome this kind of conflict without more soul baring, but as I look at my boyfriend, I know he's trying. "I'm sorry, Keats. I know I've been unfair to you and Austen. And I know you don't understand." He's trembling again, and Keaton can feel it because he still has his hand on Kent's shoulder. "But I will try. For you."

Hope blooms on Keaton's face. "What exactly are you saying, Kent?"

The trembling subsides, and Kent holds himself steady, still clinging to me, but reasserting some confidence. "I will be your best man. If that's what you want, you have it."

Shock splays across our three faces, because none of us expected Kent to agree.

I step aside as Keaton hugs his brother, and if he notices how Kent tenses up again, he doesn't make it known. Tears sneak out of my eyes when Kent slowly, cautiously, slides his arms around Keaton's back, hugging him in return. Keaton chokes on a sob, Kent's shoulders heave, and Austen rubs at his eyes.

All of us are overwrought with emotion and the significance of today. I truly hope it's a turning point for them. That they can start to heal.

Austen looks from them to me, and we share another silent promise. We know this is a temporary, tentative truce, and we agree to do what we can to make it last. I hope it lasts long enough for Keaton and Austen to have the best wedding day, because it's nothing less than they deserve.

I'm in Alex's home office an hour later, chatting to her about some pressed-flower pictures she would like to commission me to do, when there's a knock on the door. Alex opens it, revealing a sheepish-looking Keaton. He looks at me. "I was hoping to have a word with you. Just the two of us."

I nod, not surprised he has sought me out. Since the tense conversation at lunch, I've caught the concerned looks he has sent Kent's way when he thinks no one is looking, and I knew he'd find some way of reaching out to me.

"We were just done here anyway," Alex says. She hands me her business card. "Email me with pricing and potential delivery dates, and we can firm up something next week."

I have no clue how to price my drawings, but I guess Etsy could help. I'm still in shock she wants to use some of my pieces for a few of her client projects, but I won't pass up the opportunity. I am beyond excited, and Kent is thrilled for me too. Probably because he knows it means I will have to spend more time at his place, using the amazing studio he built for me. "Thank you so much. I still can't believe this," I tell her, returning her warm hug.

"You are very talented, and I like to nurture up-and-coming talent." She eases out of our embrace, smiling at me. "Besides, I would do just about anything to help my sons and their partners succeed, especially the woman who has put a smile on my Kent's face. You're so good for him, Presley. I have never seen Kent this happy. Don't let him push you away."

She must be under the misconception our breakup was Kent's fault. I would set her straight, but Keaton is waiting to talk to me, and we won't have long before Kent comes looking for me. We are due to leave shortly for the city since my shift starts at seven.

Alex leaves, closing the door behind her, and I waste no time getting to the heart of the matter. "I don't know what happened, and even if I did, I could never betray Kent's confidence. He will have to tell you in his own time."

Keaton props his butt against the desk while I remain seated in the chair. "But he has said something? Something did happen to him?"

"I think so," I truthfully admit. "But it's only a recent discovery, and he's not ready to talk about it, if he ever will be."

"I feel sick," he whispers as tears well in his eyes. "Kent was so out of control when we were teenagers, and I never stopped to question why. None of us did. We just accepted that was the way he was. Wild and out of control. An attention-seeker."

"You don't know it wasn't that," I say because we don't know what Kent is hiding. Just that it's difficult to talk about. "And he wouldn't want you to upset yourself over this." I might think that's why Kent doesn't want to say anything this close to his brother's wedding, but the fact he can't even tell me confirms it's more than that.

"I feel so stupid that I didn't do anything before now. I haven't said anything to the others and—"

"And you shouldn't." I place my hand on his arm. "I know you're worried about him. So am I, but Keaton, he's happy. We're happy, and I know there is something there, something from his past, something that he needs to face up to, but you and I can't make him face up to it. No one can. He has to face up to it by himself. All we can do is love him and support him and let him know we are here for him if he ever wants to talk about it."

He wipes his tears away. "Do you love my brother, Presley?"

"With my whole heart and everything I am."

His answering smile is wide. "I'm so glad he has you. Will you let me know if there is anything I can ever do or if anything happens and you need me or he needs me?"

I stand, hugging him without hesitation. "I will, Keaton, but in return, you have to promise me something."

"Anything," he says when I pull back.

"Don't worry about Kent. Let me take care of him. Focus on the important things like getting married to a wonderful man and having both your triplets by your side."

I'm not sure exactly why Kent agreed to do it, but I know he pushed past his demons to do the right thing for his brother, and I am going to do everything within my control to ensure Keaton gets the wedding day he deserves and that Kent has my support every step of the way.

Chapter Twenty-Seven
Presley

"**P**res?" Kent asks as we are en route to the castle resort and spa in Vermont where Austen and Keaton are getting married tomorrow. We've already been on the road for over three hours, so it shouldn't be much longer now. The rest of the family arrived earlier today, since they wanted to get the kids settled, but we should make it in time for dinner.

"Yes, honey?" I ask, barely lifting my head from my phone. I'm scrolling through Pinterest, pinning items of inspiration. The pictures Alex commissioned are due in a couple of weeks, and I've been working around the clock to get them finished in time.

Alex has also spoken to me about setting this up as a legit side business. She thinks there is a market for one-off handcrafted pressed-flower drawings like this, and she has already confirmed she will be placing more orders, so I'm seriously considering the idea. Eva has offered to help with a website and online store, and Cheryl has said she'll take photos for my catalog, so the only obstacle is time. God knows I have enough supplies because Kent buys me flowers at least a couple of times a week, and everything else is in the cupboards of my art studio.

It won't derail my long-term plans. I'm still determined to be a tattoo artist, but perhaps this will help me achieve my goal quicker.

"That therapist you're seeing, is she helping?" he asks, and I put my phone away, giving him my undivided attention, because I sense this is serious.

"Yes. She is." I haven't talked to Kent about it much because my sessions with Jenna have been heavily focused on Chris in recent weeks, and I don't want to upset him.

"I went to therapy, on and off, for years," he admits as he drives one-handed through New Hampshire.

"You did?" I swivel in my seat, tucking one leg underneath me.

He nods, glancing at me briefly. "When I started acting out, my parents sent me to a therapist. When that one didn't help, they sent me to another one. Rinse. Repeat." A muscle ticks in his jaw, and he's gripping the steering wheel tight.

"You didn't trust any of them?" I surmise, remembering the horrible therapist my social worker sent me to when I was nine and I refused to speak in the initial aftermath of the car crash.

Intelligent eyes lock on mine. "You sound like you're speaking from experience."

"I told you I didn't speak for a year after my parents died, so my social worker arranged for me to see this therapist in the hopes he would help me to deal with the trauma. The guy gave me the creeps."

His head jerks to mine again, his eyes alert, and I know where his mind has gone.

"He didn't touch me. It was nothing like that. Just that he was clinical, and I couldn't warm to him, so I certainly wasn't going to open up to him."

"That's exactly how I felt," he admits. "And I didn't trust they wouldn't turn around and tell my parents everything I told them, even if they spouted oaths of confidentiality, blah, blah."

"Well, Jenna is different," I say, reaching out to rub his arm. "Maybe you just haven't found the right therapist yet."

He is quietly contemplative after that, and I don't pry even if I'm dying to know what's going through his head. He turns the radio on low, and we both laugh when Elvis's "A Little Less Conversation" comes on because it couldn't be more apt. We sing some of the words to each other, and it helps to lighten the mood.

Fifty minutes later, Kent swings his SUV into the long castle driveway, and I press my nose to the window, absorbing the pretty scenery. "Wow, this place is stunning." Majestic trees, neat trimmed hedges, and colorful flowerbeds border the driveway on both sides. A line of twinkling lights guides our path, and with the dusky sky overhead, it adds a magical feel to the place.

I gasp when the castle comes into view up ahead. The grand two-story gray-brick structure with turrets, towers, and various arches and pillars has clearly been well-maintained. Vines of ivy creep up the sides of the castle, and I'm glad we're staying in one of the detached cabins on the grounds, and not in the castle itself, because one look at this place and I just know it's haunted. A shudder works its way through me, and I try to avoid thinking scary thoughts.

There are only ten bedrooms in the castle itself, and I know Austen's family, Alex and James, Cheryl and Keven, Keaton and Austen, Keanu and Selena, and a few of their friends are staying there. The rest of Kent's family chose the more spacious cabins, and it's where the rest of their friends are staying when they arrive tomorrow. Tonight's pre-wedding dinner is just for immediate family.

We park the car, check in, and are driven in an old trolley to our cabin. It's a beautiful gray-stone structure with exquisite views of the gorgeous woodland and mountain backdrop. We have a decked area off our bedroom with a seating area and a hot tub.

"I'm going to fuck you in there before the weekend is out," Kent purrs in my ear, his arms going around me from behind.

"I think you love torturing me," I say, spinning around in his arms as desire tightens in my lower belly. "You know I'll be squirming the whole way through dinner now."

"That's just how I like my woman," Kent teases, nipping at my neck with his teeth. "Panties soaked and dreaming of my cock."

I swat at his chest, pushing him back. "Careful or I'll cockblock you all weekend."

He swaggers toward me, pushing me down on the bed, pinning me in place with his hard body. "You can't last twenty-four hours without my cock inside you." He presses his hot mouth to my neck, and my pulse aches with need. "You would never last three days."

"Always so fucking smug," I rasp, even though he's right, biting back a moan as his hand trails a path up my body, his fingers brushing against my breast through my shirt. He pivots his hips, pressing his erection into me, and I can't take it any longer. Gripping his waist, I yank his face to mine. "Fuck me now, and make it quick." I still need to freshen up, get changed, and make it to dinner in twenty minutes, but we can do it.

He chuckles. "We'll be late."

"You're wasting time," I chastise, unbuttoning his shirt as I yank his mouth to mine for a passionate kiss. "Less talking. More fucking."

"Yes, ma'am," he says, smirking as he removes my skirt and panties, plunging two fingers into my wet warmth to check I'm ready. I strip him out of his jeans and boxers and roll a rubber over his shaft. Then he's driving inside me, and fucking me into the bed with that dark intensity I love so much.

"You're late," Alex chides when we finally show our faces in the main castle restaurant.

"Traffic was murder," Kent lies, holding out my chair for me to sit.

Kalvin snorts out a laugh. "Nice try, dude. We all saw you pulling up over an hour ago."

Kent pins him with a smug look. "We're here now." He slings his arm around the back of my chair. "And my woman's needs always come first. Always."

"Kent!" I shriek, glaring at him. Not only has he confirmed we were late because we were fucking, but he's also thrown me under the bus.

A chorus of chuckles ring out around the table while I just wish the ground would open and swallow me. Thankfully, the conversation moves on, and Alex takes her time making introductions, insisting we play musical chairs, so by the end of the evening, everyone is well acquainted with one another.

Kent has been on his best behavior, and he's in great form, laughing and joking, and I let go of the slight anxiety I was holding on to earlier. Kent hasn't said much about the wedding since he agreed to be Keaton's best man. I know he went with Keanu to meet Austen, Keaton, Orwell, and Colton for their suit fitting, but he was pretty tight-lipped when he came back.

"Austen's family seems nice," I say as we are walking back to our cabin later with me tucked under Kent's arm.

"His mom looks like she has a stick up her ass," he says, his words a tad slurred. I figured he was a little drunk because he was knocking back the beers and he finished out the night with a few whiskeys. "But his dad, brother, and sister seem all right."

"Orwell is something else." He is studying engineering at the University of Denver and about to enter his senior year in September. I chuckle as I remember some of the risqué college stories he was telling us earlier. From the sounds of it, he'd give a young Kent Kennedy a run for his money.

"He's a punk," Kent says.

I giggle. "A bit like someone else I know, or so I've been told."

Kent tickles me, and I shriek, pulling away from him, but he's fast, even inebriated, and he hauls me into his chest, wrapping his arms around my back, caging me to him. "Not anymore." He leans down, kissing the tip of my nose in an infinitely tender gesture. "You reformed me, Presley baby."

Circling my arms around his neck, I tilt my face up. "You reformed yourself, Kent. Never forget that no one can save you if you don't save yourself first."

Chapter Twenty-Eight
Presley

"Kent looks like he's going to pass out," Eva whispers to me as we sit in the first row of seats the following day, waiting for Keaton and Austen to make their big entrance.

All eighty guests are here, and the best men are lined up on either side of the stone platform waiting for the grooms to arrive. The officiant smiles widely as he surveys the beautiful setting. The elevated stone platform where the ceremony will take place rests at the edge of the twenty-acre property, overlooking the plush woodland and breath-stealing Green Mountains in the distance. Overhead, an open stone archway has been decorated with gorgeous white and orange flowers with green foliage interspersed between the columns.

"He's nervous," I admit, working hard to hide my concern because Eva is right. Kent is pale and sweating bullets as he fidgets, pulling on the end of his black suit jacket, running his fingers along the collar of his white shirt, as if it's choking him, and constantly dragging his hands through his hair. "Keanu will reassure him," I add, watching as his triplet whispers in his ear.

I don't think any of Kent's family understand how big of a deal this is for him. And why would they? As far as they are concerned, Keaton and Kent have repaired the rift in their relationship and everything is peachy. Except I know they have only papered over the cracks, and everything is far from resolved. This weekend is hard for Kent, for reasons I still don't understand, and I'm proud of him for pushing himself out of his comfort zone to be here for his brother.

The music starts, and everyone stands. I lock eyes with Kent, conveying he can do this and I'm proud of him. His shoulders relax a little and he mouths "I love you." I blow him a kiss, repeating the silent words, smiling as I turn to watch the procession.

The kids are up first, and they all look adorably cute in their little suits and dresses. Hewson is the ring bearer, and he goes first, proudly holding his chin up as he walks along the stone path toward the platform. The rest of the nieces and nephews follow, and everyone oohs and aahs as they skip up the aisle, excited to be a part of the day.

Then the grooms appear, on either side of the garden, as the strains of "Truly, Madly, Deeply" by Savage Garden pulse out of the mobile speakers. James is escorting Keaton, and Alex is escorting Austen. I'm not sure why one of his parents isn't giving him away, but there must be a reason.

I watch Austen and Keaton walk toward one another with a lump in my throat. They only have eyes for each other, and I can feel the love emanating from them. A sob rings out near me, and I instinctively turn toward the sound, watching tears pour down Faye's face. Kyler wraps his arms around his wife, looking like he's struggling to hold on to his emotions too.

Austen and Keaton meet at the end of the aisle, and they move as one, pressing their foreheads together as Alex and James step back. Kent's dad pulls his mom into his side, and they share a loving look. Austen grabs Keaton's hand, and they stare at one another with tears in their eyes.

"I love you," Austen says, his words ringing out clear enough to be heard over the music.

"I love you too," Keaton says, swiping tears off his cheeks.

"Let's do this, baby," Austen says, and Keaton nods.

With matching smiles, they face forward and start their walk up the aisle. They are wearing similar black suits, but Keaton has a white button-down shirt with a deep orange tie, and Austen is wearing the same shirt in black with a white tie. They both look so handsome and so in love, and my heart is bursting with joy. As I look around, I see I'm not the only one. This is the very first wedding I've ever attended, so I don't know if the outpouring of emotion surrounding me is normal or out of the ordinary.

The grooms reach the platform, sharing some banter with the officiant before turning to face one another, holding hands as the ceremony begins.

My eyes return to Kent, noticing the glaze in his eyes and the hard set of his jaw. He holds himself rigidly still as he stares off into space. Unless someone was concentrating on him, nobody would notice how his gaze is trained just above Keaton's and Austen's heads, or how his foot is tapping anxiously, or the little beads of sweat dotting his brow. The weather is warm, and we've been blessed with a glorious sunny day, but that's not the cause of Kent's discomfort.

I want to go to him so badly, but I can't.

Keaton and Austen make their vows, and they are beautiful and heartfelt, but I am only half-listening as I watch my boyfriend, praying he holds it together, at least until the ceremony is over. He will never forgive himself if he makes a scene.

Applause rings out, joined by several whoops and hollers, as the officiant pronounces them husband and husband, and Austen and Keaton share a passionate kiss. I glance along the row, smiling at the evident emotion on everyone's faces. All the women are crying, some of Kent's brothers too, while the kids stand around, bemused by all the weeping adults.

I breathe a sigh of relief when the officiant brings the ceremony to a close, and Keaton and Austen join hands, heading back down the aisle.

I slip out of my seat, moving to Kent's side. Keanu is talking in his ear as Colton and Orwell send perplexed looks his way. Keanu lifts his head when he sees me approaching, and there is no disguising the concern on his face.

"Kent." I cup his face, focusing his gaze on mine, silently cursing when I see how dilated his pupils are. *Fuck.* He's on something, and I'm not talking about the beer he chugged back just before the ceremony. My stomach twists into knots, but I know what I need to do. "Honey." I lean up, pressing my lips to his until I feel him thawing underneath me. "It's okay," I whisper. "It's over."

Kent's chest rises and falls, and he casts his eyes around, watching everyone heading toward the refreshment area off to the left. His shoulders relax as he pulls me into his chest, holding me tight. His heart is going crazy under my ear, and he's trembling. Tears prick my eyes, and I hurt for my broken man. I want to know who has hurt him, and I'm going to make them pay.

Selena comes up behind us, and Keanu tucks his wife into his side, shooting me a troubled look. "We're good, guys," I say, plastering a reassuring smile on my face. "You should join the others. We'll be there in a minute."

Keanu looks uncertain, but Selena pulls him away, and I shoot her a grateful look.

"It's just us." I circle my arms around the back of Kent's neck. "Talk to me."

"That was harder than I thought," he admits, planting his hands on my ass.

"That was the hardest part, and you got through it." Every part of me hurts for him. He should be able to enjoy his brother's wedding like everyone else. It shouldn't be something he has to "survive."

"You look beautiful," he says, peering down at me. "I knew the second you tried this dress on that it was the one for you." Kent insisted on taking me to Saks Fifth Avenue, and he spent an outrageous amount of money on this dress, a matching purse, and shoes.

I joined the other Kennedy women in Alex's room earlier to get my hair and makeup done. Alex hired a few professional hairdressers and makeup artists she knows from her fashion empire days, and they worked their magic on all of us. I've got to admit I feel like a million dollars.

I left my hair down, because Kent loves messing with it, and it tumbles in sleek soft waves to my shoulders. Although it feels like they slapped a ton of makeup on my face, I was pleasantly surprised that it looks understated and natural, and it complements my green dress perfectly. I love how the knee-length silk and lace Dolce and Gabbana dress swirls around my hips and sashays as I walk. The top is pretty plain, and it goes up to my neckline, but it plunges into a V on my back, meaning I couldn't wear a bra. Thank fuck there was one built in because my boobs need the support.

"I'm a lucky bastard to have found you," he says, pushing his hand up under the dress and sliding it up my thigh. He fixes me with a cheeky grin as his fingers brush against my panties.

I want to rage at him for the way his eyes can't even focus on me. One part of me understands why he felt the need to take something to get through the day, but another part of me is pissed he did. He promised he would stop using drugs, and for the most part, he has. Sure, he still smokes a joint most nights and he enjoys the occasional few beers, but he has reined in that reckless part of his behavior, and I haven't had any recent doubts.

Until now.

But today isn't about me, and starting an argument with Kent is not part of the agenda. I need to play my part to ensure he gets through this weekend without causing any trouble. So, I'll bite my tongue until we return to Boston, but then I'm letting him have it.

I will not tolerate my boyfriend turning to drugs instead of me.

I will not go down this slippery slope again.

If Kent is serious about me, he's got to find a way to completely stop. Otherwise, there is no future for us.

"Not here." I pull away from him when his fingers move under my panties, rubbing against my hot flesh.

"I need you, Presley baby," he murmurs against my neck, yanking me back to him, pressing his erection against my side so I can feel how hard he is.

"Kent, the wedding has only just started." I'm conscious we've been standing here for longer than is explainable. Taking his hand, I pull him off the platform. "Let's mingle, and we can find someplace to sneak off to later."

But Kent is not one to be deterred, and I'm guessing whatever he's taken is to blame for his current horny status. He leads me into the castle, holding my hand tight as he storms down one long hallway, pulling me into the first unlocked room he finds. It's a small library with rows of books surrounding a seated area with two couches, a few comfy chairs, a desk, and a big ornate fireplace.

Kent locks the door and presses me up against it, crashing his mouth down on mine as he fumbles with his belt. I help him, tugging his pants and boxers down, freeing his straining length. "I'm so hot for you, Presley baby. You get me so hard."

My fingers curl around his shaft, and I pump him in fast measured strokes as he yanks my panties down to my ankles and shoves my dress up to my waist. "Don't rip anything," I warn him, because he likes rough sex and it's not uncommon for him to tear my panties or articles of my clothes in his haste to get inside me.

"Don't worry, baby," he says as he rolls a condom on. "The only thing I'll be ripping is your pussy because I'm gonna fucking destroy it."

I'd thump him for that crass statement in any other situation, but right now, he needs me and that takes precedence.

Kent slams into me without warning, and I bite down on my lip to smother my screams. He stretches my arms up over my head, holding my wrists in one hand, as he drives his cock inside me, holding one of my hips in his free hand. He rocks into me, slamming me back against the door, and I pray no one is outside in the hallway. His mouth descends on mine in a punishing kiss, and God help me, but I love when he just takes what he wants, using my body to sate this unquenchable thirst inside him.

Releasing my wrists, he slides his arms under my ass, lifting me. My legs go around his waist, and he holds me up as he fucks me into oblivion. Kent works out like a beast, and he has a body carved of hard muscle, but I'm still impressed. Holding on to his shoulders, I grind my pussy down on his cock as he thrusts up inside me, and we both come a few minutes later.

"Holy fuck, baby." He staggers a little as he lifts me off his dick, planting my feet on the ground. "You are so damn good at that."

"So are you," I rasp, pulling my lace panties up my legs as he pulls the condom off, tying a knot in it and dumping it in the small trash can under the desk.

"I've had lots and lots of practice." He laughs, winking at me as he tugs his boxers and pants up his legs, as if it's funny.

Bile swirls in my gut, and anxiety prickles my skin.

I have no idea how I'm going to get through this day unscathed.

"Thanks for that," I hiss through gritted teeth. "That's exactly what a woman wants to hear just after her boyfriend's had sex with her." Sarcasm drips from my tone.

"Baby." He reaches for me, but I push him away, his words upsetting me more than he realizes.

"Don't fucking touch me." I know he wasn't a saint. Far from it. But I purposely don't think about all the other women, and he doesn't usually reference his previous sex life. Today is the last day I want to be thinking about how much sex my boyfriend has had with copious random women. Today is a day to celebrate love and everything that is wonderful and intimate between two people.

"Come on. You know I have a past."

"Like I have, but you don't hear me throwing Chris or Lync in your face."

He purses his lips. "Don't be petty, Presley. And you're completely overreacting."

I don't think I am, but I force my own feelings aside, for the sake of peace. "Just drop it," I say, grinding my teeth to my molars as I struggle to get a leash on my hurt and my anger. "And we should head back before your family sends out a search party."

He chuckles. "They probably already have, but who fucking cares?" He slings his arm over my shoulder, clueless to how much his words have hurt me, before opening the door.

We almost fall face-first into Austen's mother.

How wonderful.

"Oh my God. You gave me a fright!" she says, planting a hand on her chest. Her gaze bounces between us, her eyes widening with recognition. Slowly, she looks us over from head to toe, and acid crawls up my throat. The skirt of my dress is wrinkled, and I'm sure my makeup is in need of repair. Kent forgot to button the top button of his pants, his tie is askew, and his hair is messed up from my fingers. It's obvious what we were doing in that room.

Her lips pull into a disapproving line. "This is the height of bad manners. Especially with you being your brother's best man! I have read some very unsavory articles about you online." She looks down her nose at us. "I can see they didn't exaggerate."

"You're one to talk," Kent hisses. "No one asked for your input, and your own manners could use polishing."

"You can't speak to me like that!" Her nostrils flare, and her cheeks redden.

"You know what your problem is?" Kent says, his lips tugging up at the corners. I brace myself for it. "You need a proper dicking and for someone to remove that stick up your ass."

"You are disgusting, and you have a filthy mouth." She rakes her gaze over him like he's vermin.

"Fuck off," Kent snaps. "And mind your own business." Taking my hand, he guides me out into the hallway, brushing past her.

"Your parents will hear about this!" she calls out after us.

Kent spins around, shoving his middle finger up at her. "Do I look like I'm five or like I give a shit? Do your worst. Stuck-up bitch."

I virtually drag him outside, rubbing at my throbbing temples.

Reforming Kent

Though it looks like I'll be on babysitting duty for the rest of the day, I stop a waiter and grab a glass of champagne off his tray because I have a feeling I'll need some liquid courage.

I'd like to say things improve as the day turns to night, but they don't. At least the wedding is almost over, and Kent hasn't caused any other trouble. I spoke to Keanu, explaining about our altercation with Mrs. Hayes, and he smoothed things over with Austen's mom. She will never be Kent's biggest fan, but I doubt either of us will lose sleep over it.

"Let's dance, Presley baby," Kent proclaims, coming up behind me and taking my hand, even though I'm mid-conversation with his sister-in-law.

"Sorry!" I shout at Lana as Kent hauls me out onto the dance floor.

He's been drinking and dancing up a storm while I watch from the sidelines, mostly sticking to water and the odd glass of champagne. Kent is trashed, and one of us needs to be sober. His family doesn't notice, or maybe they're used to it, or they're putting it down to wedding exuberance. Whatever it is, I seem to be the only one concerned. I've noticed he keeps his distance from Austen and Keaton, which I consider a good thing. The happy couple is loved up, and they've been showered with congratulations and goodwill today, and everything has gone without a hitch.

The music changes, and Elvis's "Can't Help Falling in Love" comes on. Kent grins, waggling his brows, as he spins me around, and I realize he must have planned this. My insides soften, and I smile at my boyfriend, all tension temporarily forgotten. He reels me into his arms, a quirky lopsided grin on his mouth, as he sings to me in his terribly bad yet terribly cute Elvis impersonation.

He is loud, so damn loud, and his brothers move in closer to us, all of them dancing with their wives, grinning and laughing, as they watch Kent serenade me. At the very end, he dips me down so low my hair trails the ground, and then he whips me up into his arms, forcing my legs to go around his waist, holding me in his strong embrace while he kisses the shit out of me.

In front of everyone.

Catcalls and hollers ring out around us as Kent finally sets me down. I clutch him when he sways a little, keeping him steady. "I love you, Presley," he says. "Love you so much, baby." He buries his face in my neck, pressing his hot mouth to my ear. "I couldn't have done this without you. You are my rock, baby. Don't ever leave me. Please."

Chapter Twenty-Nine
Presley

Kent falls in the door of our cabin an hour later, and I lunge for him, grabbing the back of his shirt and stopping him from face-planting the floor. He laughs, rolling to the ground on his back, pulling me down on top of him. His leg juts out, and he slams the door shut with his foot. "Baby, I wanna sex you up," he slurs, his hands fumbling under the hem of my dress. He's been insatiable today, mauling me any chance he got. His brothers lost no opportunity to tease him over his grabby hands, and Mrs. Hayes sent disgusted looks in our direction whenever she noticed how amorous my boyfriend was.

I attempt to climb off him, but he slaps my ass, holding me in place while he thrusts his hips up, ensuring I feel his rock-hard erection digging into my stomach. "Feel that, baby. That monster is all for you."

"Honey." I smush his face in my hands. "I want that monster, but I also want to wear this gorgeous dress again, and if you don't let me up, I know you're going to rip it off my body, and that will make me mad." I lightly slap his face. "So, if you want to put your cock in my pussy, let me up." I drill him with a "don't mess with me" look that works.

He stumbles to his feet with me, and we strip out of our clothes, tossing them on the couch. Kent is a mess, falling on his butt as he tries to pull his pants off, and I crawl toward him, helping him to undress. Then he's on me, grabbing at me like he can't get enough, driving his tongue in my mouth while he pumps his fingers inside me. I'm already wet because he's been working me into a frenzy today. "Sit on me," he commands. "Reverse cowgirl. I wanna pull your hair."

I sit up and turn around with my back to his face, sitting on his lower stomach, stroking his erection. He hands me a condom, and I roll it down over his thick length before positioning myself over it and slowly lowering down. I like this position because he can fuck me and play with my tits and my clit, but I miss the intimacy of seeing his face.

Kent wraps his hand around my hair as I use my legs to move up and down on him. He yanks my head back, using my hair like a leash, and his free hand wraps around my throat, squeezing. Kent likes it rough a lot, but I never complain, because every way we do it is orgasmic.

Moans slip from my lips as I rock up and down on him, and he pivots his hips, thrusting up inside me while he tugs on my hair and presses in on my throat. I move my hands down my body, over the place where our bodies meet, reaching for his balls to play with them. Because I can't look down, not with the way he has my hair pulled back, I miscalculate, and my fingers graze against his asshole instead.

The response is immediate and terrifying.

Kent roars, letting loose a string of expletives, as his hand tightens on my neck, squeezing and squeezing until it feels like I can't breathe. Panic slaps me in the face as my air supply is constricted, and I stop moving on him, grabbing his arm with both my hands, trying to loosen his grip.

His hand tightens further, and black spots mar my vision while the room spins. I sink my nails into his arm while choking sounds rip from my throat. I thrash around on top of him with tears leaking from my eyes. My eyelids close, and the pain in my chest is so tight. My hands drop from his arm, and my body sags as my vision flickers in and out.

And then the pressure is gone, and I'm falling forward, slumping against the floor as I suck in air, my chest heaving as I drag oxygen into my lungs. Tears leak from my eyes, and my heart is pounding as relief sluices through my veins.

I'm lying motionless on the floor, on my stomach, sobbing, and laboring for breath. Pulling my knees up, I tuck them into my chest as I automatically curl into a fetal position. Behind me, Kent is mumbling and crying, none of the words distinguishable. A steady thumping sound accompanies his anguished cries, and I want to move, to turn around to see if he's okay, but I think I'm in shock.

"Presley," Kent cries, his voice shaky as he crawls to my side. "Baby, I'm sorry. I'm so, so sorry. I didn't mean it. I didn't mean to hurt you."

His hand lands on my head, and I flinch, scooting away from him, sitting up against the wall in the main room, tucking my legs back into my chest, and wrapping my arms protectively around myself. Burying my face in my knees, I cry. Huge wracking sobs rip from my chest as if they've come straight from my soul. The pain spearing me on the inside reminds me of the pain I felt the day I lost my Tillie.

"Presley, baby, please don't cry. Please, baby, I'm begging you. Don't cry. I will fix this. I will make it right. Just tell me what to do, Pres. Please, baby. Look at me," Kent pleads.

This time, when he touches me, his hand softly brushing against my leg, I don't flinch. I lift my head, staring at the man I love—this broken, tormented stranger—through blurry eyes, wondering how the hell we ever could come back from this. "You could have killed me," I whisper between sobs. "I couldn't breathe, Kent. You weren't stopping."

Tears pour down his face. "It wasn't me, and it wasn't you. I was lost to the rage, and I didn't know what I was doing." His chest heaves, and he wraps his arms around his body as he rocks back and forth. "I would never hurt you, Presley. I love you. You're the only good thing in my life. Please don't leave me, baby. Please don't leave me. I didn't know it was you. It was him. It was him I was killing. It was him. It's always *him*."

He stops rocking and jumps to his feet. Grabbing a vase from the coffee table, he throws it down on the ground, roaring and shouting. It smashes into pieces, and I stop crying, watching in horror as Kent slams his head into the wall, repeatedly hitting his forehead, while he cries and screams.

Finding strength from somewhere, I get to my feet and go to him, wrapping my arms around him from behind. He stops hurting himself, but he doesn't move, resting his forehead against the wall while I cling to his back and cry. His hand threads through mine over his stomach, and the only sound in the room is his strangled breathing and my cries.

Sometime later, I let him lead me to bed. He tucks me in, pressing a kiss to my cheek. His red-rimmed eyes are full of remorse when his gaze dips to my neck, and I'm guessing bruises are already forming. "For as long as I live, I will never forgive myself for this," he says in a hoarse voice. "I'm so very sorry, Presley."

I'm exhausted. It's been a draining day, and even if I wasn't exhausted, I still wouldn't know what to say.

He pulls a blanket off the chair and grabs one of the pillows. "I'll sleep on the couch."

I say nothing. I just close my eyes and wait for sleep to claim me. Maybe when I wake up, I'll have some clue what to do.

His lips brush against my temple. "I love you, Pres. I know it probably doesn't seem like that now, but it's true. It's the only truth I fully believe in right now."

I keep my eyes closed and my lips sealed, and he leaves the room just as darkness welcomes me.

I wake to the smell of minty freshness, blinking my eyes open in the dark room. A hint of buttery sunshine creeps through a tiny gap in the curtains, casting scant light in the room, but it's enough to see. Kent is sitting in the chair by the bed in nothing but sweatpants, staring at me as he holds a mug, little mists of steam cresting at the top of the drink.

"What time is it?" I ask, cringing at how rough my voice sounds. I pull myself up in the bed, resting my tired body against the headrest.

Kent closes his eyes, and his fingers grip the mug tight. "It's after twelve," he admits. "We both slept late." His eyes open again, and he stares at me with a host of conflicting emotions. "Here." He thrusts his arm out, offering me the mug. "I made you peppermint tea."

Our fingers brush in the exchange, and his touch sends the usual fiery tingles shooting up my arm. My lower lip wobbles, and tears immediately pool in my eyes.

"Presley, I'm so sorry," he chokes out, resting his head in his hands. "I know I've fucked everything up. I knew I would because that's what I do."

I sip my tea, as emotions and thoughts crowd my mind, so many conflicting sentiments confusing me. "What happened to you, Kent?" I ask, ignoring my scratchy throat, because I need to understand this if I'm to find some way of forgiving him for last night.

I believe he didn't deliberately hurt me.

I know that.

I know *him*.

He wouldn't consciously hurt me.

He was drunk and high, and it was already an emotional day, and me touching his ass triggered him.

Since Keaton and I spoke a few weeks ago, I have been compiling theories, and I think I know what it is. But I need Kent to tell me. There is no way we can survive last night if he doesn't give me *something*. I need to understand what drove the man I love to strangle me. "Who hurt you? Was it a man?" I ask.

"Don't, Pres. Please don't." Tears roll down his cheeks, and deep-seated pain is etched upon his face.

I climb out of bed and kneel between his legs, taking his hands in mine. He holds on to me tight as he cries, and my heart breaks all over again. Stretching up, I hug him, and he falls into me, his arms going around me as he sobs. I cry too, and even though I have no details, I know some man hurt him. He was either assaulted or raped, and I am not giving up on him until I find out what happened and help him get the support he needs.

He clings to me as he cries, and his pain is visceral. It infiltrates the air, swirling around us, locking us in an anguished cage where all hope seems gone and there is only suffering. I close my eyes as I squeeze him tight, pouring my love into him, hoping he can feel it.

Gradually, his sobs die out, but we stay locked in our embrace, just holding one another, both lost, both in pain, both clueless as to how we go on from here, where we go from here.

He moves his mouth to my ear, and his rapid breaths tickle my eardrum. "Yes," he whispers, and something inherent dies inside me at his admission.

Gently, I ease back just enough so I can see his face. "Look at me," I whisper, keeping one hand behind his back while my other hand tilts his face up. His eyes are bloodshot and red-rimmed, he has a lump on his forehead, and his skin is torn and grazed where he hit his head on the wall. I imagine I look equally ghastly. "Can you tell me when it happened? Who it was?"

His Adam's apple jumps in his throat, and he slowly shakes his head. "I want to," he croaks. "And I will, but I can't right now." He bites on his lip as his eyes fill up again. "You are the first person I have ever admitted that to," he adds, and that admission saddens me as much as it reassures me. If he can talk to me, even if it is in stages, it means he's ready to deal with what happened to him, and that is a big step forward.

"It's okay." I smooth my hand over his hair. "You've taken this first step, and that's huge."

"I'm so ashamed," he whispers, averting his eyes, and pain mingles with rage inside me.

I am going to annihilate whoever hurt him. I don't know how, but

I will find a way to get justice for my love. "You have nothing to be ashamed of, Kent. If someone hurt you, that is not your fault."

"I hurt *you*, Pres, because I thought you were *him*. That's what I saw in my head. How does that make me any better?" His fingers brush lightly against my neck. "You have finger-sized bruising all over your neck, and your voice is hoarse. I'm a disgusting piece of shit who doesn't deserve your compassion." He tries to remove my hands from his body, but I hold tight, not letting him push me away.

"It's not the same, Kent. You weren't present when you were hurting me. I don't need details to know that, and we'll get through this, but you've got to get help. If you love me, love *yourself*, you will get professional help."

He nods. "I've been thinking of doing it for weeks, and I'll do it. I swear. I never want to hurt you again."

A cell vibrates, and I glance over my shoulder, realizing Kent left my phone by the bed for me, along with a glass of water and some painkillers. I ignore the incessant vibrating, refocusing on Kent. "We can't go to the barbecue looking like this."

Today is another family event. The plan was to meet at noon outside the front of the castle, to say goodbye to most of the guests, and then convene by the pool with the kids for the afternoon before enjoying an early evening feast. We aren't due to leave until tomorrow morning, but there is no way I can sit by a pool in a bikini wearing a scarf without drawing attention to my neck. *And how would we explain the injuries to Kent's forehead?*

My cell chimes again as Kent says, "I know." He looks over at my ringing phone. "Maybe you should get that."

I stand, plucking my cell up to see who is calling me. I have one missed call from Ford and one from Mo. I toss it down on the bed. "It's work. Not important."

Sitting on the edge of the bed, I pat the space beside me for Kent as I drink some more of my tea. It's only lukewarm now, but it's still soothing on my raw throat.

Kent sits beside me, knotting and unknotting his hands. "I won't blame you if you walk away, Presley. It's what you should do."

I press a kiss to his cheek. "I'm not walking away, Kent." I scowl at my cell as it vibrates again. "But only if you promise to get help, to get clean, and you follow through. If you don't, I *will* leave you."

"I promise," he says, peering deep into my eyes. "I can't lose you over this because then it's something else that's been taken from me."

A thousand tiny pinpricks stab me through the heart, decimating the organ in my chest. I snatch my cell up, answering Ford's call, because it's clear they won't stop calling until I pick up. "This had better be good."

"I'm sorry to disturb you, but we thought you'd want to know."

Alarm bells ring in my ears, and all the tiny hairs lift on the back of my neck as an ominous sense of dread washes over me. "What is it?"

"Mikey was in here a short while ago looking for you. It's Chris. He says he's at the drug house and he's not in good shape."

"Fuck." I close my eyes. I do not need this today, but at least it gives us a viable reason for leaving early. "I'll call Clay, and we'll leave immediately."

I haven't heard from Clay in weeks, which is strange since he usually calls at least every couple weeks even when away on business. If I reach him, he's unlikely to help anyway. He is probably still in New York, and I can't see him going out of his way to come back to help Chris. They fell out years ago, and they don't have any contact except through me.

It's not like this is the first time I've had to drag Chris's ass out of the drug house, but it's a cesspit for hardcore junkies, and I can't just ignore the intel. The last time Chris overdosed was in that place.

Ford hangs up, and I explain the situation to Kent. He stands, shaking his shoulders out, the tension easing a bit from his face. "I'll make excuses with my family while you pack our shit. Then we'll hit the road."

Chapter Thirty
Kent

We are quiet as Presley drives us back to Boston. She insisted on driving, and I didn't raise any argument. She pointed out she was largely sober yesterday and I was trashed, before ripping into me. I let her vent, accepting everything she threw at me. She is right to be pissed, and I didn't even attempt to defend myself. I hate I broke my promise to her, and I hate I've disappointed her, so I didn't argue, willingly handing her the car keys. I won't deliberately do anything to jeopardize her safety or try to justify my actions when there is nothing I can say that excuses my behavior.

Pressing my head to the side of the window, I close my eyes, trying to ignore the sick feeling in the pit of my stomach. My chest tightens with a fresh wave of pain as I remember how close I came to strangling the woman I love. Tears stab the backs of my eyes, and I couldn't hate myself any more than I do. That Presley hasn't dumped my weak ass is a fucking miracle. I have never been worthy of her, and it has never been so obviously true.

"Goddamn it." Presley sighs, and I open my eyes and straighten up.

"What's wrong?" Besides the obvious—like your boyfriend is a worthless piece of shit and your worthless piece-of-shit ex is now encroaching on your headspace too.

"I can't get a hold of Clay. I've called him several times, and I must've left at least ten messages."

"We're only an hour out now anyway," I remind her. "And I'm sure he'll call you back when he can." She hasn't spoken much to me about her foster brother except to say he saved her from a nightmare situation as a child and he protected her growing up. I got the sense they were close, but that doesn't really seem to be the case. In all the time we have been together, she hasn't talked with him or met him in person. Not for the first time, I wonder if Presley has a romantic rosy memory of the past that isn't quite true. Not that I'm criticizing or faulting her for wanting to cling to happy memories, but I know how easy it is to hide the truth behind lies. Especially to yourself.

"He probably wouldn't help anyway." Her heavy exhale is laced with resignation.

"Why don't they get along anymore?" I ask, wanting to talk about anything so I don't remember what a shitty, pathetic excuse of a man I am.

"I don't really know. Both of them clammed up anytime I broached the subject, so I let it go. But it happened after I lost Tillie, and I think Clay blames Chris."

If he's as protective as Presley says he is, that makes sense. I rub at the throbbing pain in my head, wishing I had painkillers. I only had two, and I gave those to Presley before we left because she deserved them more than me.

"How bad is this likely to be?" I ask, imagining the type of drug house Chris visits being completely different from the ones I've visited in the past.

She takes her eyes off the road for a second, eyeballing me. "Bad." She worries her lower lip between her teeth. "The last time he OD'd, it was here."

Fuck. I sit up straighter, determined to get my shit together so I can support my woman. "Should we call nine-one-one?" I'm wondering why she didn't do that already.

She shakes her head. "They won't go there unless someone is there to meet them. The place is a big, old disused hospital, set across several interconnected buildings, and it's not easy to find someone who doesn't want to be found."

Nausea churns in my gut as I ponder what lies in store. I know it's not going to be pretty. Maybe seeing this will be another wake-up call. I meant what I said to Presley earlier. I *am* going to seek help because I can't lose her, and I know if I don't fix myself she will leave me, and then I have nothing left to live for.

"Jesus Christ," I murmur, gripping Presley's hand tight as we step over prone bodies on the floor, making our way into the decrepit main building. The old hospital has clearly been shut down for years. It's on the outskirts of Mattapan, near the Milton border. It's set across four different-sized structures, some in better shape than others. Ivy creeps up the sides of the red-bricked buildings, most of the windows are cracked and boarded up, and parts of the roofs are missing in places. The old parking garage is cracked and broken, and debris litters the asphalt.

Inside is worse. Although it's bright outside, you can't tell in here. It's pitch-black with the exception of faint lights that flicker from makeshift fires some of the residents have erected in old trash cans and large steel cans. I purposely scrunch my nose up, blocking my nostrils, to ward off the noxious smells so I don't lose the contents of my stomach.

It pains me that Presley knows her way around this place. She avoids making eye contact with the people we pass as we stride through the main section, heading toward a hallway at the very back, and I follow her lead, keeping my head down while subtly staying aware of my surroundings. Some people are huddled together in small groups while most are alone, passed out on the cold floor unless they are lucky enough to occupy one of the sparse, filthy mattresses. Evidence of drug use litters the floor amid rusted food cans and the occasional food wrapper and empty bottle.

"Don't draw their attention," Presley whispers, dragging me down the hallway. "Don't assume they are all strung-out junkies. Most of these addicts would gut you in a heartbeat if they thought you had drugs or money. We need to find Chris and get the fuck out of here ASAP."

"Okay." There's no way I'm arguing with her. I've never seen anything like this, and it's the wake-up call I need.

I never want this to be me.

I've got to clean all the junk from my system and stop relying on drugs to get me through the hard parts of my life.

Following her up a set of stairs to the next level, I vault over the broken steps when she points them out. The second level is different from the ground level. Up here, there are several smaller rooms, some with doors, most without, and I ignore looking at the people inside as I clutch Presley's hand.

The gun in my back pocket gives me some peace of mind. She doesn't know I have it because I store it in the trunk of my car, and I retrieved it without her noticing. There was no way I was coming into a place like this without some way to protect me and my girl.

After today, hell will freeze over before I let Presley return to this place. She can fight me all she wants, but she is not stepping foot in this hellhole ever again. I will fucking chain her to my bed if I have to. This place isn't safe, and I want to kick Chris's ass for putting her in danger.

Presley slams to a halt in front of the door at the end of the hall-way, turning around and flinging herself into my arms. I hold her trembling body, realizing now how much of a front she's been putting on. "I'm scared, Kent. What if we're too late?"

"I'm here for you," I say, pressing a fierce kiss to her brow. "You're not doing this alone anymore."

She eases back, staring up at me. "Thank you for being here."

I hate that she's thanking my pitiful ass, but I don't call her out on it. This is for her. It's not about me. "Let's get this over and done with." I link our hands while my free hand goes to my back pocket, ready to grab my gun should I need it.

Presley looks petrified as we step foot in the room. It's much smaller than the big room downstairs but larger than the individual rooms we passed. I gag at the smell of sweat, piss, shit, and vomit, silently urging my stomach not to rebel. I was already feeling nauseated before stepping foot inside this building.

There are other smells too. A clinical chemical type smell along with a familiar vinegary, acidic smell and the scent of burning plastic. There are about twenty people in this room. All of them on dirty, lumpy mattresses. Some are passed out, needles still in their arms, while others are semi-conscious, half sitting and half lying. They stare vacantly at us as we pass, and their ghastly faces and haunted eyes burn holes in my skull. An icy shiver crawls up my spine, and acid churns in my gut.

This place gives me the creeps, and I want to get my woman out of here stat.

Presley has to lean down to see their faces in the darkened room, and I hate it. I keep one hand in hers and the other on my gun as she makes her way through the room.

"No!" Her shrill cry rings out in the quiet room a few moments later. I keep pace with her as she runs to the corner of the room, making a beeline for the man slumped on his side with a needle poking from a vein in his arm. "Oh my God, Chris!" Her panicked cries bounce off the walls, but no one else seems to register them.

"I'm calling an ambulance." I extract my cell as she kneels on the floor in front of the mattress where her ex is lying immobile. She moves to take the needle from his arm, and I reach for her. "Should you be touching that?" This place has got to be germ infested, and we don't have gloves. Besides, the vial is empty. Whatever he shot into his veins is already in his system.

"Chris." Leaving the needle in his arm, she grabs hold of his face. I watch her as I talk to the operator, giving our location and explaining the circumstances. Presley turns on the flashlight on her phone, propping it against the side of the mattress. The light illuminates Chris's pale features. His dark hair makes his skin seem even whiter, and his lips are cracked and devoid of color, his green eyes vacant as he stares off into space. He hasn't moved since we approached, and Presley's fingers are trembling as she presses them to his neck. "Chris, no!"

I end the call as she looks up at me with anguished eyes. "I can't find a pulse," she whispers with tears streaming down her face.

"Let me try." She scoots back, as if in a daze, watching numbly as I check for a pulse at his wrist and his neck, not finding one either. Although it's probably futile, I push Chris onto his back, rip his shirt open, and begin compressions, pushing up and down on his chest with my hands.

Presley doesn't move, doesn't make a sound, just sitting there, watching as silent tears course down her cheeks.

I'm just about to give up when a strangled sound emerges from his throat and his eyes blink.

"Chris!" Presley shrieks, crawling forward and hovering over his face. "Oh my God," she sobs, crying into his shoulder. "You died!"

I'm still looming over him, and his eyes flit to mine. His pupils enlarge, and his body shakes and jerks, his limbs thrashing about. Presley lifts her head, terror etched upon her face.

"You," he croaks, staring at me. "No." He turns his head to Presley, opening his mouth to say something, but no words come out. He makes a last gasp for air, and then all the light extinguishes in his eyes.

Chapter Thirty-One
Kent

"How is she?" Mom asks when we are back in our apartment after the funeral.

"Not good," I truthfully admit. "But I'm taking care of her." It's been ten days since Chris died right in front of us, and Presley has withdrawn into herself. I'm beside myself with worry, doing everything I can to help while not knowing if it's truly helping at all.

She pats my arm. "If you need me to do anything, you only have to ask."

"You've already helped so much." Mom helped me to organize the funeral after the morgue released his body. We chose to wait a while before having the service to put some distance between the wedding and the funeral and to give Presley the opportunity to grieve in private and some time to try to track Clay down.

Mom has given Presley more commissions to work on because creating art is the only thing keeping her sane right now. I like to think my arms around her at night are helping too, but she is so quiet, barely saying anything, that I can't tell. "Just keep the commissions coming because art seems to be her only salvation," I tell my mom.

My family has been great. I managed to get a few days off work, but I can't push it because I'm only an intern. I was prepared to say fuck it and let them fire me, but it's the one thing Presley was vocal about—that I go to work and not lose the internship I've worked hard for. I have spoken to Rafe, her boss at Ramshackle, and he was understanding and supportive. Ford has hired another waitress temporarily to help while Presley is on leave, and Rafe has told me she can take all the time she needs.

Mo and Ford have wanted to visit, but Presley hasn't wanted anyone but me. I've been keeping people away, which is hard when I have to go to work and leave her here alone. But she locks herself away in the studio, working on her commissions, sketching, and drawing, and she's begun working on a mural on one of the walls.

"Hang in there, darling." Mom kisses me on the cheek. "She's grieving the loss of her baby all over again, but she knows you are there for her. I'm proud of you, and Presley is lucky to have you."

She wouldn't be proud if she knew what I did to my girlfriend, but the bruises on Presley's neck have faded now, along with the cuts on my forehead, so none of my family is aware of what went down the night of the wedding.

I'm still so ashamed over my actions, and I've had renewed nightmares since it happened. I'm careful not to disturb Presley when I wake up shaking, soaked in sweat, feeling like my heart is trying to beat a path out of my chest. The doctor prescribed her some sleeping pills, and she conks out most nights. I'm glad because she doesn't need to deal with my shit on top of everything else right now.

My family knows who Chris is to Presley and that they lost a child because she gave me permission to tell them. Keeping my brothers, sisters-in-law, and my parents away since this all went down has been challenging because they want to help. Austen and Keats are still on their honeymoon, and Presley made them promise not to return early. Thankfully, they abided by her wishes, staying in Italy and sending flowers instead. Cheryl has been dropping off home-cooked meals some evenings while my other brothers have been sending food and care packages along with flowers because everyone knows how much Presley loves flowers.

Everyone attended the service today, and I'm so fucking grateful for my family and Presley's friends. Clay was a no-show, along with Gerald and Anna Cates—the foster parents Chris, Clay, and Presley grew up with—and I know that upset and angered Presley. She anticipated the Cateses' indifference, but she expected Clay to show up for her. He hasn't returned any of her calls, and it's as if he has just dropped off the face of the earth. I'm pissed at him for letting her down. She needed her brother, and he wasn't here for her. If I ever meet him, I will rip him a new one for disappointing the love of my life.

Presley says goodbye to everyone before heading upstairs to take a shower. I reassure my family she will be fine, showing them out before cleaning up the kitchen and loading the dishwasher.

"I'm worried about her," Imogen says after Kady has gone downstairs to the car with Ford and his girlfriend, Michelle. They stayed to help with the cleanup.

"I am too. I think she needs to speak to her therapist, but I don't want her going alone, and the only available appointments are during the day when I'm working."

"I can go with her," Imogen offers. "Just tell me when and where, and I'll be there."

"I'll mention it to her." I won't force Presley to do anything she doesn't want to, and it'd be super hypocritical of me considering I haven't done anything about finding a therapist for myself. I want to, but there hasn't been time. Presley remains my priority.

She squeezes my arm. "I'm happy to help anytime. Presley has been there for me, and we've been through a lot of shit together. I'm happy she has you, and you're being incredibly supportive, but don't forget I am here too. If you need me for anything, just call."

"I will. Thanks." I kiss her cheek and show her out, closing the door after her.

I go upstairs, expecting to find Presley in bed, but she's not in the bedroom, so she must be in her studio. The door was closed when I passed by, and I didn't think to check. Stripping out of my monkey suit, I throw some shorts and a training top on. I'll check on Presley before using my small home gym to alleviate some stress.

I knock on her studio door before opening it and poking my head in. "Hey."

"Hey." She turns to look at me, holding a paintbrush in one hand. She's wearing black yoga pants with one of my old Harvard T-shirts and no shoes on her bare feet. Her hair is in a messy bun on top of her head, and her face is clean of makeup.

She looks beautiful, and my arms ache to hold her.

Though we fall asleep wrapped around one another each night, we haven't been intimate since the wedding. I miss sex with her, but I can be patient forever if that's what she needs. I would never put my desires above her needs. However, I really miss feeling close to her, and it seems like with every passing day we grow more distant. The prospect of losing her looms larger, and I'm scared in a way I've never been scared before.

"Can I get you anything?" I ask, gingerly stepping into the room.

"I'm good." She graces me with a smile.

It's the first one I've had since everything went down, and I latch on to it like a dehydrated man who finds an oasis in the desert. I think she's relieved the funeral is behind us now. It's been a very stressful ten days.

"Thank you for the fridge, the coffee machine, and the kettle," she adds.

"No problem. I should've thought to add them in the first place." I come to a stop beside her, and my mouth trails the floor as I look at the stunning mural. "This is fucking incredible, Pres. I can't believe you are nearly finished already."

A huge tree dominates the mural. Its roots run deep, flowing the length of the wall at the bottom of the drawing. The tree's branches are wide and far-reaching, like spindly fingers extending toward the heavens. Delicate pink and white blossoms coat the branches and flutter softly to the ground. They look so lifelike my nostrils twitch as if I can smell the floral scent. The branches stretch to a cloud overhead where a little baby angel with fluffy wings rests on her stomach, her chubby fingers reaching out to catch the swirling flowers.

"Do you really like it?" she asks, tilting her head to the side.

"I wouldn't lie to you. It's amazing. You are so talented. It's nearly a shame to confine yourself to inking people when you're capable of doing all this." I wave my hand at the wall, admiring the attention to detail.

She shrugs, looking contemplative as she inspects her work with a critical eye.

"The baby angel is the same one as the one on your shoulder."

She smiles, nodding. "Yes, this one is Tillie too." She runs her fingers along the ink that stretches from her shoulder to the top of her chest, and the faraway look she has had in her eyes lately makes a reappearance. "Do you believe in an afterlife?" she asks after a few silent beats.

"I've never given it much thought," I truthfully admit. "I'm not overly religious, but I believe there is *something* after death."

"I'm not religious either. I stopped believing in God when he stole my parents from me. But I believe some higher power had a hand in creating us, and I have to believe there is a heaven or someplace our souls go to after we leave this mortal realm. I need to believe Tillie is in a good place and I have a chance to see her again one day." She swipes at the tears in her eyes, leaning into me as I wrap my arms around her. "Like I need to believe Chris is at peace now."

I nod, understanding it even though I've no personal experiences to relate to.

"Is it silly to believe he is up there now with our daughter and my parents and they are happy and content?" She looks up at me with hope in her big brown eyes.

"If it gives you comfort, then it's the furthest thing from silly. Billions of people around the world believe it happens like that. They can't all be wrong." The truth is, we will never know. I'm skeptical when it comes to God and religion. But if having certain beliefs gives you comfort and relief and helps you sleep easier at night, then fucking grab it and don't let anyone tell you differently because they don't know what is or isn't true either.

"Kent." Presley rolls over in the bed later that night, curling into my side.

I put my book down, giving her my undivided attention. "Yes, babe?"

She rests her soft hands on my chest. "Thank you for everything."

I sweep hair back off her face. "You don't have to thank me. I love you, and I'm here for you." I want to add always, but that's subjective. She could still kick my ass to the curb, and I wouldn't fight her because I deserve it. I can spend the rest of my life trying to make it up to her, and it still won't be enough. I know that.

"I know I've shut myself off, and I'm so grateful you let me be, but I'm going to try harder. I don't want to wallow in grief, not when I've been doing well finally confronting it. The best way I can honor Tillie and Chris is to live my best life." She chews on the corner of her mouth, her finger idly drawing circles on my chest. "Just be patient with me," she says, staring straight into my eyes. "Because I can't promise I won't have more bad days. But I'm ready to live again."

I kiss her lips. "I can be patient for as long as you need me to be, and there is no rush. Rafe said you can take as much time as you need. Why don't you wait until you've spoken with Jenna?" I relayed Imogen's message earlier, and she is attending an appointment with Presley on Wednesday morning.

She nods before propping up on one elbow, smiling at me with a certain glint in her eye. Her hair cascades over one shoulder with the motion, and she slides one leg over mine. My dick springs to life at that small touch because my body has missed the hell out of her. "I just need one other thing," she purrs, her voice dropping an octave. Her hand moves from my chest, down along my abs, and her fingers explore all the dips and curves of my stomach. My cock is a solid block of wood behind my sleep pants now, and there's no way she's not noticed because it's jutting up proud and tall, almost saluting her.

"Anything," I croak, trying to temper my excitement in case I'm reading the signals wrong.

Leaning down, she licks at the seam of my lips, and precum seeps from my erection. "Make love to me," she whispers before claiming my lips in a soft but passionate kiss.

My fingers wind through her hair until I reach the nape of her neck. Holding her in place, I return her kisses, exploring her mouth with my tongue in a slow, unhurried fashion. If she needs me to make love to her, I will show her I'm capable of slowing things down and worshiping her like the goddess she is.

We undress one another in between kisses, and our hands explore our bodies as if it's the first time we've done this. In a way, I suppose it is because I've never been this gentle with her. Rolling her onto her back, I hover over her as I adore every inch of her skin with my fingers, my lips, and my tongue. Nudging her thighs apart, I lick her slit in slow, tantalizing sweeps of my tongue, my fingers tenderly probing the heat between her legs while my thumb gently rubs that sensitive bundle of nerves. I keep my eyes on her face as I continue loving her, drowning in awe when she comes apart before me, her juices coating my fingers and my tongue.

She sits up, pulling me up to her so she can kiss me and taste herself on my lips. Then she rolls a condom over my straining cock while stroking every inch of my body in soft caresses that imprint on my heart.

We reposition ourselves so we're lying flat on the bed with her underneath me. We maintain eye contact as I push inside her at a leisurely pace, taking my time inching into her warmth. Our hands intertwine above her head as I start moving. I deliberately slow my thrusts, moving in and out of her with infinite care, in a way I have never experienced before.

I feel everything.

The worshipful way her tight walls hug my dick as I glide in and out of her body.

The warmth of her fingers pressed against mine.

The softness of her lips as our mouths fuse together while our bodies rock in perfect sync.

An outpouring of love so strong as we stare at one another like this is the only thing that matters. This intense connection that pumps blood through my veins keeps my heart beating and fills my soul with everything that is good and light.

"Kent," she whispers, tears filling her eyes.

"I know, baby." I lean down and kiss her, savoring every second of our joining, committing every moment of this to memory because I never want to forget what this feels like.

Forever.

"I love you," she says as tears spill out of her eyes.

"I love you too," I whisper, my vision turning blurry.

"God, this is everything," she whimpers as we continue gently thrusting against one another, content to wallow in these languid, heavenly sensations without frantically chasing that ultimate high.

"You're everything, Pres." I squeeze her fingers. "And things are going to be fine because you and I are meant to be together. We were meant to spend our lives together, and I am going to do everything to make sure that happens."

Chapter Thirty-Two
Presley

"**A**re you sure you're okay to come back so soon?" Ford asks me on Thursday when I show up at five for my shift.

I dart forward, kissing his cheek. "I'm good. Thank you for caring. It means a lot to me."

"You're my friend. Of course, I care."

"I'm lucky I have you and Mo and Kent and his family." I truly am because the people I've had to rely on in the past have been a small group. Now Chris is gone, and Clay is AWOL, and my anger has transformed to worry that something has happened to him. "Hey," I add before he leaves the bar. "Could you do me a favor? Could you ask around about Clay? I haven't heard from him in months, and I'm worried."

He rubs the back of his head, averting his eyes, and I stalk toward him, forcing his face to mine. "Out with it."

"I asked around after Chris, you know..."

I nod because it's still hard to say the word.

"I knew you'd need Clay. He's still on business in New York." A muscle clenches in his jaw.

"Your intel is legit?" He nods, and my anger returns full steam. "I am so freaking mad at him. I can't believe he hasn't called me back and that he didn't show up for Chris." It's unforgivable. I don't care they hadn't spoken in recent times. For years, it was just the three of us, and Chris deserved better.

"Word on the street is they are brokering this big alliance with some notorious New York gang and Clay is The Vipers' main negotiator. I'm sure he would've been here if he could."

I plant my hands on my hips, narrowing my eyes. "Is that what you really think?"

He sighs. "You know it's not. I just don't want to upset you."

"I appreciate the gesture, but I'm already pissed at him."

"I'm pissed on your behalf. He's the closest thing you have to a fucking brother, and he couldn't find five fucking minutes to call you? He's got to know how this would affect you. He'd better have a real good fucking explanation for abandoning you."

"Wow, that's a lot of fucks. You're really mad."

"I am. If anyone fucks with you, they have me to answer to."

I hug him, my heart bursting with love for my friend.

"Don't let Kennedy hear you say that," Mo teases, emerging from the staff room. We indulge in a quick hug. "He considers it his job now."

"I never thought I'd say this, but I like him," Ford says, smiling at me. "He really cares about you."

"He does, and I feel the same way about him," I admit.

"Then why won't you move in with him?" Mo asks. "Officially," she adds, using little air quotes. "I mean, you already have a key, and you practically live there most of the time, and his place is fucking huge and so beautiful. Girl, if it was me, I'd have been moved in the very next day."

"I have my reasons." Although, they seem less important now. I wanted to hold on to my apartment to assert my independence, but Mo is right. I stay with Kent most nights, and now that I've asked Rafe if I can cut my shifts in half, because I want to focus on growing my side business, it doesn't make sense to hold on to my place.

Plus, if I'm honest, my apartment reminds me too much of Chris, and he's gone now. It's time to leave the past in the past and move forward. Kent promised he would go to therapy and get clean, and I intend to follow up on that now. I know he pushed it aside to take care of me, but I need to nudge him in the right direction, and moving in should give him that extra incentive to confront his fears and deal with it.

I still don't have the facts, but I know enough to know this will not be easy for Kent. I want to be there, every step of the way, to support him and help him do this. I can't do that if I'm nearly an hour away.

"Earth to Presley baby," Mo says, clicking her fingers in my face. She's taken to calling me that lately, loving to tease me about my boyfriend.

"You're right." I grin at her, pulling my cell out of my purse. "I'm doing it. I'm going to officially move in."

Kent

Nerves fire at me as I stand outside Mrs. Douglas's brownstone, wondering if I should have found a therapist by myself. I asked Selena to meet me here at a time when her mom, Sandrine, wouldn't be at home because I need privacy for this conversation. I could've asked her to meet me at my apartment, but I didn't want to risk one of my brothers showing up. I'm nowhere near ready to explain things to my family. Besides, Sel had a meeting in the city today, so this location works better. Before I knock on the door, my cell vibrates with a new message. I open it up, and my smile grows wider as I read Presley's message.

"Good news?" Selena asks, and I almost drop my cell.

My heart careens around my chest in sudden panic. "Shit, Sel. You're like a freaking ghost. I never even heard you open the door."

She smiles, stepping aside to let me enter her family home.

"It's good to see you so happy," she says, closing the door behind me. "You deserve it so much."

"Presley just agreed to move in with me," I tell her, needing to share the good news with someone.

Little lines pucker her brow. "I thought she was already living with you?"

I follow her into the large living room, sinking onto one of the couches. "Mostly, but she still has stuff at her place, and she still stayed there some nights. Now, it's official, and she's agreed to fully move in. She's just given notice to her landlord."

Selena sits on the couch across from me, with only the coffee table separating us. A tray with a large glass jug, two glasses, some cookies, and fresh fruit rests atop the table. "That's great." Selena's genuine smile confirms what I already know. Keanu's wife is naturally sweet and compassionate, and it's the simple things that make her happy. Like her cranky-ass brother-in-law finding a strong, courageous, gorgeous woman to put up with said cranky ass. "I adore her, and she's perfect for you."

"She really likes you too." I love that Presley gets along with my family but especially Selena and Eva because they are both special to me.

"So, why did you want to meet?" she asks, getting straight to it.

My stomach dips to my feet as nerves flood my system again. Sitting up straighter, I wipe my clammy hands down the front of my pants. I came straight here from work, so I'm still in my suit.

Selena pours homemade lemonade into two glasses while she waits patiently for me to explain why I asked to meet her alone, in her mother's house, and not to breathe a word to anyone, especially not my brother—her husband. It's a tall order, because those two tell each other everything, but I think, instinctually, she knows I need this, and she didn't argue, readily agreeing to meet me.

"I want to speak to a therapist, and I thought you might be able to help me with that." Selena and Keanu are setting up a massive facility that provides a wide range of support services to victims of sexual abuse, and she has vast contacts in this area. I could've Googled it, but I would rather see someone who is personally recommended, and there is no one I trust more than Selena.

She nods, removing a card I hadn't noticed resting on the arm of the couch until now. She passes it to me. "Denise is my therapist. She's wonderful, and I think you will like her." I take the card, looking down at the words. "She doesn't have a conventional setup, which was important for my recovery, and I get a sense it will be important for yours too."

Everything locks up inside me, and my hand shakes. I gulp over the lump in my throat as I lift my head, looking at Selena, seeing nothing but compassion and understanding. "You know?" I croak, fighting the panic swirling inside me.

"I've suspected." She gets up, coming over to sit beside me. She peers deep into my eyes as she takes my hand in hers. "I see the signs because of what I've lived through. I thought, several times, of asking you outright, but I know better than anyone that you can't force someone to confront things until they are ready. I will never ask you to tell me anything, Kent, but I want you to know I am here if you ever need me to listen. If I can help in any way, you only have to ask." Tears cling to her lashes. "I see your pain, and it reminds me of my own."

"Please tell me it gets easier," I whisper, clutching her soft hand.

"It does, but it never fully leaves you, Kent, and it takes a lot of hard work to come through to the other side. But you can compartmentalize it, and you have a solid foundation, a family who loves you, and I believe you are strong enough to deal with it and move forward with your life." She pauses for a second. "Does Presley know?"

"Not the details."

"To truly, fully confront your fears and move on, you need to tell those you love what happened. When the time is right and you feel strong enough to do it."

Panic jumps up and bites me on the ass. "My family can't know!"

It's one thing to consider telling the girl I love, but my family is way more complicated than that. If she has said anything to my brother, I will die. Pressure sits on my chest, constricting my air supply, and I tug at my tie, loosening my collar, struggling to draw enough air into my lungs.

"Kent." She palms one side of my face. "Breathe deeply." She breathes in and out with me, nice and slow, until I've regained my composure. "I haven't said one word to Keanu," she adds, knowing what I need to hear. "You know we don't keep secrets from one another, but I would never breach your trust with something like this. Anyway, up until now, I only had suspicions." She chews on the corner of her lip, looking unsure.

"What?"

"I think Keaton and Keanu have begun to suspect."

That shouldn't surprise me. "Keaton asked me outright a few weeks before the wedding, but I deflected. I should've known he would speak to Keanu about it."

"Keanu never mentioned it to me. I think he's concerned it will upset me, but I overheard them talking. I know how scary it is, Kent, and it's not for me to tell you what to do, but if you were to tell anyone in your family, it should be your triplets." A single tear seeps from the corner of her eye. "It's why you reacted so strongly to Keaton and Austen," she quietly says.

I nod. "I'm a shitty brother."

"No. It's not your fault, and you're taking the first step to make things right. I'm proud of you."

"You shouldn't be." I automatically think of what I did to Presley.

"I just have one more thing I'd like to say." She withdraws her hand, lifting my glass and giving it to me, urging me to drink. I guzzle the sweet, refreshing drink while she composes her words.

"It's wonderful you have Presley, and I'm sure she is more than willing to support you, but you've got to do the heavy lifting by yourself, Kent. I stood behind your brother for years, letting him shelter me, and it was only when I stood on my own two feet and took active steps in my recovery that I began to heal. I'm not saying that is what you are doing, or will do, but make sure you are not hiding behind her because it will only complicate things and delay your recovery. You have been on your own dealing with this, so I'm glad you have Presley now. You *will* need her, so don't push her away. Let her support you, but don't let her become your crutch or your enabler."

I'm sitting in my car at the curb outside Sandrine's townhouse ten minutes later, tossing the therapist's card back and forth between my fingers. Selena said Denise knows she might be receiving a call and I can call her anytime because she doesn't keep regular office hours. Selena's reassuring words and Presley's commitment have bolstered my courage, so I stop acting like a pussy and dial her number.

A few hours later, I'm walking toward Ramshackle with a massive bouquet of flowers in one hand and a palmful of hope in the other. I did it. I called Denise and made an appointment for tomorrow after work. I'm terrified. Like really fucking scared. But I also feel weirdly elated. It feels good to be taking back control of my life, and though I know I have tough times ahead, I feel ready to face the challenges head-on.

Bugger scoffs at me when I appear in the doorway, and I flip him the bird. The bar isn't that busy for a Thursday night, and I fight a smirk as I stroll across the room. Imogen said the female clientele has been disappearing in droves since word got out about Presley and I being together, and I wouldn't be me if I wasn't a tiny bit smug about that.

Presley is chatting to some dude at the bar, and she looks angry. She is the only one behind the counter because Ford's shift ended when hers started. Imogen is out on the floor, taking orders at one of the booths, so no one is watching the altercation between my girl and the mystery dude. I can only see his back since he's straining across the counter, waving his hands around as he appeals to her. He's tall and broad, wearing a black leather jacket with some snake emblem on the back. It's too dark to read the words, but it looks like a gang affiliation jacket.

Clayton.

He's in a gang and up to his neck in illegal activity, or so Presley has hinted at.

This must be her errant foster brother.

I enjoy a slight chuckle as I watch her spew venom from her mouth. She's giving him hell, and so she should. He let her down when she needed him, and that's not cool.

She hasn't noticed me yet, but the few females in the bar have. They stare at the flowers in my hand with a mixture of envy and derision. I have Presley's note tucked into the inside pocket of my suit jacket, and I've missed doing this. It didn't seem appropriate to continue showering her with flowers and notes while she was in mourning. But today is a day for celebration, and I'm not to be deterred.

I close the gap between us, keeping my eyes on Clay. He wears his dirty-blond hair in a messy man bun on top of his head—a look I always think looks ridiculous on any man. Prickles of apprehension sweep over me out of nowhere, and my heart accelerates for no reason. I move a little closer, and Presley's head jerks up when she hears my approach. Her face lights up, and it does funny things to my insides. Clay straightens, turning his head a little, and the prominent dragon tattoo on his neck is hard to miss.

An image flashes behind my eyes, and the smile drops off my face. *I've seen that tattoo before.* My pulse pounds in my neck, and blood rushes to my head. The flowers slip from my hands as he turns fully around and I come face to face with the man who has haunted my dreams and tormented my soul every day since the attack. Shock splays across his face as he stares at me. The flowers scatter across the floor, and water gushes all over the place. I'm vaguely aware of Presley calling my name. Rage pummels my insides from all angles. A red haze creeps over my eyes, and naked fury charges through my veins.

His throaty laugh reverberates in my brain, and the smell of stale cigarettes and sweat assaults my nostrils. My cheek burns, and my skin crawls like a thousand fire ants have burrowed their way inside me. Pain reverberates around my body, and I puke as blood leaks down my legs and tears pour from my eyes. Taunts surround me, and I double over as booted feet kick me on the ground.

I'm moving before I've even processed the motion, jumping over the counter and grabbing the bat I know Ford keeps back there. Clay snaps out of it, moving for his gun, but he's too slow and no match for the pent-up aggression I plan on unleashing on his ass. I swing the bat, my inner voice rejoicing when it slams into his skull with a loud thwack. The gun flies across the floor out of his reach, and he staggers back, clutching the side of his head.

Screaming surrounds me, but I switch off, cloaking myself in the darkness that reemerges from the black hole inside me, hopping back over the counter and swinging the bat again before he can retaliate.

I hit him repeatedly with the heavy wooden bat until he's down, flat on his back, blood covering his swollen face, his body incapable of fighting back. Then I jump on him, pounding my fists into his face and his upper body, letting vengeance have its moment because I have wished for this day for over eight years, and there is nothing or no one who can stop me from destroying this asshole. Because he did his best to destroy me, and payback is long overdue.

Chapter Thirty-Three
Presley

"Bugger," I yell, screaming at the bouncer. He's standing by the doorway watching my boyfriend beat the shit out of my foster brother, doing nothing to stop him. He jerks his head in my direction when I call him. "Do something!" I roar. I'm terrified Kent is going to kill him, but every attempt I've made to pull him off Clay hasn't worked.

Kent isn't present. He's locked in his head again, and my touch and my words are falling on deaf ears.

My head and my heart hurt. I'm confused and scared, and different theories are already floating through my mind. But the *why* will have to wait, because right now I need to ensure Clay isn't murdered in cold blood in front of an audience and that Kent doesn't spend the rest of his life behind bars.

I stomp toward Bugger, ready to grab the bat off the floor and beat him myself if he doesn't do something to stop this. Seeing the look on my face spurs him into action, and he grabs Kent by the shoulders, trying to pull him away. Kent resists, his torn fists still pummeling Clay's almost unrecognizable face, but Bugger is a fucking beast, and he yanks Kent back, holding him in a headlock, talking low in his ear.

"Call an ambulance," I tell Mo. She's standing by my side, her face frozen in terror. "Now, Mo!" Clay isn't moving, and I drop to my knees to check if he's still alive. My heart is racing, and adrenaline pumps through my veins, but my head is numb, and I'm just going through the motions, doing what needs to be done because focusing on practical stuff is the only way I can cope.

Pressing my fingers to Clay's neck, I'm relieved when I feel a pulse. It's not very strong, but he's still alive.

Bugger releases Kent, and I slowly climb to my feet, walking carefully toward my boyfriend. "Kent," I whisper, fighting a sudden onslaught of tears. "It's me." I hold my hands up when I see the wild, crazy look in his eyes. "It's okay. We're going to fix this." I take a step back so I'm not crowding him. His eyes narrow, and he stumbles a little, glaring at the motionless body of my foster brother on the floor. Then his gaze swings to mine, and he pins that dark, menacing glare on me. "Honey. It's me." I try to get through to him again, keeping my hands raised as errant tears flow down my face. For a few seconds, the rage drops off his face, replaced with the most tormented expression I've ever born witness to. His pain is visceral, and a sob rips from my throat.

I can't believe this is happening.

I want to be sick.

But I've got to be strong.

Confusion clouds my mind again, and a throbbing pain pierces my skull.

"Kent." I risk taking a step closer, and his eyes turn to anger again.

He staggers back a few steps. "Stay the fuck away from me, Pres."

His words baffle me, but I power on. "Let me help you."

His lips curl into a snarl. "I think you've done enough," he hisses.

What the hell does that mean?

Bugger sends him a pointed look, and Kent nods. My brows knit together as my gaze bounces between them. Kent sends one last daggered look in my direction before racing out the door.

"Kent!" I scream, running after him. "Stop."

A meaty arm pulls me back. "Let him go," Bugger whispers in my ear. "He needs to get out of here because it won't take long for word to reach The Vipers."

"Do you think I'm a fucking idiot?" I hiss, slamming my elbow back into his stomach. "Why the fuck do you think I want to go after him?" Bugger wheezes, but his hold on me doesn't falter. "Bugger, please," I plead, tears pouring down my face. "I love him! I need to go after him."

"You're going to get him killed. Probably yourself too, but it's your funeral." He lets me go, and I whirl around, glaring at him. "You and me are going to talk." I prod him in the chest before my gaze darts around the room. Most everyone has their phones out, recording. "Shut the doors, and no one leaves until we have their cell phones," I instruct.

"I'm on it," he says, and I run outside, pulling the inner door shut behind me. I sprint out onto the sidewalk in time to see Kent's SUV tearing off up the road, tires squealing as he floors it away. "Fuck." I grab fistfuls of my hair, ignoring the almost overwhelming urge to bang my head against the wall.

Fear threatens to suffocate me as I jog back inside. Mo is rounding up all the cell phones while old Tommy pats everyone down. Bugger watches the proceedings with sharp eyes, his gun out and pointed at the pissed-off patrons. Thank fuck it wasn't busy tonight.

"Listen up," I holler, addressing the customers. "You will get your phones back after we've wiped them."

"You have no fucking right," Cherie slurs, planting her hands on her hips as she glares at me.

"I have every fucking right," I bark, putting my face all up in the bottle-blonde's. "And you do not want to fuck with me right now."

Sirens blare in the distance, and I urge Mo to hurry up with my eyes. "No one speaks a word of what went down here tonight. Not to the medics, the cops, or The Vipers."

Most Mattapan residents distrust the cops, so I'm not worried about them ratting Kent out to the authorities. The Vipers are my main concern, and chances are someone has already tipped them off, but I've got to try to contain this; otherwise, Kent is a dead man walking. "I will have one thousand dollars in cash for each of you next week provided you don't speak." That gets their attention. To most folks, that's a lot of money. Including me, and even if I have to pay it out of my savings, I will do whatever is necessary to protect Kent because I know he didn't go psycho for no reason.

Bile swims up my throat as I glance to where Clay still lies unconscious on the ground. My heart is splintered, torn in two. There can be only one reason why Kent reacted like that, and I can't even let my mind go there. I can't believe the guy I've looked up to my whole life was involved in whatever happened to the man I love.

But it's the only explanation that makes sense.

Kent would have killed Clay if Bugger hadn't restrained him.

The rage I witnessed the night of the wedding, when I accidentally touched him where I shouldn't, pales in comparison to the rage I saw on his face tonight.

The events are connected.

They've got to be.

As much as I don't want to think it, it seems likely that Clay hurt Kent or he was there when someone else did. And if that's true, he's going to fucking pay for it.

There is a teeny tiny part of me clinging to the hope that he's pissed at Clay for some other reason. *I know Clay's been messed up in all kinds of stuff and he's far from innocent, but this?* I can't see him doing it. So, maybe Clay *was* there, and Kent recognized him and took his aggression out on the wrong person.

"How do we know you're good for it?" Cherie asks, yanking me out of my head.

I barely resist an eye roll. "You know who my boyfriend is. Of course, I'm good for it."

"I want five thousand." Cherie smirks. "Five K a head, and we'll keep our mouths shut."

I punch her in the nose, enjoying the sound of bone breaking. "Listen up, bitch. You will accept one thousand, or I'll hand your ass over to Kent's FBI-agent brother. Last I checked, prostitution was still illegal in Boston. And let's not mention your little drug side action."

She cries, holding her nose, as blood drips down her face. Bugger is restraining her, because she's primed to retaliate and just stupid enough to try it.

Ignoring Cherie, I level the rest of the customers with a deathly look. "I know all of you, and you all have your secrets. Unless you want me to talk with the FBI, you *will* accept my offer and shut your mouths." I cast one final glance at them as the sirens wail louder. "Are we clear?" I shout.

They nod, and I look to Bugger.

"We're good."

"Get out of here," I shout. "Now."

Bugger opens the door, and they flee literally two minutes before the EMTs arrive. The medics ask me a few questions, and I confirm Clay's identity, fudging the truth about what happened to him. I tell them it was a bar fight and he was hit with a bat and the other guy's fists, but that's as much as I'm telling them. They aren't cops, so they don't care.

"You need to leave," Bugger says as soon as the EMTs have removed Clay and put him in the ambulance. "I'm sure one of those bitches had already sent something to The Vipers. They'll be sniffing around here soon. I don't want you girls anywhere near here when they come around."

"I can't leave," I say, looking at the mess on the ground. "We need to get rid of the bat and clean the blood and trash the flowers."

"We'll handle it," Bugger says as Digger steps through the door, quickly followed by Ford and Rafe. My eyes pop wide. "I called them." Bugger answers my unspoken question.

"Go," Rafe repeats, urging me with his eyes.

"I'll get our bags." Mo runs behind the bar to the staff room.

"Why didn't you intervene?" I ask Bugger.

"Because Clay's had that coming for a long time," he says, folding his arms across his broad chest.

"You should have stopped him," Ford snaps, looking angry. "You've just put a target on Kent's back. Probably Presley's too."

"He had already hit him." Bugger shrugs like it's no big deal when we both know this is a shitstorm in the making. "Doesn't matter whether he got one hit or ten hits in. Clay would still want revenge."

"You can't come back here, Presley," Rafe says as Mo emerges from the back with our things.

"I'm sorry."

"This isn't your fault," Ford says, stepping in to hug me.

"And no apology is necessary," Rafe adds.

"Why would you help Kent?" I ask because Kent isn't from around here and he's caused untold issues for Rafe now.

"Because we love you and you love him," Ford says.

"And Clay isn't a good man, Presley." Compassion is etched across Rafe's face. "I know he protected you as a kid, but there is a lot you don't know about him."

I've already reached that same conclusion. "If you knew stuff about him, why didn't you tell me?"

"Because he would've killed us for telling you the truth," Rafe says, looking apologetic.

"You are close to meeting your goal, Pres," Ford adds. "We knew that would put distance between you, and we hoped eventually all contact would cease."

"What about now? Won't he come after you too?" I'm afraid for my friends.

"Don't worry about us. We have insurance," Bugger cryptically adds. "You need to cut all ties with Clay immediately. You saw how he turned on Chris. He will do the same to you now, Presley, because it will be clear your allegiance is with Kent."

"It's not that cut and dry," I mumble because my head is a mess.

"It's got to be." Rafe pulls me into a hug. "Don't think for one second that Clay can't or won't turn on you. Whatever you shared as kids will mean nothing to him compared with maintaining his rep and keeping his turf."

"Don't go back to your place tonight, Presley," Ford says. "Give me your keys, and we'll move your stuff out after we finish here. We'll bring it to Kent's apartment tomorrow."

I remove my house key from my keyring and hand it to him. "I don't care about the furniture, just my personal possessions and my pictures." I swallow over the lump in my throat. "What about Mo and Kady? Are they safe to stay at their place?"

"They will move in with me for the moment," Rafe supplies, staring at Mo, daring her to argue with a cutting look.

She blushes, and shock splays across my face. *No fucking way.* I know she has feelings for him, because she's told me, but something has obviously happened recently, and I'm a little hurt she didn't tell me. Then again, I've been avoiding people since Chris died, and we haven't shared more than a few words lately. I'm sure she was planning on updating me now I'm back to work, and it's not like I haven't got bigger problems to deal with. I know who my best friend is, and I can cut her some slack. Truth is, I'm glad she's got Rafe looking out for her and my goddaughter. I'd only worry myself sick if they were alone.

"Take the bare essentials and move yourself and Kady into my house tonight," Rafe says, still eyeballing her. He swings his gaze to me. "Can you drive them?"

I want to look for Kent, but I won't leave my friend in harm's way either. "Of course."

Rafe kisses Mo on the lips before Bugger escorts us outside. I walk on autopilot, my brain failing to process everything that has happened. It's like a living nightmare except I know there is no waking up from this. My new reality extends beyond the fact Clay isn't the person I thought he was. The consequences of Kent's actions will have far-reaching implications for all of us. Most urgent of all is the fact my boyfriend is out there somewhere, lost in a homicidal rage, while members of Clay's gang plot ways to exact a bloody revenge.

I toss the car keys to Mo. "You drive. I need to make some calls."

Chapter Thirty-Four
Presley

The doorbell chimes, and I race to the door, checking the peephole before I open it. What Rafe, Bugger, and Ford said back at Ramshackle has shaken me to my core, and I'm on edge. I step aside to let Kent's brothers enter his apartment.

"Have you heard from him?" Keanu asks, striding past me, heading toward the kitchen.

I shake my head. "I've been calling his phone continuously, but it's turned off." I'm not telling them anything new. I am sure the second I called Keanu to tell him what happened he called his brothers to let them know Kent was in trouble.

"Keven has tracked his location through his SUV," Kyler confirms. "But he has refused to give us the coordinates until he lands."

"Lands?" I inquire because I thought Austen and Keaton were the only two currently on a plane. It just so happens they are due back from their honeymoon in the morning.

"He was in Vegas on a case, but he's on his way back now," Kalvin explains, shutting the front door.

Knots twist in my gut. "He's been gone for hours, and the guys looking for him are dangerous as fuck. We can't wait." I pace the floor, wrapping my arms around myself as a full body shiver washes over me.

"A couple of Kev's colleagues are going to check out Kent's car. Kev won't let us go anywhere without him. Not after I told him the guy Kent almost killed is one of The Vipers."

"Not just *one* of The Vipers," I say. "He's their VP."

"This is real fucking bad." Keanu places a bottle of JD and four glasses down on the island.

"Tell us what you know," Kyler says, running his hands through his hair.

"Not much," I admit, accepting a glass from Keanu. "Kent came into the bar. He was happy until he got a look at Clay. Then he lost it. Grabbed the bat we keep behind the counter and beat him to a pulp. Our bouncer let him at it until I begged him to intervene. Bugger pulled him away, and then Kent took off before I could stop him."

"I take it this was Kent's first time meeting Clay?" Kalvin asks, and I nod. "Do you know why he reacted like that?"

I take a big mouthful of whiskey, enjoying the burn as it glides down my throat. "All I have are theories."

"Let's hear them," Kyler says, sipping his drink.

I don't like admitting any of this, especially when I have no facts, but this is a life-or-death situation and my boyfriend is out there in danger, so this isn't the time for holding anything back. "Something happened to Kent in the past. I don't know what," I add before they question me. "Just that it was something sexual."

The glass drops out of Kyler's hands, shattering to pieces on the floor. His tan face pales, and he looks like he's seen a ghost.

"What?" Kalvin splutters, a look of horror on his face.

Tears fill my eyes. "He has barely told me anything, but I know enough to understand it was bad. Really bad."

Tension seeps into the air.

"Keats and I had come to the same conclusion recently," Keanu admits, startling me. "Some things started adding up." He closes his eyes for a second, and when he reopens them, they are flooded with unshed tears. "When Selena heard what happened, she told me she met with Kent earlier today. He told her he wanted to see a therapist. They talked for a bit, and she put him in touch with her therapist, Denise. I got Sel to call her. Kent made an appointment for tomorrow."

A sob escapes my throat, and my chest heaves. "He promised me he was going to get help and get clean," I say, barely seeing his brothers through the glassy film covering my eyes. "It was the only way I could stay with him. I couldn't stand by and watch another man I love destroy himself through addiction."

"Did he tell Sel anything else?" Kyler asks, his voice choked.

"He didn't give her any details, but he confirmed it."

"Fuck." Kyler leans over the counter, burying his head in his hands.

Keanu picks up the broken glass, placing paper towels down over the wet patch on the floor. Pain stabs me in the heart like it does every time I think about Kent being hurt like that. Kalvin looks shell-shocked while Kyler keeps his head down, his shoulders heaving.

"Where is Kaden?" I ask, realizing he's missing.

Strain stretches across Keanu's face. "He thinks it's another one of Kent's cries for attention, and he's refused to get involved."

What a selfish prick. I've noticed Kent's older brother seems to have an issue with him. He never wastes an opportunity to put him in his place, and they don't seem close at all, which is weird since Kent is so close to Eva. "I can't imagine that went down well with Eva."

"Probably not," Kalvin admits, pulling himself up onto a stool at the island unit. He tops up our drinks, but I place my hand over my glass before he can pour more in mine.

"Someone needs to be sober to drive." Besides, my stomach is in knots and the previous mouthfuls of whiskey are sloshing uneasily around my tummy.

"We shouldn't drink anymore," Keanu agrees. "We don't know what we're dealing with here. We need to stay sharp."

"Well, I fucking need another one after that revelation," Kalvin says, knocking half his drink back. "Mom and Dad are going to be devastated." He hangs his head as Kyler lifts his up.

Kyler's eyes are red-rimmed and his cheeks damp. His Adam's apple jumps in his throat as he pins anguished eyes on Keanu. "I should have noticed. I should have realized."

Keanu places his hand on his brother's back. "Don't do this to yourself. You think I don't feel like I've failed him too? I'm his triplet. I've been closest to him these past few years, and I didn't know."

"You can't blame one another." I rub a hand across my chest as piercing pain rips through my heart. "We need to focus on finding him before something happens." Either Kent will get into bigger trouble, hurt himself, or The Vipers will get to him. None of those scenarios end well.

Kyler turns to face me. "Was it your foster brother? Is he the one responsible?" His nostrils flare, a muscle pops in his jaw, and his hands ball into fists at his sides.

Tears well in my eyes again. "I don't know, Kyler," I whisper. "All I know for sure is Kent has a serious issue with Clay."

"It's got to be connected." Kalvin drains the last dregs of his drink. "You don't almost beat a guy to death unless he has seriously wronged you."

"I wish he'd fucking murdered the bastard," Kyler hisses, and the skin on his knuckles blanches white he's clenching them so hard.

"Ky." Keanu jerks his head in my direction.

"I won't apologize for that," Kyler says, leveling me with a fierce look.

"I don't expect you to. If Clay hurt Kent, I'll end him myself."

Kyler opens his mouth to say something else, but he's cut off by the sound of the front door slamming. We turn around as one, watching Keven approach.

"Do you know where he is?" I ask, stepping toward him, pleading with my eyes.

He shakes his head, and my stomach plummets to my feet. "His car was abandoned a few miles from the bar. My colleagues are working off the assumption he called an Uber to take him someplace because they canvassed the local area and no one saw a thing."

"They wouldn't say even if they did," I explain. "They don't trust anyone in authority. The Vipers rule the streets, and everyone would be afraid to go up against them." I'm hoping the crowd from the bar is the exception, but there is no guarantee even with the financial incentive.

"Can't you hack into his phone?" Keanu asks.

"It needs to be powered on for me to do that," Keven confirms.

"Can't you use his phone to track his location?" Kyler adds.

"It seems it was dumped somewhere on the railway tracks at Mattapan Station. My colleagues are searching for it now." Keven stares at me. "I did some research on your foster brother and The Vipers on the plane, and I didn't like what I found. It seems Clay and his merry band of thugs were under investigation for a variety of criminal activities. I wasn't on that task force, but I've spoken to one of the lead investigators, and it's imperative we find Kent before they do. Do you have any idea where he could be?"

"I have wracked my brain to come up with options, but I don't know. We don't go out much, preferring to stay in, and apart from work, college, and the gym, I don't know where he hangs out."

"I spoke with his buddy Lance," Keanu says, leaning back against the counter. "And he had no ideas either. It's summer break, and most students have gone home."

"There is someone we could ask," I blurt, just thinking of Jet. "A guy who sold drugs in the neighborhood around the bar. I know Kent has bought stuff off him before." Kent was messed up when he left, and it wouldn't be unthinkable for him to turn to drugs or booze.

"Where can we find him?" Keven asks.

I rub my pounding temples. "I don't know. He wasn't on the street corner when we were leaving, and he's one of Clay's guys, so he's probably gone underground. I can ask my boss though. He might know."

Keven talks quietly with his brothers while I call Rafe. I hang up a few minutes later, frustrated and scared. The four Kennedy men look up at me. I shake my head. "It's a dead end. He doesn't know where he lives. He also said The Vipers haven't shown up at the bar, which is concerning. They've been expecting them."

"That usually means they've already gotten what intel they need," Keven says, scrubbing a hand over his prickly jawline.

"Damn it." I quickly explain about the customers who were filming, how we confiscated their cell phones, and the financial reward I offered.

Keven listens intently, showing no emotion on his face before pulling out his cell. He places a call. "You need to swing by Ramshackle and pick up a bunch of cell phones that were confiscated. We need to examine them to see if someone sent a recording or a message externally. That might be how we trace The Vipers."

"Shit." Kalvin rubs the back of his neck. "We've got to get those recordings. If it gets out, they'll arrest Kent. They won't need Clay's statement to press charges if they have video evidence."

We all know Clay won't press charges. That's not how he'll retaliate.

"I'll get that money tomorrow and give it to Ford," Keanu says, coming up behind me. He removes his hoodie, handing it to me. "You're shaking."

I didn't realize I was or how every bone in my body feels ice cold. I pull his hoodie on, tuning the others out as I try to think of where Kent might go.

All the blood drains from my face as a thought pops into my mind.

Keven ends his call, walking toward me. With a gentle touch, he clasps my face in his hands, forcing my terrified gaze to his. "What are you thinking?"

"The drug house," I whisper. Tears leak out of my eyes. "He was with me the day I found Chris. If he wanted to get high, I think he'd go there."

We don't know that he does. All of this is conjecture. But he was in a murderous rage, and if Clay is involved in his attack, it could've sent him spiraling. I saw the same thing happen to Chris enough times to guess Kent has probably sought solace in booze or drugs. He's smart, and he knows you don't take out a gang member without swift retaliation, so he wouldn't risk going to a bar. He'd want to go somewhere to lie low. The more I think about it, the more convinced I am that is where he is.

"We need to hurry." I grab Keven's arms. "We need to go now."

Chapter Thirty-Five
Presley

"Fucking hell, Presley. Why the fuck did you bring him here?" Kyler asks when we pull up in front of the old dilapidated hospital turned drug den. He stares at me with blatant disbelief.

"I wasn't thinking straight that day," I truthfully admit. "Then I figured maybe it might've done him some good. I think it did, because I don't think he's touched anything stronger than weed since we found Chris." I can't be one hundred percent sure though because I spent a lot of the days after Chris died in a numb haze.

"Don't take it out on Presley," Keanu says as a second blacked-out SUV pulls up alongside us. "Kent would not want that."

Kyler sighs. "I'm sorry." He squeezes my knee. "I'm just so worried."

"I know. I am too."

"I think you should stay in the car. Let me and my colleagues search the place," Keven says, twisting around from the driver's seat to stare at us.

"You'll need me to navigate that hellhole," I explain. "And don't even think about arguing with me. I know my way around, and I'm local. I'll help you get out of there alive."

Two car doors open beside us, and Kalvin presses his nose to the window. "Where is everyone else?" he asks, his brows scrunching.

"Sinead and Colin are doing me a favor," Keven says. "I'm trying to keep this on the down low to protect Kent."

"Fuck that shit, Keven!" Kyler explodes, and I jump a little. "His life is in danger! We need every available person looking for him before The fucking Vipers get to him."

For the first time ever, Keven looks ruffled. "Don't fucking tell me how to do my job, Ky!" he shouts. "If I make this official, Kent will be arrested. He almost beat a man to death."

"He's a fucking scumbag criminal!" Kyler shouts, and I flinch.

"If he gets a record, his law career is over before it has begun," Keven argues. "I'm trying to protect him *and* his future."

"We need to take that fucking scumbag down!" Kyler rants. "Send someone to the hospital to give him a lethal injection."

All three of his brothers stare at Kyler like he's lost his mind.

I can relate because I'm so confused.

It's not like I don't know who Clay is, but I've deliberately never pried into his gangland activities. I'm feeling pretty stupid and naïve right now.

Why didn't I ever question it?

Because I looked the other way, not wanting to lose Clay from my life. I still don't know what he's done, what he's involved in, whether he was personally involved in whatever has happened to Kent, or whether he really is a risk to my life, and I'm so conflicted.

Am I right to turn my back on him fully without knowing the facts?

I know Kent wouldn't attack him for no reason, and I'm giving my boyfriend the benefit of the doubt.

Perhaps the fact I didn't hesitate to take his side tells me everything I need to know.

I'm ashamed to admit that deep down I've known Clay isn't a

good man. I've chosen to deny that truth to keep him in my life, and I'm disgusted with myself. Everything I thought I knew has been turned upside down, and I still don't have the facts. I have a feeling once I do I'm going to feel even more sickened and ashamed.

The guys are still arguing, and I'm done. If Kent is in there, we need to get him the hell out now.

"Stop it!" I scream, and they instantly mute. "If your brother is in there, we need to get him out now, and we're going to need all the help we can get. I'm guessing you all have guns?" Kent thinks I didn't spot the gun he shoved in his back pocket the last time we were here, but there isn't much I miss. Truth is, I was glad he had a weapon. Only an idiot steps inside this shithole without a means to defend themselves. It's why I have my small handgun in my purse.

One by one, they remove their firearms, and I extract mine from my purse, curling my fingers around the weapon and dumping my purse on the floor. "Don't worry," I tell Keven as he opens his mouth to speak. "I have a license." I nudge Kalvin. "Let's go. There is no time to waste."

We all hop out, and Keven makes quick introductions. I nod at Sinead and Colin before I lead the way, stopping just outside the door. "Do not make eye contact with anyone, and keep your guns close, but out of sight. It doesn't take much to spook these people. I will lead with Keven. We are heading toward the second floor. One of The Vipers' dealers sells from one of the individual rooms upstairs, and if it's hardcore shit you're after, you end up in the room where Chris overdosed. If Kent is in here, he's in that room."

Knots twist and turn in my stomach, and acid crawls up my throat as I make my way inside. The big room is fully occupied tonight, and our entrance doesn't go unnoticed. All the tiny hairs lift on the back of my neck as we stride through the space, keeping our heads down and our wits about us. I feel eyeballs glued to my back as we cross the room, but I can't get distracted. I need to find Kent.

There is a collective sigh of relief when we step out into the dank hallway. "Kev," Sinead whispers. "I really think we should call this in."

"I agree," Colin whispers. "I don't like our chances of getting out of here alive. We need backup."

We come to a halt. "Okay." Keven exhales heavily. "I think you're right. I don't have a good feeling about this."

"I'll call it in," Sinead says, "but keep moving."

I caution them about the broken stairs, taking my time as we ascend to the next level, pointing out the places to avoid stepping. I'm panting by the time we reach the second-floor landing, but it's not because I'm out of breath. I'm fucking terrified of what we might find.

For the first time in years, I pray. I beg whoever is up there to let Kent not be in here or if he is to let him be alive because I will not survive if I lose him too.

Adrenaline courses through my veins as I advance along the hallway, avoiding looking too closely at the occupants in the single rooms as we pass by. My heart is careening around my chest, and blood rushes to my head, making me feel light-headed. I sway a little on my feet, and Keven holds onto my elbow, steadying me.

"You don't have to do this," he says in a low tone as we walk side by side. "You can stay outside."

"He's the love of my life," I say over a sob. "I'm not waiting out in the hallway when he might need me."

"He's going to be okay," he says, and I'm not sure if he's trying to convince himself or me.

"I feel sick," I admit. "I will die if he's hurt." I rub my eyes, quietly sobbing as tears flow down my face.

Fingers thread through mine. "We've got you, Presley," Keanu says, squeezing my hand.

Get a grip, Presley. It's not like Kent's brothers aren't scared shitless too. "I'm okay." I brush my tears away. "It's the room at the end," I add, walking toward it with renewed purpose.

It feels eerily like déjà vu as I step into the room that taunts me in my sleep. The room is pitch-dark, and visibility is poor. The same disgusting smells slap me in the face, and I work hard to avoid puking. Low moaning sends shivers creeping up my spine as Keven turns on a flashlight, aiming it in front of us. Most of the beds are occupied again.

"Jesus Christ," Kyler says from behind me. "This is like something from a horror movie."

"He's not here," Kalvin says. "There's no way he would come here."

We continue walking, and Keven swings the light around, flashing it in every face. Most everyone is comatose or too blissfully zoned out to do more than utter a few curses as we advance in the room.

"No!" Keanu cries, his voice sounding strangled. "No!" he shouts more loudly, racing around us to a mattress a few feet away. I run after him, dropping to my knees, sobbing when Keven shines the flashlight on Kent's unconscious body. His suit jacket and bloody shirt are discarded on the floor, but he's still in his suit pants and dress shoes. I clamp a shaky hand over my mouth, crying openly as my gaze drifts to the spoon and lighter on the edge of the mattress. His shredded knuckles rest listlessly on either side of his limp body, but it's the tie wrapped tightly around his arm and the empty needle protruding from his vein that are my undoing.

Keanu has his fingers pressed to Kent's neck, and he's crying. Kent's eyes are closed, and I pray he's only sleeping. Keven takes Kent's wrist, checking that pulse point. Kalvin and Kyler drop to their knees on the other side of the bed, clinging to one another. Kyler is silently crying. Kalvin looks dazed. I can't stop shaking as I notice how pale Kent's skin is, and the bluish tinge on his lips terrifies me. Kalvin wraps his arm around my shoulders, pulling me into his side.

"I've got a pulse," Keven says, his voice strained. "It's faint, but it's there."

"I just called for an ambulance. ETA is five minutes, and backup is just around the corner," Sinead confirms while Colin is giving directions to someone on his cell.

Kent's eyes blink open, and he gasps for air before his body starts thrashing about, his limbs flapping uncontrollably. Keanu hovers over him, calling out his name, while I hold onto Kalvin for dear life. I pray harder than I have prayed in years, begging someone to save him.

Vomit projects from his mouth as his body continues to jerk and spasm, and I can only stare horrified at the man I love, knowing he is leaving me.

The spasming stops. His eyes roll back in his head before closing, and the silence is suffocating.

Sinead pushes Keanu out of the way, clearing the vomit from Kent's mouth with gloved fingers, opening his airwaves.

"No! God, no," Keven cries, his body visibly trembling. His eyes dart wildly about. "I can't feel a pulse! I can't feel his pulse! He's got no pulse!"

His words spur me into action, and I push past a shell-shocked Kalvin and Kyler, nudging them out of the way as I lean over my boyfriend's lifeless body. Pressing my hands on Kent's cold chest, I start compressions while I pray and I beg and I make all kinds of promises to a God I stopped believing in a long time ago.

Chapter Thirty-Six
Kent

The steady beeping of the machine by my hospital bed wakes me sometime later. I groan as I come to, unsticking my tongue from the roof of my dry mouth. "Mom," I croak, swallowing over the pain in my throat as her worried face looms over mine.

"I'm here, sweetheart."

My head pounds, and I know my forehead is clammy without needing to touch it. She brushes damp strands of hair out of my eyes. "Water," I rasp as I attempt to sit up.

Dad moves to my other side, helping to prop me up against the headrest. My body feels like a deadweight in the bed, my limbs heavy and achy and my stomach is sore and uneasy.

"The nurse only left ice chips," Mom says, lifting a few to my mouth.

I open my cracked lips, letting her drop a few inside my mouth, while my gaze quickly roams the room. I'm relieved only my parents are in here, though I'm sure the others are in the private waiting room outside. Mom presses her lips to my cheek, lingering there, while Dad holds my hand, refusing to let go.

A tall, thin man with salt-and-pepper hair, wearing a white coat with a name tag, enters the room. "Ah, you're awake." The doctor smiles. "How do you feel?"

"Like shit," I truthfully admit.

Mom sits back down, holding my hand and moving her chair in even closer to my side.

"You are a very lucky man, Mr. Kennedy," he says, and I snort, sneering at him.

What a fucking tool. He knows nothing.

Ignoring my little outburst, the doctor continues. "You were clinically dead for a few minutes, but your girlfriend and one of the FBI agents took turns giving you CPR, and you regained a pulse just as the EMTs arrived at the scene. They injected you with Narcan to reverse the opioid, and it helped to stabilize your breathing and nervous system." He checks my vitals as he talks. "Ordinarily, we don't admit overdose patients, sending them home once the drugs are gone from their system, as long as we are happy there is no evidence of suicidal or homicidal tendencies. However, your parents demanded privacy, and as they are large benefactors of the hospital, we are always happy to accommodate the Kennedys."

My lips curl into a snarl. "Is that all?"

He purses his lips, ignoring me as he turns to my parents. "I see no reason why he can't be discharged in a couple of hours unless you want us to keep him here for further observation."

"We need to speak to our son," Mom says.

"I will update you in due course," Dad adds.

The man leaves the room, and tension descends. Withdrawing my hand from Mom's, I grab the cup with chips, tipping them into my mouth as I try to make sense of the last twenty-four hours. A tsunami of emotions swirls through my pounding skull, and anger competes with fear for the dominant position.

Mom clasps my face in her hands, pinning me with troubled blue eyes that are rapidly filling with tears. "Darling." She sniffs, trying to compose herself. "Why would you do this?" Her hands drop from my face, clasping my hand again. "We know what happened in the bar, but you know we would help you deal with the consequences. I can't believe you would try to take your own life!" She loses the battle, openly crying as tears stream down her face. Dad moves over to her side, wrapping his arms around her while I try to comprehend her words.

"I didn't try to kill myself," I truthfully reply. "I didn't do this."

Mom stops crying for a moment, and her eyes widen in horror. Shock splays across Dad's face

"Oh my God!" Mom starts crying again, even louder this time. Dad stands, striding to the door and stepping outside. He returns a few seconds later with Keven.

My brother looks like shit. There are dark shadows under his eyes, a heavier than usual layer of stubble on his chin and cheeks, and his clothes are disheveled, like he was sleeping in them. Most likely, he was because I've lost all concept of time, and I don't know if it's still nighttime or morning.

"Kent." Keven leans down, hugging me. His shoulders shake as he holds on to me, and I feel his body trembling. Tears prick my eyes. "We thought we lost you," he says, easing back. I'm shocked to see tears in his eyes. Keven is the steadfast one in the family. The one we call on when we are in trouble because he keeps a cool head at all times, and he usually keeps a lid on his emotions. To see him upset like this is disconcerting.

"You were there?" I don't remember anything after the heroin was injected into my arm.

He nods. "Keanu, Kyler, Kalvin, and me. Presley led us to you. We were almost too late."

I hang my head, ashamed they saw me like that. In that horrible place.

"It's okay." He sits on the seat Dad vacated, gripping my hand. "We're just glad you are all right. That's all that matters."

"I wasn't there by choice," I admit, and his head jerks up, his eyes widening in recognition.

"The fucking Vipers did that to you?"

Dad is consoling Mom over on the other side of the bed while I'm talking to my brother, and though she is quietly sobbing, I know they are listening to every word. "They ambushed me a few miles from the bar. Dragged me out of my car, took me to that hellhole, and shot that shit in my veins."

Mom cries harder.

"Did you see who did it to you?" Kev asks.

I grind my teeth to my molars, fisting my hands in the bed sheets. I tersely nod.

"Could you identify them from photos?"

I snort out a bitter laugh. I can identify them from more than just photos. "Yeah."

Kev gulps, glancing at our parents. "Why did you almost murder Clayton Cooper?"

Rage pummels my insides, and my nostrils flare. Pressure sits on my chest, and all the veins in my arms stretch tight. It all comes back to me in vivid detail. The attack. Clay arguing with Presley at the bar. The way he looked at me when he turned around. I squeeze my eyes shut, pulling my legs up under the covers, burying my head in my knees.

"Kent." Mom touches my back, and I flinch.

"Don't, Mom," I say through gritted teeth. I can scarcely see her through the rage coating my eyes. "Where's Presley?" I ask Keven, an edge to my scratchy voice.

"She's waiting outside. She wasn't sure if you'd want to see her or not."

I harrumph. Of course. "I want to talk to her. Alone."

Kev exchanges a wary look with my parents. It seems like they want to argue, but they don't. They leave, and a couple of minutes later, Presley steps into the room. She cautiously approaches the bed, staring at me with bloodshot eyes. Tears pour silently down her cheeks as she stands there, looking at me, clearly unsure what to say or do.

"Did you know?" I ask in a low tone.

She vehemently shakes her head. "No. I swear I didn't know. I still don't know."

I glare at her, and my chest heaves. "You knew he was up to all kinds of shit, but you turned a blind eye, right?"

She gulps, wrapping her arms around herself. "Yes, but I only thought it was guns and drugs and retaliating against their enemies. I didn't know..." She trails off, and her lower lip wobbles as fresh tears spill from her eyes.

"Didn't know what, Presley?!" I spit out, sitting up straighter, ignoring how my body aches all over. "That they abuse little boys? That your precious Clay, your fucking protector, took something from me he had no right to? Something that fucking destroyed me!"

"Oh God, Kent." She freely sobs. "I hoped it wasn't that. I—"

"You're still fucking blind to that pervert!" I yell.

She comes forward, dropping to her knees on the floor before me. "No, no, Kent. That's not it. I—"

I cut her off again. "He raped me!" I cry, swiping at the angry tears leaking from my eyes. "Him and his buddies."

Horror spreads across her face as she stares at me.

"I had only just turned fifteen when they cornered me in an alley one night." Pain slams into me on all sides. I continue swiping at tears, and yet they continue to fall. I don't look at her as I relive the worst night of my life. "I tried to fight them off, but they were grown men, and there were five of them and only one of me." I swallow over the burning lump in my throat, closing my eyes, and gripping the side of the bed as I dredge it all up. "Clay was the ringleader even though he seemed to be the youngest. They shoved me face-first into the wall, two guys always pinning me down, ensuring I couldn't fight back, while they took turns ramming their dicks in my ass."

Her cries echo off the walls, and I vaguely hear other sounds of sobbing, but I'm too lost in my head to care. After years of hiding the truth, burying all the pain and anger and fear, I need to get this out now. "Clay watched." I blink my eyes open, staring at Presley. "He stood off to the side, keeping his eyes locked on mine as his buddies destroyed me. I see his cocky grin and the evil glint in his eyes in my nightmares. His face has plagued me for years."

She reaches for my hand, but I pull back, her touch repugnant to me. My voice is devoid of emotion and my head numb as I say, "He raped me last, fucking my ass as blood ran down my legs."

She clamps a hand over her mouth, trying to contain her cries as her body shakes.

"But it wasn't enough. That bastard had to ensure he completely ruined me." I squeeze my eyes shut, and a full body shudder works its way through me. Sobs heave from my chest. "Your precious Clay is an animal," I spit, peering at her through blurry eyes. "A twisted, sick bastard." I clench my jaw painfully, anger replacing the numbed feeling.

"He jacked me off while he raped me. He *made* me come." Humiliation and pain thunder through me, like every time I remember it. "They all laughed. Taunting me over how much I loved it, pushing me to the ground and kicking me as they showed me the video they'd recorded on one of their cell phones, promising they'd stream it live if I breathed a word of it to anyone. Threatening to kill my family if I ever told them what happened to me."

"I'm sorry, Kent. I'm so sorry." She reaches for me again, and I yank my hand back.

"Don't touch me, Presley. I don't want you to touch me." I sniffle, brushing at the dampness on my cheeks. "His face used to be all I saw when I closed my eyes. Drugs, booze, and sex were my go-to distractions. The only way I could face getting up each day. Until you."

Even crying with flushed cheeks, red-rimmed sad eyes, and clear pain in her gaze, Presley is still the most beautiful woman I've ever seen. "You made it better," I whisper. "You calmed the storm in my chest. You gave me hope. I thought I could finally move forward."

The pressure sitting on my chest is so intense it feels like I'm having a coronary. "But you've ruined everything," I seethe. "You make me sick. You lived with that monster. You *loved* him. You refused to see what was right in front of your eyes. How many more boys were raped because you turned a blind eye, huh, Pres?"

"I didn't know, Kent!" she yells. "Clay saved me from Jeff Rinaldi. My foster dad was going to rape me, and Clay fought him off. He called social services and got us rehoused. I don't understand," she sobs. "Why would Clay do that and then hurt you?"

"I don't fucking care why!" I roar just as Kev barges into the room, followed by my parents, Kyler, and Keanu. They are all crying, and it's obvious they heard. My shouts must have brought them to the door. I'm too angry and too tired to care at this point. "You think I want to know what makes that bastard tick?" I shout at my girlfriend.

Kev lifts Presley off the floor, helping her to stand.

"The only thing I care about is murdering that fucking bastard!" I rage. Climbing off the bed, I grab one of the chairs and throw it across the room. Keanu moves toward me, but Kev shakes his head. Mom stands in the doorway, falling apart, only my dad's arms keeping her upright. Kyler looks shaken to his core, standing frozen still. "But I want payback first. I want to strip him bare, bend him over a table, and fuck him up the ass with a baseball bat, a knife, a broken bottle, the worst fucking things I can think of. I want to ruin him and cut him and make him bleed, and then I'm going to cut off his dick and let him choke on it and—"

"Kent. Enough!" Keanu cries. "Please, brother."

"You don't get to fucking tell me what to do!" I pick up a second chair, throwing it at the window. "None of you do!" I hiss at my family. "Where the fuck were all of you when I needed you?"

I glare at my dad. "You were too busy fucking your wife's psycho assistant." Mom cries uncontrollably, but I power on. Let them feel pain. It still won't come even close to what I've endured for years. "You were too busy fucking working all the damn time to care about your own kid." Jabbing my finger in the air, I point at Kyler. "You think what happened to you was bad? That's a fucking cakewalk compared to what happened to me!" I yell. I turn my rage on my triplet next. "And you cared more about Selena than you did about me. She was all you saw."

They don't attempt to argue with me, which is good because I'm not sure I won't swing for them if they dare defend themselves.

I swing my gaze on Presley. "And you!" Poison swirls through my veins, and I can't hear, can't feel anything but overwhelming rage. I can't think over the screaming in my head. "You disgust me. I can't look at you and not see him. Not see all the ways you failed me too. You should have seen. You could have stopped him."

"Kent, I'm so sorry. I didn't see, but if I had, I would have stopped him."

"Liar!" I hiss. "Get out. Get the fuck out, and stay out. I never want to see you again."

Chapter Thirty-Seven
Presley

"**P**resley. Sweetheart." Mo sits down on the side of the bed, gently touching her hand to my back. "Dinner is ready."

"I'm not hungry." I pull myself upright, forcing a smile.

"You have barely eaten anything these past few days. I'm worried."

"I'm okay," I lie, tucking knotted strands of hair back off my face.

"No, you're not, and I get it. You've had a lot of devastating blows all at once, but you can't stay locked in this bedroom forever."

"If I'm getting in the way, I can leave."

Rafe has been really kind letting me move in here, especially when I'm sure I'm getting in the way of his burgeoning relationship with my best friend. But I don't have anywhere else to go. Not since Kent kicked me out of his life and The Vipers blew up my old apartment. Thankfully, Ford and Rafe had moved all my personal possessions out the night before. The Vipers only targeted my apartment, which was empty at the time, so no one got hurt. My landlord is understandably pissed, but the insurance should pay out.

"You know that's not what I'm saying. This house is plenty big, and Rafe loves having you here."

I snort. "I'm sure that's not true."

"We love you." Mo cups my face. "And we want to keep you safe."

"That's why Rafe installed that new security system and why he's hired bodyguards for all of us?" I haven't even seen mine because I haven't left this house in a week. Not since I fled here the night Kent kicked me out of his hospital room. Kaden and Eva found me after I raced out of there, and they drove me here. Rafe and Mo welcomed me with no hesitation.

The property is in a nice part of Brookline, in a gated community, and very safe. Rafe's grandmother left the estate to him in her will, and he has spent years modernizing it. It's beautiful with six bedrooms, seven baths, an indoor pool, and gorgeous outdoor areas. I have no idea why Rafe holds on to Ramshackle when it's clear his other businesses are way more lucrative and he doesn't need the money or the hassle. Mo said he's considering selling it to Ford now Ford is engaged to Michelle and they are planning their future. I'm happy for my friends, even if my life is in the toilet.

"That wasn't Rafe," Mo admits, and I raise an eyebrow. "The Kennedys arranged the security measures. They're worried about you too."

"They're good people." This is the first occasion, where I've broken up with someone, when I've lost more than just the man. Kent's family welcomed me with open arms, and I'll miss them too. Selena and Keanu, and Austen and Keaton, have been checking in with me every day by phone. Eva came by a few days ago to tell me Kent is in rehab. He had a breakdown, but they managed to get him into rehab instead of a psychiatric facility, which would have caused problems for his law career.

She told me to hang in there, that she's sure he didn't mean the things he said. I nodded my head and smiled in all the right places, but the truth is, Kent is right. I shouldn't have flippantly ignored the things Clay was involved in.

I'm guilty by association.

I knew he was involved in bad shit, but I had no idea it extended to raping innocent boys. More fissures crack my heart as pain slams into me all over again. I don't know why I never saw that side to him. *Why did Clay protect me when he was out there hurting Kent? And how many others have there been?* I'm not naïve enough to think what happened to Kent was a one-off.

It sickens and upsets me every time I recall the things Kent said. I want to murder Clay with my bare hands for ever laying a finger on the man I love.

But I'd have to find him first, and he's in the wind.

Clay disappeared from the hospital in the early hours of the morning, and no one has seen him since. According to the news, warrants have been issued for several men known to be affiliated with The Vipers. Thankfully, I haven't seen anything that indicates Kent was arrested for the assault on Clay, but I've no idea what is going on behind the scenes.

A knock sounds on the door. "Presley," Rafe says through the wood.

"You can come in," I call out.

He opens the door and pokes his head inside. "Hey." His expression softens when he sees me. "I just wanted to let you know that Keven is here, if you feel up to talking with him."

I swing my legs out of the bed, hoping he has an update on Clay and The Vipers. I'm sure the Kennedys have Kent in some high-security facility, but I'm still worried about them going after him. By now, they would know their attempt to murder him failed.

"Tell him I'll be down in a few minutes," I say, heading toward my en suite bathroom to freshen up.

I grab a super quick shower because I'm pretty sure I smell. I twist my wet hair into a messy knot on top of my head before slipping on sweats and an old T-shirt. Sliding my feet into flip-flops, I head downstairs.

"Presley." Keven stands when I enter the smaller of the living rooms, walking toward me. He pulls me into a soft hug. "How are you?"

I shrug casually like my heart isn't broken in a million pieces and my life isn't crushingly empty without his brother in it. "I'm hanging in there." I traipse to the couch, sitting down on one end.

His eyes rake over me quickly, and he's no doubt noticing the bruising shadows under my lackluster eyes, my pale complexion, and how my clothes hang a little looser off my limbs. "I'm glad to hear it. You've been through a lot. We're worried about you."

"I'm okay. Mo and Rafe have been amazing, and your family has too. Tell your mom thanks for the care package. It was sweet and thoughtful." I pour lemonade from the glass jug on the coffee table into two glasses, handing one to him.

"You know you're not to blame, right?" he says, accepting the drink.

I shrug because I don't agree.

"Presley. Kent didn't mean those things. He's traumatized and lashing out at all of us."

"You don't have to explain, Keven. I'm traumatized remembering the things he said, so I can only imagine how difficult it's been for him, and he's had to live with this for years." A sob escapes my lips, and tears stab my eyes. I can't speak over the messy ball of emotion clogging my throat. The thought of what they did to Kent and what he's endured in the years since the attack is almost too much to bear. I never thought I could feel this much pain again, but the throbbing, aching torment slaying me on the inside is constant every time I think of what was done to Kent, and my heart bleeds endless rivers.

"I'm sorry. I didn't come here to upset you." Keven rubs the back of his neck.

I hurriedly compose myself because he doesn't need to worry about me when his focus should be his brother. "How have you been?" I ask. "It's been hard on everyone." Especially Keven, because on top of dealing with Kent's upsetting revelation, which I'm sure has sent his family into a tailspin, he's working around the clock with his FBI colleagues trying to build a case against Clay and The Vipers, as well as trying to locate them.

"We feel huge guilt," he admits, staring off into space as he sips his lemonade. "We always knew something was troubling Kent, but never in a million years did we imagine it was something like this. We all feel like we've failed him."

"Yeah. Me too."

He jerks his eyes to mine. "Presley, out of everyone, you were doing the most good. You were helping him to move forward. He was happier than we have seen him in years."

"Until my association with the monster who hurt him took all the good away." It's just another thing to hate Clay for. He has taken the only good thing I had in my life. Taken the love I shared with Kent and twisted it into something ugly.

Keven hangs his head because there is no refuting that truth. Even if Kent hadn't broken down and kicked me to the curb, the demise of our relationship was inevitable. *How can you ever come back from something like this?* I will always remind him of the man who hurt him, and he will forever remind me of my abject failings and my naivete in trusting a man who has no humanity.

I wonder if I have ever known Clay. *Was the boy I knew from my childhood a monster too, or did that side of him only emerge in adulthood?* It's this question, and others, that also keeps me awake at night. I need answers though I don't know if I will ever get them.

"You both need time to heal," Keven adds after a few heavy, silent beats.

"What was it you came to ask me?" I say because I can't talk about Kent and all I have lost anymore.

"My boss has set up a joint task force, and he finally relented and let me help. I'm on a tight leash so my involvement doesn't jeopardize my brother or the case. The team is building evidence against Clayton, and I'm hoping we can nail that bastard to the wall so no charges are brought against Kent."

"They're planning to charge Kent?" Disbelief threads through my tone. After everything The Vipers have done, you'd think they would let what Kent did go. The assholes tried to murder him, for fuck's sake, and they almost succeeded. I dig my nails into my thighs, shaking with anger.

"I hope it won't come to that, but he's not in the clear yet. I've explained the circumstances, and Sinead and Colin have backed me up. However, one of the women in the bar that night sent the recording to a known associate of The Vipers, so it's out there. We're trying to locate it so we can remove all trace of it. But if we can't—if it surfaces and the public finds out the FBI was aware of it and didn't take any action—it could jeopardize the entire case."

"They can't charge him, Keven. He wants to be a lawyer so bad." Now that I've had time to think about it, it's no wonder Kent wants to go into family law. He wants to protect other innocent kids and see justice served in a way he was denied.

"I'm determined to fix it, but it's a delicate balancing act. I'm also concerned about the recording The Vipers have of the assault. That needs to be found and contained."

"Surely, it would incriminate them if it came out? I thought that's why they hadn't released it."

"That could be the case, or it's insurance, and they were keeping it in reserve for the right moment."

I lean my head back, closing my eyes. "Fuck. This is like a never-ending nightmare." If that tape gets released into the public domain, I don't know if there will ever be a way for Kent to come back from it.

I will slaughter Clay and every member of that fucking gang if that tape ever surfaces.

I don't care if I have to gun them down in broad daylight.

I will gladly sacrifice my life to end theirs if they do that to Kent. *Hasn't he fucking suffered enough?*

Kev clears his throat. "It is, and what I have to tell you will only strengthen that sentiment."

Reinforcing the crumbling walls around my heart, I brace myself for whatever he's about to tell me. "Go on." I drain the rest of my lemonade, ignoring the biting pain tearing at my insides.

"How much do you remember about growing up in the Cateses' house?"

"Most everything because I lived there from the time I was ten until I aged out. Why?"

"We've been talking to some of the other foster boys who lived there at the same time Clayton lived there, and it has uncovered some new lines of inquiry."

Anxiety prickles at my skin. "Like what?"

"Did you ever think it strange that you were the only girl they fostered that entire time?"

"Strange? Not really. I do remember asking Anna if she could foster another girl so I could have a sister. She told me girls were too much trouble and they preferred less drama."

He clasps his hands in front of him, pinning me with somber eyes. "It appears there was a different, more sinister, reason why they always fostered boys."

I have an awful feeling I know where this is going. "Like what?"

"Gerald and Anna Cates were abusing the foster boys in their care. We've spoken to several men who have confirmed they were regularly sexually assaulted and raped."

"Oh my God!" I place a shaky hand over my mouth. "How did I not know this?"

"A couple of the men we spoke to remember you and Felicia, the girl who lived with them before you arrived. We've checked back through the fostering records, and the Cateses always had a little girl staying with them. Only one girl at a time. The men we talked to believe you were a decoy of sorts. They said you were treated well, and you always had new clothes and shoes, and they paid for lots of afterschool activities. Is that correct?"

I nod. A sick picture is forming in my mind. "The only time Anna would bake cakes was the day the social workers came to visit. I would help her in the kitchen, and she would let me ice the cupcakes myself. I always had to wear my prettiest dress, and she'd take time with my hair. She encouraged me to talk about my various activities. I did dance and art classes, and I played a variety of sports."

"They were putting on a show," Keven confirms.

"Why did none of the boys say anything?"

Shards of pain glimmer in his eyes. "Because they were ashamed. They felt less manly because of the abuse. Some of them were confused about their sexuality. They didn't just abuse them physically but mentally and emotionally too. And they were afraid of what would become of them. Unfortunately, stories like this are not uncommon in the foster system. There are a lot of good foster homes, a lot of compassionate foster parents, but there are a lot of bad ones too."

I blow air out of my mouth. "Kent is right. I've been so blind. How was this going on under the same roof and I didn't see anything?" I stab him with a piercing look. "I thought I was smarter than this. More observant." I bury my head in my hands, feeling utterly ashamed.

"Presley." Keven places his hand on my arm. "Look at me." I lift my head, barely able to look him in the eye. "You were only a kid, and you're not at fault. You haven't done anything wrong either in the Cateses' house or with Clay. You didn't know because they manipulated you so you wouldn't look. The Cateses weren't just signing you up for activities so it would look good when the social workers came around. It was a way to get you out of the house. A couple of the men also said they saw Anna put sleeping pills in your hot chocolate so you wouldn't wake during the night when a lot of the abuse went down."

That's why I had difficulty sleeping in the initial months after I aged out and moved out of their home. Because that fucking bitch was drugging me at night. "I've been surrounded by monsters most of my life, and I never even knew it." *Is there no end to this horror?* Just when I think there couldn't possibly be anything else, I learn something new. I wrap my arms around myself to ward off a bout of shivers.

"There is more I need to tell you, and this is going to hurt." Kev lowers his hand back to his lap.

I have a feeling what he says next will tip me over the edge, but I won't shy away from this. I need to understand it all. "Hide nothing, Keven. I need to know everything." I say it with more confidence than I feel. I honestly don't know how much more my brain can cope with.

"We arrested the Cateses three days ago. We have enough evidence and enough witness statements to bury them. They are singing like canaries, trying to deflect blame." He rubs his thigh, and I know he hates having to be the one to tell me this. "They cherry-picked Clayton to come and live with them. They knew Jeff Rinaldi, and they met Clay through him. Apparently, Jeff was abusing Clay."

Bile collects at the back of my throat, and I don't know how to process that revelation. "Clay was eager to get away from Jeff, so they coached him on how to make it happen. They knew Jeff would put his hands on you, and they had Clay primed and ready to leap to your defense. They were the ones who told him to report Jeff, and they then put in an application to foster both of you."

"None of it was real," I blurt. "Even back then."

"Clay helped prepare boys for them," he adds, gulping visibly. I'm guessing he's used to hearing all kinds of harrowing shit in his line of work, but knowing this is so close to his brother means this has got to be ten times harder to stomach. "He befriended all the new foster boys and groomed them. He almost made it seem normal. That's what one of the men told us."

I have no words, so I just stare at him blankly, and he continues. "He raped them too, Presley. Clay had stopped being a victim."

Daggered pain rips across my chest, making breathing difficult.

The man I called my brother was an animal who preyed on vulnerable kids.

And this all went on around me.

Nausea swims up my throat, and I'm on the verge of throwing up.

"Chris's name came up in conversation, Presley," Keven quietly adds.

"No!" I burst out crying, already knowing what he's going to say.

"They abused Chris too. The Cateses and Clay. Apparently, he was their favorite."

Chapter Thirty-Eight
Presley

"**A**re you sure you want to go through with this?" Keven asks as his colleague Sinead finishes fixing the rhinestone pendant brooch to my jean jacket. Apparently, there's no such thing as wearing a wire anymore because they have all kinds of miniature digital recording devices. Like the brooch I'm wearing with a recording chip embedded in the middle. All I have to do is press down on it to activate it. "It's not too late to back out."

"I'm not backing out," I say, smoothing a hand down over my black and red shirt. I'm wearing ripped jeans and sneakers, favoring a comfortable casual style that is my usual daytime summer look, so I don't tip Clay off. "I haven't gone to all this trouble, setting this meeting up, to back out now." It was my suggestion to use me as bait to lure Clay out of hiding. In exchange for me doing this, Keven's FBI boss has agreed, in writing, that there will be no charges made against Kent. I want to help my ex. Not to assuage my guilt—of which there is a bucketload—because I love him.

We might not be together anymore, but the way I feel about him hasn't changed. I will do whatever it takes to protect Kent. Even standing in front of the manipulative bastard who hurt him, pretending to be concerned, if it means I get him to fess up.

It wasn't easy getting a message through to Clay. His phone has been disconnected, so Rafe helped me get the word out on the street. It took two weeks, but eventually, Clay set up a meet and sent word to me.

"No one would blame you if you did," Keven says, scrubbing a hand over his five o'clock shadow. He looks tense, which doesn't help to calm my nerves.

"Keven." Sinead squeezes his shoulder. "Presley will be fine. We have a full task force on this, and we'll have eyes on her from all angles. Nothing is happening to Presley on our watch."

I know why he's concerned. The meeting location has obviously been chosen to avoid surveillance. The warehouse sits on a vacant lot across from an abandoned building in a derelict part of Roxbury. The FBI had men inside the building for the past twenty-four hours, and they will have sniper weapons trained on the heat signatures inside the warehouse once this all goes down. The hidden microphone in my brooch has a unique heat signature so they can tell who I am in case shit hits the fan and they need to open fire. Keven, and a bunch of additional FBI agents, will be waiting around the corner for the signal to move in.

It's not ideal, but these men and women are trained for all kinds of situations, and I'm prepared for all eventualities. I've got to do something to help. I won't let Clay and those other bastards go underground. Kent deserves justice and not to be looking over his shoulder for the rest of his life. So do the other men who have bravely come forward. And I need to avenge Chris because there is no one else who will care to ensure Clay pays for the torture he inflicted on my ex.

"I trust you," I tell them because I do. I know Kent's brother would not let me do this if there was a serious risk to my life.

"Kent will string me up by my balls when he finds out about this," he adds, eyeballing me.

"He'll forgive you when he discovers Clay and those other animals who hurt him are behind bars."

Keven nods as a tall, thin man with salt-and-pepper hair approaches. He offers me his hand, and I shake it. "Presley. It's good to meet you. I'm SSA West. I'm leading the operation today. Do you have any questions for us?"

I shake my head. "I know what I need to do."

We head out a few minutes later, and Keven drops me off at my car—the one Kent bought me. It's been at his apartment, and I haven't gone back for it. We are no longer together, and I'm no longer deserving of the gift, but Clay asked to meet in a run-down warehouse on the outskirts of Roxbury, and getting an Uber to the location would only raise suspicions, so I'm driving my car one final time.

Keven arranged for the car to be driven to this parking garage, about five miles from the meeting destination, so there is no risk of being seen. He hands me a large brown envelope. "There's the cash, and you've got the pepper spray, right?"

"One in each side of my sneakers," I confirm. They are only tiny vials, and I doubt they will be of much use, but I took them to appease Keven.

"I hate that you are going in there defenseless." He drags a hand through his hair.

"I might not have a weapon, but I'm not completely defenseless. I have a few tricks up my sleeve. Ironically, it was Clay who insisted I take self-defense classes when I was seventeen. He didn't want me going out into the big bad world without the ability to defend myself."

"Presley." Keven grips my shoulders almost painfully. "I need you to promise me you won't take any unnecessary risks. When things turn bad, get away from him and let us handle it. I won't forgive myself if anything happens to you."

"It's not on you, Keven. This is my choice. That bastard played me for years. He hurt Tillie's father, and he hurt the man I love. He needs to pay, and I need to be the one to set things in motion." My voice cracks as I let emotion best me. "Don't you get it? I won't be able to sleep at night if I don't try to put this right. Clay has hurt so many people, and it ends now."

Slowly, reluctantly, he nods. He pulls me into a hug over the console, holding me tight. "You are so strong. It's no wonder you're the only woman to ever capture and hold my brother's attention. I can see why he's so in love with you." He eases back, staring into my eyes. "Kent needs you. Remember that, and stay safe."

He climbs out of the car, and I give him one final nod before I reverse out of the parking spot and hightail it out of there.

I get out of the car with my breath lodged in my throat and butterflies running crazy in the pit of my stomach. It's ten p.m., and it's dark out. There are no streetlights in this part of town and only scant illumination from the crescent moon in the sky. My hands are clammy, as I clutch the brown paper envelope in one hand, and walk across the debris-strewn ground toward the entrance to the dilapidated warehouse. My eyes adjust to the dusky night sky, and my vision becomes clearer. Part of the corrugated iron roof is missing, and most of the windows are cracked or boarded up. The door creaks as I open it, and blood rushes to my head as adrenaline courses through my veins.

My sneakers crunch over something hard on the floor as I step inside. It's pitch-black and creepy as fuck. My heart is racing a hundred miles an hour, and I'm having a hard time containing my fear. "Hello?" I call out, hating how my voice quakes. "Clay?" I add, purposely shouting louder and with more confidence than I feel. I step forward, my feet crunching over the uneven ground, clasping the envelope to my chest. I purposely didn't bring my cell, as I've no doubt Clay would just take it off me, so I have no flashlight.

All the tiny hairs prick at the back of my neck and bile pools at the base of my throat when I sense a presence behind me. I move to spin around, but a hand juts out, wrapping around the front of my throat. "Hello, baby sister," Clay hisses, his warm breath fanning across my ear, making me shiver. "Did you come alone like I said?"

"Yes," I croak, unable to hide the tremor in my voice.

"It's clear," another voice says from the far right. A light shines in my face at the front, and I shield my eyes from the sudden brightness. Clay moves his body up close behind me, and I fight a full body shudder, repulsed at having him so near.

But I have a role to play, and it's too important to mess up, so I shove my repulsion aside, concentrating on doing what I need to do.

Pushing me forward with his hand tight around my neck, Clay thrusts me into the arms of a much older man with a long straggly dark beard. I recognize his face from the mugshots the FBI showed me. He's one of the guys who raped Kent, and it takes everything in me not to lunge at him and gouge that sneering smile off his mouth.

The asshole manhandles me into a chair, tying my hands to either side of the wooden slats while Clay grabs the envelope. He dumps the contents on a small dirty table on the left, grinning at the bundles of cash. Two other assholes sit on crates in front of me while a fourth man counts the money with Clay. They are all holding flashlights, shining them over every part of my body, making my skin crawl. Ignoring the panic racing through my veins, I jut my chin up, keeping my gaze focused straight ahead. I can't examine my surroundings because it's too dark, and I pray the FBI is in place and that their technology is working.

I clear my throat. "Why are you treating me like this?" I ask, angling my head in Clay's direction. "I came here to help you. I'm not your enemy," I lie.

Clay lifts his head from counting the money, narrowing his eyes. "That's to be determined, li'l heartbreaker." His eyes lift to the man with the long grubby beard. "Pat her down."

"It would be my pleasure." He guffaws, and dread washes over me. I swallow my distaste, schooling my expression into a neutral line, as he comes around in front of me and starts checking my body, his disgusting hands lingering too long in places they shouldn't. His hands dive into the pockets of my jeans, and I almost puke as his fingers dig into my pussy through the denim. The assholes on the crates laugh, their eyes firing up as they devour me with hungry gazes. Ice creeps up my spine because it's clear they don't trust me. If their behavior didn't give it away, the guns poking out of the pockets of their jeans do.

"She's clean," Beardy says, and I breathe a silent sigh of relief he didn't find the microphone.

"Put that in my bike," Clay says, shoving the envelope at the man standing beside him.

He nods, walking off behind me, and I'm guessing they have their bikes somewhere in here.

"Ten K won't last long, but it's a start," Clay says.

"It's all I can spare," I lie. "But I'll try to get you more."

Clay kneels in front of me, gripping my chin. "Why are you here, li'l heartbreaker? What's your agenda?" His face has healed well in the three weeks since Kent beat him up, but he has a couple of new scars on his face, just under his left eye, and from the way he's holding his upper torso, I can tell he's still in pain. Kent broke a few of his ribs, and they will take longer to heal. At least I know where to kick him if I get the chance.

I prepare to put on the show of a lifetime. My lower lip wobbles, and tears fill my eyes. "I'm sorry for what Kent did to you. I'm sorry I didn't go to you straightaway, but he tricked me. Told me lies and had me confused. I'm going to make it right now. I'll help you get overseas. You just tell me what you need done, and I'll make it happen, but you have to hurry, Clay. The FBI is asking all kinds of questions, and they have Anna and Gerald, and they are making up all kinds of horrible lies."

"What kind of lies?" Clay asks, straightening up and hovering over me like a dark menace.

"They are saying you raped boys. That you were involved with the Cateses in abusing all the boys they took in."

An evil glint flickers in his eyes, and his mouth curves up at the corner. "I did love you, you know," he says, running his fingers across the top of my head. "Even if you are a dumb bitch." He laughs, and the sound raises goose bumps on my arms. "You are so fucking naive. The things we did in that house and you never knew."

Chapter Thirty-Nine
Presley

A chorus of chuckles rings out as the assholes laugh at my expense.

"It's true?" I croak, keeping up the ruse even though it's most likely futile. It seems he came here already knowing I've washed my hands of him. Clay has always worn arrogance like it's something to be proud of. I'm betting he asked me to meet, knowing I was no longer playing for the same team, because he wants the opportunity to gloat. To break me apart for betraying him.

Grabbing my hair, he yanks my head back, stretching my neck at an awkward angle. "Let's quit the pretense, Pres. Even you're not *that* dumb." Forcing my knees apart, he steps between them, lowering his face to mine. "Do you want to know the real reason Chris and I stopped speaking?" He doesn't wait for my reply. "It was at Gerald and Anna's. A couple of weeks after you lost your beautiful little baby." His mocking tone has the desired effect. I want to yell at him and kick out with my legs, but they didn't tie my feet and I figure I'll need the use of them if I'm to get out of here alive, so I swallow my pain and focus on the big picture, ignoring his attempts to bait me.

"We'd just finished fucking your precious Chris six ways from Sunday." He smiles as a single tear rolls down my face. "He was supposed to have left after we showed him a good time, but he decided to be a hero. He chose to sneak back in, to try to find some evidence to use against us." He scoffs. "Fucking dumbass."

I guess that explains why Chris went back to that house. Tillie's death must have forced him to confront all the shit that had been done to him, and he decided to do something about it. Poor Chris. I hate he went through all that abuse and couldn't tell me about it.

Clay tilts his head to the side, easing his hold on my hair, running the tip of his finger down my face.

"Don't fucking touch me," I hiss, done playing games.

He shoves his knee between my groin, yanking my head back again. "Shut up, bitch, and you only talk when I say you can talk." His features even out, and he smiles at me like a bona fide psychopath. "Chris discovered us watching our home movies. We filmed all the boys over the years, and I always recorded my extracurricular activities to show Mom and Dad. They were always so proud of me." His creepy smile freaks me the fuck out, and I'm only now seeing the real Clayton Cooper.

"Kent's video was Anna's favorite," he goes on, and all the blood drains from my face. "She loved watching him bleed as I destroyed his ass." His crotch is in my face, and the bulge tenting his jeans makes me sick.

"Bet she loved watching him come all over your hand more," one of the assholes behind Clay says, and they all laugh. Rage thunders through me, and I wish I could get at his gun so I could riddle them full of bullets.

"That was my favorite part," another asshole says.

"Hearing him cry and scream was *my* favorite part," Beardy says, and I squeeze my eyes shut, silently telling myself to hold it together. They are giving us what we need. The FBI is listening in, and they will intervene soon.

"He fucking loved it," Clay says, thrusting his disgusting groin in my face. "He fucking loved my dick in his ass, just like Chris did." He leans down, putting his face all up in mine. "Most of those times Chris crawled into your bed in the middle of the night, it was after I'd taken his ass over and over again. All those times he curled around you, tried to lose himself in you, it was because he couldn't forget *me*. I was a part of him, and he fucking loved it. You were the consolation prize, Pres. Never anything more."

"Fuck you, asshole," I hiss, losing the tenuous hold on my emotions. "He hated you. I didn't understand it before, but it's crystal clear now."

He slaps me across the face, and my head whips back. My cheek stings, but I grit my teeth, making no sound.

"Want to know how we kept him in line?" he continues as if he hasn't just slapped me. "After we beat the crap out of him for daring to try and blackmail us, I told Chris if he ever went to the cops or told another living soul what he knew that I would kill you. Why else do you think I hung around you? It wasn't because I enjoy your boring company or that I wanted you because you don't have the right equipment, baby." He rakes a derogatory gaze down over my body.

That's why Chris kept coming around. He was checking up on me. Making sure I was okay. That Clay hadn't done anything to hurt me. Chris was trying to protect me, in his own messed-up way. Pain slams into my gut, almost winding me.

"But I'm gonna make an exception tonight." He grabs my chin, digging his nails into my flesh, breaking skin. "Because you're going to pay for betraying me with that cunt Kennedy." His eyes flash manically. "I fucking protected you, Presley! Things could've been so much worse for you growing up, but I kept you safe, and this is how you repay me?" He yells the end part, slapping me hard across the face. "Give it to me," he hisses, and one of the assholes hands him a cell phone. He thrusts it in my face. "You left me bleeding on the fucking floor while you went running off into the night after that fucking cunt!" he roars, playing the video from the night of the bar attack for me.

"My only regret is not killing you myself that night," I say, my tone cold and calm. "And in every situation, I would pick Kent over you."

He rams his fist into my face, and blood spurts from my nose. Stars explode behind my eyes as pain rattles through my skull.

"I don't enjoy fucking women, but I'm gonna fuck you, li'l heartbreaker. I'm gonna fuck every hole. We all are. We're gonna make you bleed worse than we made Kennedy bleed that night in the alley. We'll record it, of course, and make sure Kennedy gets a copy so he knows there is nothing of his we won't destroy if he doesn't cooperate. We'll keep you as insurance until he plays ball. Then we'll dump your dead ass at his door as a reminder to keep his silence or more people he loves will die."

"But first," he adds, scrolling his finger over the keypad on his phone while one of the assholes fumbles with the button on my jeans. "Here's a little video to get you in the mood." He steps aside to give his buddy space to remove my jeans, shoving the cell at me again, grinning wickedly as horror washes over me.

The image has changed, and I cry out as I see a teenage Kent being slammed into a wall. "No!" I scream, squeezing my eyes closed. I can't watch this. The video continues, and the sounds of Kent's struggle fill my ears, as he tries to fight the group of men off. Tears roll down my face, and I'm officially done. I have reached my breaking point. The FBI has enough, and I'm betting they are on their way. "Phoenix!" I shout out the code word as I lift my legs, kicking the guy crouched in front of me in the head before using my body weight to push my chair back. I slam to the ground, still tied to the chair, legs up in the air as bullets rain through the window and shouting echoes around me.

A loud crash from behind confirms the cavalry has arrived.

"You fucking whore!" Clay shouts as a swarm of FBI agents rushes into the room.

My eyes widen as he stands over me, gun pointed at my face. "Do it, Clay. I've made my peace with it. You've lost, and that's all that counts." His finger curls around the trigger, and I silently beg Kent to forgive me as my last moments are consumed with thoughts of him. I pray he heals and moves forward with his life.

A shot rings out, and I scream.

Chapter Forty
Kent

"**A**re you nervous?" Dr. O'Dwyer—my personal therapist— asks as I wait in the meeting room for my family to arrive. I wet my dry lips and nod.

"It will be okay, Kent," Nancy says, fixing me with a reassuring smile. "I will stop the session if it upsets you too much. Your family is visiting for a few days, and we don't need to cover everything at once."

She told me to call her by her first name, if I liked, and it's helped me to see her as more than just my doctor. I thought it would be difficult talking to a stranger about the stuff that happened to me, and there are times where it's a struggle, but mostly it's been easier than I expected. I've locked this shit up inside me for a long time, and now the walls have come crashing down, I've no desire to rebuild them. Although it's painful, I need to get the words out.

It's been over three weeks since I arrived at this private rehab facility in the mountains of Arizona, an hour outside Phoenix. My parents chose this place because it treats addiction and PTSD and they hire top experts in their field to provide a truly holistic approach to treatment. They offer a wide range of alternative therapies too, and they have a pool, basketball court, large gym, and a running track on the grounds of the twenty-acre site. It's peaceful here. We're completely shut off from the outside world and I didn't realize how much I needed that.

I'm halfway into my forty-five-day program, and it's family week, which means the first group meeting with my family is due to commence in minutes. My foot taps off the beige carpeted floor of the small room as I anxiously wait for them to arrive, thinking of everything that's happened since I got here.

The first two weeks of my stay were largely focused on detoxification, and this is the first time in years I am completely sober and clean.

Not gonna lie; it's been hell on Earth.

Sleepless nights have become the norm, and on nights when I do manage to grab a few hours of sleep, I usually wake either screaming from a nightmare or drenched in sweat as all the crap leaves my body. That first week, I spent half of it worshiping the porcelain gods as I repeatedly emptied my stomach. And let's not mention the headaches or the intense involuntary body tremors I have no control over.

Going cold turkey sucks, but I'm feeling better this week, so I hope the worst of that part is behind me.

Now the real torture starts—facing up to my trauma and finding a way to move forward in a nondestructive manner. Once I return home, I will be continuing my therapy with Denise, Selena's therapist. Nancy has already been in touch with her, and they are working out a treatment plan. She has a couple of other suggestions, for complementary tools to aid the healing process, but the most important thing is I can go back to Harvard Law, with them none the wiser, and work on my recovery while I'm continuing my studies.

The door opens, and my parents step inside the room. Nancy rises, walking toward them with a smile on her face. Nausea swims up my throat, and my knee jiggles at a greater pace. I'm still a mess of conflicting emotions, veering from anger to shame, between fear and remorse.

I didn't ask Presley to come here today—although I'm dying to speak to her—because I want to meet with her separately. My feelings for the woman I love are a clusterfuck of epic proportions thanks to that sick bastard she grew up with. It's all so fucked up.

The only things I know for sure is I love her, what we shared was the real deal, and I hate the shit I said to her at the hospital. I was wrong to vent my pain in her direction, but I can't help how I feel. She's had a ton of horrific revelations dropped on her, which can't be easy to handle. I know she loves me too, but I don't know if love is enough to overcome the mountain of obstacles in our path.

"Our other sons are waiting outside," Mom says, looking between me and the doctor. I asked my brothers to come without their spouses. I couldn't handle a room with that many people. Saying what I need to say to my parents and my six brothers will be challenging enough without adding their partners to the mix. There will be time to meet with them when I return home.

"You can ask them to come in," Nancy says, helping Mom into the seat beside me as Dad goes out to get the others. The room is rectangular in size, and there are ten chairs in a half-circle on this side of the space, all facing the white board in front. Nancy asked me who I wanted to sit beside me, and I couldn't even decide that. She suggested I sit at the end and let Mom sit beside me, so I'm doing that.

I'm still processing my anger and my hurt, and I have no idea how this session is going to go down.

One by one, my brothers walk into the room. My lips tilt at the edges as I watch the good doctor try not to react unprofessionally, but it's a struggle. And I get it. My brothers are all tall, good-looking, and famous. A lethal combination where women are concerned. The wedding bands on their fingers don't deter the die-hard fans who are convinced the marriages aren't real. It's ridiculous. You only have to look at any of my brothers with their partners to know they are in love and very happy.

My brothers glance at me and then the doctor, hesitant on whether to approach me, unsure of the protocol. Nancy regains her composure, asking them to take a seat. Keats enters the room last, and he walks straight toward me, leaning down and hugging me. Tears prick my eyes, and my arms tentatively go around him. He's the only one who wasn't at the hospital to witness my meltdown because he and Austen were still on a plane. By the time they landed, I was already en route here.

"I love you," he says when he pulls back, his eyes clouded with tears.

I nod, swallowing roughly, wondering how the fuck I'm going to get through this with any semblance of sanity intact.

Nancy introduces herself, gives them a quick audience-friendly summary of what I've been doing since I got here, and explains how this session will work. Then she gives me the floor.

And I clam up.

My tongue darts out, wetting my dry lips, and my heart is pounding so hard it feels like I'm dying. My brothers all look at me, and the weight of their expectation presses down on me.

"Kent. Take a deep breath," Nancy says, reassuring me with her kind eyes and her soft smile.

I inhale and exhale, and gradually, the panicky feeling in my chest settles down. Mom takes my hand in hers carefully, like I might break. It's too much. I know she means well, but I just can't right now. Extracting my hand from hers, I wrap my arms around my body as I try to form words.

"Kent." Nancy looks directly at me. "Why don't you tell your family how you are feeling right now, and we can take it from there?"

"I'm on edge," I admit, looking at no one in particular. "And I'm scared. Ashamed too." I drop my eyes to the carpet. "But mostly I'm angry." I lift my chin, looking at my family. They all look nervous too, which should help, but all it does is make me angrier. "At those assholes who did this to me. At myself for letting it happen. At Presley for not seeing that bastard Clay for the monster he was. At all of you for not ever seeing *me*."

"Kent, we tried. We—"

"No, you fucking didn't, Mom!" I shake my head, looking at both of my parents. "You shipped me off to one useless therapist after another, never stopping to ask why it wasn't working. You blamed me for not opening up to them instead of asking me why I was behaving like that in the first place. You cried over where you went wrong with me, but neither of you ever asked me what happened to change my behavior. It was always why can't you be good like Keanu and Keaton? You are disgracing the family with your reckless behavior. You're such an embarrassment. We have given you everything you need and this is how you repay us?" Those statements, repeated to me so many times, are imprinted in my brain. "It was always about *you*. Never about me."

Mom pales, but she doesn't try to defend herself. Neither does Dad.

"You're right, son," Dad says, a couple of seconds later. "We didn't handle it correctly, and we are deeply sorry for failing you."

"I've felt like an outsider in this family for so long because you were all so dismissive of me. Even in the way I was introduced to your friends and your partners. Like, oh that's Kent, the black sheep of the family." I sniff, chewing on the inside of my mouth. "Yet none of you took the time to understand why I was like that."

"Would you have told us if we asked?" Keanu asks.

I shrug. "I don't know, but none of you even tried. Not in any real, meaningful way."

"Why didn't you tell us?" Kalvin says, leaning forward, placing his elbows on his knees.

"Could you have fessed up if this happened to you when you were fifteen?" I ask, and the expression on his face tells me all I need to know. I doubt any of my brothers could've spoken out if this happened to them at that age. But I need to try to explain it in a way they will understand. This is a hard truth to admit. "At first, I was too scared. They recorded it and threatened to stream it on the web."

"I could've gone after them and gotten rid of it," Kev says. "I was already hacking government systems by then."

"I know you could have, and you think I didn't want to ask you for help? I did, but then I'd have to admit everything, and I just couldn't do it." I glance at Mom and Dad. "They threatened to kill my family if I said anything, and I was terrified they would kill you or my brothers."

"Oh, honey." Mom's fingers twitch, and I know she's longing to touch me, hold me, but I can't say what I need to say with her clinging to me. Dad tightens his arm around her shoulder, comforting her with his touch. "We had the resources to ensure they never got anywhere near us, and we would've gone after them with the full extent of the law."

"Would you? You were all so fucked up back then. So involved in other drama. There wasn't time for me." Not to mention I didn't want cops and lawyers knowing about it. And I knew if I reported it, it would make the news. *How the fuck could I have faced the kids in school if that got out?*

"Honey, that's just not true," Mom says. "If you had only told us."

Is she not fucking listening? I grip the edge of my chair, digging my nails into the wood. "Mom, I was *fifteen,* and I was terrified they were going to come after me and my family! I knew they were in some gang because they were wearing identical leather cuts. And I was so ashamed."

I gulp over the golf-ball-sized lump in my throat. "I felt so stupid, so weak that I had let them do that to me. I tried to fight them off, but I was drunk." A bitter laugh escapes my lips. "It was the very first night I drank alcohol. I was staying over at Vincent Channing's house that night, and I told you his parents were there, but they were in The Hamptons for the weekend. A few of us went into Boston using fake IDs, and we got smashed. I got separated from the guys when we left to go to a club, and I wandered into the wrong part of town. The

Vipers saw me, recognized who I was, and decided they were going to teach the 'rich prick' a lesson."

Kyler stares at me, his face twisted in pain. He understands some of what I'm feeling. "I was in so much pain. Physical and emotional. After a few weeks passed and they hadn't come for me, my fear gave way to rage, and I needed to lash out. That's when I started partying and drinking and doing drugs. I was having flashbacks and nightmares, and I just wanted it to stop. Getting high and drunk cured that issue. And I fucked around a lot because I needed to prove I was a man. To know I was into women and that they hadn't ruined sex for me." I glance at Keats, and we stare at one another. "I needed to prove I wasn't gay," I add. "They messed me up in the head. I'm not proud to admit it, but they created a hatred within me for gay men."

"It's okay," Keats says. "It's understandable."

"No, it fucking isn't! It's just something else those sick fucks did to me. Something else they took from me." I owe my brother an apology. He's the only one in this room I plan on apologizing to, but I want to do it in private. "I need to speak to you alone when we're done here."

Keats nods. "I'd like that."

"Why didn't you say anything when I fessed up about what happened to me?" Kyler asks.

I exhale heavily. "That fucked me up, Ky. Knowing you had been through something like that and even you hadn't noticed anything wrong with me. I'm sorry for what you went through, but I was so fucking pissed after you came clean because everyone rallied around you and it was all poor Kyler, and once again, I was relegated to the sidelines. No one noticed I was sinking to the bottom of the pool."

"We're not mind readers, Kent," Kaden says, speaking for the first time. His tone is softer than the hardened voice he usually uses with me, but it still irritates the fuck out of me.

I narrow my eyes at him. "Doesn't matter if you were though, Kade, right? You'd still hate me."

"I don't hate you, Kent. I've misunderstood you, and I am really fucking sorry about that."

I scoff. "Whatever."

"I am truly sorry, Kent. I'm ashamed to admit I'd written you off as an attention-seeking troublemaker. Even when Eva was telling me you were hiding deep-seated pain, I refused to believe it." He hangs his head. "I don't know how I can ever make it up to you. I'm your older brother, and I should have protected you instead of pushing you away and ignoring what was right in front of my eyes."

"You didn't try to find me," I croak, my anger giving way to hurt. "The others were there with Presley the night The Vipers tried to murder me. But you were absent. You didn't care whether I lived or died."

"That's not true." He shakes his head, swiping at tears. "Of course, I don't want you to die!"

"So why the fuck weren't you there?" I shout.

"Because I thought it was another attention-seeking move on your part and I believed we should try a tough love approach this time, but I was wrong!" He stands, pacing the room. "I was fucking wrong, okay, and I have to live with the fact I turned my back on you that night."

He breaks down, and I haven't seen my brother like this since the night he found out James wasn't his bio dad. "You could have died, and I wasn't there. I let you down, again, and I can never forgive myself for the way I've treated you." Tears stream down his face, and I'm struggling to breathe over the strangled ball of emotion clogging my throat. "I am so fucking sorry, Kent. More than I can express."

I can see he's genuine, but he doesn't understand he has damaged our relationship in a way we might never recover from. I don't know if I can ever trust Kade. Maybe with time, but I just don't know. I shrug, averting my eyes.

"If I could go back and rewrite history, I would do everything different," Mom says, and I lift my chin up.

"But you can't," I say through gritted teeth because it's not helpful.

"No, we can't, but we're here now, and we want to help," she says.

"What can we do, son?" Dad asks. "How can we help you now?"

I force myself to calm down, and it's a little easier because some of the tightness in my chest has lifted. "I need you to wipe the slate clean. To let me start over. To not hold my mistakes against me because I'm sick of everyone in this family judging me."

They all nod, and air whooshes out of my mouth in grateful relief. "And I need you to be patient with me," I add. "Because I've got a lot of shit still to process, and I've gone cold turkey, and I've most likely lost the only woman I have ever loved. I'm not going to be easy to live with, but I need you to understand." I cast my gaze around the room. "It's not me being an asshole; it's me trying to pick up the pieces of my life and glue them back together."

"We can do that," Dad says, and everyone else nods again, murmuring their agreement.

"I think we'll leave it there for today," Nancy says. "And maybe in the next session, we can discuss how your family feels after hearing all of this today."

Chapter Forty-One
Kent

"I reserved a table for all of you in the dining hall for seven," Nancy explains. "And you are welcome to avail of the other facilities. All I ask is that you keep the conversation casual. Kent has been making amazing progress, and just getting to hang out with his family, with no pressure or expectations, will help him enormously."

My parents shake her hand as Keven approaches me. He pulls me into a hug. "I'm glad you are getting better. I do need to talk to you, but it can wait until later. I know you need to speak to Keats." He must have an update for me on the FBI situation, and it's been on my mind. I still don't know if they plan to pin an assault charge on me. I can kiss Harvard Law goodbye if that happens.

Mom, Dad, Kalvin, and Kyler take turns hugging me, and I arrange to meet my brothers in an hour for a game of basketball. Kade lingers, looking unsure. I jerk my head in acknowledgment, folding my arms across my chest, because I don't want him touching me. He can't just throw out words, no matter how heartfelt they are, and expect everything to be peachy. He has hurt me a lot. More than my other brothers. He has been so cold and ignorant at times, especially in recent years, and it's not something I can get over just like that.

"Can you stay too?" I ask Keanu because I think he needs to hear this as well.

"Of course." He squeezes my shoulder before dropping onto a chair.

Nancy stays in the room with me, Keanu, and Keats, but she tucks herself away in the corner, pulling her notepad out and jotting more notes down.

"I want to try to explain," I tell Keats when he sits down beside me. "I know I hurt you and Austen, and I feel bad about it. I've always felt bad about it, but you coming out was a trigger for me. I have hated gay men since I was raped. Anytime I saw two guys together, it reminded me of the attack and it enraged me. It sounds silly, and it's so fucking unfair, but they became synonymous in my mind."

"Did you ever question your sexuality?" Keats quietly asks, his face radiating compassion.

My stomach twists into knots as I nod. "Did they tell you what Clay did to me?" I'm too emotionally drained right now to say it out loud, and it's the part I'm most ashamed of.

Tears flood his eyes as he seethes. "I want to gut that fucking bastard and hang him by his entrails from the roof."

Keanu nods in agreement, his nostrils flaring as anger shines in his eyes.

Nancy lifts her head, her brow puckering in concern.

"Careful or Nancy will book you a room in here beside me," I tease Keats.

Keanu's lips twitch, and Keats swats his tears away.

"I was very confused for a while, and I was terrified it meant I was gay. Fucking lots of women helped, because I loved sex—with girls—and it helped me feel more in control, but there was always this niggling doubt at the back of my mind."

"Did you ever experiment with any guys?" Keanu asks, his face curious.

"Hell no. I might've been confused, but the thoughts of letting any guy touch me made my skin crawl." Too late, I remember my other brother. I wince a little as I eyeball Keaton. "No offense meant."

"None taken," Keats says, offering me a reassuring smile. "Did me coming out bring it to the surface again?" He chews on the corner of his lip.

I shake my head. "Not in that way, no. It brought everything else about the attack to the surface at a time when I had felt like I was finally getting a grip on it." I look at Keanu. "Selena moving in with us helped me a lot. I saw how brave and strong she was, and she inspired me to clean up my act and try harder. I almost confided in her so many times."

"Why didn't you?" Keanu asks.

I shrug. "I convinced myself it was too late. Too much time had passed and I was doing better. Not drinking or smoking or popping pills as much. I graduated and got into Harvard Law. I told myself dredging up the past would do no one any good after this long."

"You can't bury that shit. It eats away at you until you explode," Keats says. "Our circumstances were vastly different, but I was a ticking time bomb for years."

"I'm sorry for how I treated you and Austen. It wasn't personal. It *isn't* personal. It's all tied up with the shit in my head. It enraged me you were gay and I hadn't seen it. Every time I saw you with him, it made my blood boil. It dragged up a lot of old feelings, and the flash-backs and nightmares were more recurring. I started floundering."

"I hate that," Keats says.

"It's not your fault."

"It's not yours either," Keanu says.

"I said some really nasty things to you, Keats, and I hate myself for that," I admit. "I should never have slept with Melissa either, but I'm glad it helped to uncover her motives." He nods, and I know, deep down, that was the least of the issues between us. "I have never hated you, and I'm happy you're happy. Austen seems like a great guy, and I'm just sorry I ruined any chance of a relationship with him." I've seen the way Keaton's husband looks at me, and I don't blame him. I would want to kill anyone who treated Presley with such disdain and disrespect.

"Nothing is insurmountable," Keats says. "I know my husband. He will give you another chance. He's pissed because I've been hurting so bad, but he isn't unsympathetic. He was really upset when we found out what happened to you."

I clamp my brother on the shoulder. "I have missed you so much, and I hope, in time, we can get back on track." I need to work through a lot of my anger, but I'm determined to do it—*for me*—and so I can recover my relationship with my brother and my family.

Keaton pulls me into a hug, and I reach over, grabbing Keanu into our circle. "I'm going to need you." My voice is choked with emotion. "Out of everyone, I will need you both." Especially if I don't have Presley.

"We're here for you," Keanu says.

"Whatever you need," Keats adds. "I have already talked with Austen. I can move back to Cambridge with you if you like. I can do my show from anywhere, and Austen is busy now the season has started back, so we can make it work."

"You'd do that for me?"

"I would do anything for you. You only have to ask."

After an energetic game of basketball with my brothers, we all go our separate ways to shower and freshen up before meeting our parents for dinner in the dining hall. I'm quiet during dinner, just listening to my family talk about their lives. The banter flows naturally, like anytime we are all together, and I hate how I still feel so much like an outsider. I guess it's not something that can be resolved overnight either.

The stark contrasts between me and my brothers have never been more obvious. They are all married. All in loving committed relationships. Some of them with kids. I'm the only one who is still studying. The only one without that special person in my life, and not for the first time, I regret the things I said to Presley. I blamed her when she was only a little kid too. It's not her fault, and I'm ashamed for how I've treated her. I wouldn't blame her if she never spoke to me again.

"Can we take a walk?" Kev asks after dinner ends.

"Sure."

We say goodbye to the others and head off outside, following one of the less popular paths. We don't talk at first, but it's not awkward. Keven has never been a big talker anyway. "I spoke to Nancy before dinner," he says, and I arch a brow. "I wanted to check if it was okay to bring this up. She gave me the green light."

"I'm all ears," I say, purposely rolling my shoulders to loosen the knot there.

"Clayton is dead, and we have the rest of the assholes in custody."

I slam to a halt. "What?" I splutter. "How did it happen? When did it happen?"

He jerks his shoulder. "Let's keep walking."

I walk beside him in a daze. I've dreamed of this day, but in my visions, I was the one to gut that motherfucker Clay until all the air left his body. I listen in shocked silence as he starts to explains.

"Before I explain, Presley is fine."

My eyes widen in alarm, and intense pressure sits on my chest.

"Kent." He grabs my arm. "She is *fine*. I would never let anything happen to her."

"She was involved?"

He nods. "It was Presley's idea to use herself as bait to lure Clay out of hiding."

"And you fucking agreed?" I shout, glaring at my brother. He has the audacity to chuckle. "Bet you wouldn't find it funny if Cheryl offered herself up as bait to a psychotic rapist!"

His chuckles die out. "That's a bit too close to home, brother, and we're getting sidetracked. We set up a sting operation, and Presley got Clay to admit to everything. We have it all on tape. Plus we got all copies of the recording from the bar and the night they attacked you. The deal Presley made with my boss was her help in exchange for them dropping all the charges against you, so you don't need to worry about anything coming back to hurt you. Mom also spoke to your boss at the law office. They were really understanding, and they have offered you an internship next summer. They also said if you wanted to take those bastards to trial, they would represent you."

I'm knocked sideways by all those revelations, but Presley is the priority.

"How did Clay die and was Presley hurt?"

"I shot the bastard because he had his gun aimed at Presley," he admits. "She walked away with a few minor scratches and some bruising. That's all."

I grab my brother into a hug. "Thank you for taking care of her."

"She's your girl. I was always going to look after her." He glances at me as we walk again. "Everyone has been looking out for her. The whole family has been involved."

My heart swells with emotion. "I said some awful things to her."

"She doesn't hold it against you. She's been really worried."

"How is she?"

"Honestly, I think she's struggling," he says, and pain stabs me through the heart. "It's been a lot for her to process too."

"I want to be there for her, Kev, but I can't support her when I'm like this." It's hard for me to admit that, even to myself, but it's the truth. The best way I can take care of Presley is to take care of myself first.

He stops walking this time, turning to face me. "She knows that, and she's in the same boat. She wants to be there for you, but she can't." His expression turns sad, and acid churns in my gut.

"What are you not saying, Kev?"

He removes a small white envelope from the back pocket of his jeans. "Hide that quick. We're not supposed to give you anything." I slip it in my jeans, trying to ignore the sudden pounding in my chest. "Presley asked me to give you that before she left," he says.

"No." I shake my head, pain slicing through me. "No, Keven. Do not tell me she's gone."

"I'm the only one who knows," he says. "She asked me not to say anything to the others until I had told you."

"But you know where she's gone, right? You know where to find her so when I'm better I can get her back."

He shakes his head. "She wouldn't tell me, and she made me promise not to look for her. She said she needs time to heal, and she can't do that with you. She loves you, but it's too painful. She needs a clean break, and her belief is that you do too."

Chapter Forty-Two
Presley

Six Months Later

"What's up, Pink?" Pete says, holding his hand up for a high-five as I step through the door of Denver Ink to start my shift.

"Same ole, same ole, boss." I flash him a grin as I toss my dark hair over my shoulders. The pink-tipped ends are new, but after my colleagues christened me Pink, as in P-ink, short for Presley Ink, I decided to add some pink highlights to my hair. Everyone has a special artist's name in this studio, and it adds to the family vibe.

Inspiration came to me five months ago after I'd left the little house I'd rented on Jensen Beach.

After I fled Boston, I craved solitude and the soothing comfort of the ocean. Ford's fiancée, Michelle, suggested I head to Florida. She spent some summers with her family on Nettles Island, which is close to Jensen Beach. It was the perfect hideaway, and I took long walks on the beach, inhaling the fresh salty air, letting the heady sunshine warm more than just my skin, as I began the difficult healing process. My therapist, Jenna, was a great help in those early days, making herself available for biweekly video calls as I struggled to untangle the jumbled mess in my head.

I couldn't afford to stay there forever, and wallowing in guilt and remorse with little distraction wouldn't have been healthy in the long-term, so I knew it was time to put my tattoo artist goal into action. Thanks to Alex Kennedy's steady stream of commissions, I had enough money saved to make it a reality. I recalled the conversation I had at the wedding with Austen and booked a flight to Colorado the next day.

Pete gave me an initial trial, and I was thrilled when he offered me a full apprenticeship after my first week. I haven't looked back since, and there's no doubt getting to fulfill my lifelong dream has helped me to get through the dark days when I felt so lonely, like I had little to look forward to. Immersing myself in Denver Ink, and in my little sideline business, has saved me. I have continued my pressed-flower picture business, but I mainly sell at the local weekend market and via word of mouth.

I settle behind the reception desk, pulling up the schedule for today, and I begin the prep work before the others arrive. Pete makes coffee, regaling me with outrageous stories from the eventful dinner party at his in-laws last night.

The rest of the crew arrives in drips and drops, and the place quickly fills up with excited customers. Before I know it, it's lunchtime. Wrapping up warmly in my coat, scarf, and gloves, I walk to the little deli a couple of blocks away to fill everyone's order.

When I arrive back at the shop, everyone is standing in the waiting area, fixated on something playing on the wall-mounted TV.

After placing the paper bags down on the counter and unbuttoning my coat, I turn around to see what has everyone so intrigued. I suck in a gasp as my eyes latch onto a familiar face. Although it's been almost seven months since I last saw Kent, I haven't forgotten how vibrant his blue eyes are, or how firm his strong jawline felt under my fingertips, or the soft warmth of his lips. Not a day goes by where I don't think about him, miss him, pine for him. Some days the craving for his strong, protective arms is so intense I have almost given in and called him, but I resist.

I can't interfere with his recovery, and he probably wants nothing to do with me anymore anyway. Maybe it was cowardly to leave while he was in rehab, but my fragile heart couldn't cope with the prospect of fresh rejection. I know Kent was speaking from a place of hurt that day in the hospital when he said those things to me, but he can't help how he feels, and he should never be made to feel guilty for it. And I was hurting too. My heart was an empty shell, and I had nothing left to give anyone. Not even the man I love with every facet of my being.

No, I was right to walk away. There was too much hurt on both sides, and I had to get away from Boston to leave all the painful memories behind. I've worked hard to absolve myself of responsibility for Clay's actions, but it's still a work in progress. I have a new therapist here and I attend weekly sessions.

Despite my best intentions, my heart still clings to the memory of my lost love. I haven't washed Kent's Harvard T-shirt even though the spicy scent of his cologne barely lingers on the fabric anymore. I keep his picture by my bed, and I regularly reread all the notes he gave me. The first picture I made—with the first bouquet of flowers he sent me—hangs proudly over my bed.

"Shush. It's starting," someone says behind me, snapping me out of my head.

I refocus on the TV screen, trying to keep a neutral expression on my face so no one figures out my secret. But it's hard because my emotions are veering all over the place. Kent is the only man who has ever fully owned my heart, and being away from him is torture even if I know, deep down, I'm doing the right thing.

Kent is giving a press conference at some swanky hotel in downtown Boston. I know this must be about the case because TV stations, gossip sites, and newspapers have been carrying reports of the trial for weeks. Gerald and Anna's case came to trial first, and I celebrated when they were locked away for fifteen years with no prospect of parole. I thought I might be called to give my testimony, but the FBI hasn't been in contact with me, about either case, so I guess they have enough to nail the bastards without me.

Kent sits behind an elevated table at the front of the room alongside a pretty woman with auburn hair and a distinguished-looking man with a mop of dark hair. I recognize them from media reports. They are his attorneys, and I was pleased to see the law firm he interned with over the summer was representing him because it must mean things are good between them.

The male attorney taps the microphone on the table, preparing to address the large assembled crowd. The camera zooms in on the Kennedy family in the front two rows. They are all out in support of Kent. His parents and all his brothers and their spouses. Understandably, none of the children are present. A pang of sorrow slaps me in the face. I should be there supporting him too because I'm sure he's scared shitless. This can't have been easy, but I'm so proud of him for doing the right thing. It only makes me love him even more.

Reporters shout questions at his attorney as he leans in to speak. "On behalf of my client, I would ask for complete silence, please." A deadly hush moves over the room as reporters wait with bated breath for him to continue. "Mr. Kennedy is going to read a pre-prepared statement. He won't be taking questions. This has been a difficult time for Kent, and his family, and we ask that you respect his privacy." The man nods at Kent, giving him the floor.

Kent's Adam's apple bobs in his throat as he stares directly into the camera; it's the only subtle hint he's anxious. He holds himself confidently, his expression betraying none of his nerves. Bowing his head slightly, he clears his throat and begins to read his statement.

"A CDC study found that, in the US, one in seventy-one men had been raped or suffered an attempt within their lifetime. One out of every ten rape victims is male. More than one-quarter of male victims of completed rape experienced their first rape when they were ten years of age or younger."

He lifts his chin up, staring into the camera. "It is a myth that only gay men are raped." His jaw pulls tight, and there is a pregnant pause before he lowers his eyes to the page in front of him and continues. "Today, four of the five men who raped and assaulted me when I was only fifteen have been sentenced to life in prison for that crime and other related crimes."

I'm familiar with the charges as I've been avidly following the case. They must have been convicted on all counts—serial rape, attempted murder, and drug and gun offenses.

"This is not just a personal victory for me," Kent continues, "but a victory for all victims of rape, most notably male victims of rape. Male rape still carries so much stigma in our society, and we need to change that culture. No person, male or female, has the right to force themselves on any other person, and I am grateful to the justice system within the state of Massachusetts for counting rape and sexual assault as one of the gravest felonies and handing down sentences today that carry the weight of that conviction."

Kent looks up, setting the statement aside as he speaks from the heart. "As a frightened teenager, I told no one what happened to me largely out of fear. Fear of retaliation. Fear of humiliation. And I was so ashamed and confused. I felt weak. I felt like less of a man. I felt like I should have been able to fight them off, but none of those things are true. They took something they had no right to take, and the blame squarely lies on their shoulders. For years, I used alcohol and drugs and sex to mask my pain and as an outlet to reassert control over my life. The men that abused me tried to murder me seven months ago so this story wouldn't come out. I almost died, and I had a breakdown, but with the support of my loved ones, I am clean and sober and I have taken back control of my life. That gave me the courage to pursue my rapists through the legal system even knowing this story would become public knowledge because of who my family is. I don't regret it because if my story helps even *one man* to come forward and tell his story then I have done the right thing. Then it is worth it."

The haunted look that used to linger in his gaze is nowhere to be seen as he stares confidently into the camera. "If you have been the victim of rape, I urge you to come forward. To report the crime and to seek out the support that is available. My legal team has set up a temporary support helpline. The number is at the bottom of the screen, and there is an abundance of information about various support groups on their website. I would like to thank my therapist and RAINN for their dedicated support over the past few months and for providing some of the statistics I referred to at the start of my statement."

His features soften. "I would like to say one final thing before I go." His tongue darts out, wetting his lips. "During one of my darkest days, I lashed out at the woman I love. I said things I felt at the time, but they were things I never really believed. Things that *aren't* true. I understand why you did it," he adds, speaking directly to me, and my heart stutters in my chest. "I understand how badly you were hurting too, and I wish I could have been there for you. I hope you are okay and that you have found some peace." He leans forward, and he might as well be in the room with me. "I still love you, and I want you to know I'm ready and waiting. You are the only woman I will ever love, and I haven't given up on us. I would wait an eternity for you, if that's what you need."

A sob rips from my chest before I can stop it. I can barely see the screen through my blurry eyes as the press conference comes to an end and someone switches off the TV.

"Presley." Pete slides his arm around my shoulders. "Why don't you take the rest of the day off?"

"I'm fine." I swipe at the hot tears coursing down my face. My colleagues glance at me, their expressions a mix of compassion and curiosity. I haven't told any of them about Kent, for a variety of reasons, although they know circumstances forced me to leave the love of my life behind. They also know I'm from Boston, so I'm sure it won't take them long to connect the dots.

"Go, sweetheart." Pete pushes me gently toward the door. "Go do what you need to do."

Chapter Forty-Three
Kent

Six Months Later

My cell pings in my pocket for the third time in a row, and I put my niece Ciara down on the ground. "Uncle Kent has to take this," I tell her, trying not to laugh at her cute little pout. "Go play with your cousins." I nudge her toward the playground where Hewson, Hayley, and her twin brother Cathal are hanging off the climbing frame under the watchful eyes of the babysitter. I am at my parents' place for the weekend, and Kalvin and Kyler dropped by with their kids. Their wives are at Cheryl's baby shower today. Keven finally put a bun in her oven, and they are expecting their first child in six weeks.

Removing my phone from the pocket of my shorts, I'm surprised when I see it's Austen calling me. Things are much better between me and my brother's husband these days, and my relationship with Keaton is back to what it was. Keats stayed with me the first few months after I left rehab, and it was good to spend that time together.

Keanu and Selena stayed over some nights too, but they couldn't permanently stay in Cambridge, not with the Moonlight build being at such an advanced stage. I really appreciated how my family came together to help me, especially my triplets and their partners. Eventually, I made Keaton return home. He was a newlywed, after all, and while Austen was cool about it, I knew they were missing each other like crazy.

I hold the phone in my hand, wondering why Austen is calling me now. He has a game tomorrow against the Denver Broncos, and I'm sure he must be at the training facility.

"What's up?" I ask when I answer my phone.

"Eventually, he answers," he drawls, and I snicker. Austen has a unique sense of humor.

"Dude, aren't you at practice?" I ask.

"I'm on my way there right now, but I need to tell you something."

"Okay. I'll bite." I'm more than intrigued.

"I just saw Presley."

What? That was the last thing I was expecting to come out of his mouth. Butterflies swarm my chest, and my heart does funny little jumps.

"Kent, did you hear me?" Austen says when I don't respond.

"Where is she?" I ask, quickly checking the time on my watch.

"She's working at the tattoo parlor I used to go to. Seeing as I was in town, I decided to drop in on Pete, and I couldn't believe my eyes when I saw her behind the reception desk. I remember talking to her at my wedding about how I'd planned to do an apprenticeship there if I didn't get an NFL contract. I never even stopped to consider she might've gone there."

"Send me the details," I blurt, already racing toward the back door. "Do you think she'll run?"

"I don't think so, but I spoke to Pete. I gave him a quick rundown, and he's agreed to call me if she gets spooked."

"Thanks, man. I owe you."

"Go get your girl, Kent. Text me when you land."

I rush through the kitchen, ignoring Kalvin and Mom, heading into the living room where Dad is chatting with Kyler. "Dad!" I shout, running toward him. "I need your help."

It's a miracle I thought to grab the envelope while I was hastily throwing shit in my duffel bag before Dad and I left for the airport. He flew me here himself. Now, as I'm being driven from Denver International Airport to downtown Denver, where Presley works, I pull out the letter she sent me after the press conference. The pages are dog-eared and wrinkled from being read so many times.

The picture and letter arrived three days after I poured my heart out to her via the TV. It was the only chance I had of talking to her. I knew my press conference would make global headlines because the level of interest in the trial was off the charts. I also know my girl. I knew she would be watching and reading and following it with interest, so I knew there was a strong chance she'd be watching the TV that day.

She sent me one of her drawings. It's a side profile of a lion, and his large mane is constructed of the most vibrant yellow and orange pressed flowers. On the bottom of the framed picture, written in her elegant handwriting, it simply reads: For those who are truly brave.

Does it make me a pussy that I cried looking at the picture knowing how much thought, time, and effort she'd put into it? And that I cried again when I read her letter? That I've cried, several times, rereading her letter?

Fuck it. I'm a man who is finally in touch with his feelings, and it's taken me a long time to get to this place, so I'm going to own this shit. It's okay to cry. Especially for the only woman who matters.

I trace the tip of my finger over her words as I silently read her letter. "It takes a very special, strong, courageous man to face his fears knowing the entire world is watching and listening. Your bravery will inspire and empower the very people who need it. I know that's why you did it, and I couldn't be prouder. I think about you every day, and

I hope you are healing. You are the most amazing man, Kent Kennedy, and I am so blessed to love you. You have my heart, now and forever. All my love, Presley."

I'm not gonna lie. I loved it and hated it at the same time. It bolstered me to know she still loved me, but I thought she'd come back, and when she didn't, I realized maybe there wasn't going to be a future for us after all.

I told her at the press conference I would wait patiently for her, and I meant it. But I'm a fucking Kennedy, and we don't give up without a motherfucking fight. So, I'm putting myself on the line today, hoping I'm not too late and that our time has finally arrived. Mostly, I need to see her for myself to know she is okay. If she's still not ready, I'll step back once I'm satisfied she understands I will always be here for her, and I will welcome her back with open arms whenever she feels the time is right.

Holding the flowers against my chest, I open the door to Denver Ink and step inside, urging my racing heart to calm down before I have a heart attack. My heart deflates with disappointment when I spot an older dude behind the desk.

He looks up and smiles. "I've been wondering when you'd show up." He steps out from behind the desk, holding out his hand. "I'm Pete."

"Good to meet you," I say, shuffling the flowers under my arm so I can shake his hand, hoping he doesn't notice how clammy mine is. "Is she here?" I ask, looking around. The waiting area is large and clean with floor-to-ceiling windows at the front, a colorful wall on the left, and a long hallway in the middle, stretching the length of the building. My eyes pop wide as my gaze roams over the stunning mural. "Is that—" I splutter.

"Yep. Your girl did that. She's crazy talented."

My chest bursts with pride. "She is."

"Let me get her for you." He pins me with a genuine smile before walking to the first door in the hallway and rapping on it with his knuckles. "Pink. You have a visitor," he hollers, and I arch a brow.

Pink??

"I saw your press conference," Pete says, returning to the reception desk while we wait for Presley to show her face.

I don't shy away from talking about what happened to me, but I'm loath to get into specifics with any of the people who broach the subject. Right now, I'm glad of the distraction because my knees feel shaky and my heart is pinging around my chest like a canary being chased by a rabid cat. "I can't even begin to imagine how difficult that must have been, but you're an inspiration to men everywhere. Respect." He jerks his head in acknowledgment.

"Thank you. That means a lot." I've been pleasantly surprised at the reaction since everything came out. Of course, there will always be jerks spouting shit, but most people have been compassionate and supportive. I have had so many letters from other men, who were victims of rape and sexual assault, telling me my courage gave them the push they needed to come clean to their loved ones and to report their crimes. I don't have words to express how that makes me feel. To know I have made a difference means everything.

Clasping the flowers closer to my chest, I will my errant heartbeat to calm down. *Where the hell is she, and what is taking so long? Doesn't she know I've been waiting over a year to see her beautiful face again?*

"I had a feeling you were talking about Presley that day when she started crying," Pete adds.

"She didn't mention me?" I ask, trying not to feel disappointed.

"She told me there was a guy. *The* guy," he adds, helping to eradicate any disappointment I was just feeling. "But she remained tight-lipped, and I didn't pry because that girl was in a world of pain when she first got here."

At one time, I'd beat myself up that I wasn't here for her when she needed me, but not anymore. I'm learning to let go of some of the excessive guilt. Truth is, I was of no use to Presley this time last year, and she was right when she said we needed time to heal away from one another. "And how is she now?" I ask.

"Terrified, if I had to guess," he says, chuckling a little. "I think she's been expecting you since Austen showed up."

"Fuck, I know the feeling," I truthfully admit. "I'm sweating bullets here."

"It's going to be okay," he says, patting my arm.

"You got a crystal ball or something?" The longer I'm standing out here like a spare tool, the less confident I feel.

Pete grins. "I'm a sucker for true love, and I heard the things you said to her, and I saw the way she reacted. Besides, she's never hidden the fact she left her heart behind in Boston." He squeezes my arm. "There has been no one else. She doesn't see anyone but you." That's a relief because it's been one of my fears. That she'd meet and fall in love with someone else. It's been six months since she wrote those words to me, and I know a lot can change in six months.

"It's been the same for me." I haven't as much as spared any woman a parting glance. Presley is the only woman I want, and everyone else pales in comparison.

"Yep." Pete grins again. "True love. I want an invite to the wedding," he tacks on the end. I can see why Austen likes this guy, and I'm glad Presley came here. I don't need her to tell me this guy has looked out for her to know it.

His words spur me into action, and I stalk toward the hallway, ready to claim my girl, when the door opens and she steps foot outside.

My heart stops. Seriously. It, like, legit stops beating for a few seconds. All the air leaves the room as I set eyes on her for the first time in a year. She is even more beautiful than I remember. Her gorgeous hair is still long and wavy, but the ends are pink now. That's not the only change. She's got this gorgeous diamond stud in her nose and new ink on her arms. She's wearing black jean shorts with an off-the-shoulder black, red, and white shirt. The strap of her red bra is showing along with a tempting glimpse of olive-toned skin. She has diamante-studded black flip-flops on her feet.

Effortlessly stunning, like always.

But it's her eyes that undo me. They suck me in, pulling me closer, as I drown in the deep, decadent, chocolaty depths. Her lips part, and her soft breath trickles out. Her eyes turn glassy as we stare at one another, rooted to the spot, unable to tear our gazes away. Her gaze roams me from head to toe, her chest heaving as emotion electrifies the air.

"Kent," she whispers, and a single tear leaks out of the corner of her eye.

"Hey, Presley baby." Ignoring the nerves firing at me from all corners, I walk toward her with my heart in the palm of my hand. "Boy, are you a sight for sore eyes. I have missed you so fucking much."

She just stares at me, unmoving and barely blinking. Behind her, a few doors open, and I spot a few heads poking out.

"These are for you," I say, holding the flowers out to her.

She takes them, keeping her eyes locked on mine as she buries her nose in the rose petals. "They're beautiful," she whispers. "Thank you."

I hand her the first envelope, hoping she doesn't notice the sweat beads on my brow. I hadn't thought of doing this in front of an audience, and I'm even more nervous than I was stepping through the door.

She hands the bouquet to a tiny blonde lounging in the doorway of the room Presley just emerged from. The blonde gives me a slow once-over, cocking her head to one side and grinning. *Okay then.*

Presley opens the first note, smiling as she reads it.

"What's it say?" the blonde asks, and I want to tell her to mind her own business, because this is our thing, but Presley must like this chick because she reads it out loud to her.

"Come back to me because 'I Want You, I Need You, I Love You.'"

The blonde looks less than impressed.

"It's Elvis," I explain, handing Presley the second envelope. "It's our thing."

Presley beams at me, and it's like getting sucker-punched in the nuts. I almost collapse in a heap on the floor with the force of her smile and the impact it has on me. "Another one?"

"I thought the occasion required a little extra cheese." I shoot her a flirty smile.

This time, she reads it straight out before her nosy coworker asks for the details.

"Come back to me because 'You're the Reason I'm Living.'"

She giggles, and the sound embeds deep in my heart.

Our fingers brush as I hand her the third one, sending delicious tremors zipping up my arm. From the way she jumps a little, I know she felt it too. We always had amazing chemistry, and sex with her was out-of-this-world incredible.

I watch her elegant fingers open the final envelope and extract the last note. She gulps, and tears roll down her face as she lifts her head to look at me. Her voice is shaky as she reads it. "Come back to me because 'I'm Yours.'" Sniffing, she takes a step toward me, holding all three notes in her hands. "I'm yours too, Kent. I always have been, and I always will be." Her eyes drill into mine. "I wanted to run straight back into your arms when you said those things to me at the press conference, but my head wasn't in the right place yet. I needed more time to heal, but it didn't mean I wasn't missing you like crazy because every day without you has been difficult."

"Come here," I say, barely able to speak over the emotion choking my throat. All I know is if I don't hold her in my arms, I'll explode.

She closes the gap between us, slowly at first, before flinging herself into my arms. I lift her up, and her legs go around my waist as she buries her head in my neck. I hold her close, nuzzling my nose in her hair, inhaling the familiar smell of her vanilla shampoo and the musky notes of her perfume. I close my eyes, absorbing how incredible it feels to hold her again, tightening my arms around her back, silently promising to never let her go.

"Presley, baby," I murmur, as she slowly slides down my body a couple minutes later. Tilting her chin, I force her gaze to mine. She stares at me through tear-filled eyes, but she has a bright smile on her face and she's clutching my arms as if she can't bear to not touch me. I can feel her happiness as if it's a tangible thing. My heart swells to bursting, and a deep sense of contentment washes over me. Her eyes lock on mine, and they are full of so much emotion it almost knocks me over. "I love you," I say, winding my hands in her hair. "I love you so fucking much."

We move at the same time, and our mouths collide in a passionate kiss that injects new life into me. I slide my tongue into her mouth as I angle my head, needing to deepen the kiss, to ensure she understands everything I'm saying with every brush of my tongue. I don't care that we have an audience as I taste her lips over and over, holding her flush against my body, feeling her heart race in sync with mine.

This, right here, is the missing piece.

We might have needed the time apart to heal, but now we need to be together to glue back the remaining broken pieces of our hearts.

Epilogue
Presley

Two Years Later

"Okay, I'll admit to being a little horrified when Rachel showed me the design for your dress, but I've got to hand it to both of you; it's exquisite, and it works," Alex says. "It's perfectly you." Her eyes flood with tears as she looks me over in my nontraditional wedding dress.

I swirl in front of the mirror, admiring my reflection. The gown is a plain strapless white dress with a full skirt that swings out from my waist, ending at my calves. It's the fine layer of delicate black lace, covering the fitted top and creeping onto the skirt, and the silky black and red wraparound belt that elevates it from plain to spectacular. I even dyed the ends of my hair red for the occasion, to match my dress, and I've chosen to wear my hair down as Kent loves it like that. If we'd had a winter wedding, there's no doubt I would've opted for a full-length black and red dress, but we wanted an early summer wedding so Austen could come. His season starts next month, and he wouldn't have found time for a weekend wedding with his busy schedule.

Kent and I have become super close with Keaton and Austen, especially now they are back home in Boston with Austen having transferred to the Patriots last year under a record-breaking deal. Kent wouldn't get married without them here, and he was happy to adjust our plans to accommodate his triplet and his husband. *Isn't it amazing how things can completely change?*

Kent and I continue to attend monthly therapy sessions, and I'm sure we will for a long time, but we have come through the tough times and are out on the other side.

"It *is* fucking sensational," Rachel says, waddling toward me. "Even if I do say so myself."

I turn around, wrapping her in a gentle hug. It's hard to do anything else with the large baby bump getting in the way. Rachel is due to give birth to their second child next month, and everyone has been teasing her and Brad like crazy since we got to the cabin last night, joking it's triplets or quads.

I seriously thought Brad was going to stab Kent in the eye when he asked a typically inappropriate question about how much bigger Rachel's boobs had gotten. He still likes to wind Brad up any chance he gets, and I'd like to say his big mouth doesn't get him into trouble these days, but that would be a lie. I love that Kent is still uniquely himself and what he's been through hasn't altered his personality too much.

"Thank you," I tell her. "I'm honored to be the first woman to wear a dress from the new Rachel McConaughey brand." Rachel left Miranda Fanning last year to set up her own label, and her first launch is only three weeks after the new family addition is supposed to arrive. She is ridiculously busy, and I felt very loved when she insisted on designing and making my dress. Alex made Shania's flower girl princess dress and Selena's matron of honor gown.

We didn't want the whole extravagant hotel wedding, so when Faye and Kyler offered us the use of their Connecticut cabin for our big day, we jumped at the chance to hold it here. It's only family and our small network of friends, including some of Kent's colleagues from his law firm and our employees from Tenley Ink.

Lance is here with his wife Emma. He's the only one of Kent's former Harvard buddies in attendance, because Kent isn't in contact with Mitch or Topher anymore. Mo, Kady, and Rafe are here too, as is Ford and his wife Michelle. Even Pete and a couple of my ex-colleagues from Denver Ink made the trip, and I'm touched they went to so much effort.

Things were good after Kent and I reunited the day Austen found me at Denver Ink. We had no choice, but to do the long-distance thing for the first six months. I didn't want to walk out in the middle of my apprenticeship and Kent was in his last year at law school, so it meant living apart during the week, in the short-term. But we spent every weekend together. Either I traveled to Boston or Kent came to me.

Until I got pregnant, and that changed everything.

We had stopped using condoms when we got back together since I was on the pill. Plus, the chances of getting knocked up were slim, given my condition. Or so we thought, which was why we weren't as careful as we should have been. Shania wasn't planned, but she was the best surprise ever.

When I discovered I was pregnant, I immediately handed my notice in to Pete, packed up my stuff, and booked a seat on the next plane to Boston. I didn't tell Kent until I showed up at his door, crying tears of joy as I explained we were going to have a baby. He was beyond thrilled, and his excitement matched my own.

Someday, when Shania is old enough, we will bring her to Tillie's grave and explain she has an older sister watching over her from heaven.

Turned out, I wasn't the only one keeping surprises, because Kent had been in talks with Austen for months about opening a tattoo shop in Boston as a joint venture between Austen and me. They had just signed a lease on a state-of-the-art premises in a prime city location, and Kent was planning to tell me when he flew in for the weekend. All the paperwork was in my name, and Kent handed the reins to me then because he knew I would want to be involved in every aspect of setting up my own business.

And that's how Tenley Ink was born. Austen and I have a fifty-fifty partnership deal, but I actively manage the business. He helps out off-season, and we both have a select number of clients we personally look after. The business has only been up and running a year, but it's already a massive success. We are in the process of setting up a franchise business, and once everything is in place, we plan to look for partners to open branches across the US.

It's more than I could have ever dreamed of.

And it's all thanks to the man waiting outside to marry me.

Kent has made all my dreams come true in more ways than one.

When he proposed last Christmas, I couldn't stop crying tears of joy.

Now, today, when I marry my soul mate, with our baby daughter by our side, surrounded by family and friends, my life will be complete.

Kent

"You nervous?" Keanu asks as I rub my hands down the front of my black Armani jacket for the umpteenth time.

"What groom isn't nervous on his wedding day?" I arch a brow. "You were shaking like a leaf the day of your wedding and so pale I thought you were gonna puke."

"That's a lie," he replies, straightening his tie. "I was nervous, but it was the good kind of nervous. Exactly the kind you are experiencing now."

I roll my eyes, but my brother isn't wrong. So far, everything has been perfect, and I want to keep it that way. I want today to be a day we will both cherish for the rest of our lives.

I stare at the placid lake in front of us, grateful we chose to have the wedding at my brother's cabin. It's beautiful here and completely private. We've managed to keep today a secret from the media, and that's helped to alleviate a lot of stress.

I cast an appreciative glance at the gorgeous garden surrounding us. Kyler and Faye's property extends for miles in all directions, and there are several places on the vast estate we could've chosen to conduct the ceremony, but the rear garden behind the luxurious cabin is the perfect spot.

The grounds are beautifully landscaped with an abundance of shrubs and colorful flowers. We built a temporary deck right in front of the lake for the ceremony, and Mom did a great job decorating it with pretty flowers. Presley's love affair with flowers continues, as is evidenced by the sheer volume of flowers on display today. We are virtually drowning in flowers, and I know my girl is planning on pressing all of them and using them in her artwork.

She has given up her side business as she just didn't have the time to manage it, but she still loves creating pictures in her spare time. All my brothers have at least one Presley creation in their homes, and Mom and Dad have pieces all over their Wellesley house.

We bought a house a few miles from my parents, just before Shania arrived. Our place is close to my other brothers who live in the area, and while I never imagined I would return to live in Wellesley, we are happy there. Shania gets to play with her cousins daily, and my parents are very active in our lives. Mom has taken a back seat in her interior design business so she has time to spend with her grand-children, and she's always willing to babysit or help out if we need it. Dad too. We are lucky we have them because life is hectic, but I wouldn't want it any other way.

My eyes skim over the rest of the grounds, landing on the large marquee where we'll conduct the party. We hired a party company who will play games and other fun activities with the kids, in the small side marquee, while the adults feast on lobster and champagne. And we have a guy coming in an hour with a few bounce houses to keep the kids entertained. He even has one for the adults for later, after the kids are in bed. That should be fun. My lips twitch at the possibilities.

"Oh, here comes Rachel. That's a good sign," Keats says from his position beside Keanu, and we turn to watch Brad's heavily pregnant wife waddle up the aisle.

She's not the only family member pregnant today. Both Lana and Cheryl are also pregnant, but they are not as far along. Lana is expecting her third child with my brother Kalvin, and Cheryl is expecting her second child with Keven. Their son, Taylor, turns two in August.

I'm expecting an announcement from Keanu and Selena any time now. They are the only couple in the family who haven't had kids yet. Both are exceptionally busy with their jobs, and Keanu previously said he didn't want to bring any babies into the world until they have the time to devote to their family. Now that Keanu's fashion brand and his modeling agency are well established, and very successful, and Moonlight finally opened its doors last year, I think they will take some time out to start a family.

The music starts, and my shoulders relax as Elvis's "Love Me Tender" plays over the loudspeakers. Everyone should expect Elvis to be played *a lot* today because he's played a big part in our love story.

My heart is full to bursting point as I turn around with Keats and Keanu by my side. All nerves disappear as I watch the first of the bridal party appear on the deck at the back of the cabin.

I'm so ready to do this because I can't wait to make Presley my wife.

Our guests stand, and I share a knowing look with a few of the guys from work. We've attended a lot of weddings this year, as many of our friends settle down.

Reforming Kent

After I passed the bar, Stearns and Westfall offered me a full-time position, and I didn't hesitate to accept. From the first summer I interned there, it has felt like home. After they took on my case and ensured I got justice, I knew there would never be any other law firm I would want to work at. I also offer free legal services to residents of Moonlight in my spare time, and it's good to be in a position to help other victims of sexual abuse.

Kyler captures my attention just as Selena and Hewson step down onto the red carpet. Kyler, Keanu, and I laid out a temporary decked path, which is serving as our aisle today. Kyler has tears in his eyes—joyful ones—as he looks at me, and I know he's happy for me. We've spent more time together in recent years, and we've talked a little about the things that happened to us as kids, and it's brought us closer.

Kyler wraps his arm around Faye, holding her tight as she clutches a wriggling Caoimhe in her arms. Their youngest daughter is fourteen months old, and she was born three months before Shania. I can already tell the girls are going to become the best of friends because they always gravitate toward one another whenever the whole family is together.

Selena and Hewson walk toward us with matching smiles. Hewson turned eleven last month, and he's one of the few family members who has always accepted me as I am. Of course, he doesn't know what happened to me, because we shielded the kids from the news as they were too young, but he was always happy to hang out with his Uncle Kent. Probably because I was the craziest one back then. I can't believe he's eleven, and he's so freaking tall already. His arm is looped through Selena's as he escorts her up the aisle, holding the ring boxes in his other hand.

When they reach the top, he lets go of Selena's arm to shake my hand. "Congrats, Uncle Kent. Presley's a total babe."

I hear Mom murmur how he's a miniature Kalvin, and she's not wrong. He's a total little charmer in the making. We do this elaborate knuckle-touch maneuver he taught me before I pull him in for a brief hug. "Thanks, dude, and she so is." He walks off to his parents, taking a seat in between his mom and his sister Hayley.

I kiss my sister-in-law on the cheek. "You look beautiful, Sel." She's wearing a knee-length red silk and lace dress that clings to her killer model curves.

"I'm delighted for you, Kent." She hugs me warmly. "Be happy because you deserve it."

A massive lump swells in my throat, and I wonder if I'll get through this day without crying.

Of course, Keanu can't resist kissing his wife even though it's not exactly protocol. But the minister doesn't mind. Eva beams at me as I glance over my shoulder at her. She asked us if she could officiate the wedding when we told her we didn't want a religious ceremony, and we accepted her offer on the spot.

Things are still a little strained between Kaden and me, but I appreciate he doesn't let it affect the close relationship I have with his wife. In time, I'm hoping we'll be able to fully leave the past in the past and have the kind of relationship I now have with the rest of my brothers. I think it helps ease Kade's guilt knowing how much I still adore, respect, and rely on Eva. Milly and Matthew stand beside their dad in the second row, giggling excitedly as Shania comes into view.

I give my daughter my full attention as Austen lifts her off the deck, placing her chubby little legs down on the aisle. He has to bend his legs and crouch down to hold her hand, but he doesn't mind how silly he looks because Austen and Keaton adore our little girl as if she is theirs. Shania only started walking three weeks ago, so she's a little wobbly on her legs.

"Dadadadada," she shrieks when she spots me, trying to run to reach me faster.

Not gonna lie; the way my little girl looks at me, like I'm the center of her universe, turns me to mush every time. I didn't think it was possible to love anyone as much as I love Presley, but the instant Shania entered the world, I realized how wrong I was.

I held our daughter for the first time as the medical team was stitching Presley up, and when she stared up at me with these big trusting eyes, I knew I would move mountains to ensure she grows up happy, healthy, and safe. From the second she curled her tiny little finger around mine, I have been completely and utterly in love with my daughter. This perfect little creation that is part Presley and part me. She has my eyes and my cheeky disposition, but she's the spitting image of her mother in every other way.

My little princess is gonna break hearts someday.

Someday in the distant future, very far away.

Like, I might permit her to date when she's thirty.

Or maybe forty.

I bend down as they approach, opening my arms wide, and Austen lets go of her hand when they reach me. Shania barrels into my chest, flinging her small arms around me, babbling "Dadadadada-da." My heart expands, like it does every time she calls me Dada. That shit will never get old. "Hey, princess." I stand with her snuggled in my arms, dotting kisses all over her pretty face. She giggles, pressing noisy, wet, slobbery kisses to my cheek in return.

"You good, dude?" Austen asks, clamping a hand on my shoulder.

"Never better, man. Thanks for being a part of our day." I wasn't surprised when Presley chose Austen and Selena to be her best man and matron of honor today. She gets on well with all the spouses and my brothers love her too, but she is closest with Austen and Selena, so it was a no-brainer.

"I wouldn't have missed this for the world." He looks over my shoulder, blatantly eye fucking his husband, before he steps over beside Selena to await the bride.

Eliot cries out, and Keats and Austen almost give themselves whiplash turning to look at their son. Mom is struggling to hold the normally placid two-year-old in her arms. He has his arms outstretched, crying for his dads.

They adopted him a year ago, shortly after they moved back to Boston, and they are complete naturals with their son. My dad takes Eliot into his arms, whispering in his ear, and whatever he says works like a charm as the little boy settles down. I can visibly see the strain lift from Austen and Keaton's shoulders, and I smile. I love how happy my triplet is, and I'm thrilled he got everything he has always wanted.

The music changes to "Loving You," and I move Shania to my hip, pointing at the end of the aisle. "Look, there's Mommy." Mercifully, Shania keeps still, looking as mesmerized as I am by the vision walking toward me.

Warmth blooms in my chest, and a messy ball of emotion clogs my throat as Keven leads my bride up the aisle. I thought Presley might have asked Ford or Rafe to give her away, but she asked my brother, giving me another reason to fall in love with her all over again.

Presley and Keven share a special bond after he saved her life, and I'm glad she asked him. I can tell it means a lot. Keven is the unsung hero in our family, and I like that my bride wanted to acknowledge his importance in her life, in *our* lives, by asking him to walk her up the aisle. As they walk toward me, I can see how proud he is to be a part of our wedding because he's not hiding his emotions today.

My eyes stay glued to my love as she approaches. Presley is perfect. Absolutely stunning. So beautiful she steals my breath, and I can only stare as she comes toward me, wondering how I got so lucky, how I ended up with this amazing life.

Tears cling to her long lashes, and her eyes are glassy and glimmering with emotion when she finally reaches me.

"You're so beautiful," I rasp, barely able to get the words out. "And I'm the luckiest asshole on the planet."

Mom rolls her eyes while Dad fights a smile.

"I'm so happy for you guys," Keven says, smiling. He takes Presley's hand, planting a kiss on her knuckles. "Thank you for this honor, Presley. I will cherish this moment for the rest of my life."

One of my brothers murmurs, "Pussy," and a few chuckles ring out. My money's on Kalvin, especially when Mom whips her head in his direction, drilling him with a warning look, no doubt. Dad passes Eliot to Mom before stepping up beside us. He clamps his hand on Keven's shoulder. Kev releases Presley's hand, nodding at me before he leaves to take his seat beside Cheryl and their son.

Shania wriggles in my arms. "Mama," she screeches, almost jumping out of my arms.

Presley takes our daughter, kissing the tip of her nose. "Love you, baby girl." She hugs her for a few seconds before passing her to my dad.

Dad holds Shania close, smoothing a hand up and down her back as her lower lip wobbles. Our daughter hates to be apart from either of us, and like me, she hates to feel like she's missing out on something.

"I'm so happy for you, son," Dad says, his eyes alight with emotion. "And I wish you both every happiness for the future." He leans in, kissing Presley on the cheek. "You're already a part of this family, Presley, but it's good to make it official."

He steps back, walking away to take his seat beside Mom. Eliot claps his hands in glee when Shania arrives, and Eva asks everyone to be seated.

The music cuts out, and I take Presley's hand, stepping forward until we are in front of Eva. We turn to face one another, and I hold her hands in mine, my heart soaring toward the heavens as I prepare to make my beautiful bride mine forever.

Presley

"I can't wait to see everyone's faces," I say, purposely avoiding looking at my husband, because I know I won't be able to hold my laughter in.

My husband.

It's only been a few hours since we got married, and I still have to pinch myself to believe this is my life. I am so unbelievably happy I could scream.

"Red better have kept it a secret," Kent says, sliding his hand up under my skirt. "Remind me to thank her later for this."

I swat his hand away, forgetting I'm not supposed to be looking at him, as Rachel takes control of the microphone in the marquee. We are standing just outside, hiding so we don't ruin the surprise before it's time to make our grand entrance.

I burst out laughing as I take in the state of Kent in the fitted white, black, and red sparkly Elvis jumpsuit. Kent's motto is go big or go home, so he's wearing an Elvis wig on his head with matching fake sideburns, and he's got a pair of gaudy shades on too. He looks ridiculous, but I'm glad he's a good sport and that he instantly said yes when I suggested doing this. We've been rehearsing for the past few weeks, and we have the lyrics and the routine down pat now.

It's just after ten, and the party is well underway. The kids are tucked up in bed, our guests' bellies are full of food, and they are enjoying the complimentary bar. The band is taking a short break so we can do this.

Kent swats me harder on the ass. "Keep laughing and I'll have to take your naughty ass outside afterward and spank it."

I lean in, kissing the corner of his mouth. "Is that a promise, Mr. Kennedy?"

He reels me into his chest, planting a hard kiss on my mouth as Rachel demands quiet inside the marquee, preparing to introduce us. "It is, Mrs. Kennedy, and one I intend on delivering in full." He bites at my earlobe. "You look fucking hot, and I'm so screwing you in this later."

"I wish I'd been born in the sixties," I say, admiring the gorgeous dress Rachel made especially for tonight. It's got a fitted black bustier top with wide straps, a full black skirt with white and red polka dots, and a wide belt with a big red bow. My hair is up in a ponytail with my bangs puffed up high and styled back off my brow, and I feel every bit as beautiful as I did wearing my wedding dress earlier.

"I don't," Kent says, running his hands along my sides, his fingers brushing against my breasts. "Though I love this dress, if you'd been born in the sixties, we never would've met, and that'd be a travesty."

"The worst kind," I agree. "It's showtime," I add just as Rachel announces us.

Kent takes my hand, flashing me a wide grin. "Let's get our cheese on."

The room erupts into a chorus of laughter and a round of spontaneous applause when we burst into the marquee to the opening strains of "The Lady Loves Me." It's a song from *Viva Las Vegas*, a movie Elvis made with Ann Margaret back in the sixties. They duet on this song, and the lyrics are hysterical, reminiscent of how Kent and I first met, so when I went looking for an Elvis song for us to sing at our wedding, this was the perfect choice.

We step up on the stage, taking the microphones from Rachel, performing our routine exactly how we rehearsed it. Kent's Elvis impersonation has improved a little over the years, but it's still pretty terrible, and I'm not exactly the world's greatest singer either, but we make it through the song, and it's the most fun I've had in ages. The audience is laughing, dancing, and singing along, and Kent's brothers are whistling and hollering while recording it on their cell phones.

When we get to the end, to the part in the movie where Ann Margaret pushes Elvis into the pool, Brad throws a jug of water over Kent, and it's so unexpected, and so fucking funny, that I can't sing the very last line, breaking into fits of laughter as I fall to my knees, clutching my sore stomach, while looking at the shell-shocked expression on my husband's face.

"You're dead, motherfucker," Kent says, wiping water off his face as he jabs his finger in Brad's direction.

"Payback is a bitch, Kennedy," Brad shouts, chuckling as he pulls his pregnant wife into his arms.

"Oh my God. That was classic." Faye is giggling as she approaches with Kyler, and they are both red in the face from laughing.

"I can't decide which was more entertaining," Kyler says in between bouts of laughter. "You two doing that or Brad finally getting his revenge after years of you fake hitting on his woman."

Kent helps me to my feet. "You can add a third option to your list." He smirks as the song switches. "This one's for you two." He blows them a kiss as he helps me down from the stage just as "Kissin' Cousins" starts playing, and the crowd cracks up laughing again.

We race around the marquee, laughing hysterically as Kyler gives chase, shaking his fists, pretending to be mad.

Keven approaches with his pregnant wife when Kyler gives up, returning to Faye. "That was the fucking funniest thing I have ever seen." He shakes his head, grinning as his gaze roams the length of Kent's Elvis costume.

"How the hell did you even get into that thing? Looks tight as fuck," Kalvin says, materializing alongside us with his arm slung over Lana's shoulders.

"You're telling me." Kent tugs at the silky material pulled tight around his crotch. "My balls are fucking constricted and turning blue as we speak."

"We'd best let you attend to that," Cheryl says, winking at me, as Keven leads her out onto the dance floor, quickly followed by Kalvin and Lana.

Kent pulls me into his arms, and we sway to the music. "Today is the best day of my life. Well, it's tied with the day Shania was born," he adds, correcting himself. He leans down, kissing me slowly. "Are you happy, Presley baby?"

"Happier than I ever thought I could be," I admit, wrapping my arms around his neck. "And that's all down to you. Thank you for giving me everything my heart has ever desired, Kent."

"Thank *you* for sharing your life with me, Pres." Tears pool in his eyes, and it's not the first time today. "I didn't imagine I'd ever get to have this, and now I have everything." He tightens his hold on my back. "I promise to never take what we have for granted. We have fought so hard to get here, and I will never forget that."

"I love you, Kent."

"I love you, Presley baby. Now and every day for the rest of my life."

Moonlight in Massachussets is the next book in the series. Available now and free to read in Kindle Unlimited.

Support Contact Details

If you need to talk to someone regarding sexual assault, please call the National Sexual Assault Hotline in the US at 800-656-4673

1In6 is a website for men who have had unwanted or abusive sexual experiences in their childhood. They have partnered with RAINN to provide a 24/7 hotline for men at 1-800-656-4673 /online.rainn.org

If you need to talk to someone regarding any mental health illness, please call the National Alliance on Mental Illness in the US at 1-800-950-NAMI (6264) or email info@nami.org

If you require support dealing with PTSD, please contact PTSD United: http://www.ptsdunited.org/contact/

The Childhelp National Child Abuse Hotline in the US is available 24/7 at 1-800-4224453 https://www.childhelp.org/hotline/

If you require help regarding drug or alcohol addiction/abuse, please phone the SAMSHA national helpline at 1-800-662-4357 https://www.samhsa.gov

If you live outside the US, please contact your local support center.

Acknowledgments

So, that's a wrap on *The Kennedy Boys* series, and I hope you enjoyed *Reforming Kent* as much as I enjoyed writing it. I wanted to end the series with a bang, and I hope I delivered that. This book was so emotional for me to write because the subject matter was harrowing in parts and it's the last Kennedy Boys book! Gah! I'm not ready to say goodbye to this crazy family even if I know it's time to let them go.

Ending any series is always bittersweet for me, but especially this one as I have spent four years writing about this fictional family who seems so real to me at this point. Although, I had only initially planned on writing Kyler and Faye's story, all the Kennedy men were speaking to me from early in the series. All their stories have been crystal clear to me from the outset. I always knew something this traumatic had happened to Kent, and his pain and his inner turmoil has hurt me so much throughout the other books in this series.

If you have been reading my books, you will know that I like to tackle topics that don't often make their way into romance books. While my books, especially within this series, are often deliberately dramatic and angsty, I try to inject authenticity and real life through the subjects I choose to write about.

The statistics Kent shared during his press conference are real statistics my critique partner unearthed for me. There is such little real data about male rape available, which is disappointing but not shocking. There is still such a stigma about rape in general, although the MeToo movement has done a lot to help undo that, but male rape is particularly taboo, even if it happens a lot more frequently than you might think.

My heart hurt for Kent in this book, and I cried a lot while writing it. I also read some real-life interviews with male rape victims and cried for their pain and suffering too. If you have been the victim of rape, I hope this book hasn't upset you too much. I want to raise awareness while treating the subject sensitively yet not shying away from the harsh reality either.

I need to thank the following people: Ciara Turley, Kelly Hartigan, Sarah Ferguson, Sara Eirew, Shannon Passmore, Robin Harper, Fiona Jayde, Daisy Zorman, Sinead Davis, Danielle Sanchez, Lola Verroen, my ARC and Street Team, Siobhan's Squad on Facebook and all the bloggers/booktokers/bookstagrammers who help to spread the word on social media.

Huge thanks to all the readers around the world who took a chance on *Finding Kyler* and who have stuck with the series throughout the years. I only wrote the other Kennedy brothers books for you, and I hope I haven't let you down.

Lastly, a big shout-out to my family. My husband, Trev, and my sons, Cian and Callum, make a lot of sacrifices so I can write my little heart out. They are my biggest supporters, and I couldn't do this without them.

I hope I haven't forgotten anyone (always my biggest fear when writing acknowledgments) but if I did, please don't take it personally. It doesn't mean I don't appreciate you because I appreciate everyone who supports me. It just means I have a head like a sieve (Ask my husband; he'll tell you all about it, lol!).

I love connecting with my readers, so feel free to reach out to me via social media or email (siobhan@siobhandavis.com)

Thank you so much for reading *Reforming Kent,* and I look forward to entertaining you for many more years to come. Big hugs from Ireland.

MOONLIGHT IN MASSACHUSETTS - The Kennedy Boys
Book #11

Find out what is going on in the lives of your favorite family and their offspring. Set five years after the series end, this story begins with Selena receiving a prestigious award for Moonlight, the support center she opened to help survivors of abuse.

You can expect laughter, camaraderie, steam, a little drama and angst, and lots of love! The Kennedys are as close-knit as ever, and family still means everything to them.

This is a multiple POV short novel, including chapters from all the main characters in the series.

Available now in ebook, paperback, and audiobook.

pain. Until Jared rocks up to the art gallery where I work, with his fiancée in tow, and I'm drowning again.

Seeing him brings everything to the surface, so I flee. Placing distance between us again, I'm determined to put him behind me once and for all.

Then he reappears at my door, begging me for another chance.

I know I should turn him away.

Try telling that to my heart.

This angsty, new adult romance is a FREE full-length ebook, exclusively available to newsletter subscribers.

Type this link into your browser to claim your free copy:

https://bit.ly/TITMHFBB

OR

Scan this code to claim your free copy:

About the Author

Siobhan Davis™ is a *USA Today, Wall Street Journal,* and Amazon Top 5 bestselling romance author. **Siobhan** writes emotionally intense stories with swoon-worthy romance, complex characters, and tons of unexpected plot twists and turns that will have you flipping the pages beyond bedtime! She has sold over 2 million books, and her titles are translated into several languages.

Prior to becoming a full-time writer, Siobhan forged a successful corporate career in human resource management.

She lives in the Garden County of Ireland with her husband and two sons.

You can connect with Siobhan in the following ways:

Website: www.siobhandavis.com
Facebook: AuthorSiobhanDavis
Instagram: @siobhandavisauthor
Tiktok: @siobhandavisauthor
Email: siobhan@siobhandavis.com

Books By Siobhan Davis

NEW ADULT ROMANCE
The One I Want Duet
Kennedy Boys Series
Rydeville Elite Series
All of Me Series
Forever Love Duet

NEW ADULT ROMANCE STAND-ALONES
Inseparable
Incognito
Still Falling for You
Holding on to Forever
Always Meant to Be
Tell It to My Heart

REVERSE HAREM
Sainthood Series
Dirty Crazy Bad Duet
Surviving Amber Springs (stand-alone)
Alinthia Series ^

DARK MAFIA ROMANCE
Mazzone Mafia Series
Vengeance of a Mafia Queen (stand-alone)
*The Accardi Twins**
*Taking What's Mine**

YA SCI-FI & PARANORMAL ROMANCE
Saven Series
True Calling Series ^

---

*Coming 2024
^Currently unpublished but will be republished in due course.

www.siobhandavis.com

www.ingramcontent.com/pod-product-compliance
Lightning Source LLC
Chambersburg PA
CBHW070643310726
48982CB00001B/390